THE MAYOR OF
NEW ORLEANS

THE MAYOR OF NEW ORLEANS

JUST TALKING JAZZ

by

Fatima Shaik

CREATIVE ARTS BOOK COMPANY, BERKELEY
1989

For information contact:
    Creative Arts Book Company
    833 Bancroft Way
    Berkeley, California 94710

Typography: QuadraType, San Francisco
Cover Design: Charles Fuhrman Design

Library of Congress Cataloging-in-Publication Data

Shaik, Fatima, 1952–

    THE MAYOR OF NEW ORLEANS

    Contents: The Mayor of New Orleans • Climbing Monkey Hill • Before Echo.

    1. Louisiana—Fiction. I. Title.
PS3569.H316M39   1987   813'.54   87-71147
ISBN 0-88739-050-1 (cloth)
ISBN 0-88739-071-4 (pbk.)

Printed in the United States of America.

Table of Contents

When I look upon the waterfall
And feel that every drop has known some land
Whose captured harmonies must now expand
In bursts of praise that rock the spirit's wall,

I think the Lord made poets of us all.
What matter if in tongue, or eye, or hand?
The spirit yields but to His own command
When sudden light and love and grace enthrall.

—Lily LaSalle Shaik
April 14, 1948

THE MAYOR OF NEW ORLEANS

JUST TALKING JAZZ

"YOU MIGHT THINK I'M SIMPLE," SAID WALTER
Watson Lameir, "but they ain't nothing black or white."

He had reached the beginning, his crescendo of story, with the
young man who walked into Buster Holmes' restaurant at Bur-
gundy and Orleans streets. It had taken Walter a few beers to get
the visitor into a listening mood, primed as they say on the farm,
oiled as the hookers might repeat who worked in the classy districts around St. Charles Avenue.

Walter knew a man needed preparation for stories. Up the
Mississippi River in Garyville, Louisiana, where Walter claimed
to grow up, people might commence over a piece of sugarcane.
It took a lot of jawboning by listeners and participants before the
tale was sucked sweet and the husk dry.

"Shoot. I'm in New Orleans, Louisiana, the U.S., the world.
Ain't nothing simple about that. Looking at me, you might
could imagine you know all about me," Walter was coming to an
arpeggio, the bridge. It would be repeated and resounded until
the audience cheered. Walter, besides being a storyteller, was a
musician, "his true heart," as he might say. He was a Dixieland
trumpet player, a Coltrane saxophone imitator, an appreciator
of Mangione, and a "mayor of New Orleans," he told the young
man. "You, son, are looking at the former mayor of New Orleans. Now don't go and asking me none of that political stuff,
like legislation, jurisdiction. I say like I want to say. Politics is of
the people. And I am of the people. That's why the people
elected me."

1

Walter looked at the visitor, a sorry little young man, as people go. Jack, he said, was his name, Walter believed. Looked like his mama had slipped a too big T-shirt over him and stuck his legs through baggy white shorts. If he tucked in his shirttail, Walter knew, he'd be wearing elastic waist.

"Well, ain't you sick and tired, Jack," Walter continued, "of them officials in starchy white shirts, neckties strung up so tight they face look like blood on the banquette." Walter pointed to the sidewalk to indicate the place he meant.

"You tell him, Yonar," a patron called from the back of the bar.

Walter continued, "Those fancy politicians, they cross they legs at the knees, how a friend of mine Jim used to call it, they push they thighs so tight together, they squeeze all their good juices up to they brains."

"Hot dog," the bartender hollered, testifying like church.

The clients hooted.

"Far shore," exclaimed a man alongside Walter who had been listening. He wore a cowboy hat scrolled tightly on each side.

"Look out," the bartender called again, nodding his chin to the side in the direction of the cowboy.

The men at the bar cackled some more.

But Walter looked a little disappointed, which is hard for a man like him. He was too tall, too healthy a physical being to look downtrodden. His chest was broad, although its focus was slightly lowered. His arms still showed ripples even though they were now under a layer of fat. Walter had the wide rubbery face of a man who knew what to do with his mouth when the situation demanded it. He was the kind of presence that people like Jack in their hometowns of New York City and Detroit would either cross the street to pass or else ignore.

Walter took some offense that his story had been interrupted and he looked down into his draft Dixie beer. The bubbles separated themselves like the past, present, and future. Some settled under the foam, some dissolved into the air.

Still, it was Jack's flimsy and insular-cultured self that Walter wanted to address. People like Jack believed too little, especially about people like Walter. His sensation sometimes about this circumstance was akin to madness.

"Look, little brother," Walter leaned over to Jack who was rocking slightly from alcohol, "it is obvious this your first time in New Orleans; let me take you aside. Let's go for a ride in a carriage. I got a friend. I will tell you how I got to be the mayor of New Orleans and show you the best reasons for why you came here."

The men left the bar, stepping through the screen door into an ice white sun. They reduced the clientele in half when they left. But patronage was always forthcoming at Buster's. A plate meal could be eaten for less than a dollar. Everyone did his part to entertain for free and educations were doled out with as little as possible pain.

Walter and Jack headed for a step across the street on the corner. "So we catch my friend when he ride by, if in either direction," Walter pointed out. The cement was hot. But there were two wide natural seats where the banister would have been. Giant steps framed each side of the little pyramid stairs up to the door.

Walter sat on the top level with his feet on the second level. Jack, on the left, did the same.

"The sun ain't too much for you, is it, boy?"

Jack shook his head no. The heat was sobering him, making the big, black man next to him appear frightening.

Walter said, "You not ready to go, huh? Listen.

"How many time you vote in your life?" Walter asked Jack as they sipped the ice water that Walter had returned to Buster's to get. Walter guessed that Jack was in his mid-twenties, but pretty sheltered. So Walter had given Jack an opportunity to leave if he got too afraid.

"I suppose about three times," Jack replied. "Only in presidential elections." Walter figured he got Jack's age about right.

"I never did vote until I was old as you. But that's because I couldn't. At least I used to did tell myself. Come integration and all that, and voting rights, and I could have march and things. But I never did it.

"Nothing, nothing in this world mattered more to me than playing my horn. I used to wake up the people next door to me. Lord, when I was a boy, they used to complain. And I lived in the country. I came to New Orleans when I was eighteen.

"I was happy as a queen on Bourbon Street. Don't need to look around afraid like that, Jack. In New Orleans they don't mind the publicity. I been to some of their balls around Mardi Gras. Shoot, they have the best time around town."

Jack started wondering again what he had gotten into. New Orleans was such a strange place. In other cities, people were against each other or for each other so violently. But never unless there was some vested interest.

Here, he thought, life arranged itself so incongruously. The vines grew out of the bricks. He saw them in the back of his hotel. Some flowers coming into his windows and lizards crawling into his room.

The cleaning lady told him, "Won't harm you. They'll eat the cockroaches. Just let them be. They got no business with you and you got no business with them."

The streets here wound in circles and the names changed depending whether he was walking in the French Quarter or across Canal, over on the business district side. Jack wondered whether they changed the streets just for the tourists. But then he saw all those eighteenth century signs.

"This is the alley where the pirate Jean Lafitte killed most of his victims," the guide said when Jack joined a group to walk around. "And here are the slave quarters, aren't they beautiful? Some of our finest and richest people have darling quaint apartments there now. For two-fifty more, you can get another tour that will take you inside."

Walter tapped Jack on the shoulder, "I guess you be wondering how I got to be mayor. I'm getting around to it. Was because of unemployment. But first here comes my friend."

"Say, Edward," Walter called, "make some room in there for me and this young man from out of town. Where you going at? To water your mule? We just hop in and ride for a while and wait until you begin again."

The mule stopped in the middle of the intersection. It was tired of the foolish ways Edward drove. It was the mule's intention to embarrass the people. But the cars following it waited quietly and patiently until the men stepped up.

"Ain't this the coolest outside place in the city? Up here under the shade brim with the breeze coming through. You have to learn to love the simple things, Jack. That's what I learned from all my jobs," Walter said.

"But what about unemployment? . . . ," Jack asked.

"Whoa," said Edward, "don't be telling no sad stories in my cab. If you want to tell sadness, go cry in your bed."

"Nah, man. This is about my life. It is entirely glad," said Walter.

The mule listened too because it could not tell the difference between sadness and mirth and it wanted to know. The mule put its ears back against its head, as far as they could go with that flowered straw hat. People were always trying to dress up the mule like a lady. Genderless, opinionated but without any reason, the mule was not quite sure whether it liked that.

The men drove slowly to the trough alongside Jackson Square. Edward out of habit and pride pointed to buildings along the way. "That's the museum of voodoo, where they got Marie Laveau in wax and also the monster Lagniappe."

"Man, they must have took Lagniappe out of there years ago," Walter said. "I remember when I brought my kids. Had to buy them some ice cream they got so scared. And then me trying to explain to them what *lagniappe* meant when we were children, going to the store and getting a little bit extra than what you paid for."

"You the fool," said Edward, "I think your kids well understood that."

Jack asked, "Longyap is such a funny name. Is it Spanish or French?"

"I don't rightly know. Do you, Mr. Ed?" Walter asked.

"I think it got something to do with the revolution or pirates or something. Anyway, it's a real word. They always use it in the *Times-Picayune*," said Edward. The mule didn't read the daily newspaper. So it just looked all around.

"In New Orleans, isn't anything as it seems. Which brings me back to this truth I want to impress upon you, about my life," added Walter.

"I got to be mayor of New Orleans because I wasn't interested in nothing but music. Let me take you back.

"When I come here, there was many more gigs in the city. People didn't have Victrolas, except the rich. But on the

summer evenings there was music all over. Just on my block—
picture this—opera coming out of the long French doors like
bouquets of roses. Piano like good-time girls if you sat on the
step. Man and trumpet, that was my baby, coming sweet clean
at you from a window like a woman's lips, wet and delicious,
wishing with her heart you would give her a kiss.

"I was right in there. I'd go over to Jackie's and we'd talk-like
with music. And then sometimes Earl would come over, after
his job on the waterfront. If Delesepps could get away from
his beer and his wife after his day of painting houses, he'd break
out his violin. Man, you couldn't get a more beautiful situation
that that.

"Those were nights. And the days were like heaven too because no matter where you were you carried a song. Your feet
walked it. Your ears put the sound of the streets into it. Shoveling gravel, shoveling gravel, carhorn, carhorn."

Jack smiled at Walter, maybe this wasn't going to be so bad
after all. The mule came to an abrupt stop. Cars slammed on
brakes and drivers hollered out behind them. Edward gave them
a calm wave of his arm to pass by. Walter continued.

"And we made money. Because nobody, like I told you,
bought records. Come Saturday night, they'd hire us as the
band. House parties. Baby. You can't believe, liquor made in
the tub out of sugarcane. Dancing. Some of those girls like to
come out of Africa. They did their shoulders, they hips. Make a
man cry.

"Morning, somebody fix grits for breakfast and we go to
church. That's how a person stayed purified."

Walter had begun sweating. He took out a rag, which at one
time could have been a handkerchief, and wiped it tightly across
his forehead and neck. "Jack, do you believe me?" he looked up
into the young man's spellbound face. "I knew you would on
that part." There was a glossiness in the older man's eyes.

"People believe in our souls," Walter's wife had told him
when things started to become rough, "so we must." She reminded him that no one gave them anything that they didn't
work for or deserve. "So, baby, the truth is to trust," she said.

Times had gotten harder when the sweet music and life were
passed on to the youth. Like the children that multiplied out of

this union, hundreds of them all playing instruments, having contracts and managers, there was more music than parties, more parties than jobs. The days became tough. Such began Walter's search.

"So I began taking my music out to the streets," Walter waved his arm across the narrow French Quarter street caves. "Walter, Your Man in a Moment, my sign said," he laughed. "But nobody was looking for fast jive."

Walter remembered some part of this to himself. There was much to be done educating Jack, but personal had its points. There was a scene at his uncle's house when Walter was out of work that still pained him. His folks were his life and they felt the same way. But hunger put the devil in the best.

"Music has had its time and so has you," his uncle, Fredrick, had said, hard on gin. Walter's aunt, T'Ma, said, "We got plenty to feed anybody who comes to our table." She said it to defend Walter but she would not go as far as against her husband. But she made the money then anyway. She took in sewing for rich people. Walter wished he could play like that lady stitched, tiny threads close next to each other with bare swellings for knots near the buttonholes, big, firm even strokes around the hem.

The rich ladies never came over to fit. So T'Ma carried the clothes uptown. Until she left the neighborhood, she walked with the package sitting on her head. She'd bring back a French bread, quartee rice, quartee beans—each a quarter's worth—from the Italian grocery around the block. Then she'd cook it up so good you would never know meat wasn't in it.

T'Ma passed away so skinny that it hardly took men to carry her wooden box. Walter always thought it would have been better, although crazy if he had suggested it, if women balanced her coffin to the grave on their heads.

She didn't go much after that big argument in their house, Walter remembered. So he followed not far behind. He took his trumpet, and a little lace and a scapular with the bleeding heart of Jesus on one end and Mary on the other. He carried the smaller things next to a few dollars that he enclosed in a hand-sized piece of leather tied with a string.

Lots of his buddies were on "skids" as they called it back

then. He never knew why it was referred to as that, nobody got to slide. Nothing was smooth about those days, nothing rode. Still there was laughter and sharing and music. This was New Orleans; no pain was let to last longer than a tide.

"Sheet. 'Mama,' I tell her, 'this is New Orleans. You better get up off some of that cash.'" Sweet Percy was in rare form when he discussed his women, called himself a rider. He said, "Like the insurance man."

Percy was one of the few men, if you could call him that, Walter remembered, who made money when everyone else's things went bad. He gave them all entertainment for free. "That's all that's free around here," he reminded the men. He appreciated their laughter at his evil side.

Sweet Percy, Herbert Latousse, and Sam Miligan, "the Milkman," they called him because he was so white. Might have been real white, Walter remembered, but he acted so awful, who was to know or to care.

All the men joined at a bar on Rampart Street in the early morning. Walter learned to stop over there to see if any of the houses needed someone to play. "We got players and playees plenty," Walter was told by Sweet Percy, eating a big breakfast. He said, "My first meal of the day." Walter just laughed rather than hitting him. Times were hard.

Lavergne was a beautiful, sweet, generous woman. It pained Walter to think about her out in this sun. She was from south Louisiana, skin colored sunset like a peach and just as juicy inside. Lavergne made some of the best money for Sweet Percy, gave Walter some and sent the rest to her mother. "I do this because God gave me something to use to help others," she would tell Walter. He never knew whether she meant her customers, her mother, or him.

"This is New Orleans," Edward was saying to Jack. "It's a part of Louisiana, the South, the U.S., America, and the world. Ain't nothing different about it what goes on here, no. Just like anyplace else. But it's all the way different because all goes together when it happens here."

"How can that be?" Jack was laughing.

"It's funny. It's funny, you right. Ain't nobody to argue that with you," Edward went on.

"Like this here mule, beast of burden. But would you burden yourself with a mule? Before I goes home every day, I take and brush it. I waters it, feeds it—sweet hay and maybe a little molasses. I takes off that hat and straighten it out. Make it pretty for tomorrow. Then I make sure its bed all straight since it got nobody to sleep with. Then I goes home to my wife. What she tell me? I smell like a mule. I say, 'you look like a mule.' Then we could get on with dinner and I could play with my kids. I'm up early in the morning before my mule wakes up to take care of this animal here."

Jack was leaning back laughing. He was sipping a Dixie out of the can. Edward had reached into the cooler that he kept next to the horse trough and gotten them all cold beers.

"But it's the truth, I tell you," he was laughing also now and Walter had returned to the present and joined in. "Don't make me tell you again," Edward was standing in the front seat and addressing Walter and Jack as if they were children. They laughed. "If I tell you again, I might tell it different."

"And it still be the truth," Walter toasted Edward in the front and then Jack at his side.

"I'll tell you what is the truth. Columbus discovered America," Walter laughed.

"No. No. I got better than that," Edward added. "This is a genuine antique, miss. I give it to you for three dollars."

"How about . . . This Mississippi River water is the purest in the United States of America. Drink up," Walter said.

"Good girls don't kiss and tell," shouted Jack.

A moment of silence.

"Where you from, boy," Edward asked.

"Why? Uh. New York."

"Not in that shirt," said Walter.

"Well, really, just outside the City. In Connecticut."

"You ever had a good girl?" asked Walter.

"I guess," Jack said, "I don't know."

"Well, now you getting close to the truth.

"The only difference between yellows, browns, blacks, reds and whites is colored skin," said Walter, "And that ends it there, 'cause all them women got it and it runs all over them, covering them up.

"A woman will tell you the truth as she knows it and believes it and wants to think about it. That is the goodness of a woman and the foolishness of a man."

Edward leaned over his seat in the front looking intently at both of them, "My woman is as sweet as the rain in her heart. Her head, that's another story. And her behind, hot mamacita."

"Music and love is both women and truth is too. But what women ain't is politics. Women don't sleep with everybody just for a dollar. Not even the whores. They put some of their souls on the line," Walter concluded.

"You're going to tell me about when you were the mayor," Jack prompted Walter.

"I'm getting to that."

It was two in the afternoon, the sun blazed like a spotlight on the story Walter was about to tell. The men left the mule alone so they could go and get sandwiches "in the air condition." They entered a room that had the smell of oyster shells and the feel of sawdust underfoot. A waitress came up to them.

"Look here, baby. I want a hot sausage po-boy and, what you want, Walter?"

"Just a half loaf dress shrimp."

Jack looked at them both. "Do you have an American cheese sandwich and a salad?"

"I think we could find it," the waitress said and continued writing as the older men smiled.

"Women," Walter said, "they just full of truth.

"So, okay. I was out of a job, right? My woman, she say to me, 'Lameir,' she call me by my last name to get serious, 'What we would do if I have a child?'

"'Honey, don't account on that,' I tell her, 'I ain't got no job.'"

Walter explained he got a woman because times were so hard, he "could at least afford to have love.

"It was excellent. But more than anything, it was mine. Something I owned. I worked it and I deserved it.

"But love is a funny thing. There is lots in the world, all around. But you got to pick it out, like one of those wishes, you know those little cotton puff flowers that float around in the spring. You got to see it in the air, then chase it, then catch it. No matter if you look like a fool.

"The thing I had to learn was you got to hold it in your hand for a minute to make your wish, then you let it go. Even the children know that. But people get more stupid as they grow," Walter said.

"Now don't go getting ignorant, fool, just because we're talking about love. Ain't there is a sentimental in every man in New Orleans? I swear," Edward said.

Jack was about to ask if that was a question. But Edward shook his head the width of the bar to the air. No.

"What this Romeo is trying to say is that his Juliet left him," Edward continued.

"Went with a heartless man to the North," Walter said. "What could I do if she was pregnant? We had no money. I couldn't be happy. How I was going to support my boy, if it happened?"

"First of all," Edward said, "you don't know if it was a boy. Then you don't know if she was pregnant. Next, you ain't really sure she just didn't want to go North anyway. Case closed."

"Man, you want me to hurt you?" Walter stood up. "You give me some better words."

"Look, Lameir. Your second wife is with you now. She loves you. I love you. You my brother. Don't be moaning over no common-law gal. Besides, you told me yourself, she never could cook," Edward said.

"Man, she soak a pot of beans until you get sprouts," Walter smiled, "or either you find one of those rocks in your dinner. You swear you eating some of Laplace."

Jack chuckled, "Where's La Place? Is that a real place?"

"Man, real, what we trying to tell you, young son, is relative," said Walter.

"Relative, that's right," added Edward. "Like your first wife, your second wife, hope to God you don't get no third wife. That poor woman you got now if you don't start treating her better I'll trade in her for my mule. And maybe your mama too."

"Your mama, fool. What, she eat ignorant beans when she was carrying you?" Walter said as the beers arrived.

"So here I is . . . ," Walter was describing his past. The men leaned over their beers, their sandwiches gone to reveal only the white waxy paper they were served on covered with juice, a mixture of tomato catsup and mayonnaise. They looked into each others eyes, were attentive and teasing, and gave themselves over to the afternoon. "So I is here in the city then, with no first wife no more . . ."

"Done flew the coop," added Edward.

". . . out of work for a long time, if you call musicianing work, meaning only you get money. My sign, now, Walter in a Moment, people seen so much they think I'm stupid . . ."

"Well, there's some truth to that," Edward said.

". . . so like I say, I take to the streets.

"The streets of New Orleans are beautiful things," Walter continued. "You notice, Jack, how on some they laid in brick. Hand by hand, somebody's daddy did that, maybe their mama for all I know. But it was a person, a people thing, not like this here what they got—running over the tar squishing it to all sides like some skunk you done ran over in your car. Anyhow, on some streets, they got brick. On some they got gravel, uptown. Some of them streets out in the seventh ward, London Avenue for instance, was nothing but oyster shells, grey white with a pearl finish if you look at it on the right day, in the right frame of mind. But it smell; Lord have mercy.

"I know about all of these streets because I walked down every one of them. Carrying my trumpet in my hand, had sold the case. My scapular and my lace in my wallet, if you could call it that. And praying, baby, I prayed every day, sometimes twice.

"They were building Corpus Christi Church, putting up that nice stucco on the side, like Mexican style. Of course it was for the colored, how people was called in those days. The missionary priest and sisters came to New Orleans just like they went up to the Indian reservations in the north. One day I think I'm going to meet a real Indian and I'll be able to ask him, 'You ever have a run-in with Mother Ignatius? She box your ears?' I think that's half the reason I can't hear so good out of one side right now."

"Man, you know you hear what you want to hear. Don't talk about the nuns. The nuns kept you from being illiterate," said Edward.

"That's the truth, I'm not going to deny it. I'm not going to deny prayer either. As I was going to tell you before I was rudely, and I mean rudely, interrupted. I prayed like hell and I walked like them put on they shoes angels, 'all over God's heaven,' well, over earth. And come to be that a lot of people start recognizing me.

"'Hey Walter,' they be hollering, 'hey baby, how's it go?'

"'No dice,' I sorry to tell them all the time. But the people, they give me hope. They concern. 'Honey, I'd get my husband to put you on, if you knew how to do bricklaying work,' one lady tells me.

"'Miss, I'd do anything,' I tell her. And she knows I'm telling the truth because she smiles. I won't never forget that pretty blush smile. But her husband tells me, times is hard and he got to hire his relatives and you know how many relatives they got in the seventh ward, count all the way to cousins fifth and sixth and cousins by way of living next door."

"So look, tell this poor boy what happened. He's getting older front of my very eyes," said Edward.

"I'm okay," said Jack.

"See, now. He's starting to get the hang of how we do things down in New Orleans," said Walter. He called the waitress for another round for the group.

"So I ain't walking the streets just to walk the streets, you know. I ain't no beggar," said Walter.

"Not unless you got the money to pay for that round you just ordered," said Edward.

"Not to worry. If I ain't got it, Jack got it. Right Jack? And we'll move around the corner where I know people for some more beer," Walter said.

"Sure," Jack told Edward.

"The reason I'm walking the streets," said Walter, "is because I am a musician. And you seen those jazz funerals where they march, right, Jack?"

"Sure," he said.

"Well, I was parading. I was parading myself from the seventh ward to the ninth ward, from Treme to the second ward. Back of the garden district to St. Roche cemetery. I was going to play me some music to get the people happy enough to give me money."

"Did it work?" asked Jack.

"Kinda. But you got to listen to my songs. First, I start off with 'Just a Closer Walk With Thee,' just like at the funerals. The people feel sorry for me and they think of all they old dead folk and how they wish they could hear that song. So they start singing along to themselves, you know, so the dead can read their minds. Then I do 'God Bless the Child,' like I learned in them roly-poly joints. The old ladies get sort of hushed on this one, like they're going to go away. But they know they stood outside of those places, at the farthest, and they like that music same as everyone. Then, 'His Eye's on the Sparrow . . . So I Know He's Watching Me.' They hooked then, they don't know whether to stay or go. You know, like the Lord caught them red-handed."

"Man, do we must hear all this?" Edward asked.

"You drink up, partner," Walter said. "Anyhow, I end with 'Way Down Yonder in New Orleans' and they begin to second line. Always got a few of the loose ones will shake their behinds and pass the hat for me."

"So you made out all right, then?" Jack asked.

"Well, not with money, with popularity," answered Walter.

"I think you going to be very popular here too," said Edward. "Here come the waitress to ask for your autograph."

"You got two dollars, Jack?" Walter asked.

"Sure," Jack put a five on the table.

Walter laughed, "Don't go show yourself, unless you ready to share."

They stepped through one half of the swinging door and it banged back and forth, slamming against the lip of the other and squeaking.

"I used to could make my music off of stuff like that," Walter said.

Edward called, "I got to go check on my mule."

"We with you," Walter responded.

They had not left the French Quarter but Jack felt transported. He was thrown to a time that he never lived. It was comfortable sometimes. Then he would feel totally out of place. He did not know these men. Both were old enough to be his father, or maybe his grandfather. He was not a good judge of black men's ages.

Although race wasn't the issue either. He had gotten over that back at Buster Holmes' when he decided to stay on the step. It was like he was handed some test of manhood by Walter. At the time, Jack thought, "Well, who is he anyway?" But he was glad he had waited. For himself, even, he felt that he had passed.

Why did they look at him so strange when he said, "Good girls don't tell" or "do tell," which was it? Anyway, didn't they think he knew women at all? He had been screwing since he was fifteen. Betsy Crinoline let him have it. She, he smiled, was very good.

"So you think I don't know anything about loving women, huh?" Jack caught up to Walter as he stood reading the weekly newspaper's headlines through the tin-enclosed stands while he waited for Edward.

"I got no problem with you and women," said Walter, "but you are wrong if you think you know about love."

He went on, "Who knows about love? Christ Jesus was the only one I heard of who I could say put the finger on it. It's just like truth. Mother Mary was the only one who knew perfect truth, never sinned. And then, what was done unto them, was that the truth or was that a lie? Was it love that killed him or hate? Did she and Joseph like each other or just suffer the presence of the Holy Ghost? Are we reading the Bible or is it some story people made up along the way?"

Jack's head was swimming with beer and with symbolism. "What does this have to do with women?"

"You say you know love. You think it's women. I say it is music."

"Walter, you bending this man's head," Edward approached them. "Why don't you let him come up for air? Anyhow, you supposed to be telling him when you was the mayor of New Orleans."

"Edward, where's your mule?" Walter asked.

Edward looked down at the ground and said weakly, "I think it's sick from the heat. I went over there and it's foaming a little around the mouth. I couldn't tell. And it ain't saying a word to me."

"You talking to it now?" Walter asked.

"Don't make me out no fool," Edward said. "You know how I rapport with that mule. Lay one side of the rein on his back, that mean turn to the left. Sing 'Watermelon, red to the rind,' it turn to the right. Most of the time I don't need to tell it the way home. I sleep from the French Quarter all the way to the stables. It stop at the lights and everything."

"Man, I just got a few beers in me. I'm sorry. I don't mean to make fun. So what you going to do?" Walter asked.

"Well, I figure I sit with it for a while, see if it get worse. I already put a little water 'cross his neck and sponged the back."

Walter pointed to Ursuline Street. "We just going around the corner. You know my place. Jack here ain't never heard music like what they got there. I want him to know."

"I hope your mule feels better, Edward," Jack said.

"Thank you, boy. I do appreciate to hear that."

The young man and the old man walked slowly from the horse trough to the cathedral. The ironwork fence around Jackson Square ran alongside them. It was upright like bars and open to show children playing games freely inside, the bums sleeping under the shade trees, and pigeons circling in packs.

Painters set up small easels every two or three feet. They brought ice chests and seat cushions along with their paints. People decided who was serious by what subject they chose to paint. There were caricaturists at the bottom of the list, then portrait artists in charcoal, then near the top of the list were the ones who did French Quarter scenes. Of course, people discounted the artists who just took little butter knives to apply oil paint from the tubes to raise the lines of a print that had been pressed in by machine. You could get them for far less money than the others, except the caricature people. So the knife people were the most popular.

"Wait, stop here a minute," Jack halted Walter by the arm. "I want to go into this postcard shop."

Walter waited outside next to the Mammy in a red-checkered dress with an apron and her head tied. She was stuffed cotton, like a big rag doll or something a taxortionist, he thought they called them, would do. People from out of town took their pictures with it. Children lifted the woman's dress to see if she had on underwear, or her scarf to see if she had hair.

Walter could imagine he lived in the old times of those Mammy laws, even though they were at least a hundred years before. His grandmother repeated the stories to him when he was a child: "They made it so we had to tie up our heads, all the colored women. It was against the law to show hair. They was afraid of our beauty. Had so many black, yellow, red ones having white men. They was as much afraid of our power, too, that we would put the love of white into our colored children. See, they wanted to keep pure their race."

As a boy, Walter had not believed her. But then later, he read the law in a book. His grandmother had been one of the greatest reasons he took up trumpet. "Play it loud so I can hear it from both ears," she said. She was a little deaf. She never seemed to notice when there were mistakes.

"Here, I bought you a postcard," Jack exited carrying a small brown paper bag. It was of a scene in Preservation Hall of old men playing Dixieland and Sweet Emma on piano. They looked sort of waxy and unreal, Walter thought. But he appreciated Jack's gift.

"You all right," he patted the young man on the shoulder. Jack was leaning up against a building and writing out a postcard against the old stucco wall. His handwriting was bumpy and scribbled. "This is for my girlfriend in New York." He handed the card to Walter when he finished it. It said, "Music is love. Jack."

"You going to be an old sentimental yourself, as Edward say," Walter told Jack and patted him on the shoulder a little harder than before. "Come on, let's get around this corner a minute. You make me wonder what I'm talking for."

Walter had seen so many young men come and go in New Orleans. Visitors, he was thinking about. Not that they had to be white. He remembered a young man he befriended from New York, said he was a writer. He wore a watch chain across his stomach, which was pretty wide. It went from one pocket in his vest to another. He wore the vest over a white T-shirt. Edward didn't want to pick him up. He told Walter that was some kind of sign.

"Well, I was the fool to make a friend with him," Walter told himself. That time, he remembered, it hurt. Walter saw his life's story in a newspaper someone brought back from New York, except the man had written it into fiction without even mentioning Walter's name. He wrote in the paper that he had a vision of the South in his head, although he preferred to live in the North.

"I'm a friend to every man," Walter remembered his conversation with Lapin at the bar where they were going. "Ain't it true that I reap what I sow?"

"True. You reap friendship, not fame, Walter. But maybe that's not enough. Look at you now, you got no place to go," Lapin said.

This friend had encouraged him to run for mayor. "You out of a job anyway. What can you lose?" Lapin was called that since he was a child because of his buckteeth in the front and later for the quick staccato style that he blew clarinet.

Walter got into the mayor's race more for Lapin than anyone, at least anyone he could name. He felt for Lapin, being made fun of all his life. Lapin was a most excellent musician. But because of his funny looks, he never was given serious fame. The others Walter ran for were the people. He knew that sounded crazy when he told it to his wife.

"You some kind of revolutionary? Walter, you not on LSD or something you picked up in the French Quarter, are you, baby?" she said. He explained he was doing it for her, for her friends, and for the beauty of life.

"I knowed when I married you, I married a sweet man. That's one of the reasons I love you," she had said. "God bless us, baby, for what we about to do. But why not?'

Walter went back to Lapin the next day to tell him to begin the campaign. Lapin said, "What? You already got one."

They put flags all around the bar and crepe-paper ribbons outside that washed color onto the building with the first good rain. People who had been saying, "Hi, Walter," when he walked around town with his trumpet and sign came to the bar to have a beer, hear him talk and play.

Walter felt his message then. He blew for the lady with the "rag round her head," he told the people, who lived on the corner of London and Rocheblave where she hung up the wash. "Washwoman Blues Monday," he told the audience that the song was called. It sounded like the call of a goose. His music was like that, sort of funny, sort of pitiful. Everyone who came there could relate to that.

From the bandstand, Walter could see big men wiping their eyes in the dark, and ladies and children who came during the day were singing along.

He did "Washwoman," "Schoolteacher's Vacation," and "Garbageman's Strike." The last song he was inspired to create during the police boycott of Mardi Gras. When the television cameras asked a garbageman if his union would go out in support of the police, the man said, "Them what you go to support today be the same ones who tomorrow beat you in the head."

Walter himself had gotten swung at a few times. When he was a teenager, he and Lapin went to the parades. Lapin jumped up to catch some beads and came down accidentally on a woman's foot. Even though he apologized, the woman screamed and screamed. Walter tried to reason with her, "Miss, you can have one of my doubloons. Don't be upset on Mardi Gras." But she was from out of town.

The police came at them swinging. Walter and Lapin got struck a few times. But they were able to run. "Just remember, what you don't say when a cop got a stick at your head," Walter told the crowd to prepare them for the music, "is 'please, mister don't hit me.'"

The audience laughed.

Walter's memories, sometimes he felt, were like waves. Like out on Lake Pontchartrain where he sat on the seawall steps. First you could sit on the fourth step up from the water, then the sixth up and soon you had to sit up at the top. The water in the evening would be coming, rolling, splashing, never really announcing that it could do you real pain. But if you were fool enough, Walter remembered, like Bootsie, to stay planted on the step in defiance, the waves could sweep you off and take you away.

"Bootsie, that was a fool," Walter smiled, "a man who would try damn near anything and see if he live." Most of the time, like that evening at the lake, his friends loved him so much because of his foolhardiness, they would save him. Walter himself, not much of a swimmer compared to the other guys, had also jumped in.

"But didn't we have a time?" Bootsie asked Walter once after they got older and Bootsie worked in a wrecking yard. They leaned up against a hollowed-out car. Bootsie said, "Man, I loved ya'll brothers for that so hard."

"Sheet, you a fool, Bootsie," Walter had tried to make it into a joke. But after, he thought maybe it was the wrong time. Bootsie's wife left him not too long after that and Bootsie committed suicide.

Jack told Walter, "You got awfully quiet. Is something wrong?"

"Shoot, not no more than I'm thirsty and somebody better be buying the next round."

"Not me," Jack said, trying to joke as he had heard the men do before.

"How you know?" Walter asked him.

"Well, uh."

"Jack," Walter started laughing, "You got a lot yet to learn. Come on in."

Walter escorted Jack by the shoulders alongside him up to the bar. "Lapin, where you is at?" Walter called. "I want service from your hands."

"Wait, man," Lapin called, "I got to go to the bathroom . . ."

"Isn't that thoughtful," Jack said, "for him to go wash his hands?"

". . . I ain't dirty enough." Of course, Lapin didn't go to the bathroom. He came directly over to them at the bar. "My friend," he said to Walter, going to hold palms and shake.

"Your mama," Walter said, shaking his hand.

Jack was getting dizzy, not understanding what was real. Who was good? Who was bad? He looked up, north to the sky, for assistance. Then he saw one of Walter's campaign posters. "Is this some kind of joke?" he asked the men.

"You know, Lapin," Walter said, looking at Jack, "You tell people the truth and they don't believe you. They want to think the worse about you. But never that you could be something."

"I'm sorry," Jack said, "I'm not trying to be offensive. It's just so . . ."

"A joke, man," Walter said, "It's a motherfucking joke and so am I. That's what you think?"

Jack reached for his beer. What had he done? This man was trying to be nice to him. He apologized again. "I'm sorry, Walter. I'm from New York. Things don't happen like this up there," he said.

Walter responded, "You'd be surprised."

"Now, Connecticut . . ." Walter said, "I would believe anything about Connecticut. Ain't that is where they got the New Haven slums and Yale? Remember Laurent went up there after St. Augustine High School when Yale came recruiting. Went to Africa and then became a Communist, as I remember. Ain't that right, Lapin?"

"Yes, but he is a peaceful man and he still go to church," said Lapin.

"Well, he want to be buried by Corpus Christi Parish and you know how they strict," said Walter.

"I'm sorry, Walter. I am from Connecticut," Jack looked down over Walter's beer.

"Look, young man, don't get all worried about that," Walter said. "Just don't bullshit me. There's a lot of truth going on here."

"You know what's the truth?" Lapin called out to both of them. "That fat women taste like candy kisses."

The men laughed.

"I swear," Lapin sang. "Look at my own sweet wife." He handed to Jack a black-and-white photo that was stuck in the cracks between the frame of a mirror behind the bar and the glass. "You might not think she is a lot to look at," Lapin said to Jack, "but she is as good as a summer day is long. And the nights," Lapin gazed into the air, "thank God they so short. I'm getting kind of old to keep that load lifted for hours."

"For hours, sheet," said Walter, "not for that long in many years, Lapin. But me, like the song says, 'I'm the sixty minute man.'"

"Music," Lapin reminisced, "Music is what brought me and my sweet lady together." He looked at Jack, "You ever been to hear James Brown?

"Well, let me tell you," Lapin continued, "here, every year, they used to have a James Brown concert at the municipal auditorium. The auditorium, you know, is back of Congo Square. That's the place outside, where when in slavery, they used to bring the slaves on Sunday and the people would have parties and socializing. That, they say, dancing and socializing, is the difference in the slaves of the English and the French.

"Anyhow, about this time as I was a young man, I'm talking about twenty-five, thirty years old. Walter here is older than me. I used to go every year, hear James Brown. He wasn't so popular those days. At least not with all the people buying his records, like now. Then they put his face on the cover and, anybody know in those days, wasn't nothing but us going to look at us on the cover of albums. Not even Johnny Mathis, they didn't put him on for a long time. But anyhow, in person, JB, Lord, he put on a show.

"Well, the white people never came to those concerts either. Because people be partying so hard, they about to kill each other to death. Always was one humbug or another there. But nobody except the troublemakers really get hurt."

Jack watched in amazement. Lapin seemed to have forgotten he was telling the story to him. Lapin looked out over the bar into the air as he talked or sometimes he would direct his conversation to Walter.

"Anyway. One night at the JB concert there was a shooting. Bam. Bam. Bam. People started flying down the aisles and out the door. Me, I ain't no fool either. I go running straight to the St. Bernard bus. But guess who I'm following behind?"

"Your wife?" asked Jack.

"You right, young man. There she was barefoot as she want to be, running with one shoe in her hand. She jump on the bus and sitting there either between laughing or looking foolish, she telling everybody who could hear that she left her good shoe under the seat in the balcony. Well, I liked her way about life. We got to talking after that."

"Lapin, that is a love story if I ever heard one. You ought to go get somebody to write it up in one of those magazines," said Walter. "I don't see why the *Times-Picayune* wouldn't publish it in the 'Lagniappe' section, the lagniappe being ya'll got married besides being in love."

Lapin looked at Walter, "You know that's a thought."

The sun felt like it was still high. It might have been four or five in the afternoon. But no one was going to go outside to look up and see. There were no clocks in the bar. "That's bad for business," Lapin told Jack. None of the men wore watches. Jack, because he didn't want his stolen in a strange city. Walter and Lapin, because in their words, "our time is our own."

"Still, now, you ain't heard me out about being the mayor. You know, I don't believe you want to know?" Walter swiveled his chair to face Jack.

"No. That's not true, Walter," Jack apologized.

"I'm just playing with you, boy," Walter responded. "We're all over that."

Lapin prompted Walter, "Tell him about the time we had the big parade. Started and ended right here at this very bar."

"OK," Walter said and leaned over to Jack, "do you know the difference between marriage and death?"

Before Jack could answer, if he could answer, he was so busily searching his mind, "Participation," said Walter, "that's the truth. This is how I want to tell you about that parade."

"Once," he began, "once a man marries, he has full knowledge of what he is doing. Oh, him and a few women, they been around. And his kin, they so happy, he's joining them under the wedded yoke. They come to the church as if something was free. And it is. And then they dance at your reception.

"Man, if you never been to a Creole reception. How long you be here? I should take you. There is so much dancing and drinking, rival any house party or whorehouse. But there is not a bit of evil on anybody's mind. Not big evil, at least. Maybe some venial sins, like your sister get soused and call her mother-in-law a name or maybe everybody dividing up who going to dance with the single girl and one of the men break the group and ask her all alone.

"Well, marriage is like that. Joy, drinking, dancing. Then you may ask, 'Then what, I do not see it, is the difference with death.' True, then all the same things go on. And all of your family takes part as well, bringing their sins with them. Except there are other guests.

"Some people who come to your funeral be glad to see you is

dead. Others come because they are still with the living and they misses you as one of their number. They don't know you either. But Lord, do they cry. Well, that's what I'm getting at," Walter said. "The difference between marriage and death is the same as political parades."

"I don't understand," said Jack.

"It's the same people what do all of these things. For the same reasons. Except quicker. They love you or hate you and dance with you, for you or against you all in a few months' time," Walter concluded.

Lapin showed Jack mementos on the walls of the bar. There was a sign saying, "Walter, the Candidate for the Moment." Stuck in the mirror were photos of Walter with the president of the United States, a lady with a fruit basket on her head, and a child dressed up in an outfit like a ham. On the costume was a blue ribbon; it said First Prize. "That was a lawyer friend of mine daughter," Walter said quietly. "They too had they hard times."

"We used to have lots of his literature in here," Lapin said, "but I had this waitress once who used all the flyers for bar napkins because we ran out. Can you imagine? I had to let her go the next day. Some people don't have no appreciation or respect."

"Must have been every musician in town came to that parade. The old ones who come dragging they feet and the young ones who played nothing that hadn't been electrified. They all came to strut, like I said, for all their different reasons. But Lord, that was a day. We covered some ground," said Walter.

"We started right here at Lapin's bar. Everybody got the first round free. He's such a good man. Then we took to the street. We went down to Buster's to pick up some people, over to Esplanade and up to Simon Boulevard. He was a war hero, you know. Go look at the statue. We went over to Charity Hospital, stood out there and played for the sick for a spell. Then we came up the back, right to City Hall.

"They got a big spot full of grass in front of the mayor's office, you know. So we played and we played. Some women I knowed in grammar school, who were then secretaries, took our literature and went pass it around inside."

Jack could picture this. He knew lots of secretaries. He saw women in suits and high heels, knocking on every door in the tall City Hall building and giving each office worker a pep talk.

"Shoot, that girl Irene went home and got her slippers." Walter reminisced. "She said she was going to walk around City Hall plaza for me all day.

"But it was the sound that got me over, I know. Everybody playing his own tune then coming together at the bridge like that. You heard what they call Dixieland music, huh Jack?" Walter asked.

"Yeah, I studied it once. It's A-A-B, A-A-B," he said.

"Well, you could say that," Walter patted Lapin's arm. He was always impatient. "But it's more like, listen, 'Let's go around, ba-rump-bump. In low down, ba-rump-bump. Old New Orleans, ba-bump, ba-bump, ba-bump ba-bump bump.' You could do a big lot of shaking on that." Walter saw from the corner of his eye Lapin was now smiling and humming along to himself.

"Well, that's what the people did. They shook they behinds so bad, they made up they minds to vote for me. Lots of people. You couldn't count how many yourself. They checked those machines on election day for three times. Nobody could believe I got the votes. The politicians said, 'How this fool done come in here with no power, no organization, no people backing him and win, come to be the mayor.' I say to them, 'Fellas and some of ya'll who is ladies too, that's where you wrong. I got people who always wave to me when I go down the street. I got power 'cause power is people. And I got organs and organization, the head connected to the neck bone, the neck bone connected to the shoulder bone, the shoulder bone connected to the chest bone, the chest bone connected to the . . . well, you know that song, don't you Jack?

"Anyway," said Walter, "that's how I come to become mayor. But a man is not a job. So that's not my story. That's just the half of it."

"I was no more or less a man as the mayor than as the unemployed," Walter told Jack.

"Is this a morality tale?" Jack said, a little drunk, showing his youth.

"Ain't no tale at all. This is the truth," Walter answered. He was drunk by this time also and did not understand the offense, as it was slight.

"The difference between where I was before and then," Walter said, "was words. I still had the heart of a musician. I still had my natural gift of gab. But because they named me the mayor, people looked at me in a different way."

Edward walked into the bar. "How's it going?" Lapin greeted him.

"Man, I'm messed up," he replied.

"What are you angry about?" Walter asked.

"My mule ain't sick. Not really. Somebody just went and gave it some ice cream. All of that white round his lips. The mule got milk and sugar drying up all over his face. Drinking water to get the sweet taste out of his mouth. I tell you people are crazy," Edward said. "A mule ain't a child. If they didn't have nothing to do with they ice cream, why did they buy it? Now I'm going to waste a whole evening working because that animal is nauseous. But you know I think I saw him smile?"

"Give the mule some peace," Walter patted a chair for Edward to sit down. "Come trouble us. We used to your kind."

"Walter was just telling Jack the difference between a job and a man," Lapin called out.

"Well me myself," said Edward, "sometimes I would like to know that."

"Remember when I was the mayor?" Walter asked Edward, "remember what happened then?"

"All kind of people want to come up and shake his hand, ask him his personal business, make him pronounce how the black people felt," Edward turned to Jack.

"Well, at any time, anybody can tell you I be glad to talk about all of that," Walter said, "but it was because I was the mayor they asked me. Not because I was Walter. It was like that children's story, remember that fairy tale about the boy who couldn't take off his hat.

"They be asking me this and that. Not 'cause they had no respect for me. But because they wanted to hear the mayor's words. And if I tell them, they laugh, meaning to hurt in a way because that's not what they expected from the job," Walter was interrupted.

"You know what the black man's burden is, Walter?" Lapin asked. "It's that he speaks the things that people don't believe. They can't or don't want to believe or something. I ain't figured that part out yet. But I know it's the truth."

"You right, my friend. I could tell you from firsthand experience," Walter said, "remember I was the mayor and lots of folks couldn't even listen to me. Oh, it was all right to them to vote for me as long as I was a musician. But being the mayor, by their own rules, deserved respect. And couldn't many—black or white—give that to a black man—mayor, musician, or what."

Walter remembered he'd had to get bodyguards for his wife because she shunned some men in the grocery store. She never was the kind of woman to play along with men. But after he got elected, people said she was trying to act stuck up.

"Who is the mayor's wife now?" Walter remembered the newspaper headline. She was who she always had been. But now, men were calling at her, reporters following her down the street, women studying her hair and wanting to hear her speak. But she just wasn't the kind of person to give her opinion. At least, not to the public. Just to Walter, he smiled, just to Walter.

"Having a job was hard as not having a job," Walter remembered to himself, "and it was all on account of words." Not only was he named new and people had a particular suit for him to fit, but they started dragging for him about the way he used English and what books did he read and why did he attend the Catholic church.

At that time, Lapin did Walter the favor of going to the library and bringing back some books for him. "Look here," Lapin handed him a novel, "I thought this one would be interesting. It's by a man-woman, James Joyce. I don't think that name is totally for real. But the lady at the library said it had a lot to do about speaking in different ways. He's from Ireland and you like them."

"Yeah," Walter had said, "my great-grandfather was from Ireland, Conden. So I got no problem there. That guy Milkman we used to know, I think he was Irish too. But he was kind of rough. Then look at his company, Sweet Percy. So I guess all peoples is about the same."

Walter still remembered the story he had read about the girl who was going to marry a sailor. It reminded him so much of his little cousin. Except his little cousin took the boat and left New Orleans with the man. She had so many in her family to support. Went to Miami and came back home without him, rich.

But Walter remembered, he did learn something from those books. Everybody talked as bad as him. Some of them might try to act more proper or like they owned the English language. But the books showed that people put words together all kinds of ways, just like music. And Walter knew about music; in music, there was no such thing as more right.

A man could play a horn sweeter, Walter remembered, like Miles. Or a woman could sing worse sad, like Billie Holiday, queen of the blues. But to say that an aria, Walter knew opera too, was better than a riff, only a true fool would presume.

Outside the evening was falling like a cheap window shade, the best buy for the people who loved summer because it still let the breeze and some light in too. It gave a blue mood to an old-fashioned room. On one side of the big double doors, the grandmother would be kneeling in the reverent half-brightness and saying the radio rosary. On the other side, by the round lion-footed table, the mother would be setting out plates.

The evening smelled like onion smothering down into brown gravy, if you strolled on your way home past windows in the seventh ward. The voices of children playing would surround you like music. And in fact, many times, they would be singing. "Miss Mary died. Oh, how did she die? Well she died like this. One, two, three, four. Miss Mary died. Oh, how did she die? Well she died like this. One, two, three, four." The little girls would be following the leader in the middle, holding their backs or their sides or their chests, in repetition. "Well, she died with a heart attack in her sleep. Never coming back to live on this street." Then they'd pick a new leader. "Miss Sarah died. Oh, how did she die. Well she died like this." The new child might spin her forefinger around her ear to show Sarah died of insanity.

Each child would go inside, some before darkness fell, some much after, as their people called them.

"I was not a happy politician," Walter told Jack.

Jack was looking out of the open door to the street. It was beginning to get dark. He felt, for no reason he could put into words, like he wanted to run away.

"Man," Edward called Walter, "are you buying beer for people or what?"

"What." Walter said, "Could you put one of those cold ones out for me. I'll take care for Edward with you tomorrow."

"I know where you live," Lapin said, "not to worry."

"I was happiest," Walter said, "most entirely happy playing music. There is nothing more pure than sound alone."

"Think about it," Walter put his hand on Jack's shoulder. Jack jumped just a little, coming out of his personal thoughts— subways, money, getting a cab from the airport.

"Listen to what I'm telling you. If you are by yourself sometimes in the middle of the night, you can hear the earth spinning," Walter confided.

"Oh no. There goes crazah," Edward called. "Man slow down a little bit on those beers."

"Don't pay no attention to him," Walter leaned back to Jack. "I got an idea *why* you can hear it. It's a proven fact that you can. Ain't that the truth, Lapin?"

"Well, man, I ain't never listened to it with you. And you say you can't hear it unless you alone. And me, I got a house full of children," Lapin replied. "But I ain't going to argue with you about it. Stranger things done been proved."

"Well then, all of ya'll listen. The earth, you see, she is like a big, twenty-five-cent gumball. You know, like those jawbreakers we used to buy when we were kids . . ."

"You talking about the day-old donuts from Dequoux?" Edward asked.

"No, not them kind of jawbreakers," Walter said, "the kind you used to suck on, the hot ones, like you used to put in a handkerchief and try to crack with your teeth if you was in a rush, you know. You'd have all the little pieces in your handkerchief and you'd sneak to eat them bit by bit during class."

"I know what you talking about," said Lapin, "the children who used to study a lot would just suck on them real slow until they melted to a tiny round ball of sweet in the middle."

"That's the jawbreakers I'm talking about," Walter said. "Well, big like that in comparison to a circle that you would draw in the dirt to play chinees. Ya'll might have called it marbles, Jack, where you was a boy. I know that's just New Orleans.

"Well, imagine a big blue jawbreaker sitting in a circle of chinees, everybody staring at it, wondering what it's doing there? who's playing with that? will it stick to the ground? Just then a bully comes by, picks it up, and throws it farther than can anybody see. And this being a special blue jawbreaker, it just keeps flying, humming out into the air. Scooting away forever. That's the universe.

"And then what would all the children say? There would be so much commotion, laughing, fussing, teasing. Maybe even some of them who really wanted to find out about the jawbreaker's reasons for being there would cry. But I can tell you, wouldn't it be loud then?"

"Most assuredly," said Edward.

"I hear you," said Lapin.

"I've been in a situation like that before," said Jack.

"Yes, it would be loud," Walter went on. "Now imagine yourself, you a little bitty tiny ant. In size, less than an ant . . ."

"A uncle," Edward joked.

"Shh," said Lapin.

"So you this little living speck, on this big jawbreaker. And you stuck on it. So when the bully throws it, you go too, flying faster than you could ever imagine in the air. What does it sound like, children hollering, you flying, the wind all around you whistling by? It sounds like the earth spins. I don't need to see it to know it's a fact.

"I am not a visual person," Walter said. "I once had a college woman tell me that. She must have been right. Said she learned in school, some people are visual and some people go by what they hear."

"Aw, that's a story," said Edward.

"No, for real," Walter said. "Like Edward here," he told Jack, "he is visual. Me, I listen for things. But Edward, he could tell you what things looks like all over New Orleans."

"Well, that's the truth," said Edward. "What you want to know?"

"How does the city look during Mardi Gras?" asked Jack.

"Huh, you asking for a lot of seeing," said Edward, "get me another beer."

He began, "At Mardi Gras, you know that's a religious holiday, all over the city, the people are colored. Got on red suits, bright blue dresses, dirty brown baby diapers, wearing big green palm trees on their heads. And I'm just talking about the grown men.

"The woman, they are the most beautiful, drunk as they want to be, too. But some of them put on they sexiest clothes, bikinis, backless evening gowns. Some of them dress like nuns.

"It's the spirit that makes everything look different then. That, plus they mask. In New Orleans, if you masquerade you can really come out with yourself. But don't let people recognize you. They'll holler, 'I know you Mardi Gras.' Then you been found out."

"Tell him about the Indians," Walter encouraged.

"You ever seen a black Indian?" Edward asked.

"Well, I guess," Jack said, "like some of you have Indian blood, right?"

"No, I'm not talking race Indian. I mean real Indian, like for Mardi Gras. The Wild Magnolias or Wild Tchoupitoulas. Some named after the uptown streets. That's where lot of them were born.

"When I was a boy, you'd wake up early on Mardi Gras to go see the fights. The uptown Indians would fight with the Indians that lived below Canal Street. My mother said don't get mixed up with all of that. But I went," said Edward.

"Us too," Walter spoke for himself and Lapin.

"You could know they was coming if you look on the street and see the flag boy arriving up front. The scout probably passed already but you missed him. It was his job to be sneaky and spot them who they was going to beat up on. Then he'd go back and tell the chief.

"By noon, they be so full of firewater, the most they could do is just give out a few bloody cuts. So that's when they had the good times. Be in a circle on the neutral ground, you know, the grass dividing the uptown from the downtown sides of the traffic. And second-lining. The best.

"Now, talk about looking pretty. They costumes was full of beads making pictures, yellow like a egg sunnyside or black like a good racing horse. Every bead, the warriors sew on themselves by hand. And I think they really be wishing not to get into no fights to get all covered up with blood."

"Edward," Walter interrupted, "was you ever an Indian?"

"I was for a few months until Mardi Gras," Edward said. "Then my mama catch me going out of the house and stole my clothes. They laugh about that too hard on the block. So I decided none of them really was my friend worth giving up my life."

Edward continued, "But the saddest thing I ever saw was a Indian burial. Much like the shouting Baptists, some of them anyway. There was screaming and falling out on the ground. A little girl, about fifteen, she was this warrior's lady. He was the same age. She went up to the hole and threw his costume in. I thought she was going to go in herself. But I think she wind up having a baby. Then going back to high school."

"I never heard that or even read about it in the guidebooks before I came to New Orleans," said Jack. "I thought I covered everything."

"Might never would 'cause it's our story and that's about history, man," Walter said. "Lapin knows all about history."

"Man, you trying to tell me I'm old or something," Lapin joked.

"You could be old as you want to be," Walter said. "I know you remember and you read."

"Don't be spreading that around, man. I'll lose my reputation as a good bartender . . ." Lapin leaned toward the group to do his part for Jack.

"History, she's a funny thing, Jack," Lapin said directly to him. "Each person has one and everybody has one. So can't never anyone agree on it."

"Yeah, like that time you say that wasn't no vision that they had on Laharpe Street," Edward said. "Look Jack, it was the Blessed Virgin Mary appeared in the bathroom. I seen it myself. At least what she left. There was a little shadow right next to the tub in her image and likeness. Just like her."

"Well, man, you know how I feel about that," said Lapin. "The Blessed Virgin Mary don't need to go to no bathroom. She give her vision to other places, where people need her. Like in Mexico, remember how she did them roses in Guadalupe," said Lapin.

"I don't know about no Guadalupe. I'm talking about Laharpe Street."

Walter stopped Edward, "Let the man talk."

"We'll settle this later," Edward said.

"See, like everyone knows history. But they know it in a certain way. And ain't none of it true. Then again all of it is. It's like America. The things you learn in school go up against the things you know from the street. Like, they say in New Orleans, the Spanish did the ironwork balconies. But I know for a fact that one of my people was the best ironworker in town. And he was pure de black.

"But then black is not a real people color anyway. It's not a race, it's a political term. . . ."

"I'm going to finish telling you to about my political term, Jack," said Walter.

"Yes," said Lapin, "he definitely got to hear about that. I'm just going to be another minute . . . black neither white is nobody's skin color. You ever seen it?"

"Maybe some of the African people?" said Jack.

"Not to be offensive," said Lapin, "But hell no. Even them, they ain't black. They might be purple-brown, or oil-mud color. But never just black. Ain't nobody white. They might be egg-shell or ivory or milk-cream. So why do they call all of us that?

"Because of history. Because somebody wanted to read everything in a certain way. First, they have the war, the revolution of immigrants. Then they got to make they own history and system. So they decide to make it in a black-and-white way. When the first American people choose to take on that name, they have to make a thing out of their race. Is you white? Is you black? Is you other? We is all other—Italian-Chinese, German-Cherokee, Haitian-Irish, ain't that what you is, Walter?"

"Just on my grandmother's side. I got French, Spanish, two or three Africans and Indians, and some other stuff," he said.

"See, that is history and that is his right," Lapin concluded.

"But I don't quite understand," Jack said. "You are saying that there are racial differences. But you don't want to call it that."

"Of course, everybody is different. That's what I'm saying makes them the same. That's what makes real history. Everything told in between black and white," Lapin answered.

"So what does a person believe? How does a country unite itself?"

Edward spoke up, "I don't see where nothing is falling apart. It's about the same as it always was, in my life. Except now, some is trying to make you think we wrong unless we all think the same thing 'cause we stuck together by land north and south."

"Look out now," said Walter. "Out of the mouths of fools."

"I be reading the paper too, man," said Edward.

"I know it, baby," Walter replied.

"What a person has to believe," Lapin said, "is the truth. That's what you have faith and trust in. And the truth can come from any side."

"Now ya'll ready," said Walter, "this here has to do with why I am not the mayor no more today.

"They ain't room for the truth in mayoring," said Walter. "Not like music playing or basketball or swimming."

"Man, remember how we used to go swimming at Lake Pontchartrain before it got polluted?" Edward said. "Shoot, do a mile before you know it or play pitch the can, see through the water clear like in your bathtub. Now, you couldn't see you hand in front of your face, was you was to put your face in that mess."

"Well, there is mess all over and in politics, it come up to your knees," said Walter.

He remembered his first day in office. He felt so proud. By the time he got to actually be the mayor, in between the election and the inauguration, he had a lot of ideas.

He couldn't help but have them. People dropped by his

house, asking him what he was going to do about so many things.

"I think they should be a commission or department or how ever they call that on sink fixing," said the old lady from across the street who came with her grandson and a fruitcake. "I swear, Walter, I be cleaning my pipes, this boy here can tell you. He does it for me. He's a good boy. But still the drain go down so slow. I think it is 'cause of something in the street."

Walter suggested that she follow the line from her kitchen to her yard before he took this suggestion to his office. "You getting uppity, Walter?" she asked. "Now I'm gonna look for you to announce this in the paper. My baby here will read it every day to check for me."

That was one of the easiest requests Walter got. There was already a department in pipes, except in a different name. But many painful, impossible tasks came, too, that Walter tried to do something about. "My baby," a young mother stopped by Walter's front-yard fence to talk, "he is retarded, Walter. I didn't get the right formula to him when he was a child. Or either it's 'cause of my husband's family. I don't know. But Walter, I don't know what to do either. Since my man left, I got to work and there ain't nobody I can put him with. You know, I don't take welfare, Walter. I don't want charity. Can you help me to get a permission for a school at my house so I can mind him and other children too?"

Her house had been in the wrong neighborhood for zoning and changing it would have cost the city too much money and for her to fight it cost legal fees. Plus she didn't have a degree. Walter still saw her now walking around the streets with her son following on her arm. He thought she was taking hand washing.

"The truth was, what could I do to really help anybody?" Walter asked. "Soon as I come in, the others who were politicians set up against me because I was not one of them. Everything I tried to do, they stopped in the city council. It was like they didn't want me to do anything but parade. Greet the visitors. Pass out the key to the city. Sheet, now if that ain't a lie I don't know what is. Please tell me, what does the key to the city unlock?"

"The bathrooms at the Lake Pontchartrain shelters," Edward said.

"Some room in city hall?" asked Lapin.

"Opportunity," said Jack.

"None of that," Walter replied. "The key to the city is something that if it was smaller you would wear, like a white rose or a red rose on Mother's Day or a boy scout pin. Except those things are more true than what the key means. It means favorites, like you finally got in.

"No problem with favorites, except if you got some that you like, you got some that you don't. Except the city is supposed to be for all of the people and most of the people without the key, the ones you don't give nothing to, you don't even know.

"So look here, Jack, this is what I did to the cause of being fair. I said to myself about serving the people, 'I know what is a true answer, what don't take no councilmens, and I know it won't cost the city a thing.' So any time anyone want to talk with me in my office, when they sit down I play them a song. Then I send them away to think about it, to make up their own mind. And then to do that for everybody, I went back out on the streets."

"What? Walter, that doesn't make sense," said Jack.

"Cents is just only cheap money," said Edward.

"That's right," agreed Lapin.

It was pitch-dark all over New Orleans. Some might say darkness fell all around deep. Out in the country, places like Garyville, Hammond, and Laplace, the evening smelled sweet like invisible night-blooming jasmine and tall grass. The pasture's blades attracted little bits of water from the air. They bedded down with each other clinging to each other in spite of not appearing the same. One was tall, green, and rooted in the earth. The other tiny, round, and a traveler. But it disappeared in the morning as dew.

In New Orleans, the city, the nature of earth was harder to see. The nature of man came first. It was a house-building, singing and dancing being. And, because it was not as easy to understand as the physical world, the man had to search for his truth.

So under the cover of darkness, a darkness of sky solid as a good gumbo pot, conversation bubbled through the night to get at the reasons for everything being. And as anybody would say, that was good.

In the bar, laughter was good too and truly not easy to perceive. "Funniness," as Edward would say, "that's what they call them men dress up like girls." He might add too that, "Yeah, my little cousin was with them, went all the way to France. Came back speaking the language and with a college degree. Made us proud."

Jack had almost given up thoughts of leaving on the plane in the morning. He had also, pretty much, given up fear. Every once in a while he would take in a pause in the conversation. The other men never stopped for even a breath. Jack would have to think about why he was here. He didn't know how to explain to his girlfriend or his parents, or especially the guys, the situation he was now in. It was as if he had know these people all of his life, and they cared for him. But he felt that in any other place or time, they would be opposed.

Jack couldn't imagine sitting in a bar in the middle of the night in Connecticut or, God no, in New York with three big black men who hardly spoke the same language as he did. What would they all have to say to each other?

But here he was. He never spent this much time talking to even his father. "I mean," he tried to think of explaining it, "I spoke to them all day."

Maybe if he told them it was one of those situations like on the *Twilight Zone*, where the hero is captured by his own curiosity and totally forgets his fear. But Jack regretted and apologized to himself for that thought. He wasn't heartless, maybe sometimes confused. But there was no threatening here.

Quite the opposite in fact. But so strange, these men conjured up awful images of each other in words. Jack couldn't picture his father calling anyone a fool without being ready to fire them or walk away from them. Here these men were calling each other terrible things and, seemingly, liking each other more for it.

This was something he'd have to think about for a long time. Or not think about, just let the idea come. These men advocated faith and trust, but not believing. Every once in a while, as they spoke, Jack felt he really understood that there was a genius to that.

"Drink up, boy. You a young man," Walter was patting him on the forearm and encouraging him. "You not going to slow down now, are you? Don't be no chump. I'm about to get to the best part."

"Who you calling a chump, sissy?" Lapin defended Jack as he raised his heavy head to look up.

"I'm calling you, your mama, and his cousin," Walter pointed at Edward.

Edward toasted Walter and Lapin, "That's right."

Jack said, "I'd like to propose a toast to friendship and special times."

"Well, all right, boy," said Walter as Lapin and Edward also lifted their glasses. He added, "As it was in the beginning, is now and ever shall be."

"Amen," Edward said from his habit.

"I'll really tell you about friendship," Walter said. "Lapin let me play here when he opened the first time and I met my wife here . . ."

"His present wife," said Edward.

". . . and there was no better occasion, a trinity of friendship —my woman, my music, and Lapin. The place started to fill up around five in the evening. People coming in after dinner. Most of them work in the trades, you know, so they do everything early from the time they get up. There was even some of my friends from grammar school here, Canard, PeeWee, plus one of my schoolteachers, old lady Judice.

"You know, when I was a child, I thought she was the most beautiful woman. It was the way she treated us, that made her appear like that. By the time I got in high school, I recognized what she really looked like—a straw hat frayed at the brim where she always put the hat pin, stockings twisted around her skinny legs like somebody just spun them, and that nylon dress with the shoulder pads falling down to the front above her flat chest. But that time, when I was a teenager and saw her on the street, I said, 'Good afternoon, Miss Judice.' And she said, 'My smart boy Walter. How are you doing in school?' You know, the sound of her voice changed her in my eyes, like she had been wrapped all of a sudden in a beautiful blue sheet, the color of the lake when we was boys, and thin like a new bride's negligee."

"Damn, man, that's beautiful," Lapin said, resting his face in the palm of his hand, his elbows on the bar. "I had Miss Judice in second grade too. She sounded just like that."

"I think ya'll got some kind of mother thing," Edward joked to lighten their load.

Walter smiled, "You should know, mule."

"Now, don't talk about my best friend or my wife for that matter," Edward said.

"Oh, look, isn't that her walking across the street with that young man?" Lapin pointed.

Edward spun, "I don't see nothing."

"You must have missed her. The guy looked like Creole Clark Gable," Lapin said.

"Sidney Poitier," said Walter.

"Muhammed Ali," added Jack.

"Ya'll joking me," Edward said. "OK, I'm the fool."

"The fool of the heart is a wise man," said Walter. "Let me tell you about my wife. Like I said, when I met her, she came with her cousins to listen to me play. We knew each other as children, yeah. Went to the same school, just different grades. But we never talked. She was always helping the nuns, wiping the blackboard, taking out the trash. And me and them, well, we just couldn't get along.

"I pretty much thought the same about her at that time. You know, when all the little fellows getting their first girls, ten or twelve years old, you don't want nobody you can't feel. So you get you a girl, just as curious, ya'll show each other things, go about your business. This woman, she up with the nuns all the time, I tell the boys, 'She ain't got no appeal.'

"Come to find out, after we married, one of my friends told me he was her secret all the time. I got no hard feelings on anybody 'cause of that, no. So, she had hers. I had mine."

"Tell the man your wife's name, brother," Lapin encouraged Walter.

"Wanda Yvonne Notburga, don't that have a ring? It kind of whispers up on you. Then rumbas. She is really a saint. But she knows what to do with her women things. I don't like to talk about my personal business, but in the bed, she can really make a man satisfied. Not that she don't make you work for it. But she be working too, you know. It's like, very much together, something you doing. I think that's a form of love," Walter said.

"Back to the bar, the bar, man," said Edward. "I don't know how far I can go on this tumbling hayride."

"Hey . . . I might see your wife again," said Lapin.

"Ok, just go on with it," Edward heard him but addressed Walter.

"Anything you want to say is all right, Walter," Jack said.

"Thank you, boy. Thank you also for your attention, peanut gallery," Walter looked at Edward.

"When Lapin first opened and my wife come in with her cousins and I pick up my horn, heaven on earth. Pure beauty. Feeling like falling asleep after you and your good woman have done it, except without no humanly tiredness, only with your blood running smooth and steady like a good tap faucet. That's what it was like to be playing up on that bandstand.

"That's why too, when I was the mayor I took back to the streets with my music. Couldn't nobody argue with anything that is true. Well, some of them could, and did. But I'm getting to that later. First, I got to tell you about my full term."

"Good as dancing the slow drag, wasn't it, Walter?" said Lapin.

"And just as dangerous," he replied.

Jack had never danced the slow drag but Edward told him it was like the two-step except without moving your feet and bringing your partner so close "ya'll forget who stops where."

"As I was saying before," Walter continued, "I took to communicating by trumpet. Like when I wanted my secretary to bring me a pitcher of water from the fountain, I'd play 'Little Brown Jug' or if I was leaving City Hall for the day and I wanted to let the people know, I'd do 'Old Man River' and end it with that part 'He just keep rolling along.'"

Jack put his beer down on the table, "This part you are joshing me, right? I mean I believe you were the mayor. But you played music instead of talking for everything?"

"Well, not for everything. I mean, it was just not fit for everything. When things were important and sad, like that retarded school I was telling you about, and had to be done, I tried to reason with folks. But they wasn't good on being reasonable either.

Seeing how I become the mayor, they stayed upset about that.

"So seem like anything I be for, they be against, and also the opposite. I couldn't claim to do anything big the whole time I was there," said Walter.

"How long was that?" Jack asked.

"In days, hours, or minutes?" asked Walter.

"However."

"About four months."

Lapin spoke up quickly, "But them was the best 120 days ever had in New Orleans by anybody. Don't you see? When Walter was in office there was no taxes passed. The police stayed home. Nobody was starving. Everything was handled out on the streets."

"See, the politicians was against me. But none of the people was. I took my horn to City Hall Plaza outside every day to play. I used to make up these blues, you know. And all the cleaning ladies and the men who stand at the doors in the big hotels would come down and it just tickle them. One I had, 'I may be low. But don't you tread on me. I may be low. But don't you tread on me. I'm the bestest mayor as could be. You wish I leave. But then I think I won't. You wish I leave but then I think I won't. I got in here by the people's vote.'

"Well them people loved it. Whoo, they would laugh. But them on the city council and all the rest of the politicians, I think they was ready to hatch chickens right on that lawn. I heard one of them saying once, 'Frank, we got to do something about that mayor. This music playing is making us laughingstocks.' Me, I stepped up to them. I ain't afraid of no coat jacket wearing fracas. I say, 'If you is laughingstocks, you belong in a stockyard.' And then I walk away."

"That's telling them, Walter," said Edward.

"You got good courage, my friend," Lapin agreed.

"Plus, 'cause they was wrong. I was doing fine for the people. For a good while at least. I tell my secretary, 'We don't need all these desks and these telephones and all this carpet and chairs.' You think I got all that carpet and chairs in my house, Jack?" Walter turned to the young man.

Jack shrugged.

"Well, I don't. Tell him, Lapin. And tell him if any man lives better than I do," Walter looked to his friend.

"It's the God truth," Lapin said.

"So my wife, who runs a good house as any man can tell you, but especially me, she say, 'Walter, I know you been complaining about how all that furniture be collecting dust up in city hall.'

"'Yes, my dearest,' I tell her. She say, 'Well, why don't we give it to the nuns. They help the poor and the sick. And I bet you they could do something with it. So it don't all be wasting like that.'

"Now this here is a woman who could take a penny and buy something with each side. So I know this is an exceptional idea. What be better than to help the poor? And who be more good than nuns? Can't nobody complain with that. Or so I thinked."

Walter refreshed himself with a gulp of beer at this point; right after his glass was refilled quickly by Lapin.

"It's a crying shame," said Lapin, "when people don't follow the good, no matter what kind of clothing it wears."

"That's right," said Edward. "People always want to see the wolfs in sheep's clothes. But what if the wolf in wolf clothes? Most of the time, seem like that to me anyhow."

Jack was a little puzzled by this turn of the story. But he was learning to wait by now to find out what was going on. He sipped his beer more, although he was trying a little to keep awake by this time.

It was about midnight, Jack guessed. He wondered whether the hotel would look for him if he didn't arrive tonight. He was glad he had taken the key offered to him by the desk clerk.

"I bet you that you want to keep this in your pocket," he'd said. "We leave at quarter to three. But lots of times people what got hotel rooms don't ever be using them to sleep, no way."

At the time, Jack thought he was being solicited. He still, at this moment, wasn't sure.

"So man, you should have seen this," Walter said. "Me and my boys. Lapin was with us. Also Edward here. And Bootsie, that's before he was dead, and the St. Augustine High School band and football team and we even had some of them Harry Christians. They said they would pitch in for the cause of the poor people and it didn't make them no never mind whether the poor was helped by the city or them or the nuns.

"I had told my secretary the night before: 'You put all of this furniture what I got a piece of tape on, you put it in the hall.' And I went around all the rooms in the City Hall building. Taping all those chairs that people never sit in and them plushy couches and some of them big telephones and empty water coolers. Anything that look like it never been used or ain't being used enough, I put the red tape on. That was on a Friday. Then Saturday morning, we got in our trucks with all those people I told you about and the football team and the band, and we loaded it up.

"It was a beautiful sight, if you ever wondered about it. Beauty, that is. You tell him, Edward, you is more good with this," Walter said.

"I tell you like this, Jack," Edward began. "Since you been in New Orleans, you ever go to Jackson Square?"

"Yes. We passed by there earlier, today. I guess it was today, right Walter?"

Walter nodded to Edward, yes.

Edward continued, "Well, you know how the bums, they be sleeping in the shade, the children be playing, and mules be drinking water and pigeons flying around. Well, either two things could happen. The pigeons could peck the mules, and the mules break aloose and kick the children, and the children run frightening-like right over the bums. But no. The mules and the pigeons, they drink from the same water, and the pigeons they fly over the children and become part of their game, and the children don't disturb the bums, till they ready to wake up. So they all work together, kinda natural. Well, that's just like how it was on that day.

"Them St. Aug boys be carrying that furniture over they shoulders like book bags and the Harry Christians be putting it up on the trucks. Lapin brought the cold beer for everybody who was of the right drinking age or pretty close. And me, I supervise and Walter play his horn," Edward said.

Walter remembered that day as his best in office. It was the culmination of his aspirations and his wife's thoughts.

"A big crowd gathered listening to the music and started to help when they found out what it was that we was doing," continued Edward. "And most of them, lot of folks, got in their cars and followed us out to the nuns' house. That was Saturday.

"Well, by Sunday, wasn't a stick of furniture that wasn't sold or swapped or something. We got commitments like, a year's worth of restaurant meals for a family of six for one of them twelve-button telephones. Shoot, lots of people wanted the keys to the city. Got a man said he would pick up three old folks a week from the home take them to the social security office for a key. And people paid money. The nuns counted two, three thousand dollars just off of rugs. Do you know how much poor people that could feed, Jack?" Edward asked.

Jack said no.

Walter calculated it for him. "The nuns ain't what you call extravagant when it come to meals. So you figure on beans, rice, and chicken wings. That's about sixty-five cents a plate.

"My sweet wife," Walter said, "was so happy, I thought she'd arise right into heaven when they said they could feed all those poor folks."

Lapin said, "You was the bestest mayor, Walter. The most good-hearted, righteous one of the bunch."

"But as we be trying to tell you, Jack, the truth has its limits. More, I figure from my experience, than lies," Walter said.

"When you become a official politician," Walter explained to Jack, as Lapin wiped off the bar where the men sat, "you can't believe nothing except what you have to at the time. Any other thinking about truth's just wasted baggage. You know, they tie you up. Keep you beholding to something or somebody. And politicians got to be able to change their minds.

"It's like the law. The law says things is one way, and if you don't go with it, you against. No matter that you trying to do good. Good don't necessarily got no part to it. Good is for individual peoples to think about. That ain't got much to do with what the law sees as right or wrong. It's like this fella in jail told me . . ."

"You went to jail?" Jack exclaimed.

"Just for a little bit. Not to worry. Not for too long," Walter said, "Anyhow, this guy in there told me, 'Sure I stealed out of Schwegmann's. I ain't had no job. My baby child was sick. We needed something to eat and we ain't had no money. I ain't did nothing like beat on or hurt nobody. You think that's a crime?'

"'Sure do,' I told him, 'is against the law. That's why they put you in jail. See, I was hungry at one time or another and I never took nothing that didn't belong to me. I played for my money at the houses and such. But that's . . .'

"'So why,' he say, 'are you in here, you so smart?'

"'Well,' I tells him, 'I just thought being I was the mayor, what was in City Hall was mine.'

"See I explained it to that guy like this . . ." Walter went on.

But Jack was looking outside through the window and around the bar. No one was there except the three men and himself. And Jack imagined or realized, he drank so much he wasn't sure, that it was beginning to dawn.

He could hear no sound but talking and maybe distantly a little music was playing. A shadowy aqua-green light seemed to bathe the street. When cars passed they either did or didn't have on headlights.

The room where he sat was wooden and old, as if it had been saturated with years of cigars and talk. You could have put a match to it, Jack figured, and nothing would burn. The floorboards and beams in the ceiling looked plump and swollen. The place reeked of liquor. But to Jack it smelled simply sweet.

He looked at the men he was with. Edward was sort of pigeon-faced, pinched around the nose and eyes and sagging around the rims. Lapin had a forehead that stretched too far back from his eyebrows. It seemed that his whole appearance took a shape swept off from his teeth. And Walter didn't seem at all frightening now, even though he had just told Jack about jail. Walter was not the tough guy that Jack conceived him at the first bar before they all started to talk. Then Jack had him in his mind for a criminal of a certain type.

It was almost as if, in the sodden atmosphere of New Orleans, all the hard opinions that Jack had formed while he was growing up had suddenly become waterlogged and soft. Their edges became blurry, like looking into a fish tank or, even more, like looking out. Jack wished that he had some way to hold onto the conversation, like he had tape-recorded it or something. He wondered after all of this drinking how much would stick. He decided he would catch the plane after all and he could almost hear the sound of his jet landing at Kennedy airport, a high-pitched whistling, sliding down the scale and then hitting the ground. Junk shake. Junk shake shake.

"What kind of music you like, Jack?" Walter was asking him. "I want to play you a song."

"Well, Mozart, the Grateful Dead, Neil Young, Leon Russell, Stevie Wonder . . ."

"Good," Walter said, "I'll make up as I go along." Walter stood in the center of the floor. Empty chairs supported him on all sides. The trumpet began like an old lady humming aloud to herself "Summertime." "'One of these mornings,'" Edward sang softly, even though Jack could still hear him, "'I'm going to rise up singing. Gonna spread my wings and take to the sky. But till that morning . . .'" Here Walter departed into a light staccato tune, sort of sweet. "Hubert Laws," Lapin told him, "Ain't that fine?" Then the beat changed again, one more time accompanied by Edward, beating on the bottom of his chair. It was Brazilian sounding, almost like a rumba. "Go on man, parade," Lapin called. He was strutting from one end of the bar to the other, waving his dishrag above his head. Three steps up, three steps back, two steps, two steps, one to the side. "Go on," Edward called to Lapin, "shake, shake, shake it, now."

Walter held his trumpet down by his side and finished this part singing, "My kind of town. All around. Down in New Orleans, but . . ." he paused. And he began slowly, "'Them that's got will get. Them that's not will lose . . .'" He picked up the trumpet again and played with the words Lapin stopped and sang, "'so the Bible says, and it still is news. Your mama may have. Your papa may have. But God bless the child that's got his own.'" And the song changed again, and Lapin moved with it as if he had been doing this for many lives. "'I've been so many places in my life and times. Sung a lot of songs, made some bad rhymes. Acted out my life in stages. Ten thousand people watching. But we're alone now and I'm singing this song to you.

"'I love you in a place where there's no space or time. I love you for my life, you're a friend of mine. And when my life is over, remember when we were together. But we're alone now and I'm singing this song, singing this song to you, to you.'"

Jack applauded. And so did Walter, Edward, and Lapin.

Plus, Lapin snapped the air with his dishrag and Edward wiped his eyes.

"What was it like in jail, Walter?" Jack asked.

"Black man, very, very, very black."

Walter moved back to the table. "I don't mean in color, not at all, even though it was us mostly who was in there for one reason or another and that makes you think too. But man, what there was was an absence of sound. The door close behind you with a clunk, you know, like slamming the tailgate of a truck. Except it be you in the truck and there is no open top or sides.

"Sure there is talking, plenty talking. But most of it is quiet and all of it is words. Even when you would hear guys screaming or fighting, it come at you like if you was breaking a glass. It was those kind of sounds, nothing good that I heard."

"Come on, man, let's not talk too much about that. It's all over and done," Lapin said.

"Well, you know, kinda," Walter replied. He took Lapin's dishrag and wiped off his horn.

Edward said, "Tell him about when you went to court. Now boy, that was a scene."

"Like Mardi Gras," Walter said. "I was just trying to do good, selling that furniture. The people, they knew, that was just me."

He continued, "Them councilmens, they was the first ones. And I sort of think my secretary was in on it too. When I come into my office on that Monday afternoon, they was all standing in there waiting, saying, 'What the hell's going on here.' One of them tells me, 'This is public property.' And I say, 'Well, that's what I thought, so that's where it goed.' And another one of them said, 'You done broke the law, Walter; we knowed you was going to tear your drawers some time.' And I tells him, 'Well, at least I wear some. Who know what happen to yours.'"

"I'll tell him this part," Edward cut in. "So they got sheriff and such and law and bring him to court. But sheet, child, we pack up that room with more people than they got seats. And all of them seats in there, all was permanent. You know, nailed to the floor."

Lapin picked it up, "They was lined up against the wall, thick as thieves on one of them Arabian Nights. Had the newspapers, the televisions, the grandmas, and the babies in there. Had the high school boys and the nuns. Remember," he called to Walter, "Sweet Percy came with all of his girls."

Walter said, "Sure do. Looked like a flock of parakeets in the front row in they yellow evening gowns, red business suits, big blue matador coats. And they hardly let the judge get in one good word.

"'I'm going to have to put all of ya'll in contempt,' the judge said," Walter reminisced.

"'Contempt my behind, baby,' one of them called out. 'Tell him girl. Speak the truth, darling,' said one of Sweet Percy's boys.

"Well, man, that whole court was just a laughing. Some of them old ladies brought picnic food. All of the time the councilmens was up on the stand, the old ladies be wrapping and unwrapping they brown bags and wax paper. 'Shush,' the officers kept trying to tell them. But you could hear those old girls whispering back asking them, 'Honey, you can have some if you want. Don't you? This is good.'

"Well, of course, I got to get up in front of the people. But I ain't ashamed. I did what was right and I got some pride. When I'm walking up to take the stand, somebody in the back blow one of those big plastic horns, you know, like they got at football games. 'Baraam,' it goes. The police hustled that fool out there quick. But everybody had to laugh on that one.

"I say, 'Yes sir judge mister. I realize now it was public property. But the nuns, they just can't give it back.' The sisters, even old Mother Ignatius in the wheelchair, is sobbing, pulling they handkerchiefs out of their sleeves. I say to the judge, 'Look at them. You ever seen a more pitiful sight?'

"'Walter,' he tell me, 'that's not no question. You done broke the law. The sisters neither the Harry Christmas is public, you know that. So now you just got to go to jail.'

"'But am I still the mayor, your honor?' I ask him.

"'I'm sorry to tell you, Walter. But you ain't even got that.'

"Then my lawyers go talk to them other lawyers and whisper up with the judge in his robe chambers. And when they come out, he say, 'Hear this, ye everybody. This here what we going to do. Walter, to keep us from all being the national laughingstocks, you just go to jail for a few days, pay back the money so we can buy some new furniture, and we call that that.'

"'But your honor,' I tell him, 'I'm unemployed. Where I'm going to get the cash?'" Walter leaned over to the young visitor. "Jack, if you don't remember anything ever, remember, what comes around goes around," said Walter.

"He don't need no lecture," said Edward. "Tell us the rest."

"Well, don't you know, when the judge bang down his hammer, all the people begins to boo. Hollering, 'That ain't right.' 'This no kinda justice.' Mother Mary Ignatius, she even throw up her fist.

"But next thing you know, as me and Wanda leaving the courtroom, people start handing us dollar bills. Some never said nothing. Others whistled, 'Come over here.' I must have got two, three hundred dollars from each one of Sweet Percy's girls. Of course, Sweet Percy hisself, he don't give me a dime. In fact, he come tell me, 'You just a fool. Need to be in jail.' My wife, she look at him in the eye, tell him, 'Jail is in the person. You already inside your own walls.' I separated them. But I swear, I was sure proud of her every minute since that. That's a good woman, Jack. She tell what need to be told, when it need to be. You try to remember it."

Edward began talking. "Damn if they ain't had the pilgrims over to his house for months after. You know lines, just like the holy shrines running from his yard down the street."

Walter said, "Yeah, people dropping by bringing me quarters, fifty centses, fat ladies bringing me plate dinners to eat. Shoot, we had more than enough money to give back to the city then. They fix up City Hall like the lap of luxury. But after we returned the cash, and we were broke again, you know, we still felt rich.'

"My wife say to me, 'Walter, we got love and memories plenty.'

"'And music,' I tell her, 'You can't never forget that.'"

The sun surely had risen by now, Jack thought. He could see bright rays painting the floor. Whether that light would bleach the wood or make it look stained, he didn't know. But then, he remembered, it moved evenly all day, from one wall to the other.

Edward had gone to the bathroom. "Oh Lordy," he said.

"Getting too drunk with ya'll. Made me forget all about my mule." Lapin was just about finished washing glasses. He planned to leave in a half-hour, he told them, "Soon as I get my relief."

"You about ready to go, young son?" Walter asked Jack, "I'll walk you over to your hotel."

Jack said, "I'll wait for you outside. I'm going to get some air." He thanked all the men and he promised to look them up when he returned to New Orleans. He was definitely coming back.

Jack stepped out of the bar and looked to one corner, then the other. The street was practically empty. It must have been about 7:00 A.M. He could hear trucks passing with a "Vaaroom" on nearby blocks. He thought, probably delivering sweet corn to the French market he had visited. He saw in the slight morning fog the vague shadows of old ladies turning every few minutes or so into the doors of the cathedral. He wondered for a little while if it was important for him to know why they entered. A couple of men holding hands walked past across the street and waved lightly at him. He returned their greeting with a slight nod and a smile. A tall woman in a bare red dress approached him from behind, strolling, it seemed, with her mother. The old woman told him, "You ought to do like I tell her. You young people don't listen. You got to rest yourself once in a while."

Jack took a deep breath and walked with a drunken sway to the corner, his hands in his pockets. There was so much to think about. He looked at the pavement, then the street. The cement was cracking in places, showing old brick. In the middle of the block, across the road, he could see one of the eighteenth century markers plastered onto the building. He went over to read the sign.

It began, "In this house in the 1780s lived an African of French descent . . ."

Edward and his mule passed at the intersection. "All right. Take care, boy," Edward called.

". . . who from all accounts was a tribal leader in his home town . . ."

Lapin sped by in his Volkswagen.

". . . and in New Orleans became a popular figure uniting

white immigrants—Irish, Spanish, French and others—and blacks. His profession was not known. But he is believed to have been at different times a musician, providing entertainment in Congo Square, or an educator or storyteller. Legends also recall him either as a sorcerer or a saint. His name is the cause of much dispute among historians because it was translated into so many local languages. But he was called mostly . . ."

Jack saw Walter walking quickly in the other direction of the street on which he was standing. So he ran stumbling to catch up with him. But the man turned the corner and when Jack finally reached him, it was not Walter. So Jack tried to return to the bar.

But he had turned so many streets, he was a little lost. He couldn't figure out for the life of himself where he was. He wandered around searching for the bar until people began filling the streets, going to breakfast, church, shopping. Finally, Jack got in a cab.

"The hotel, please." He looked at his key to make out the address.

"Where you from, boy, with an accent like that?" the driver asked him.

"New . . . Connecticut. I'm from Connecticut."

"Well, isn't that nice, you visiting us. Oh, here come on the radio a good record. I'm going to turn it up a little. You don't mind, no? Music. I swear, I live for music. I'm telling you the truth. What about you? You do that?"

CLIMBING MONKEY HILL

IT WAS CAUSE FOR EMBARRASSMENT IF BLACK
children climbed on Monkey Hill, even after they had integration. The boys and girls who ran from their nearby homes to
play in Audubon Park after school did not arrive with their
freedom only given by the law.

When they ran up the hill, they were ridiculed by the parents
who called down their own pale children. The adults stared at
the black ones as if to see them for the first time. Although some
were their over-the-fence neighbors, they replaced with bitterness the casual greetings of earlier times. "Look at them little
monkeys on Monkey Hill," the parents agreed to each other
over their children's heads. They spoke in a jovial way that encouraged their sons and daughters to adulthood by sharing the
laugh.

Watching from a distance away, Levia knew what occurred.
The adults stood confidentially close to one another, but arro-
gantly. Phrases of sarcasm carried to her in the air, although only
slightly because there was no breeze, as is usual in New Orleans
in summer. Levia did not expect to hear more of their words, because to shout at the children made the adults appear reckless
under the law. She recognized they used their only remaining
tool, ridicule, and, legally, the children were not bound to care.

Still, she held the hands of her brother and sister to keep them
away from Monkey Hill. "Don't let yourself be a joke for nobody," she told them, just like her mother.

Levia's mother warned them not to wander too freely while
she walked to get soft drinks. They were all safer if the children
stayed on the blanket she placed on one patch of grass while she
alone went to the concession stand.

But Levia now told her brother and sister, "Here, take some

money and go get on a ride," to make them feel better. She wanted them to know they could afford to go places. And she watched their figures walking away, like miniature adults hand in hand, little shadows of a man and a woman walking across a horizon sharp as tightrope while around them the world offered itself bleached and bare in the midday sun.

Levia sat on the scrap of lawn looking at Monkey Hill. It was a big lump in the middle of a flat, dusty field of Audubon Park, like one bucket of sand a child upends at the beach. Any grass planted once on Monkey Hill had died from the heat or underfoot from children running. Before development in this area, the park was a corner of swamp near the Mississippi River. It still had in spots the aura of unforgettable melancholy like most of New Orleans. But it took on an irony. Huge oaks with moss waterfalls fringed the dry field where Levia sat.

Monkey Hill was an even more incongruous site on the barefaced and dusty plain. Mud and river sand piled up about three dump trucks high, Levia figured. She pictured men in white uniforms building Monkey Hill and molding it with their hands like a giant, clay ice cream scoop. After Monkey Hill took on popularity, politicians on television proclaimed it a site for the education and freedom of enjoyment of the children of New Orleans. Levia knew who they meant.

Anyone offered something by television in 1965 had to be only one race. And that specification excluded Levia, who was many things, but not white.

She was a girl who now at adolescence molded her two fat plaits into one rope of hair that followed her long neck and turned up naturally where her shoulders took hold. She was nearly as tall as her squat mother and glowed healthily like her dad.

"You're a miser's penny," he told Levia to let her know how precious and beautiful she was to him. She was copper-colored sometimes when he looked at her. Other times she showed more red or gold. He teased her, "Maroon," like that kind of person sold for a time in New Orleans after she ran very fast. So Levia was actually black and as yet a threat to the people who wanted only one kind of child on Monkey Hill and in Audubon Park.

But that didn't bother Levia. These days she cared less about what people thought and more about what she was feeling. Specifically, she wondered if Monkey Hill was high enough to see New Orleans in a different way.

No one in the city, adult or child, who did not travel ever experienced both going up and coming down another side of a hill. The closest they ever got was the levee, which extended itself to one high point, then made a sheer drop. A child running against the breeze had to stop suddenly at the peak of enjoyment or fall into the river.

Levia once went alone to the levee. At the plateau was a path where people rode barebacked horses or walked south to the left and north to the right. Levia wondered how far they could go before the levee was no longer needed, either because the earth held back the water enough by itself or the waves of the gulf took over.

Levia wished she could go to the river now. The day was so hot and uninspiring. The adults that Levia and her family joined in the park now bickered at a picnic table a hundred yards away. The topic, as usual, was who got hurt in civil rights demonstrations this week, and how everyone else should react. Levia just wanted to go some place where it was high, quiet, and she felt free. At thirteen, she wasn't anxious to join them.

Her mother said Levia should begin making decisions. The first one she gave her today was to watch the children near Monkey Hill. "Olevia, mind them till I come back. Show a little responsibility," her mother said. Levia felt responsible already. But she could not talk back. "Yes ma'am." That's all she was allowed to say as yet.

"Yes ma'am. No ma'am." Who gave Levia credit for thinking? She felt she considered a lot but everyone said she was daydreaming. "Just a stage, you know," her mother told people all the time to explain Levia.

Levia had stared out the window this morning while they drove to Audubon Park. It was about one half-hour from their house.

The scene changed from small wooden homes that were painted to match the same shades in their gardens to half-block estates with stained glass windows and ironwork.

While they loaded the car to leave—shoving in the blanket and ice cooler along with a box of sandwiches their mother promised to bring for her friends, the neighbors came out to their porches and watched. They nodded approval, or showed envy at the picnic by waving down to them like shoo-fly as the car drove off. The children were bound out of respect to reply to either greeting.

"Hello, Mrs. Dee. Hi, Brown. Good-bye, Irma Ann." They had to catch each personally or the one they missed would try to convince even the others who got a hello that the children—because they were going to white places now—were growing stuck up.

By the time they neared Audubon Park, they could quietly look out the window. The houses here were so big, even if people wanted to they couldn't wave to their neighbors because no one could see another from porch to porch.

Everyone called this area the garden district because the big plots displayed huge flowering trees. Not only did hundreds of flowers grow there but almost as many people were hired to take care of them. Levia's father, who knew people that worked outdoor parties in this area, said anyone black who wore a uniform was welcome here. In this neighborhood, no one flinched at the mention of slave quarters attached to a house.

Levia studied those estates in the city magazine that her mother ordered to come weekly to their home. And when she and her mother drove around, exploring the city, as they did often, Levia counted streets and streets of these massive and imposing buildings. Some had four big, square, brick front-porch pillars, that her mother called, "grandiose Creole." Others had smooth, round, white columns, "southern Greek." Shingled roofs came down low to just top the cut-glass front doors that sparkled like diamonds. Levia liked to believe these doors were locked like the treasure trunks in her mythology books and held great mysteries and came from secret places. But Levia's mother reminded her as they drove that everything she saw was the product of "hard work." And, occasionally, as they passed the houses, she said, "Slave labor."

But she didn't say that often because it stopped both of them from talking and she knew Levia liked to dream aloud.

"I'm going to have a big house on St. Charles Avenue someday."

Her mother said, "You better learn first to keep clean."

"And I'll have a library of books in two rooms and a horse in a stall near the back by the park."

"And who's going to pay you to waste time?"

The conversation usually developed into an argument soon after that or else Levia's mother ended it quietly, "My child, you can have anything that you really want."

Except recently, Levia wanted to go to the garden district by bus and walk around by herself like she did in her neighborhood. But her mother said, "That won't do." Because of integration, people in the city were angrier with each other than ever before, especially when they were separate.

Levia considered going without telling. Their anger had nothing to do with her. She'd have to change buses and streetcars three times. Even the transportation system allowed for the separate traditions of New Orleans communities. Different people did not live side by side. Instead, their houses were back to back. So there were white streets and black streets and most traffic followed the major white avenues, where Levia thought to get off and walk.

If she went on the bus, on entering she got a thin piece of tan paper to make the transfers. She had to be careful not to clasp it too tightly or sweat because it could melt in her hand. Many seats would contain workingmen who smelled strong from their day jobs and women with their arms draped tiredly over the back part of the chairs where their small children sat. Levia had to avoid the old ladies because no matter who sat next to them, they talked and she could miss her stop.

For the first transfer, she would be on Canal Street, where she could see anyone. A neighbor might tell her family. A stranger might hurt her. There were sailors and tourists, shopgirls and businessmen, teenagers much worldlier than Levia and foreigners who wanted to stop and talk. But people said that was pointless because they were dumb. Levia wasn't sure whether that was actually true. But it was safer, she felt, not to speak to anyone at all.

At Canal and St. Charles, where she boarded the streetcar,

there would be a crush to get on. But by Magazine Street, all the pushy ones—men from the business district, transients, and the women who shopped in the expensive stores in the daytime, but who lived other places—would have left. Those remaining stayed in either big St. Charles houses or the small communities organized to serve them, located a couple of streets behind. But both of these people accepted their destinations with leisure. Some pulled down the wooden shade and dozed out of the sun, as the train rocked on the tracks to the end of the line.

The problems, Levia imagined, would only come when the streetcar had only a few empty seats. A great deal of confusion occurred about who would sit first since the curtain was gone behind which black people sat. Now if a seat became open, a white person might come to the back of the bus to claim it or a black to the front. Both movements were considered rude if others in the predominant race in that section stood. Even a young boy would not get up for an old woman, unless they were the same.

Once Levia's friends rushed to a seat to prevent a white woman from sitting. "Come. Here. Olevia," they called. "You shouldn't stand."

Levia kept her head down for the remainder of that ride while the others joked. She felt she couldn't look up to see the old woman, swinging on the strap and panting for air in the hot bus. Levia repeated to herself, "Slave owner. Miss Anne. She's not so fragile." Levia wondered then, would her mother think this was rude or just?

Levia did not want to encounter trouble if she went by herself but she did want to take the ride. She knew her mother would say, "No. Everyone is just too upset now over integration."

Integration, that's all Levia heard and she was sick of it. New Orleans became possessed with the idea. It seemed good enough to think about, when it was planned. But now it just appeared too much trouble to Levia.

People were always protesting and others moved from places they lived all their lives. Where blacks and whites had lived willingly with their differences, now they were bitter. Too much change, Levia thought. Too much fighting, supposedly because of their children.

For years, Levia looked forward to high school. But now the

first question everyone asked her was whether she wanted to go to school among blacks or whites.

Next summer she'd have to make up her mind. "Does it matter?" she asked people who looked dumbfounded when they heard her reply. That was another occasion when her mother asked everyone to excuse her child. Then whoever posed the question to Levia in the first place would say she had a duty to her race. Of course, she had a duty. Levia understood that.

For what other reason would she be going to school at all? Lynne Carre's parents let her wear miniskirts and boots and date boys who were five years older, and Lynne said she wasn't going to school because she first had to please herself. Actually, she was pregnant last fall.

But Levia's parents "expected things" of her and a baby was not part of their plan. If fact, her father warned, "If I ever see you on the corner with those neighborhood bums, don't come home." So she didn't stay out late. Not that she thought he was fair. But she believed he would not let her back in the house and she couldn't figure out how she would take care of herself alone.

But everyone else made too big a deal of things she would do naturally, like go to high school, while Levia had better plans. For example, Levia made herself a promise to enjoy living day to day. And she was keeping it, not worrying too much, thinking about the things she wanted to do and not the requests of others, remaining free like a child.

She thought, this was the prime of her life, the summer beginning, and she was in the park. Levia lay in the sun, idly thinking, alone without her sister, brother, or mother. She took the quiet for granted, rested and watched the shadow of Monkey Hill grow as the sun marked time.

"New Orleans has too much of a mixed-up society to be bothered anyway," Levia heard one of the adults talk against integration at the kitchen table one night. "Now, who's going to tell me how they going to draw the line around here?" The grown-up said no one would want real race relations legalized: "With where the poor whites live and the St. Lima whites with black people from Corpus Christi Parish right back of them, politicians going to be zigzagging that color line all through people's front porches to keep everyone separate and still follow the integration law."

Levia listened to only this part of the conversation, then she went out into the backyard. Maybe it was unnatural to force people to change. She wouldn't mind people keeping a friendly distance like she did with the white country people around the block. They were a family of six pale, big-boned boys and girls whom she really didn't mind.

Once their pet armadillo climbed under her fence.

"Watch him, watch him now," the oldest boy told his sisters as he ran around the corner to get into Levia's yard. The armadillo buried itself into the mud where the chain link ended near the ground. The girls poked it with a stick to send it to their side. But their backyard was concrete. And the armadillo acted as if it were embarrassed to run away but obligated to go where it was greener because it burrowed under the grass behind Levia's house while they called it, going deeper and deeper into a hole.

The boy arrived with a wood and screen box, the kind, Levia knew, that was used to keep pigeons in. He stopped the armadillo by cornering it with a board. He kept blocking its moves until the animal tired of the places it originally wanted to go. Then he picked up the armadillo and showed it to Levia, "Look here." She studied its slate-colored shell, long fingernail claws, and little unprotected parts around its legs on the underside.

"Won't hurt yer," he said by way of thanks. "You could come play with it if you want." Levia shook her head yes to be polite. But it seemed too unfair to both man and animal, she felt, to play with something that you had to catch.

Instead, in the evenings she played with the children in the houses that faced hers on the block. They attended the black public school up the street or went to Corpus Christi, the elementary attached to the church.

Their games were mostly inventions, like Coon Can where they hit a rolling ball with a stick and ran back and forth from one square drawn on the ground to another, scoring points. They played Red Light to see who could sneak to the light before getting caught or Fassé with everyone keeping the ball against one another and a Hide-and-Seek called I Spy.

Before night fell, all the children sat on the steps and talked.

Levia felt they made their own sidewalk family, besides being involved in separate ones at home. Elanore wanted to be everyone's mother with her bossiness, "Girl, you ought to take off that short skirt with them bony legs," "Johnson, come over here."

Philip was "doo-fuss," the children said. He allowed his mother to tell the barber to cut his hair too short and one time he even showed them a part shaved crookedly right onto his scalp. Philip never spoke first to anyone and only talked back to Elanore if she pushed up against him. Once he told Levia that when he grew up he wanted to be a policeman.

"Why you want to do that, to have a gun?" she asked.

"I'm sick of white people telling us what to do," he replied.

Levia looked at him hard for a few minutes, then took up conversation with another child on the step. She didn't tell anyone Philip's desire and she even avoided Elanore some after that. Levia wasn't quite sure why. But Elanore, Levia sensed, would force Levia to choose sides. And all Levia knew was that she felt bad talking about white people all the time, as everyone did, and now she didn't feel good either talking with Philip.

Levia preferred to spend time with her cousins. Charlene was a cheerleader now for St. Augustine. The two black Catholic high schools, St. Augustine and Xavier Prep, had a football rivalry so intense that nothing else mattered for weeks in the neighborhood.

"Go, St. Aug," people called from their porches to youngsters dressed in purple and gold. Young mothers balanced their baby children on their hips as they stood outside the St. Augustine schoolyard fence watching the band practice in cavalier helmets. Girls not yet pregnant lingered with one arm hooked above their heads in the chain link to display themselves to the male musicians. Many a trumpet and saxophone player was inspired to further a musical career by the sight of female S-curves on the horizon, a line that stretched from the school's Hope Street to Law Street boundaries.

The night before the game, Charlene gave Levia and her friends a demonstration of cheerleading in the street. The boys who wanted to watch promised to keep an eye out for oncoming cars. Levia and the girls sat in a pyramid on the steps and waved their hands like paper shakers for Charlene to begin.

"We're really rocking them, really rolling, really pushing them down the field. Look at Purple Knights, a real swinging deal. We push them back, and roll them back, and knock them to the ground. Look at our team, we really rocking them down. St. Augustine. Go St. Aug. St. Augustine. . . ." Every time Charlene said St. Augustine, the girls on the steps put their hands on their hips and directed their shoulders from one side to the other, like mini-Supremes.

Every cheer these days was a little angry with a newfound pride. Black cheerleaders had always done the latest dances and "finger-popped" while the bands played. However, they got a greater appreciation for the way they looked while dancing after they saw new, sophisticated female groups on television. But they also got laughed at during cheerleading competitions against the white schools. Where their cheers were acrobatic, the blacks' cheers were musical. The result was that the cheerleaders for St. Aug, Prep, and many others held their heads with a little higher tilt under bouffant hairdos that took advantage of their full hair, and they smiled a little less these days for every occasion.

On the day of the game, Levia accompanied Charlene. Then Levia took a seat near the top of the stadium. The air was clear and cool, hinting of the arrival of fall. The oppressive heat in summer that made a poor choice of any seat close to the sun was gone.

Levia looked across the field to Xavier Prep. Bodies rocked in unison as if pulled side to side by the music. Levia heard from the competition an occasional shrill snatch of trumpet or a couple of drumbeats. It gave her a sense that she wanted to dance too. Except she felt it inside, like a stirring in her body or a shiver in a place she could not locate. While she waited for the St. Augustine band to begin, she pulled against the collar of her sweater in a way her mother disapproved because she said it would stretch. But that made Levia relax a little and she looked more closely at the stands below her.

People brought umbrellas to open and bob with the band's music. Others waved handkerchiefs in their enthusiasm. Like two hundred flags, an army of individuals bound by music and rivalry, they slapped the air to the right and left.

The movement was one of sureness. Levia felt part of a single voice raised for enjoyment of the day. Support for a team was so unlike Levia's picture of high school, if she had to go there under the laws of integration.

When she watched television at dinnertime with her parents, the white people protested blacks coming to their schools. "Two-four-six-eight, we don't want to integrate." Levia saw their spokesman address a reporter, "They will lower the standards in our classrooms to where our children couldn't learn anything."

"Why do we want to be where they don't want us, anyway," Levia asked her mother.

"For the future, Olevia. Pass your plate." She went on serving dinner.

Levia's father said, "Education is the only way to move up. Whatever high school you go to, Levia, we want you to apply for college."

Levia remembered complaining, "Do I always have to think about this?"

But alone at the football game, Levia conceived an easy picture of high school. She would go to a black school and be safe, just like she was today, or all her life in her neighborhood, and with her family.

From her seat, away from the crowd, Levia saw her neighbors—Philip and his mother, Elanore and her boyfriend. Many other people looked familiar to her, like cousins, in shapes with rounded shoulders, in sun-lacquered hues and clothes she knew from the local stores. She nodded hello to a soft, masculine face that she recognized from the neighborhood or was even related to. But when he smiled, Levia saw from the crookedness of the teeth and the way the lips were hooked around them, he was no one she knew.

But he rose from his seat a couple of sections away and began walking over to her. Levia didn't know what to do. If she moved away, he would think she was rude. Plus, she already was sitting at the top, so she would encounter him if she tried any route to leave. She waited, pulling her sweater across herself with both hands, making an X. She was shivering when he arrived.

"Are you cold? What's your name?"

"I came to the football game with my cousin," Levia replied.

"I'm Roger. Want me to get you warm?"

"I have to go to the bathroom." Levia got up.

"What high school do you go to?" He caught her arm.

Levia shook herself away, rushing now, down the steps. She called back, "I'm just in eighth grade."

Levia hurried with her head down and her arms across her chest, to the bathroom under the bleachers. It was dimly lit and where ceiling lights were broken in places, electricity buzzed in the dark. She slowed her pace to think in the dark places because no one could see her there.

She wondered if she could hide from Roger and if she returned to her seat if he would still be there. She was angry because he touched her arm. She wondered what she would do. He can't make me talk to him, Levia thought. But she knew she felt bad because of her confusion. Other girls, like Elanore, could have been slick or jive.

"Does that feel good to you," Elanore had once replied to a boy who had pushed her up against the house. She told Levia, the boy let her go right after that. "I didn't have to fight. You just got to be smart," she advised.

It was just like with white people, Levia thought. Always someone was telling her, "We have to outsmart them to get what we want." When people told her that, Levia could not remember a thing that she wanted from whites. How could she want anything that people were not willing to give? And if she got it because she was smarter, why didn't she have it all along?

Her mother said civil rights was a problem for white people, because "then they will have to see we're the same."

A cheer went up from the stands above Levia's head. This year Xavier was winning. The championship moved between it and St. Aug because they were so evenly matched.

Levia stood still and looked around her. Pretty high school girls flirted with boys in the bright places near the concession stands as they waited to get treated to soft drinks and sandwiches. They laughed with their faces tilted up, just so the light flattered the curves of their cheeks and slid over the bones in their jaws.

Levia considered that men challenged women just to see who would win. Another cheer broke from the stadium above her head. Levia tried to laugh like the girls did who were standing under the light. But she only succeeded in making a dumb sound like little grunts linked by a strained desire.

Suddenly people came running down the ramps of the stadium. "They say there's a bomb in the stands," someone yelled as he passed. Levia looked around for Charlene or anyone she thought she might know. She saw no one. So she ran with the crowd, out of the gates of the stadium into the parking lot.

People stood around looking confused and disappointed. Levia walked from group to group, peering into them to see who she knew. When she got farthest away from the stadium, she saw a motorcade coming. With horns blowing and convertibles alternately speeding up and screeching to a stop, crowds of white teenagers drove past shouting to the people who were leaving the game, "Dumb niggers. We fooled ya'll dumb niggers."

More protests were on the evening news during dinner. This time, mothers were crying and fathers were mad. "How can my child be safe anymore in her classes?" one woman said, full of tears.

"They just don't want our young men fooling with their girls," Levia's father called at the TV from his seat at the kitchen table.

"Marvin," Levia's mother told him, "please hold your tongue in front of this child."

"I'm going outside anyway," Levia told them. "I don't see how no boy can do anything to a white girl that he wouldn't do to me."

Ever since the game Levia was wondering about the rules of being kissed. Was it like something you said you wanted to do? Or was it like being ambushed? People in the movies clung to each other, the man holding the woman's head in his hands as if something precious was there. Levia would have to think harder, like the women on TV, to be able to say the right things and get kissed for her smarts. She resented that people thought white girls would get kissed more than her. Levia felt she had just as much brains.

The question of school, too, still hung before her. But worst, her parents wanted her to consider going to a white school with all girls.

Levia saw them many times on the bus. They wore white blouses where the ironing seemed to melt by the afternoon and blue pleated skirts that they rolled so short it called attention to their legs, yellow like chicken parts. Their mothers let them shave to their knees and many carried big, square, adult pocketbooks.

The girls at Xavier Prep were not nearly as free. A hint of wiped-off lipstick carried three afternoons of cleaning the nuns' windows, and any objection to punishment made necessary a trip to confession.

"You're not going to school to socialize," Levia's mother told her, "and you might make a few friends." That time Levia walked into her bedroom without answering. She did not tell her parents either about the boys she saw pass in the car. She knew they would say "rowdies come in every color."

She was losing her arguments, too, about all white people, because the whites who stayed in the Catholic schools had to agree with integration. The bishop threw out of the church that year any of the others who did not want to mix. It was un-Christian and un-Catholic, the bishop said. Levia and her mother had seen it on television, and they cheered as the bishop refused to talk to the people who protested blacks entering.

"Finally, somebody is putting their foot down on real sin," Levia's mother said. "It is never too late," Levia agreed. But now, as the decision acutely affected her, she wondered, what about blacks who did not want to go to school with whites? Was it as bad for black people to be against white people, as whites were against them?

Elanore said no, once when Levia asked her. "They be always on our case. Why you so polite to them? You some kind of Oreo, black on the outside, white on the inside. Or oleo, yellow all the way through."

Levia answered, "I don't like white people."

"So let's go then," Elanore called her along.

Levia had said, "I don't like white people," a little louder than she would have liked for her parents to hear. They told her because she had freckles from one Irish great-grandfather, that she should not be quick to draw lines. "You just focus on what is just and what is unjust," her father told her, "and don't choose your sides by the color of skin."

But wasn't it true that white people hated them because of appearance? "So why," Levia argued, "do we have to be nice?"

"It will keep you from being a fool to the wrong kind of people, girl," her father said like he didn't want to hear anything more.

But that day with Elanore, Levia did not hesitate to follow Elanore's convictions. She was dark and she had freckles too, like they could be sisters, she said, as she once flattered Levia.

"I know how we can get them," Elanore whispered after they entered Richards, the dime store around the corner on the white street. "I'm going to make a fuss with that woman at the cash register. You pick out some candy for me."

Levia got a few Tootsie Rolls, some gum, and a mint. Then she walked to the front. "That's the one with her," the saleswoman called to a man coming toward Levia as she saw Elanore run out of the door. "Check her pockets. You got money to pay for that?"

"But it's not for me."

"You think I'm going to put it back on the shelf?" the saleswoman glared.

Levia left with her pockets empty of change and a bag of candy in her hand. As she turned the corner, Elanore appeared from behind one of the shady oak trees. "You got some gum for me? You are some sucker." She stood with her hand on her hip laughing at Levia.

Levia drew back her arm and popped Elanore in the face with the candy bag. The candy flew out of the bag as it broke and stayed spread over the sidewalk because Elanore chased her all the way home.

When she got to her house, Levia went straight to her room, to be alone and to be quiet. Both the whites and her black friend had turned against her and she did not want to be around anyone anymore.

"Some people just want to stay stupid," Levia's father, with a drink in his hand, badgered her because she refused to discuss anymore where she was going to high school.

"Maybe I'll just get books and read at home," Levia said.

"Oh, what we got here is a separatist," he called to the air. "You into black power or white?"

"Daddy, shoot." Levia left the room.

She didn't think she could learn at home. But she saw many people on television who took their children out of the public schools. Black parents who feared violence and insults took their children to schools formed by church parishes. Whites who didn't want theirs to mix formed small teaching groups at home.

All these adults claimed to be right. Others said, "Trust in God," for all answers. "His justice will reign," said one woman who came to Levia's door selling religious books. She dropped to her knees and prayed on Levia's wooden porch when Levia told her she'd better start to go home because the radio just predicted a hurricane on its way.

"God's going to whip the slate clean," Levia's neighbor, old Mr. Gontier, stopped to tell her on the way to the grocery store. He had seen many hurricanes, "Lola, Darleen, Sylve, Ethel, Darleen." Levia nodded her head with each one, especially for the hurricane he mentioned twice, thinking he might get the message that she had to go and was getting bored. But that just seemed to encourage him to go on.

"Out of respect," her mother said pay attention to old people. So Levia felt caught by his stories, and she blamed her parents for her delay now. "God always work in mysterious ways. But I'll tell you, He always send a message for you while He's doing it. Something for you to learn from." Levia was beginning to back away from old Mr. Gontier, and he noticed. "Now you hear me well," he hollered. She had backed off far enough to be able to turn her face away, with one last shake of her head, "yes sir."

Levia hurried to the Circle Food Store. The lines were long. Before any hurricane, people stocked up on canned food and candles, liquor, water, and ice. If she ran out of money, Levia wondered which of the necessities she should choose out of that group.

But her mother gave her enough to buy two bags of ice and four tall votive candles. They had enough, Levia guessed, of the rest.

While Levia waited in line, she watched old people gather under the arches right outside of the entrance door. Circle Food Store was more a tradition in the neighborhood than a full-service grocery. It was a rambling building, erected in parts, like occasional Spanish memories, probably as the owners got more money in their cash registers. With several red-tiled roofs and upside-down U's linked side by side to make an open wall for a breezeway that extended over the sidewalk, the Circle gathered the old and the romantic. Nothing in the vicinity was new. The check out clerks were over sixty-five, the pigeons that lived under the arches were balding, and some boxes of food were usually damaged by rain or outdated and sold at discount. The floor was worn in spots from black-and-white linoleum squares to a smooth, sloping plywood.

That the old people came to the Circle in numbers to discuss the hurricane seemed right on time. Levia thought that a good wind could destroy either the building or the people with one gust. The idea made her wish that she had spent longer listening to Mr. Gontier.

"We will be closing in twenty minutes," an announcer said. The checkout clerks sighed and people began rolling their baskets quickly in Z patterns up the aisles. The way their carts jingled over the floor as the people shoved them, then crashed into others when their drivers left them, struck Levia as funny. "Miss, will you hurry up. Is something humorous here?" Before Levia answered, the clerk said, "Next."

The sky was dark by the time Levia reached her house. There were marbled patterns above her of black and white, changing constantly with an unpredictable pace. "Thank God," Levia's mother stood on the porch. They closed the door and latched the long, cypress shutters behind them, just before the wind began shaking the wood.

First it rained like a thunderstorm, except without lightning. Then the wind hit the front of the house like someone was throwing debris. Soon a noise rose like all kinds of people shouting at once. But above it, Levia's family could hear parts of the house next door bursting against its own windows, garbage cans rolling down the pavement, car horns going off and on like bleating—sounds that made Levia think of the instruments in a band running away from the musicians. Tree branches scraped down the street like fabric being ripped. The lights went out.

Levia, her mother, brother, father, and sister moved into the same room and gathered around one votive candle. "First, let's say a prayer for the people who will suffer through this," Levia's mother said. "For the good and the bad, may they find Your Wisdom." The family said, "Amen."

The next morning a neighbor from across the street rattled the door blinds to wake them. Levia's father jumped from the floor. "Man, I thought you were the hurricane," he said after he opened the door.

"You got to see this, brother," the neighbor pointed to the corner as they walked away. Levia ran down the steps to follow.

Water tapered off to become level with the street where it rushed into the drainage sewers about two blocks from Levia's house. Beyond that, St. Bernard Avenue was a canal. People launched skiffs into it and paddled downtown.

"They say it gets deeper and deeper farther back. To the ninth ward, it's over the roofs," the neighbor called to her father over the sound of others saying the same thing.

The street was also filled with children playing. They laughed and splashed in the shallow water as if all of a sudden God gave them a public pool. The city had ordered all swimming facilities closed a year earlier since too many people complained about such intimate mixing of whites and blacks. Levia's mother spoke to the television when she heard the reports, "That's OK, city, we always swim in the natural lake."

Neighbors slowly returned who had left their houses to stay with relatives during the storm. They carried stories up the street, crossing from porches on one side to those on the other. The telephones didn't work. So they had the only news for everyone.

"In the ninth ward, the water is over your house," one man said. "They claim lots of us drown." He carried the contents of his refrigerator, offering meat and eggs to families as he went along. "I rather do this," he said, "than to let it spoil."

Levia went to the corner to find other children. Only Philip was out. "They say Elanore's family went down to the ninth ward."

Elanore's grandfather approached her house dressed in the suit and straw hat he wore every day to go to the horse races.

"They not home," Philip said and told the grandfather about the floods in the ninth ward.

Elanore's grandfather sat on the step with his head in his hands, "It's the white people."

Levia went to the edge of the water at St. Bernard Avenue and waded. Then the water got too deep, near the curbs where the street sloped down or near intersections. So she swam. The water was brown like the river and it smelled like the London Avenue sewerage canal. People passed in small motorboats, making soft wakes. They shouted, "You ought to get out. This water's filthy."

But Levia wanted to swim downtown as far as she could. She could go two miles in the lake and had since she was little. This water was shallower and porches jutted above it along the way where she could rest.

Once when she stopped, bits of clothing and then a suitcase floated past. "Didn't get away fast enough," Levia thought, then she wondered where was the person they fit. The water held boards and tree branches, plastic toys and food, like a box of cereal. Levia watched most of the day from that porch about one mile from her house. She did not go further because all she saw ahead of her was just drifting and she decided not to just follow along.

When the radio came on in a couple days, reports said the levee had broken downtown. By that time, Levia and her family already heard a different story from people arriving in boats docked near their street. People said the levee was torn away by the city at a section in the ninth ward. That made the water pour into the black neighborhood and relieve the flooding of whites on the other side. Everyone who drowned during Hurricane Betsy was black, Levia heard. A movement began for revenge.

Elanore never appeared and Levia prayed constantly, asking God to forgive her for hitting Elanore in the mouth. Soon after, she saw Elanore getting out of a car. Levia ran up to hug her. "Is you crazy?" Elanore jumped back waving her hand at Levia as if to drive away a bad smell. "Nobody got to worry about me, I could swim."

Elanore's mother told Levia that Elanore saved her grandmother as the flood rose. She pulled her in the water from the roof of a house to the three-story school building across the street.

"I'll tell you one thing, I'm not going to be nice anymore," Elanore said.

People sat on their porches more than usual for the next week while the telephones were out. Daily came news, less about dead people now, more that pet cats were bloated and found in backyards when the water receded, or new furniture was ruined with no insurance to pay for it, and of permanent watermarks near the ceilings of houses.

Where Levia disbelieved everything before the hurricane, now she listened to anything. "They say the Black Panthers are going to defend the ninth ward from now on," Levia told her mother, "and they're going to stop school integration."

"Cheer up," Levia's mother smiled. But Levia could not figure out what she meant. Levia was frightened like most of the old ladies she visited on the block. One told her, "I guess God just don't want people to mix. If He did, wouldn't he see to it that we could get better along?" Levia thought for a second that her father said people were together more at one time in New Orleans, until they started black and white separate justice. But Levia said nothing. The old woman kept talking, "I think them Black Panthers is right. We need protection."

"The Panthers say, if you don't put something black on house, you have no respect for the dead in the ninth ward and you will be hurt," Levia brought a new rumor home.

"That's crazy," Levia's father answered. "Who doesn't know we're for black people doesn't know us. So it's none of their damn business."

But in the same way as Levia brought that requirement to her house, other children and childish minds spread the rumor down the block. The neighborhood soon accumulated drapes of sympathy all day in varying degrees from solidarity to fear. Flags of red, black, and green hung out of some windows. In others appeared pieces of black material, a coat jacket, a navy blue towel, and a negligee.

"What is she giving up for the revolution?" Levia's father called to his wife.

"Hush up," her mother laughed.

Levia followed her father into the bedroom and watched while he opened a dresser drawer and got out his gun. "I can take care of this family good enough."

But when they went to sleep, Levia took her grammar school uniform out of the closet. Although it was navy blue, she planned to hang it out on the porch. She unlatched the shutters and pushed the blinds open to see if anyone was outside. But the electricity had not yet been restored so there were no streetlights.

Levia tiptoed out to the porch, clutching her school uniform in her folded arms over her nightgown. To think of a place to hang it she sat on the steps. She tried to get her eyes to adjust to the darkness all around her. She could make out a few lit front rooms in the neighborhood where people sat up, or where they left the lights on because they were afraid. Levia felt cold sitting on the steps in her sheer gown. But she didn't want to go inside.

There was something going on all around her, and Levia felt if she sat outside long enough she could smell it. The air held the salty moisture of breeze off the river, the rancid smell of moss and wet grass, and a tinge of something burning. Levia thought to hang her school uniform on the door. But then she remembered that she would have to wear it tomorrow and her father would be the first one out of the house. She thought maybe he was right about keeping the gun loaded. If the white people came inside, he would just blow them up.

"The big fish eat the little fish, and we, the people, eat all the fish," old Mr. Gontier joked with Levia as she watched him unload his boat. His nephews stood in the skiff on its bed pulled behind the car parked in the driveway. Mr. Gontier handed one of the older boys the garden hose to wash the stench of dead bait and catch out of the boat, while the other gave him the ice chest.

He dragged it into his unfenced front yard and took out fish one by one to show the children. "This here is my dinner. And this," he picked up a dead shrimp, "was his dinner." The children laughed as he made gulping noises and pointed to the fish.

But some fish were still alive. The children stared at their big, unblinking eyes and sighed while the fish drew air deeply through their gills. These produced a collective "Aw," in sympathy, speckled trout that lost their rainbow as soon as they were lifted out of the ice by the tail and croakers who made long, painful belches as they gasped to flop slowly from one side to the other on the pavement.

"Ya'll too soft," Mr. Gontier fussed at them. "Where ya'll get hamburgers? From Old McDonald's cow!"

"Ugh," children groaned and covered their mouths. The old man continued, "And you know how they kill them, pow, they shoot them right in the middle of the head."

"I don't believe you," Elanore said. "Old stupid man," she called ahead of herself so he could not hear from behind her back as she went home. Levia decided it was time for her to go too. Philip remained next to the step until the sun went down and the old man said he had to go inside.

Levia went to the kitchen table, "Do we have to kill animals to eat?"

Her mother replied, "Well, there are some things that we grow. A person could eat vegetables and grains all the time."

Her father entered the room, "No. Listen to me child, in life, you are either the hunter or the hunted."

"That's not true, Marvin," said her mother.

"You tell me why then, if it's not man against animal, it's man against man. It's either kill or be killed, Darwinism, the philosophy of the hunter. Have people ever been able to get away from that? No, it's a jungle and until people first understand that it is, they will never get beyond it."

"Well, that's the survival of the stupid if you ask me," Levia's mother said.

"Thanks," answered her father. "What are we having for dinner?"

"Pork chops."

Levia ran out the back door, holding her stomach. "The poor pig."

Twilight was falling when she sat on the backyard steps. She tried to make out the outline of the things she enjoyed. The bay-leaf and pecan trees, the tomato bushes, her mother's planters with pansies, the doghouse and the dog's silent pacing in his fenced off section.

She heard evening bugs around her. Something big like a bee flew near her head and she tilted her ears on an angle to the ground, and held herself stiff. After she relaxed, she stared at the dark grass. Its stillness was calming and every once in a while, she'd notice a faint little glow, a lightning bug, low to the ground. Levia stayed outside even though the mosquitoes were beginning to bite.

In the daytime, mosquito hawks ate the mosquitoes. Like fly-ing dragons, someone once told Levia, mosquito hawks were all over the yard. She used to catch them by their transparent wings and feed them tobacco. Now she just liked to watch them. They were getting too fast for her, Levia's mother said, to encourage her to act more like a lady. And Levia began to take pleasure just noticing their prettiness. The mosquito hawks had different tints; some were shaded blue, some green, others black, silver, gold from their flat, fly noses to their crispy wings.

If she caught them, she did not see the color. She had to con-centrate on keeping them still. Half the time the wings broke from the pressure of children holding. Most pinched the wings harder if the mosquito hawks tried to get away.

Once Levia's mother caught Philip shaking a mosquito hawk by the fragile wings to make it release the tobacco in its mouth.

"Philip, what are you doing? You gave it to him."

"Ma'am, I don't know."

"That thing didn't do anything to hurt you. So leave it alone."

Levia wondered as she began to go inside and slapped the mosquitoes now stabbing her arms if it was all right then to kill something that first comes after you?

She hit at the site of a prickly pain and squashed the insect

into a fragment of rolling fabric under her hand. When she tried
to pick the dead bug off her arm, what she felt most was the wet-
ness of her own blood.

Her cousin carried a gun with him all the time. "Once I was
fishing," he said, "and I nearly got bit by a snake." He was a big
man and a hunter like most of his friends. Sprouting along the
walls of their houses were necks, faces, and antlers.

He taught Levia how to shoot. "You don't have to act all the
time like a girl," he said. "Besides, you'd better learn how to
protect yourself." He placed his hand over hers as she held the
base of the weapon. "Now hold it straight up and shoot it into
the air."

Levia pulled the trigger. A vibration traveled from her wrist
to the center of her chest. "There you go. Now that wasn't bad,
was it? You want to do it again?" he asked.

Levia said no. He had shown her the proper way to load and
carry the weapon. Shooting it once was all she could stand.

When he let her shoot, it was New Year's Eve night so no one
noticed the ringing sound. In fact, shooting rifles and handguns
was part of the fun in New Orleans. In neighborhoods where rifle-
men did not have time to buy blanks the sky rained buckshot.

Everyone drank and hugged out of tradition in the background. Overhead was pitch-black. But the shooters stood safe
distances from each other, or in groups that would not face head-
on, and from the ends of their weapons, quick, deadly fires
blazed. It was like one hundred matches lighted at once, or a
burst of anger, a scar on the sky. Levia wondered if the woods at
night stayed black and lonely only to protect itself.

The children that year played a new game called "Killer."
One girl's cousin brought it from California for the holidays. He
lived in Watts. They would sit in a circle and wink at each other
before another winked at them. Once you caught the wink of another, you were dead.

Levia played once and lasted a long time. But she did not like
the way she felt during the game. "Come on, girl," the boy from
Watts challenged her, "I could do better this time and it's more
fun with lots of people."

"Didn't I tell you I don't want to play?" Levia pushed his

shoulder away from her in the circle where they sat. But before he could push her back, tears came out of her eyes. She did not know why and they dried up immediately from her own shock.

The boy walked away from the other children, telling the others, "Where did you get this weird one?"

While the party was still going on, all the children were called into the front room. The television was on. "Look at Dr. King," the grown-ups were pointing. It was more news about civil rights, Levia thought. She didn't want to listen too long. But everyone was quiet. He was talking about marching for non-violence. He kept using the words "Love" and "Peace."

"He don't know these crackers down here in New Orleans," one of the adults said. "I rather listen to Malcom X." Then the adults began arguing and Levia returned to the other room. The children were talking about the same thing. "I'd rather see them all die," the boy from Watts said, "than to live with them."

By spring of her eighth grade year Levia had to start thinking about high school. Elanore would attend the junior high in the neighborhood for a couple years, she said. Philip told everyone his father wanted him to work.

Levia stopped going around them because they kept asking her what she was going to do, and bragging about their own choices, which Levia felt they had not really made. If they were telling the truth, she told herself, how were they able to decide so easily?

Surprisingly, in one year, some parts of the the city had gotten more accustomed to integration. But now pressure came from other sides. Her teachers encouraged Levia to be the first. "Go there and get on the volleyball team." Or, "It would be nice if they had a black girl debate."

Levia would have to fight for these things as well and she was not sure she even wanted to try. Others in her community showed her another way: That blacks did not need to be among whites at all. That made sense to Levia from the life she had experienced so far.

A man visited every Saturday morning selling *Muhammad Speaks*. He talked to Levia's mother at length each time. She liked the way he looked. He was dressed out-of-date as far as

Levia was concerned, hair cut too short, a bow tie and a suit that was too shiny, especially for Saturday morning. But Levia enjoyed the way he paid attention to her.

"Good morning, beautiful sister," he addressed her. "Is your mother here?"

On days that her mother was busy, he handed Levia the paper to bring inside and her mother swapped back to him the weekly newspaper of her Catholic faith. Levia wished she had something intelligent to say to Brother then. She had always sneaked out of mass off and on so they couldn't talk about that. But in *Muhammad Speaks* she had read the cartoons that called "shameless" the women who wore their dresses too short and tight. Levia had not yet developed a figure like in the cartoons but she did feel she could comment on that.

So the next time Brother came, Levia tried to seduce him into a conversation about clothes. She was standing in front of the house watering the garden. She was barefoot because of the especially warm spring day and had on a short playsuit. Every few minutes she would run a stream of water across her legs and feet. That stopped them from scalding on the cement for a time.

"I think you are right about women not wearing their dresses too tight, Brother," Levia smiled and looked him in the eyes.

"That's right." He watched from the blush on her shoulders down her long arms that ended at her thighs to her toes. "Are you cool or warm?"

"OK, I guess. But I think it's right about self-respect and the way ladies put on dresses. My parents always told me that."

"Is your mother home?"

"No. But you can talk to me."

"Give her this, beautiful sister. And if you want to have a conversation, there are many women who would like to give you guidance, if you wish to consider visiting the Mosque. In the meantime, young sister, be aware of yourself, like your mother says, and at least put on a dress."

Levia felt very hot. The soles of her feet burned. Suddenly she realized why. She had been standing the whole time with the water running into the bushes. She picked up the hose and now pointed it at the cement as the Brother left. Then she held it up like a fountain and let it shower her like when she was a little girl.

Charlene called to ask Levia what about going to St. Mary's. If she did go to St. Mary's like her cousin Charlene, Levia might be popular. St. Augustine picked most of its cheerleaders from there. It was a black, Catholic girl's school and having a cousin could help, especially since Charlene was awarded the title of school queen during her senior year.

Levia considered the possibility of an active social life based on her royal blood. She remembered Charlene's coronation in the auditorium. Folding chairs covered the floor except for a wide center aisle. Parents sweated in their Sunday clothes. Some women wore tall white hats iced with net in their high school sororities' colors, while men had on shiny striped suits and several kinds of official emblem ties.

That day Levia sat on the aisle so she could photograph Charlene. Everyone smiled as much as the queen did as she passed them to the stage. Charlene was as gracious as if they all were her servants applauding. She waved her scepter like the bishop sprinkling out blessed water with a holy enthusiasm that the people shined under like they were catching some summer rain. Levia wondered if everyone felt like she did that Charlene was looking just at them and if they looked back, they would have some of her beauty.

When Charlene arrived at her aisle, Levia snapped a picture and waved. Charlene stopped then and blew Levia a kiss. A sigh rose from the crowd, sweet like candy air floating up to the sky from the cotton-making machine. It was as if everyone puffing softly could make Charlene nicer.

Charlene got the most roses, red long-stemmed ones, of any of the girls on the stage. The runners-up received flowers according to rank and Levia took pictures of each one of them, even though the man sitting near Levia said, "Save your film for the best."

Later, after the photos developed, Levia pinned them to the bulletin board on her wall. While she studied and listened to the radio in the evening, she stared at them every day until she knew by heart what they all looked like.

She imagined that these girls were like starlets who were kissed in the movies, each one more favored than the next. The ones who were the least pretty were the least admired. The one who was beautiful, Charlene, was not only well-liked, but rich and famous.

But the day Levia was studying and thinking about going to high school and she looked at the pictures, an idea occurred to her. She was not nearly as pretty as Charlene. Levia glanced quick to the mirror; there was hardly a family resemblance. How would they know she and Charlene were related? And what if she told them and they could not see Levia was as pretty as her cousin, so they didn't care? What if people didn't like her still after they knew she had a famous relative? She would be a total failure.

Levia suddenly felt like a little fish in the high school pond that was already eaten by Charlene. What could she do to change this fate?

Levia sat still thinking with her hands on her books and listened to the radio. It played the Supremes' "Nothing But Heartaches." Then the Temptations came on with "Just My Imagination (Running Away with Me)," and then followed a new group called the Jackson Five.

Levia had danced to this music by herself many times around the room, pretending that she would grow up to be somebody that a special person would like. No one like that had yet arrived, although a kind of love life happened already for some of her friends.

Like Elanore. Levia hadn't seen Elanore for months. But someone told Levia that Elanore was sighted on Canal Street. "She was sticking out this big." That person put their hands right about in the spot of a beer belly.

"Who is the daddy?" Levia asked.

"Who you think," the other said, "Philip."

Levia wondered now how someone like Philip could be a good father at all. The men she imagined herself dancing with were at least a foot taller than Philip, broader and had deep voices.

"Why haven't I seen you before?" one whispered to her.

"I guess because I'm inside studying a lot."

"There is nothing I like more than a woman with brains." The handsome man pressed his hands softly against her head and tilted her up to kiss.

"I can spell constitution," Levia whispered back, "C-O-N-S-T-I-T-U-T-I-O-N." She returned to her lesson. There must be some benefit for spelling.

Her eighth grade teacher said that men liked women smart as much as they liked them pretty. Levia as yet saw no evidence of that. She saw that men just wanted the pick of the best women. But then they all had their definitions of best. She had asked Philip once. He said, "I like them sexy." Brother said that women should not be sexy at all. And her father just said, "Stay a good girl." Levia did not know a woman yet whom she could be like and yet not compete with. Everyone wanted to tell her how to grow up. But Levia thought the grown-ups made too many rules about life, just like the white people.

The white people said blacks were lazy and ugly, athletic and stupid. Levia knew that didn't apply to her. So why should anything else?

The radio announcer said it was 5:45. Looking out of her window, Levia felt that was about right, although she could never guess the time in early evening when the sun was no longer visible but the sky wasn't yet dark. It might actually be only a few minutes long. But Levia felt she spent several hours of every day in twilight.

Perhaps that was because she sat so long thinking about everything lately, particularly herself, not nearly as grown up as she wanted to be, but much more than a child. She was tall and lean. Her face had pushed out in places that promised to be attractive. Her body even showed little bumps and curves, plumpness where she was once all hard running muscle.

But her thoughts seemed to grow only in spurts, then completely shrink, so that lately she had no control over her mind. Where she once had contentment, peace like her little brother and sister had who played and hummed all day to themselves, Levia now was uneasy. There was nothing to do. Nothing could hold her interest. Nothing satisfied. All one day she spent worrying over a cowlick that appeared in her hair, until her knees ached. Her mother called that growing pains.

If hurt meant something was growing, Levia thought, so was New Orleans. Now people were breaking the windows of government buildings and setting houses on fire, in response, they said, to the hurricane. New Orleans ached all over from integration. Levia didn't know if it was worth all that much. Why couldn't everything have stayed soft and comfortable like when she was young and a baby?

Then, the family went on picnics out at the lake. In a special place, Levia learned to swim, between two identical pilings. They were actually broken telephone poles hammered into the lake's bottom for a construction that never came. They were the same because the tops of both of them had been split by lightning.

She was just a baby when her parents let her float inside a life preserver tied by string. They sat on the shore, on a step that rose out of the water, letting her paddle out with the soft tide, then reeling her back in. Only once did she get in trouble, when she drifted against a construction piling. She bumped it and tried to hold on. But her parents tried to pull her back, thinking she had just grazed it and was not clinging.

The life preserver got caught on a nail, holding her just at water level. Every time a wave passed her head went under and she had to hold her breath. She screamed for her parents in the wake of the water, when the low, sucking part of the tide came. A couple of times, she hollered too late and a salty flood filled her nose and mouth, and she was choking.

"I will die now," she remembered thinking. "My life is short." But she actually had no choice then. Her mother arrived to take off the life preserver and wrap one arm around Levia to pull her to shore.

They continued swimming that afternoon, Levia's mother said so they would not become afraid. Her father, who never learned to swim, stood anxiously watching from the steps while holding the string and life preserver. From the water, Levia could hear him continue to curse the broken pilings and construction wood junked in the lake's "colored side."

Levia remembered those years when the lake was divided into separate areas where the blacks and whites swam, that the white side had a sand beach; they could see it when they passed in the car. On the colored side, a slope into the water was built with tossed off street construction material—bricks, rocks, and broken oyster shells.

At the time, she thought the shells where pretty. But her cousin, the hunter, said, "That's because you were a kid." Levia wondered, if she went to the colored side of the lake right now, how would she feel about it?

Levia's father got a phone call from a man on his job. "Stay out of trouble," the voice had warned. Her father had told the family at the dinner table. He made a joke out of it, "I was in trouble just by being born. I don't know what side's doing the calling." He explained at his job, there was a continual fight between blacks and whites. "I try to stay out of it until it gets to me," he told the children. "Then I got to act."

Levia saw him in the morning, getting ready for work. He was taking his gun. She volunteered to get it for him. "I know how to handle one," she said.

Levia lifted the case from the drawer of her father's dresser. She set it on the bed and unzipped the leather holder. It opened like the inside of a small animal slit up from the belly to the throat.

The body of the revolver was a metallic brown. Levia brought it to the light to see it up close. With the white bulb shining hard, the gun appeared a mean grey, the color the bank looked that night when she and her father got there too late and were locked out.

She heard once on the radio that everything living has colors, like emotions. Peace is green and anger is red. She wondered how she looked in the light of the bedroom lamp, if it had the power to diagnose her feelings as it did with the turncoat gun. Levia wondered if people turned colors when they were afraid. Would a crowd of people marching, if incited, suddenly turn orange like a clamoring flame?

And were the colors of rage and happiness the same for white people and black, or were they darker and more melancholy for black people since they seemed sad more of the time? Or were colors just reserved for the halos of saints, glows that surrounded their heads on top of their hair?

As she was thinking, Levia loaded the gun for her father, to do him a favor. She took out the box of bullets from a different drawer. She broke the revolver like her cousin showed her and spun the chamber, putting in bullets one at a time like thumb tacks.

People have to defend themselves, Levia thought. If they didn't, who would? She thought that her mother would answer the question with God. Her father would say himself. Levia wondered who would defend her if either one of them died. Would she get married for her husband to protect her? Nobody like Philip would ever do, she thought. Nor would anybody who didn't think I was pretty enough.

Levia continued to load the gun slowly and carefully. She could hear her parents arguing in the back of the house.

"Are you crazy, you going to be like the rest of these crazy men. Shooting at shadows? What is going on with you?"

Her father said, "I just got to show who is the boss around there. If I don't show some strength now, everybody will be able to push me."

"But a gun, Marvin," her mother said. "Isn't there something else you could do?"

"I thought integration was the answer. Hell, I pushed for it at the job. And now, everyone's turning against me."

Levia tried to listen now. She felt alone too most of the time. And for some reason, she was always afraid. But afraid of what? Certainly not whites. Not blacks. And yet something was always bothering her. Something that made her anxious. It was a feeling like a weak stomach. But she carried it around with her all the time, as if it were already a part of herself. Like no one could give her the definite truth, the right thing to do, yet they were asking her for it. What's good for the future? What's bad for it? Do you want to live around whites? Do you believe in killing for a just cause? What are the limits of race?

It was as if all the adults she knew became suddenly stupid but they continued to act. Big people shouting on television that they didn't want children to go into a restaurant or ride a bus. Her father kept his gun oiled. Her neighbors hung underwear on their porches now every time there was a thunderstorm. The city said it could not figure out how the levee broke.

And all of them were asking their children, what should we do? You are our future now. It seemed to Levia that the children were their present, were responsible for their own life and death decisions. Levia looked up from the gun, saw the picture of Charlene smiling from where she was pinned on the clothes closet, and then Levia couldn't ignore her own reflection in the mirror.

Maybe the truth always weighed on children. Mama said when she was a child she had to raise her brothers and sisters while her parents worked. She had to cook and clean and get them from school every day. She had to defend them from the bullies across the street, she said too. Once she said she hit a boy in the head with a baseball bat. "I never went to see what happened to him," she told Levia, "and I heard he was OK but I regretted it all my life."

"But wasn't it him or you, Mama?"

"The older I got the less I could tell."

Levia had just about gotten the gun loaded and snapped the barrel back into place.

Then she reconsidered. Her father just had to show he was powerful. So he could take his gun. But she would protect him. She would finally make a decision that would help her parents.

She opened the gun with both her hands, pulling the barrel apart from the body on both sides. She shook the bullets out to the floor where they hit soft like hail. Then she went into the back room where her parents argued.

"Here, Daddy," she gave it to him. He put it inside the waist of his pants under his coat jacket. Levia felt good all day. She had made a decision. Like Martin Luther King, Jr., she thought, she would tell her parents later, she had decided on nonviolence.

She felt good until her father did not come home that evening. While she and her mother waited with dinner, they turned on the news. "Oh my God, Levia," her mother called her close to the television. There were pictures of violence and sounds of shots as the camera weaved through the crowd. "That's Daddy's work," her mother said, "What should we do?"

Levia didn't know what to say. She just ran out the house. "The white people," she said to herself, she kept repeating. "They killed my father."

She ran to the corner where the children were playing. But she had nothing to say. They just looked at her as she stood silently. She ran to her cousin's house, the hunter. But he wasn't home. "I'll get a gun and I'll kill them," she kept saying to herself. "I'll kill all of them." She ran around the corner where the white children lived. She shouted to them on their porches, "I hate you."

The boy heard her and came down the steps. "My father," she hollered and she began to run home. He followed her and by the time they arrived, people from her neighborhood were all gathered around her steps. Everyone was saying, "What's wrong?" They were talking to her mother who was looking for Levia. "What's wrong?"

"My child," Levia's mother gathered her close and held her. They sobbed together on the steps of the house, while all the neighbors came near. The people were there from the front street where the blacks lived. And the children from around the corner brought their mother when they heard the news. "Oh my God," they were all saying, "dear God," when Levia said she had taken the bullets.

Then her father drove up.

He thanked everyone for their concern. He had gone to another location for work. There was too much fighting on his job. He had expected the worst and before he got out of his car, he checked and found his gun wasn't loaded.

"Then I asked myself," he told the neighbors, "what if my child felt responsible. What if I killed someone. Everyone now is too crazy. We have never hated each other before like this." Old Mr. Gontier called from the back, "Amen."

"We got to act more civilized," he said. Then he opened the door of the house. "Anyone who wants to is welcomed inside," he told them. Slowly, the neighbors came in.

They entered all night, filtering in and out. People talked from the separate streets who never knew each other except by appearance. They introduced themselves by name. Mostly, the black people stayed. But the mother of the white country people from around the corner came bringing all of her children.

Levia made sandwiches, opened soft drinks, and cut cakes that people brought and served them around. As the crowd stayed in the back room of the house, the children her age gathered off to the side.

While they talked, Levia asked the others where they decided to go to school. Nobody liked where they were going, and they wanted to stay in the neighborhood. The white country boy said most of his friends left the public school because they were afraid of the blacks. Levia said she did not know where she would go yet, "But I think I want to go where it's integrated."

"Why?" someone asked her. "Everyone just wants to fight now. Isn't it just too hard."

"Not everyone," Levia said, "and only because things are important."

When the people were leaving the house, Levia thought she wanted to ask the boy more, about what things were hard for him. She wanted to ask him if he had ever climbed Monkey Hill, and how did that feel. She thought maybe the next time. But not too long after that, his father moved their family out of the neighborhood.

And as time passed, Levia began to think less about the games of Monkey Hill played by children, the running and climbing and fighting to get to the top. And she thought more about growing up, and how in the future people could be good, but not better than others.

Before Echo

MORNING LIGHT DOES NOT ENTER THE SWAMP. Even the sunrise is dark. Still, time progresses, night into day.

A picture of bayou country is deceiving. Slow streams converge under mud to make the appearance of land that is actually water. One net of moss hangs from one hundred trees. Lightning strikes the same stump many times.

People pass the swamp's fringes in trains, on tracks that cling to the last solid ground. Out of their windows are landscapes that take the earth's colors to every periphery. Bright orange sunsets surround people like sky on an airplane. On grey foggy mornings, they ride through a dream that has no beginning or end. But time has its limits, these people know. They are expected places—Memphis by midnight, New Orleans by dawn.

Deep in the swamp, animals keep the only appointments. Birds gather at high places in trees. Raccoons make their last noisy passes for food across someone's back porch before he awakes. Fish all around splash up although they cannot see the morning coming to clean the picture of day like clothes bleaching in a galvanized tub from dark grey to light grey.

Joan looked out from the porch to the swamp she had known all of her life. Ahead of her in the veiled light were the outlines of many trees. Below and around her were the crisp sounds of nature awakening. Cupped in both hands, perched on her knees was a warm mug of coffee.

Joan got up early for no other reason than habit. If she stayed in the bed, her bones would have felt strange. To avoid their odd aches and stiffness, she rose when the dampness of morning settled on her face. She could smell the dawn since the air held a less stagnant pungency.

Usually the smell of rotten wood and dead fish came into her house. It mixed with the smell of moss, moldy but flat. But it provided a diverting aroma when Joan put her face close to the pillow or mattress.

The house was surrounded on three sides by water. Joan looked for her reflection when she first arrived on the porch. It stood out on stilts like a dock. But she did not see her appearance. The water was too dim and the morning too early.

"Is the same now as it was then, before the Savior, before the words in the Bible," Joan spoke out to the darkness and considered that little had changed since the very beginning.

Joan thought and dreamed a lot lately because she was so much alone. Her life was proscribed by the length of the days, and the bounty or scarcity of food in a season. "That's everybody," Joan reconciled her existence as the same as everyone else in the world. Perhaps she was more lucky than most to be fitted so well with nature. Everything she needed was inside her home or within the boundaries of water.

Her ideas differed little from the rare people who still lived in the swamp. When the fish ran, the oysters grew fat in their salt beds; the animals' furs thickened with the anticipation of cold; the people prospered and prided themselves for remaining in exile like their forefathers had in tribes and from Canada.

Joan didn't know history or think about it because she was still young. Her life was the present. Even the Bible she read, although written hundreds of years earlier, spoke directly to her.

Joan lived with her grandfather and she took his ways too as modern behaviors. She hunted and fished, repaired the house, and sewed crab nets. She sipped homemade wine, smoked pipe tobacco or sometimes chewed it. It occurred to Joan only rarely that other young women might not live as she did. But if she considered that briefly, she dismissed it.

When Joan sat on the porch in the morning, she waited for nothing. Now she wanted to hear the buzz of outboard boat motor that would tell her the doctor was coming. Joan's grandfather was sick.

About illness, Joan was again like the swamp folk who took sickness too personally. They saw failure in themselves or the removal of love by the Creator. That was one reason few people re-

mained so isolated. Not many could sustain such passions with
the invisible.

Joan wished for parents in her times of trouble. But they existed for her only like the dark spaces on the other side of the
trees. Joan wanted to feel in the big, empty clearing, peace and
the comfort of nothing. That was her idea of belonging. When
she was a baby, Joan's mother died, her grandfather said. They
were not ever acquainted with Joan's father.

The woman at the supply store that Joan reached by pirogue
boat suggested that Joan try to find out more about her mother
and father. But Joan told her, "I don't care." The woman tried
to convince Joan, "But what if you could know them? Don't you
want to know?" Joan said, "Non." That was her lie.

Joan had tried early in life to figure out more from her grandfather. But her mother was like any daughter, Joan's grandfather
said. That's all he knew. Joan worried, "How I could find out?
Who I could ask?" But there was no one around her. And the
concern made her days in the swamp go heavy and slow. When
she began to feel that some fault caused her to be alone rather
than God's act, Joan suffered. It was painful to think something
should have been changed. Joan's only solution, she realized
very young, was to not think about it. Only then could she experience comfort in her days that consisted of chores to take care of
the house, the dog, and her grandfather.

Joan did not venture further with her curiosity, just like at
night she did not go beyond the porch. Other animals saw better
in darkness. Then, they took over the land and the water. Joan
only heard them outside and from their weight, she guessed they
ran in packs or danced in couples, that her only recourse was to
scatter if she saw them in daylight.

Joan felt the darkness allowed the animals to conceive and to
multiply. The darkness inspired God in His time to create the
world. In Joan's darkness was quiet and mystery. She kept the
time before her and of her beginning in ignorance.

Joan heard the faraway sound of the doctor's boat for ten
minutes before he pulled up to the house. He handed her his bag
before stepping from his rocking skiff to her stairs going down to
the water.

"How you how you?" he greeted her, just like the people he visited, although they bragged he "had education." They took credit for his success because he returned to them after going away to school. They boasted to each other of his ability to move between the worlds of "smart people" and "us."

Joan's grandfather now remained in the bed separated by a fabric curtain from the rest of the house. Joan could hear his breath whistling loud like a person who sleeps with a cold, although he didn't rest. Sometimes he just stared ahead toward the door and his eyes rolled back toward the ceiling. Joan was afraid.

The last time the doctor visited, her grandfather did not awaken as his pulse was taken and the doctor placed the cold shiny thing over her grandfather's heart. The doctor made Joan listen first to the old man, then to herself, and then to him. "You can see for yourself. I'm sorry to tell you the truth, but he ain't doing too well," the doctor said. Joan held the object deep to her grandfather's ribs to hear the faint swishing and patting not quite in rhythm like clothes on the line being blown by the wind against the side of the house.

Her own heart in contrast sounded like her bare foot tapping against the planks of the porch. And the doctor, even though he was much older than Joan, but younger than her grandfather, his heart thumped like the dog's tail on the floor wanting to be let out.

After the doctor left, Joan talked to herself about the Bible and read it aloud to the dog. She unwrapped some dried fish from a piece of paper and took some leaves from where they hung in a bunch near the ceiling to make a thin soup. She tried to get the old man to drink. But most of his food drooled back on him. She drank the rest on his plate and gave some to the dog. She sat on the floor near the old man's bed. And she held his hand as he had not allowed her to do since she was a little girl. She was now sixteen.

Joan noticed her grandfather growing old when his thick hair turned flatter, and from black to grey, white, then yellow. He walked slower. But since they traveled few distances by foot, she didn't care.

A few years earlier, she had raced to their summer bathing

place by the inland river and he could not keep up. But she challenged him less often as she got older. So they walked there in a slower, actually elderly gait.

She was young and she was pretty, Joan could see in the water's reflection once the light had descended in a flat heat and the darkness erased. But she did not especially flatter herself. Joan washed her dishes, clothes, and body with the same country store soap. She changed jeans not too frequently and outgrew her only pair of good shoes while they were still in the white box that came from the mailman.

Still, the lady who ran the store that Joan reached by the pirogue boat made nice comments. And some people, the store lady said, who remembered Joan from years past when her grandfather came to the community parties, complimented her, "Now she must blossom." Joan did, with full cheeks that blushed the color of rose water lilies from new ideas and embarrassments. And Joan felt rare. These swamp flowers proliferated in the heat and the darkness, but Joan was the only young woman around.

Joan sat alone on the floor next to her grandfather's bed and tried to inhale deeply at the same time as him. At first, she thought this could help. But he didn't notice and it only served to make her feel more of his difficulty.

The first day her grandfather could not rise from bed, Joan went in the pirogue two hours away to the store where she called the doctor. They discussed taking her grandfather to the nearest city hospital. "We could make way to take him in the boat. But why suffer him?" the doctor said. "You a woman now." The doctor paused on the telephone for her to acknowledge his authority, "You got to take care of this, you. If he don't come around, if he go, you pack and you come stay by me."

Joan listened because her grandfather always said, "Go to the doctor house, if anything happen." Besides being her grandfather's friend, the doctor was the nearest advisor. The priest, sheriff, and schoolteacher all lived and worked close to each other in an area surrounded by high land. They clustered together to be convenient, they said. But that helped only people who got first to one of them.

Since the day Joan called the doctor, her grandfather lost his desire to talk and lay most of the time like a baby or how Joan imagined one to be. He slept off and on. When awake he stared ahead and his eyes filmed with water. Sometimes he drooled and wet on the bedcovers.

Joan felt he would die very soon, and she would bury him. She got pictures of herself in her mind, paddling the boat away from the burial. When she got those images, they often proved out.

Since a child, Joan saw clear pictures in her head during times of deep concentration. Sometimes, quicker than a picture a voice would give her advice. This voice too had the quality of predicting in advance something to happen. Once when she and her grandfather were hunting, the voice said, "Look over there." She saw a deer. Another time in the woods, the voice told her, "Stop." She just missed bumping into a snake hanging low on a branch.

Joan told her grandfather about these experiences. But he just advised she had good instincts, just like the animals knew a storm was coming, the birds from the North filled the ponds every winter, or the fish came close to the shore sunset and dawn. Joan had a special sense for nature, her grandfather said, and Joan agreed. She did not tell him that she knew in advance his words or requests for dinner. He might have thought her disrespectful.

Plus, the Bible assured Joan that all things were possible. Prophets saw visions. Demons took hold of people and had to be cast out. Joan felt safe and content in her special abilities. They helped her. They confirmed that her grandfather might soon be dead.

The old man called for Joan. She stood up and wiped her grandfather's face with a warm, damp cloth. His skin was thick and dry like an old piece of bark. His lips were parted and she could see the spittle collecting into one cheek. She lifted his head for a sip of water. But his face tilted to the side and the liquid spilled from his mouth like an overturned cup.

The woman at the store wanted Joan to live there, where she rowed every week for supplies. "You just a child," the woman behind the counter told Joan. "Yes, you could be a daughter to me?" But Joan shook her head no, and packed the canned food she bought into a small leather bag that she put over her shoulder. The dog waited on the dock of the store by the boat.

Joan did not know where to go. But just rowing away seemed a good start. She had taken her grandfather's body, wrapped in a sheet, out to the boat. He was light like a small animal. Joan closed the front door with the zipper of bent nails that held the screen flat when the wind was up from a rainstorm.

She took with her grandfather's body four empty half-gallon jugs that he kept for wine. He did not have too many around because he did not drink that often, only for special occasions. One remained half-full.

As she did for the more than a month of his sickness, actually for most of her life, she moved slowly and methodically. When her feelings welled up, she erased them. She had learned not to cringe when a rabbit needed to be skinned and gutted. She could watch with fascination alone when the heart of a turtle continued to pulse on the kitchen table. She had suspended her fear while her grandfather grew more sick, and she faced one new duty after another, cleaning up after him and waking to his gagging chokes in the night.

Joan was strong. Her grandfather once said her name came from the French saint set afire who went willingly into a war. So when he died, she buried him the way she knew. She rowed the boat out into the swamp, and she filled up the wine jugs with water by ducking them below the surface. Through the thumbhole for lifting the jugs she laced a rope and then tied it to her grandfather's body. Then she put them all overboard. The swamp folded her grandfather inside as he sank and she said prayers to remind herself his spirit left during the previous night, and now she submerged only his shell.

But Joan began crying and praying words from the Bible. And soon all jumbled around in her head, so that even the dog in the bow of the boat looked at her strangely. Her sobbing echoed on top of the water reaching far into the dark, empty spaces of swamp. And when she stopped, nature imitated her silence. But no longer did she feel its peace. Inside this timeless and changeless darkness, Joan felt different. She and the dog no longer belonged.

The doctor's house shone so white and brilliantly in the sun, Joan squinted. Back from the main road, the house was surrounded by grass, green and flat. Joan felt conscious of standing still when she stopped walking. Being on land that did not sink when her boot pressed into it made Joan feel strange. She did not need on this unfamiliar ground to shift her weight from one foot to the other, as near her home.

In her line of vision stood the big, square-shaped residence with its huge tapered yard and a white picket fence across the front. Joan didn't know anyone who lived like this. When younger, she took a bus ride and she saw these kinds of homes every few miles. But this time, she stood and looked without the impression of speed, or without shadow and trees framing her sight.

Joan felt dreamy. But she was unsure whether the fog in her head was due to the dream she had just entered or the dream she had just left. She knew only that her skull ached slightly and the hard sun made her sweat. Brightness surrounded her like an exaggeration of colors she saw the first moment she stood by the road.

She had waited there, not far from the supply store after leaving her boat at the dock. She walked a few miles up the oyster shell and gravel truck-path from the store to the highway.

The man who opened the door of the huge trailer truck asked her, "How much?" when she got on the cab seat. Joan did not understand, so she ignored him and gave him the address of the doctor's house. After a while, she told him about her grandfather.

She was just lucky, the truck driver said, that she got him and nobody else. How would she be safe?

"God bless you," she said good-bye when she got out.

"Mercy," the truck driver wiped his brow and wished her good luck.

Joan had felt during the ride a sensation coming from him, like sitting close to the fire. She ignored it because she felt uncomfortable. She did not want him to take pity on her. She was already afraid and only by staying quiet and keeping her distance could she not acknowledge it.

She could not see herself as he did. The man thought at first she was someone from the houses on Decatur or Bourbon Street in New Orleans who was stranded downriver. She wore such a strange outfit: the jeans and hat with animal skins laced around the band, leather bag and tall boots. She was beautiful. The plait she wore to her waist was the same color as her eyes, like rocks of tar set in a complexion of gold. But as soon as she got in the cab, he smelled the decay from the swamp. He had never picked up anyone like her.

If only she were a child, the doctor thought as he prepared to meet Joan, someone would perhaps adopt her. But physically she was a woman, although without the strength or the wit of the experience. Living anywhere outside of the swamp, she would be a victim. The modern world allowed no ignorance or indifference now on the part of participants. One moment of indecision and predators would see this girl's weakness. Then she could live the rest of her life with a wrong choice.

The transition from her quiet life would not be easy. Before he arrived almost a generation ago, the doctor remembered, he never wore shoes all day. Then, he owned two white shirts and one tie that he laundered by hand in the bathroom every night. He was expected to dress for classes in medical school. The other students laughed at him.

But he won out finally. He was accustomed to studying. Early in life, he read aloud at home. His habit became to repeat and explain to the younger children, and translate bills and letters for his mother who could not understand writing.

But the city boys, most of them monied, had as their hardest job to curb their good-time energy. Their college plans were to go out night after night. Fun did not play much part in the doctor's experience.

So many of the others did not graduate. But they returned to their rich families in uptown New Orleans and went insane like their weak fathers. Or they became drunks like their once beautiful Southern belle mothers who hungered for company.

Those medical students who did graduate now owned fine, expensive practices in the New Orleans districts where the streetcars ran. The doctor visited a colleague once in the city. This man charged fifty dollars to listen to perfectly strong old ladies' hearts and to convince them of their lingering desirability. At least this colleague spent one afternoon in the poor section of town. He ministered from the back room of a drugstore to people who really needed medical attention.

That day was more than an education, the doctor remembered. He felt better when he returned to his own rural community. He knew these people needed his knowledge. Still, his situation often discouraged him.

These people could not afford the drugs he prescribed. So while his costs rose greatly, he could not raise their fees. Most of them would do without a doctor rather than pay more than ten dollars for a visit. They depended on him to give them the drugs, just like medicine men who once practiced in this part of Louisiana. They expected lagniappe from the doctor, something extra to go along with his services, as if he were a grocery store clerk. Rarely did they treat him like a professional.

Maybe he could have achieved more success in New Orleans. But then again, maybe not. The laughter of college boys still rang in his ears. They made fun of him in school when he answered in half-French. His professors encouraged the ridicule, "The state of Louisiana has been purchased, monsieur. Please join us." He learned to speak good English once he used it every day. But when he returned to the country, no one could understand him. So he began speaking as he did before he left to get educated.

His city peers still lost no opportunity to demonstrate his unsophistication. On his last visit to a colleague, the rural doctor complained about rising costs and expenses, and his patients' inability to pay. The city doctor said, "Look at the burden they are to society now. Probably most of those you are treating were mistakes anyway."

"Mistakes," the doctor said aloud when he left his colleague's office and stepped into the too-bright New Orleans afternoon sun. What a way for a healer to think about people.

But this girl who stood in his front room was one of those kinds of "mistakes." He knew well about her. Born illegitimate and then abandoned to her grandfather, she would get nowhere in life. If she could get a job, she would be at best some kind of servant. Her lack of skills, her isolation and unrealistic religious beliefs gave the credentials for failure. The doctor just hoped that the state would not have to take care of her finally. For now, he would give her a home in exchange for odd jobs. Then she would have to leave, before his real live-in housekeeper got jealous.

The doctor wondered where in the future he could place this child. No matter his help, she would probably just run off like her mother and any number of other misfits to wind up in New Orleans. He thought the woman was there still. The old man died with that secret.

"Big thanks, Lejeune," the doctor said up to heaven. Now the responsibility was his of telling the girl her mother still lived. The old man became simply selfish or maybe he got afraid as he got older; the doctor understood that. "New Orleans she already got my one baby girl," the old man cried to the doctor in a time of weakness. He knew Lejeune just wanted to protect this next child. But the old man succeeded too well in his goal.

Here were the consequences. The child was ignorant and too stoic for a modern world. The doctor could see that just on his few visits. He could offer her few alternatives, even if she did have the sense to choose. Maybe he should send her off to a convent.

"Do they take illegitimate nuns?" he wondered. "Still, at that age, she will need the mother's approval." Her grandfather made the doctor swear not to tell the child that her mother remained alive. She left only to return to the city. "Better the girl think she got nobody than think they don't care, no?" the old man asked. The doctor agreed. But the old man ignored his part of the promise, to send her to school.

She spent only about four years learning to read and write with three other children in an unpainted frame house near the supply store.

The doctor once stood in the store as the woman who ran it tried to encourage Joan's grandfather to prepare her for the outside world. The woman wanted him to buy Joan a dress to wear to church festivals in town and for parties. She said, "Here, put your gal pretty in this here." The store owner pushed something lacy and bright yellow in front of the old man's face.

"What she go to use that for?" the old man replied in French.

"She traveling into the world at some time," the old lady, fat with the prosperity of trading flour and grease to country people for skins and fur, answered him in his own language.

"God got the time when to take care of that," he answered in English to make her understand how far he was from sharing her opinion. Then he pushed Joan by one shoulder toward the door.

But the doctor could see that Joan became first excited, then very disappointed. Before she left, the doctor handed her a bag of sugar ball candies in reparation.

"How you need that?" her grandfather told her to give them back. Joan wouldn't. Her grandfather said, "You'll see." He later told the doctor Joan ate the whole bag that night and got sick. Her grandfather said he just protected her from things "that got no place."

The doctor realized then he could do nothing as long as the old man lived. Now that she came to his doorstep, he wondered if he wasn't too late. His city colleague would say this kind of person did not need to be born. The pregnancy could have been corrected by science. She could have stayed innocent like an angel. The doctor thought of many others that his colleague would have no use for: Mrs. Labat who could not afford her pressure pills; Regaline who knew the weather on every date from the 1980s back through 1960, but who could not learn to spell; Thomas with the gimp leg that told the rain. Then the doctor thought, without them, he would have little variety in his work. Plus, he would not have them as friends. "Who can be so pragmatic?" the doctor thought. He would ask his city colleague who he would kill and who he would save. The doctor knew the answer already. His city colleague would discount most of his poor black patients immediately. But then, when the old white ladies died off, who would the city colleague have to treat, the doctor would point out. His colleague could not stand the idea of losing money.

The healing sciences were entrusted with the soul as well as the body, the doctor considered. He needed to give this girl Joan something to do. Room and board would be enough to start if she worked around the house. Maybe God sent her to him because he took care of the people who could not afford to pay. God did not want the doctor to be broke after all.

Joan awoke in the morning now to the smell of food and the feel of sunlight on her skin. She lay in bed and stretched her hand out and on the floor appeared a shadow. It moved just as she moved her hand, like an echo, except quicker and nearby. Joan was surprised to see shadow in daytime. She thought it only came on at night with the lamps.

Joan used the pitcher and jug on her dresser to wash up, although on her first day in the house Claudia, the housekeeper, bragged, "That's just for decoration. We got water running."

Claudia had walked Joan into the bathroom and showed her how turning the faucet chased the water down into the drain. Joan tried it again when she was alone. She turned it off and on seven times for good luck. No one could hear into the bathroom because the door shut tight like inside an icebox. It was cool and delicious in there. The tiles were so shiny and clean, Joan felt like licking them.

She told that to Claudia. But Claudia put her two hands to her face to hold the smile down in her mouth.

Joan saw the doctor did the same thing every time she called him to the "bird knock," the sound that whistled before someone came to the door. When she entered the "cold room" to dump the wastebasket, a person sat on a table wrapped in a sheet. He looked surprised. But Joan ignored him. When the doctor found out she had entered, he got very angry. "Don't you know how to announce yourself," his voice strained.

The next time, Joan opened the door, closed it behind her, and stood presenting the wastebasket at chest level. "I am Joan," she said. The doctor began laughing and the person on the table made a little scream and pulled the sheet up to her shoulders.

Joan felt like laughing too when she made them surprised and happy. But she did not want to be their joke. It made her feel like a small child again, ashamed in front of the adults.

She and her grandfather did the same things, Joan remembered as she dressed in the big bedroom alone. When he got up in the morning, he pushed to the wall the fabric curtain that separated their sleeping areas. Then they sat outside together for coffee. Some days they whittled pieces of bark on the porch or told stories. When his eyes hurt, she read to him. She did not feel that he looked after her any more than she looked after him. When he got older, in fact, he was the child as she told him what he could and could not do. Other times Joan spent walking in the woods or fishing with the dog in the pirogue.

Now she did not have the dog either. He was banished to the yard. Claudia would not let him in. "To have dog hair in this house?" she asked the doctor, and answered him too, "No." Joan suspected that Claudia did not even want Joan living inside.

Joan had stayed in the house for a week now, and for the first few days she had often heard, "It's her or me," coming from the front room. Then the doctor called Joan into the room to show her how to use something better or to tell her why to bring some item outside. The nutria rat that Joan caught near the thick part of the backyard and left in the kitchen was thrown into the garbage, even before Joan got to skin it. "Is good eating," she tried to tell Claudia. She did not even cover her mouth that time. Claudia screamed, "Ah!" and left the room. "Ah!" Joan knew now meant to leave Claudia alone. Claudia said, "Ah!" less lately. But when Joan entered a room, Claudia pulled her face tight to the middle like she expected "Ah!" to jump out and she was trying to hold it back.

Joan thought of her home in the swamp, her boat, the straight-backed chair where she read the Bible, and her very, very soft bed. She and her grandfather stuffed it with moss and bird feathers. Then he presented it to her as a gift for her thirteenth birthday. It was a grown person's size. She thought they were making it for him. She missed her grandfather.

They sang together in the evenings sometimes. He played the harmonica. She had a guitar. As a child he taught her a song: "Fait dodo Minette. Trois petites cochons du lait. Fait dodo ma petite bébé. Jusque l'age du quinze ans." She comforted herself now by going to sleep with that lullaby in her head.

Joan sang the song to the other children in the small school when she went. She had to leave when the teacher told her grandfather she had nothing more to teach Joan. She remembered their fight. The teacher wanted to send Joan to school in the city. She could come home on weekends like other young people did. Her grandfather said no.

"She got to go some time. She could live with the nuns in the week," the teacher argued.

Her grandfather said, "For what more she got to learn? Can't she read? The nuns to take care of her better than family?"

Joan concluded, as she overheard this conversation, that her grandfather outsmarted the teacher with too many questions. That too was the explanation he gave Joan. "She got no good answers for me," he said.

Finally, the teacher left them alone.

For a while, Joan wondered about the new school. Where would it be? What would it look like? One time, she day-dreamed a picture of the classroom into her head. Joan saw a square, white, frame house with extra rooms joined to the sides like wings. A dirt yard was adjacent, with a short flagpole. Joan saw small children in blue skirts or pants and white shirts lined up in front of the building. Then they marched inside. The hall-way was dark as they left the daylight. Joan appeared to be with them because she was temporarily blinded. The next picture she saw was inside a spacious room with many desks and oversized windows. All of the desks were filled except one.

After a while she stopped seeing the picture. And she also came to feel her grandfather right in his decision. Who could take care of her better than family? He devoted his life to raising her. Then she devoted herself to him.

Joan looked at herself in the mirror as she combed her hair. She was taller than she had imagined. She was solid and full. At sixteen, she could do just about anything a grown woman could. She compared herself to Claudia. Joan could keep house just as clean, maybe cleaner when she got on her hands and knees.

Joan could cook fresh and now frozen stiff that they took hard from the top part of the refrigerator. Joan could garden and plant. Her grandfather showed her good roots for tea that Joan found in the backyard.

But the more Joan helped out, the more Claudia seemed to get sad. Joan watched Claudia at the table with her head in her hands. Claudia would smoke a cigarette and shake her head sometimes and mumble. Joan could not tell what she said. Once, she heard Claudia say to the phone, "I know he paying her nothing. Some kind of way to get rid of me, huh?"

Claudia answered the voice on the other end, "What to fight? I'm old now. She young."

Joan felt proud at first, "Yes, I'm young." Later, she did not know whether that was a fault or a compliment.

"I'm getting too old and useless, ain't I child," her grandfather would sometimes ask Joan. At those times, she felt useless for being young. She had no answer. If she was happy about herself and her age, it would be painful to him. "I wish I was old too," she would say in response. She came to believe it. She wished she was old now so she would not have to be in the care of others and also because her grandfather in his age had some place to go. She did not.

Joan decided to lay back on the bed. She lingered long enough to follow the sun's rays with her hand as they moved across the floor.

The doctor came to the door first, "You sick, Joan?" He called her Joan with an accent that sounded soft and concerned. She was dressed so she went to the door. "No, sir. Non, m'sieur."

"But why then you still in the bed?" He continued to speak in the familiar tone in patois. She had many answers. But they congealed in her throat full of emotion. "Pas raison," she told the doctor. "Today, I work in the yard."

But there were no jobs outside. So for most of the day, Joan sat far back in the lot. The dog came up to her. He nuzzled against her calf. He smelled different since they left the swamp. This too was because of Claudia, although he did not want to adjust to his cleanliness. After his bath he ran into a nearby field and rubbed back into the mud. He ran one shoulder to the ground first then the other. Then he rolled on his back and kicked his feet up into the air.

That day, Claudia rolled her eyes over to Joan. Claudia liked to show that she knew better than Joan, and was more of a grown woman. But it was not Joan's fault what the dog did. So she shrugged and looked away. But Joan resolved to begin smelling sweet like the soap, even if the aroma was strange to her.

Now, Claudia called Joan from the back door. Claudia was silhouetted in front of the kitchen light. The sun was going down. Claudia went inside for a while. She came again to the

door, this time accompanied by the doctor. "Joan. Joan," he hollered. But Joan continued to sit under the tree far back in the
yard. When she didn't answer, she could see their heads bowed
toward one another, talking.

Joan did not want to answer because she was confused. The
wrong time to appear seemed to be when they called. What explanation would she give for hiding in the yard? Suddenly, she
felt lonelier than ever with her grandfather, although more
people were with her.

"But they're not my family," she cried to herself. "I have no
family, anymore, anywhere." And with that thought, she stayed
outside in the back lot, more comforted by nature than even the
clean bathroom. When Claudia found her outside the next
morning, she called her "a little pig." Those words were the
same as her grandfather sang lovingly, "petite cochon," but said
now in anger.

"We looked for you all night, Joan. Why you don't came
here?" the doctor said. But Joan could think of nothing to say.
He looked as if he wanted to be angry, but his eyes did not cooperate. She felt they really wanted to know.

But Joan was not sure how to tell him her feelings. She
wanted to go back into the swamp. In his house, she felt lonely
and strange. She felt more like a child with them taking care of
her and she didn't like it.

"I'm sorry to do wrong, sir," she said.

Joan looked around at the room that the doctor called
"study." It was darker than the rest of the house, and so more
comfortable for her. Joan thought the doctor liked it better in
here too. Often she heard him reading aloud or making comments to himself alone in the evenings. Books filled many
shelves and wood covered the walls. They were the same dark
silvery color the swamp trees took at a particular time before
sundown.

Joan felt the doctor watching her. He touched her shoulder so
she had to return his look.

"What to do with you, Joan, if you don't like it here?"

"I miss to have family," were her only words.

The doctor left Joan alone in the room and sitting in a big, green leather armchair after he told her, "Your mother could be alive." Joan felt at first he was playing some terrible meanness on her, perhaps for making him worry all night, like sometimes her grandfather pulled the dog by one leg to get him out of the house when Joan's cajoling wouldn't work. Seeing the dog hopping on three legs and giving pleading howls and hearing Joan say, "Leave him; leave him alone," seemed to satisfy some feeling in her grandfather.

Joan took that sense as one they did not share. She was never tempted to be that kind of mean. Sometimes she neglected her plants in the pots until they shriveled up. But she never desired to hurt something breathing. When she hunted she made sure her animals were quickly dead. She even gutted and cleaned the fish as soon as she caught them.

Now she had to consider, it could be true that her mother still lived. Joan sat in the chair and wondered, had a miracle happened? Having a mother was God's answer to Joan? "Holy Mary," Joan got on her knees, "I'll live with my mother. She could take care of me and be with me. And everything will be all right."

Joan bowed her head to consider and pray. For her the room became dark. Her eyes pulsed behind the red lids even though she tried to still them like something alive she did not want to acknowledge. Her voice said, "If your mother is living, she will just die again." But Joan could not picture her mother's death. Instead she saw herself feeling surrounded by thunderstorms. She could not make out the room. But she heard the rain heavy and hissing outside like a nest of snakes. And she heard the slamming of voices against a wall. They were like wails and negations. "No." "Stop." "Oh no." Joan's own voice was saying, "I don't want to go there." Then she felt a warm wind like a Sunday breeze when she was peaceful and sitting alone on the porch. It felt soft across her forehead like a passing hand or secure like a sucking thumb.

Joan pressed her fingers to her eyelids. It caused her picture to dim. Only her breathing resounded loud in the silence of the empty room. Her thoughts continued with a logic that Joan did not want to own.

If she was the kind of mother Joan wanted in childhood, Joan would not have to seek her. "She would be here," Joan thought. She wouldn't have had to bury her grandfather alone. She wouldn't be wondering about her future. She would have a place to be and someone with whom she belonged. Was it better to have no mother or a mother she never saw? God was invisible. But He had a reason and the power to make such a choice.

"What is Your will," Joan prayed to bring her feelings to some resolution. If she saw her mother, Joan thought, she would say, "I am a woman now too. Is there anything you can tell me?" Joan imagined herself speaking boldly and cruelly to this parent, although she really needed an answer.

"When I meet her, this is what I will tell her." Joan picked at the nails that held the green leather to the wood of the chair. The bones of Joan's fingers made a little vibration in the bones of the furniture, even though in between the wood and the leather were soft fabrics and cushions layered for reasons to stop such reverberations from happening.

"I do want to find her," Joan told the doctor when she left the study. But she pretended to be more sure than she was. "We will live together soon. I can't wait." Inside, Joan wondered still as she did in the swamp. Would she be able again to erase this mother, as necessary, out of her thoughts?

The doctor had not been in New Orleans since the last visit to his colleague. Now, he, Claudia, and Joan drove in the car. On the backseat was an ice cooler, blankets, and food that Claudia packed. Joan's cowboy hat sat in the back window.

It was not a grim task. The doctor saw the girl's desire for her parent growing, although he did expect more happiness in her initial reaction.

He tempered his offer that they seek out Joan's mother. "Maybe she's in New Orleans. But I don't know. We don't know who she is now, or where she is, or if she ready to take care of a child, I got to say it," the doctor stared at the girl when he saw her confused reaction. He thought he knew about the maternal bond. It was always existent. It stretched over time and even beyond death and living. People still prayed to their dead mothers in heaven, placed flowers on their graves every week, and carried their photographs, the doctor knew, in the town where he was born.

The mothers too kept the birth of each child as special, no matter how many. In the doctor's family were nine. How women changed these times of pain into pleasure, the doctor still wondered, although he did not dispute it. He assisted at plenty births, some of them terrible. Sometimes the women struggled for hours. And after it was over, a month or two later, they couldn't even remember how much they hurt or they translated the pain as unimportant. "Look at my beautiful boy," one woman whom he saw suffer the worst said, "and tell me how can I remember anything but God's gifts."

He hesitated then to tell her the child appeared slow, even at that young age. He waited until the third examination and took several tests before he suggested the child might be retarded. And then, how did she respond? First she appeared sad and then she said, "How my life will be full always teaching him." The doctor became speechless.

That day, he cursed God for giving a child so unworthy to this woman who was so beautiful and strong. She would not, in her old age, be taken care of by her son. In fact, for most of her days she would serve him. What justice was there to that? The doctor could not sleep at night, thinking about the plagues of the world and how God allowed it.

Later he realized one reason such experiences so frightened and confused him. He worried sometimes that he was spared. Why wasn't life that bad for him? Didn't he come from a poor family? Why did he achieve? Why were his brothers and sisters so healthy and smart and self-sufficient? And then, was self-sufficiency the most a person could ask out of life anyway? After the basics, what was there? For him, the goal had been recognition. But then he found out in medical school that the monied city boys would do the most research because they had connections to those scholarships.

The doctor had gotten far enough by just attending. At least, that's how he rationalized. He had passed into the white medical school without anyone finding out he was colored, as people called blacks in those days.

The doctor's own family came from a place not far from

where he now lived. Typical of the region, he could not locate his ancestors too far back. But he knew enough to acknowledge there were Africans, Indians, and French among them.

His admission forms were altered for entrance by another black in the same situation. This school official passed too. His pleasure was to sneak into this public medical school any of their number. It was his small stab to disturb the lies that held white purity as the only intellectual standard in the region. He didn't bother that some of these students continued on in life as white. That was their failure of conscience or politics. Others returned to their nearby black communities with the needed skills and education that passing afforded them.

The doctor was part of the latter group. He went back to a very poor town where race was an issue far behind eating and living. The people in Sagetville did not discriminate for one major reason. If someone did try to consider himself better because of a particular color or shade, he would be reminded by others of his dark grandmother who was a saint and his white grandfather who was an alcoholic, or vice versa.

Plus, only in cities was race important because it determined economics into the next generation. Unlike rural areas, where almost everyone had an individual or family enterprise—trapping, farming, or fishing—and were all on the edge of subsistence, in the cities, blacks, and everyone else, worked for institutions. The doctor heard the institutions were even larger and harder to enter up in the North. It was the place to go during his time for more freedom, people said. But the doctor heard stories of poor people freezing to death. So neither the weather nor attitudes of other states beckoned him.

Because his appearance gave few clues to his race, his patois usually first caught attention. And as an additional discrimination, many people thought he was rural and uneducated when they heard him. So because of his race, his country roots, and his arrogance to be visibly proud on all counts, the doctor kept himself apart from most people. Too many only wanted to start trouble with him. He felt his solitude kept others' bitterness out of his heart, and it allowed him to find the most efficient ways to progress. Now, he could be as he was without apology. From the whites, he desired nothing.

He, Joan, and Claudia stayed in an apartment that one of his colleagues offered for their visit to New Orleans. "You can have it, my extra place. Besides I'm flying to the islands this fall," he bragged. The doctor hadn't expected to get a place to stay so easily. He had planned to call many physicians. He did not mind imposing on some of these people. In fact, he got a certain pleasure in showing up from time to time.

That was because some of those men who came from his same background became pretentious. They spoke to him plainly enough when they were alone, sometimes even in dialect. But if another entered the room, their accents changed so that their ancestors could not be located.

"La-bas?" he loudly asked one acquaintance who changed his own character after another person entered the room. The doctor reached for the door handle to leave. The questions, "there?" and "the bottom?" referred simultaneously to the means of the doctor's exit, to the reason for his departure because of his associate's changed attitude, and to the place they all grew up. The innuendo was so well understood, it was ignored completely by the doctor's colleague. He still hid when it was no longer a necessity, the doctor resented.

Now, the doctor saw how New Orleans had changed. When he, Claudia, and Joan arrived at the concierge, they did not get a second glance although they were all black. They demonstrated their race in its variety with skin the color of pecans, porcelain, and gold. One had hazel eyes, another black, the third brown. And their hair was singularly straight, kinky, and subject to fall somewhere in between depending on the day's humidity. The doctor saw as much variation in many Louisiana families.

Joan tried to study the face of every person as the car arrived on the streets of New Orleans. But too many people blurred past the windows, just like the trees flew sideways on the road.

Joan wanted to control her anxious feeling at moving so quickly. Claudia and the doctor had helped Joan practice for the car ride while they ran errands, like people in the city let their dogs jump into the backseat.

At first Joan felt similar to a bewildered animal. She was completely alert and moved her head often toward sounds on the side and behind her. It was a wonder, she heard Claudia and the doctor say to one another, that Joan didn't stay dizzy from this continual turning. Joan overheard and took these words and other of their directions. So she tried to "relax," "calm down," and "talk slow" at the right times while at others she learned to "sit up straight," "pay attention," and "come right here" as they told her.

New Orleans was more than she imagined. It had so many different faces. She could not remember one past seeing the last.

How did people recognize each other among so many? It was different for animals. They acted on smell. Joan recognized them too. The raccoons near her home in the swamp who came from the same mother had a particular grey strip of hair on the same side. The supply store woman's pony had a diamond on its muzzle, like the mare.

Now for the first time Joan wondered, when people saw her, what did they think? She now considered if she resembled her mother. But what was that like? Did she inherit her height, her eyes, or her temper? Animals possessed emotional compositions too. Some dispersed a mean spirit throughout the litter. Others kept a skittish streak from generation to generation.

Joan tried to picture her mother. But she could only imagine a girl about the same age as herself. In this frame, the girl sat on the porch of Joan's house. Her chin rested in the palm of her right hand and she looked down into the water. Joan could not see her face and had taken that position many times herself. Perhaps she was just remembering the solitude and even the loneliness she felt sometimes in the swamp when her grandfather left in the boat to go hunting or fishing. She and the dog waited then feeling empty and fearful. There was always the chance that he would not return.

Her grandfather was gone now forever. She missed him badly. He taught her to balance the pirogue through the most thin and twisted swamp alleys. Her grandfather taught Joan direction and advised her that the largest and best body of water in the United States lay at the foot of the Mississippi River.

Joan saw it as a huge clearing emerging from an overhang of

trees. In her mind, she paddled her boat down the wide river and entered the Gulf. She thought the water was as deep as cypress were tall. Fish hurtled themselves over the bow of her boat. The air smelled of rain, salt, and deer. Although the Gulf was huge, it had a shoreline in her picture to the right and left. She could not understand the Gulf's crystal blue water or its deceptive depth caused by the sunlight. For one reason, her grandfather had told Joan only some information, and some of it was wrong.

Joan's special intuitive sense operated in this odd manner. Her pictures were more accurate if she based them on truth or if she knew nothing at all. When someone gave Joan the wrong facts, she trusted them strongly and her imagination was obliterated by her faith.

At the same time she missed her grandfather, she felt disgust that he kept her mother a secret for so long. She felt angry in a way she could not completely understand. She never felt this emotion so intensely before. She would get mad at the dog for turning the garbage or even, when she reached her teens, at her grandfather for some comment. But the anger did not gnaw her stomach as this feeling did and come up into her throat in the night so that she dreamed about faceless problems and innumerable little meanings of words like orphan, daughter, family, children.

They would enter her dreams first like distant returning echoes on water that would then stretch out visibly like a phrase on a blackboard. They became nightmarish as they grew louder and bigger like something a person in school tried to repeat to you until you understood them. But she couldn't. Joan only remembered her school days lasting a few years before her grandfather decided that was enough. So she found no connection beyond her grandfather's assertion that her mother was dead and now the information reversed.

But coming to New Orleans, Joan discovered more of her reasoning and her intelligence. She was able to read the maps and street signs. There were not many words she did not know since she had learned to read the Bible, but now the words had new meanings. The differences between the secular and religious confused Joan at first. "Don't walk" did not mean "do not follow a path for fear of reprisal." It simply meant to wait before crossing the street. It made Joan think this city life was very easy and far from the spiritual, truer meanings of living.

The doctor was handed a photocopy of Joan's birth certificate in New Orleans City Hall almost immediately after his request. The speed was unlike his experience in the small, country towns. There, he waited while clerks printed the information by hand or promised to mail it to him in a week.

In New Orleans, the effort was almost too quick and casual considering the importance of the facts these papers contained. This big, faded green office with a few scattered old wooden tables and its nervous fluorescent light held the recordings of crucial events for countless living beings.

The doctor tried to imagine all the humanity embodied in this office. He delivered many babies and never ceased to be amazed about the progression from conception to personality. He knew life was really a gift. Man could never invent it. There was a Creator as far as the doctor understood. No matter how much flesh the doctor stitched together or heartbeats he revived, he could never lay claim to making one human.

And death was a similar mystery. He saw the breath leave a number of people and never did he have any feeling but sadness, an empathy deep like a response from his own soul. Early in his career when he answered calls at Angola prison, he talked to men on death row. Some claimed to have been happy to kill their victims. "He deserved it," each justified the behavior. But later the man would whisper, "But I'm sorry it had to be me." Even the most evil prisoner that the doctor met, a man called Snake by the others, confessed regret.

"I felt like a child watching the air come out of a balloon. I wanted him to come back, to bust up alive and fight like a man. But he died right in front of me and I felt the worst. I didn't want that feeling from my hands. He deserved to be hit harder from what he said to me. But I hurt right behind it, feeling bad since after he's dead."

The doctor restrained himself from telling this man that when killing life, he took the biggest creative gift of God and through mortal pride destroyed His prerogative. That has got to be a bad feeling, the doctor could have said or he could have reminded the prisoner that the devil was acting through him. Instead, the doctor suggested to Snake that he talk to someone in the clergy, maybe to confess. But Snake puffed up his wide chest to return to the attitude he had when the doctor entered the room. "What you think I just did? I ain't telling nobody. Who you think you are anyway?" he said. The guard who stood nearby jerked the chains around Snake's ankles when his voice raised. The guard said, "Don't believe not a thing that one says, Doc. He ain't got no respect for nobody."

Where did all the people go when they died, the doctor wondered. Where did they live on earth? All those people in the City Hall files, where were they born? The doctor thought of all the strange places he assisted mothers panting and sweating—taxicabs, hospital beds, bedrooms, and bars.

According to Joan's birth certificate, attending her birth was one Irene Campland. The event took place in a house low in the ninth ward almost to Plaquemines Parish and out of the city. The doctor decided to drive to the address on the birth certificate to see if Campland still lived there and ask her about the mother named on the form: a Miss Oceola Leontine.

As the doctor walked to get his car near the French Quarter apartment, he decided to stop in a bar. He saw as he strolled that Bourbon Street had changed little since he was there last. Now the advertisements showed more skin and expressed more sexual diversity. But the same intent remained.

Inside the bar was the same as well; permanent darkness existed. A smell that probably had never left since the Second World War of liquor, stale cigarettes, and urine clung to the room. The doctor could not see the label on the bottle that filled his shot of scotch. But, the doctor remembered, that was the point.

He did not see either the face of the woman who appeared quickly and soundlessly next to him. She asked for a drink too. B-drinkers, they called these women in his time. And just like then, the bartender filled her glass with colored water while charging the doctor for alcohol.

He knew it was illegal. But here was another generation prac-
ticing the same tricks. People always seemed ready to fill the
glasses as well as the criminal ranks.

This woman's voice showed her to be very young. So did her
opinions. She liked "heavy" music. She did not believe in elections. She was "friends" with her parents, although they did not
know her telephone number. "I call them up and let them know
I'm OK. Long as they're OK, it's all right," she said.

The doctor asked if she ever considered working a job a little
bit "better." She looked at him directly and said softly, "Honey,
what did you have in mind?" Then she laughed, "Oh, you're
serious. This is a good job. What else to do? I stay out of trouble
and I get home before night." Then she asked the doctor for specific pills—Valium, Prednisone or diazepam. She thought he
could "at least do one favor."

"I don't think it would mix with the alcohol," the doctor
responded.

"Aw, this isn't . . . ," she started to call out to him as he rose
and walked toward the door. But the bartender banged the heel
of his hand on the counter near where she sat. "Oh, come back,"
she now laughed, cheerful and desperate. "Let's have more
fun," she pleaded louder as the doctor exited.

The sun was blinding. It was just afternoon. Stepping inside
that bar was like a nightmare. What pleasure had he discovered in
it when he was young? Partly, he was included in the carousing.

How quiet his life now was compared to this side of New Orleans. And Joan's home in the swamp was archaic. Visiting her
house with the grandfather was like returning into some primitive century, some prehistoric time. The darkness and the rigid-
ity of the home fixed in place, pressed in by constant isolation.
When trees fell in that part of the swamp, no one but Joan and
her grandfather heard the sound. But the doctor considered,
somewhere a ripple of water hit the river and Gulf shores just a
little harder.

Almost all day while the doctor was gone from the apartment,
Joan stood on the balcony wondering about the varieties of
women who passed on the sidewalks below. Where did she fit

among them? Some wore their hair loose and curly. From her vantage, their bare shoulders jutted square out of blouses where sleeves should go.

Joan's hair swelled up from the humidity. But instead of plaiting it Indian style on each side of her head and joining the plaits at the back as was her habit, she pulled it straight back into a rubber band as she would have early in the morning before she had time to comb.

"I see a change in our girl already," the doctor commented.

"She better not go too fast, no," said the housekeeper.

"I'm all right." Joan glanced again toward the street. The other women she saw wore dresses a lot. The ones who wore jeans, like she did, had on beautiful lacy shirts, bare sandals, or high heels. Joan was glad the apartment was just one story up, so she could study the women as they approached. She did not miss the men either. So many kinds! There were lots who appeared close to her age.

One of them, as he passed, even looked back up at her. "Hello, beautiful," he whistled.

She whistled back. Like the mockingbird she heard often in the forest, she copied the sound sliding up the scale and then quicker back down. He laughed, waved, and kept going. Then she whistled "Bob-white, bob-white," just like the little birds she knew. This time, when he waved he was no longer looking at her. She went "Caw-caw-caw" like the crows, "caw-caw-caw." But he was a half-block off and other people stood below her balcony looking up at her.

"Throw me something, sister," one of them rattled his hands high above his head as if seeking a present like the ones thrown to street people at carnival time. Joan ran inside and returned near the balcony only to latch the glass doors.

"Is too hot for you, huh?" Claudia thought Joan was escaping the sun into the air conditioning. "Is a lot different for a girl such as yourself," Claudia continued. "I know you got no mother yet so to speak of . . ."

John interruption, "But I will."

". . . but seem if you need anybody, sometime, I could be just as as good as them. You listening?" Claudia tapped Joan on the knee.

"But I'll find my mother and I'll go to live in her house," Joan insisted.

"Till then, don't throw out what I say, no," Claudia rose and touched Joan's right shoulder.

If the doctor could not find her mother, Joan had a plan. "God provide. He provide for the birds of the air, don't he," she said quietly. She did not want to depend and impose on others who were not family. Her grandfather taught her to be too proud. She could take care of herself alone if necessary. She was only confused now because of too much activity.

New Orleans was so different from the swamp where precious silence allowed her to concentrate. It was peaceful there and Joan had many tasks—quilting, reading her Bible, cooking, washing, cleaning. In the city, there was nothing for her to do. She just worried most of the day. When would they find her mother? How would she act? Would she really accept Joan? "What if she don't like the way I look," the young girl watched herself in the mirror.

She was nothing like the girls on the sidewalk, Joan thought. She was thin and repulsive. She was plain. All of her clothes covered all of her. "What if I'm too stupid for her? I got no city in me," Joan thought as she framed the ponytail around her face. "Is all a mistake," she regretted her existence.

Night was beginning to fall in the French Quarter. Lights made small faded universes at each corner.

Joan looked through the window to the dim darkness outside. She knew the sky could get so much blacker, clear and positive. There was a particular spot on the porch in the swamp that jutted far over the water where the cypress trees and their moss did not block her view. She could see straight up. That was her space, a triangle of nothing bounded by stars into the shape a child draws a house. "Look, Papa, voici cote' moin habite. Ici moin re'te," she told him, here is where she lived.

Suddenly, she wanted to see it, the deep black darkness, the vast space between the cypresses, the clear lane to heaven. She went to the balcony. But looking up, she could not see far. She viewed only the tin floor of the second story balcony and the wooden trestles that held it up. To see past, she leaned back over the railing. She wasn't thinking of the ground below or how for a moment she was suspended in air except for two points where the small of her back touched the balustrade and her toes balanced her weight off the ground.

"Joan, you crazy. You trying to break your neck, kill yourself?" Claudia rushed over and pulled Joan by the hand into the house.

Joan began weeping and could not stop. And she could not recall just one reason. Many confusing thoughts came at the same time. She wondered why grandfather, her mother, her dog, her house on the bayou, and her heaven were all gone from her now. Even if she returned to the swamp, all would be sadly different.

In the Faubourg Marigny across Esplanade Street from the French Quarter, Oceola Leontine lived this year. She was currently a redhead. More often she was a brunette with coppery streaks of hair that she called "blonde." On the nights that she wasn't too hung over or depressed, she walked into the Quarter to make her living.

"She was a beautiful baby," she thought about her daughter when she entertained new friends in the local bars with the infant picture. It showed a dark-haired newborn whose putty face had changed greatly in the intervening sixteen years, but Oceola did not know it. Oceola told people the child was born two years previously. "With her father," Oceola told those who asked whereabouts. Most of the time, no one was that curious.

The photo served as a screen for Oceola, an appropriate drama she acted out with new men. If they showed sympathy, she felt safe enough to take them where they paid the hotel.

With this type, she was more comfortable. Then she could drink and complain about her situation, a reality she did little to change. Instead, she hoped it would change itself if she were particular. Many girls just took the highest price. They were strictly business. Oceola felt herself open for the possibility of love.

Also, her logic was, if she took the man who bragged about having the most money, he intended to keep it. It was too much work to get that kind to loosen up.

Oceola's type showed her a picture of his children too. So they began with soft things in common. Their similarity, however, was not that they were parents. They discussed that "just now," "right at this time," they were in a bad state that companionship could probably fix. On the inside, they felt they would forever hurt.

Oceola did not intend to spend her life like this. But after New Orleans she could not go back to that swamp. She spent too many years with that old man, a tyrant, she explained to her old and new friends. He planned to marry her to one of his fools, one of those trappers or hunters who smelled bad all the time, and didn't have an easy hand with a woman.

And didn't she know now that those country bumpkins went straight to the houses like everyone else when they came to New Orleans? It made no difference that they were religious. In fact, it gave them something good to confess, Oceola joked to the other girls who drank together frequently to celebrate their own madness.

Nobody, including herself, wanted to be like she was, Oceola would say, "But who got a choice?"

Women, unlike the working men who patronized them, could not get jobs in construction, make cash trading stock in the business district, do cement finishing, or trap animals for a living. Women who tried union jobs on the dock were hounded until they left. And the factories hired only a few people of either sex at a time.

Let the women's righters say what they wanted, these women agreed, first of all, good work "ain't."

Of course, occupations existed other than prostitution. They could clean houses or mop floors in the downtown buildings. But Oceola and her friends had contorted their pride so that they felt keenly the diminished respect laborers got from the public. Like Oceola, the other women would not defend a righteousness in their job. But they felt, considering the attention received by them or the houseworkers, they got more of it. Women who broke their backs dumping trash cans and washing lavatories never got a wink when they walked through the corridors of the French Quarter hotels.

Besides, Oceola bragged to all, she learned quickly the tricks of dressing and walking. So easy. She was willing to instruct anyone: "Men are so primitive, so dumb, so basic." All men considered in their dealings with women were crotch and commerce, she believed. She, on the other hand, thought deeply. She often considered hell as her present and afterlife.

The doctor woke up kind of foggy, thinking all sorts of unrelated ideas. The young woman who approached him in the bar appeared in his dream like a galloping pony with a white diamond-shaped space on its forehead. Then he seemed to be in the swamp. He was so hot and sweaty. Then he was transported to forty years ago, into an old-fashioned bathtub with a woman. Then he was outside of it while she remained in. She was beautiful, soaping her body under the bubbles that stayed on the water's surface. Then she lowered her head to soap her face. When she lifted it, the bubbles remained, covering her features. The doctor waited for her to rinse. But she didn't. In a sort of innocent way, she waited for him to. That's when he woke up. He was waiting for her. She was waiting for him.

The doctor thought maybe the dream was the effect of cheap scotch. He knew half a day would pass before that poison would burn through his system. He decided to call Irene Campland first.

"I never seen her in many years. But I remember all about her still, yes," the old lady answered on the telephone. "Nice as I was too. Not a hello, dog," she continued.

The doctor, in one of the old lady's rare pauses, took liberty to invite himself over.

"It's my house," she said in the affirmative, a visit was fine with her.

When he arrived, he had to shout from the front gate for her to hold back the dogs in the yard. There were signs all around, misspelled and handwritten, and tied by wire coat hangers to the gate. "Keep Aout!" "Badog," had an S dangling below in another color like a fallen off puppy. "None your business," she pointed out for him. "I put that for those people all the time asking me 'who live here?' I say, 'What is it your business?' Want to know my name. Want to be calling me up on the phone. Want to buy property. Buy property. I say, 'How much?' They say, 'Can't tell.' I say, 'Get on 'way from here if I don't shoot you. Quick!'

"Now I think they just wait for me to die. That's all right. I'm not afraid of no spirits. I got enough of them. Bad and good," she talked continuously.

The doctor did not wonder why Irene Campland let him visit her after her next question. "How much you give me to tell?" she broke his guard with stares from two bloodshot eyes.

"About what?" he stalled.

"I don't mind dying and taking you with me," she answered. "First, the girl owe me money anyhow."

The doctor peeled off twenty dollars. She leaned into his wallet when his head was down.

"Fifty." She pushed the top of her body forward like a broken board. The heels of her hands were on her knees, which were spread wide apart over her misshapen and slippered feet.

The doctor thought of the dogs loose in the yard again and the long trip he'd taken. "Here," he frowned at the old lady in the chair opposite where he stood.

She motioned to a straight-backed wooden chair like a school-teacher's, "No need for you to make yourself comfortable. You not staying that long."

The old lady began about Oceola. "She was so stupid when she come to me. Big like this." The old woman put her hands out to indicate pregnancy.

The doctor thought that motion ironic on such a skinny old woman.

"I say, 'Girl, why you wait so long?' She still act like she not made up her mind," the old lady was frowning as she told the story. She took the butt of a small cigar out of her ashtray and lit it. "Her friend tell me, 'She religious.'

"'Well, she liable go to hell anyway,' I tell them, 'for what she done done.' Then this girl, she start to crying. Her friend, the man she was with, then he couldn't take it. 'Shut up,' he say. 'Didn't I tell you to shut up?'

"I ain't ascared of hell," the old lady blew out a puff of smoke. "I seen worse misery on earth. And that's what I tell her right then. And the boyfriend, that's what I think he was anyhow, he laugh, 'See, we got somebody here not even afraid of the devil. So what you crying for?' And the girl quieted up. I think she was mostly afraid of him. 'And I'm afraid of being poor,' I try to make her a joke. But she wasn't going that far. So I just ask for my money, 'In advance,' I tell all of them."

Most rural midwives had more compassion, the doctor thought. Money was not even the issue with the ones he knew. They were happy to bring healthy babies into the world. He remembered the woman who helped his mother on many occasions. Mrs. Amy, he thought, was her name. The way people said it, it sounded like Mrs. Aimez, Mrs. Love in French. He actually wasn't sure that was not the spelling. But she was "American." In their town, that meant Protestant.

Mrs. Amy inspired him early to medicine. "There is nothing better on earth than to bring new life into this world. Yes, people may say, 'It's too harsh. We can't afford it. That baby might be ugly.'" They both laughed. "But Ugly might invent a drug for sickness or build a town hall. Besides he looks like his daddy, I say." The doctor never saw Mrs. Amy take a dollar. They just made sure she always had enough eggs and preserves. She often said to everyone in the room when she entered their home, "First, I thank you very kindly for everything."

This woman who sat across from the doctor was not like Mrs. Amy. Her tobacco-stained teeth jutted sparse like claws out of a fish mouth. Her face was cold, and so were her pointed eyes set in that pale, waxed-paper skin. It was as if she were the devil, and that's why she was not afraid. She could have been dead already and taken form just for his visit. The doctor scared himself with his own imagination. He was an intelligent man, he reminded his fear. But it was a very basic emotion.

Once when he was very young, he heard that a child died not far from his house. This boy had been murdered, the talk around the rural community held. A stranger strangled him, people said. And they were helpless to solve the crime because everyone nearby knew each other. It was surely someone passing through, they insisted, not one of them. The sadness and inability to help the boy's family set a gloom through all community activities. People got teary-eyed upon meeting each other at market when they saw his relatives. The doctor, a boy about that age too, was told often to take many precautions. For a long time, he could go nowhere alone. But at night he dreamed he was being chased by the devil. He often woke up screaming. His mother sat by his bedside and his older brothers and sisters took turns. But they all told him the same thing, "If it's the devil, pray to God. He is more powerful."

For a while when he was teenaged and rebellious, the doctor considered his faith merely superstition. But when he got older and realized, yes, he was vulnerable, yes, he would die, he was not eternal, the doctor found a spiritual power like God as a comforting thought. Whether his belief contained a large measure of fear or superstition no longer seemed very important.

Now, he found himself saying a prayer for courage to look into the old lady's eyes. He saw nothing but hardness, no demarcation of iris. Seemingly she kept the warmth of humanity out of them by sheer concentration. She was talking now excitedly.

"I put the cloth on her face and I say, 'Here, drink this whisky.' But she shake her head no. I say, 'Here, girl. Don't be fool enough to chance your own life.' Then before I know it she jump up, run out the bathroom. Is naked. Running out the front door. She made me so angry. I called her everything. Some people on the block let her into their house. But a few months later I'm still the one he call to birth it. I didn't give her no whisky then for real." The old lady sat back in her chair and stared out into her empty room, satisfied with the punishment.

The doctor wanted to punch her. Not often was he impelled to violence. But his revulsion came out. Evil should be handled on its same terms. That was the reality of life beyond its sweetness. Some people should have been stopped before they hurt others. He was looking at one of them.

He could not think of another question to ask. He had learned more than he wanted to know. Evil was not a new invention and being born ugly was better than anything this old lady had planned for children.

"Benitez-nous, Monsieur," was all he could mumble. They were the first words he said before accepting his plate three times a day, "Bless us, Lord."

"The daughter wants to see the mother," he finally said.

"I want to see her too. She still owe me." The woman looked

up at him. The doctor was standing. He opened the door himself and went out. Whatever the scent he carried as he left that house in such anger and shame, the dogs stayed away from him.

Another old lady was standing outside on a nearby porch when he left the house. She waved hello in a shy way. But when she saw the look on his face, she called him over more urgently. "Here," she said. "Give her whatever you got to pay for that property. Just get her away from around us."

"I don't want to buy her land," the doctor replied.

"It's been too long. Too long I heard those children crying. In the night, when I'm sleeping I hear babies, 'Mama, mama, mother.' Little ones' voices. They say she got the bones buried in her yard."

"Oh, no," the doctor started to back away.

"I'm a religious woman and I stay here, just because of that," the neighbor continued. "If I can stop any of them, any young girls before they go into that house, I have done the good work." She looked at him squarely in the face and the doctor saw truth.

"You wouldn't happen to remember, maybe sixteen years ago, a girl running out of there naked?" the doctor ventured.

"Yes, praise God. That was a strange sight. He come and get her from me a couple days later. But I told her not to go. She was just weak for him. Man named Aces. Until she got pregnant, they was Aces and O.C. down at the Peacock," she pointed in the direction of a local tavern.

Oceola Leontine was O.C. to the men who whistled, amened, and applauded each of her Friday performances at the Blue Peacock. That could have meant her talent was special. But this bar was only one of a countless number in New Orleans that had to be won over. And all these places were filled. At different times of the day, audiences entered whose tastes corresponded to their work shifts.

The earliest evening crowd came from 3:00 to about 7:00 P.M. after laboring construction, plaster, or painting. They needed jukebox. At 5:30 arrived the few mildly successful men of commerce who needed peace. Those with more ambition cocktailed in the business district. From then until 8:00 P.M. came wives fetching their husbands or children their fathers. Also, families came in all together to take out oyster loaf sandwiches for dinner and sit while the parents drank one beer. They entertained themselves. Until 11:00 P.M. or later, 2:00 or 3:00 in the morning, visited people who were very lonely or out of ideas. They sought out others to excite them by new thoughts, words, or deeds.

O.C. and Aces provided the latter nourishment. She sang sad, slow, sweet blues songs. On no platform, she was directly ahead of them and level with their chairs. Some nights, her performance began as if she had simply arrived through the front door or returned from the bathroom, and rather than take a seat she began singing. For her casualness, the audience appreciated her even more.

Oceola proved to them that anyone could have a song down deep and with the right kind of spirit one could just open one's mouth and it would escape. It would fly out beautiful and melodious, grand and important. The singular feeling possessed by all that she captured was the soul of them.

Aces was counterpoint to her beauty. He was a small man full of wiry energy. That impelled him to fly, although in another direction from Oceola, as he tap-danced on floors, chairs, tables and made rhythms against the wall. "There's no stopping him," O.C. introduced at the end of her performance and the beginning of his.

But he was already stopped by the public. In those years, tap dancing was seen as a kind of plantation throwback, a degrading form that appealed to degenerates. So Aces' fate, actually, was to go nowhere and there he brought Oceola.

O.C. also sang some of the country songs learned from her father. When he was younger, and more joyful, he taught her to play guitar. In the swamps where she lived as the only child, Oceola listened to her voice—clear, light and youthful. It cut through the denseness of moss and waterlogged trees to create soft responses. Still, she learned modulation, pitch, and performance from hearing her own echoes.

When people gathered, as they did in those years, at the homes of friends on holidays, Oceola would sing to the room. Those faces were grateful to see her healthy on those few times a year, much less to enjoy her experience. In their enthusiasm, they encouraged her, "Oceola, people should hear you in New Orleans."

"Is nothing but sin in those cities," her father, who would eventually raise Joan to stay home, then discouraged Oceola. But she continued to practice and others said, "Don't waste your talents." She did not tell them to leave was forbidden.

Finally, she snuck off with a boy to New Orleans for a day on the pretense of going to fish. Her father paced from the time they should have been home, in the afternoon, to early the next morning when they returned.

Oceola did not lie. Her life would be wasted if she lived in the swamp. She had a talent, she argued. Few people still lived like they did in the swamp, she said.

It was true. Most of the people who gathered for holidays had moved, if not to the cities, to rural communities where they would be closer to other people. The old man refused. His house still served him well. The swamp was there before some people and would remain after.

And, although he did not say, he feared trying to live any place except where he was. In the swamp, he could hunt, fish, and for cash collect and sell moss. His existence did not involve streetcars and banks, telephones, automobiles, and the rush and excitement to use or own them. In the swamp, he had all he needed; that was enough. The part of his reasoning that he told Oceola was, "Enough." He said, "Enough," to her questions. Often, he shouted it.

Oceola left home feeling "enough" most applied to her existence. She had outlived her usefulness to him. If her father made do with the necessary, her desire to commit to something as frivolous as song was superfluous.

She was wrong. He was so lonely for her voice after Oceola left that his joy fell off him in pounds. The small animals he caught now resembled him in proportion. And then, when he set them on his dinner table, even they seemed too large for him to cut up and eat by himself. For a while, he thought he was dying. His only friend was the doctor who visited once a week. The doctor came around more to reassure and comfort the man than for physical reasons.

Oceola returned less than a year later. She brought Joan with her, proof Oceola was lonely too. But she had taken a woman's recourse and was too proud to let her father call it her sin. Her face was drawn tight with tension. Her body appeared aged. Her lips were too bright, and the skin around her eyes was too dark. The eyes themselves were dim. When she had left the swamp, her total appearance showed clear and lighthearted. When she returned weariness was all about her. She was weighted with this new life, the father observed. He asked her to stay and she did for a little while. But the time was too late; she could not remain in the dark and the silence.

She said when she handed the baby to the old man, "I hope you do better with her than me."

The Blue Peacock and its neighborhood was the site of her brief urban life before having the baby. Oceola was only seventeen. The boy who first brought her to New Orleans found her a room in a house close to his city relatives. But Oceola did not see him again after she refused to have sex.

"Come on, girl, grow up." He tried intimidation. He tried love. But Oceola knew better. She told him that. So finally, he tried force. She would have to listen because she was alone in the city and she knew only him. He miscalculated. She pulled out the hunting knife in her pocket.

It was about nine inches long with a blade that eased back just a little like a saber. It was capable of easily slicing a small animal from the gut to the throat.

"If you want to keep everything you got now, you leave me alone forever," Oceola advised. He listened. She did right, but after that she was even lonelier, with neither friend nor enemy.

In her single room near the back entrance of an old lady's house, Oceola passed the days playing guitar. She ate very little. The same sandwiches and hard meat went down day after day. That wasn't too bad; she was accustomed to a diet that offered little variety in a particular season.

She also knew how to amuse herself. But in the city was a different feeling to being alone, unlike in the swamp, where she took living company from the trees, water, and birds. Here was little in nature to communicate to her. And there were people all around her that she could not contact. That was the worst.

Loneliness was harder to control here when she heard daily the voices of others, yet they did not speak to her. She even saw them if she looked out of her window. Oceola could almost touch them. But she did not know them. So she felt they had nothing in common and no desire for her acquaintance.

A young man who saw her sitting outside on the porch took the initiative finally. Aces was the first person to take an interest in Oceola in New Orleans.

Aces got his name because he was a four-flusher, everyone knew. In fact, he ran out of neighborly people with whom to associate himself. He too was lonely for company of a good nature. He sought it out constantly, although when people opened their hearts to him, or their homes, he took advantage.

He sensed Oceola's purity. He practically smelled it from where he stood in the street. Her face was almost bright with innocence. All he said was "Hello" and her conversation gushed out.

He invited himself to her porch step that afternoon and then daily. By the time the old lady in the front of the house told Oceola that Aces was bad, she could not agree. He showed Oceola only his kind side, as he did with most new people. From her perspective, she never met anyone so concerned with her so sweetly.

He learned that she played guitar. He danced. "A match made in heaven." He found her soft spot. Her first job was through Aces at the Blue Peacock. She did not realize that because of her singing, he would rest more instead of dance and he collected more than a fair share of the paycheck.

She was just thrilled to get money for performance. She invited Aces one night for dinner. He stayed overnight, sealing himself to her. She got pregnant almost immediately.

As she grew big, he removed the embraces. She thought at first, maybe her want had increased. Or perhaps her memory was skewed from the too-clearheadedness of not drinking alcohol in the club as she did between sets, eating more, and going to the bathroom often. Did Aces care for her less? Sometimes she sat, observer to his affection. No, he did not massage her shoulders anymore, pass his hand down her back, kiss the part in her hair.

At the Blue Peacock she saw him treat other women. And she

believed half of what she saw, like the blues song said. But she believed all of what she heard, as it advised against.

Aces introduced her to the abortionist. Oceola was one month farther along than she told anyone. But she was less afraid of this lie than of Aces. Just as sweet as he was at first, now he was evil. He had no in-between.

Oceola never was in the company of a man except her father. Still Aces' threats did not seem right. They fought bitterly when she ran away from Irene Campland. She planned to leave after the baby was born. And she did. Back to the swamp. But she could not stay there. She had acquired a taste, however bad, for the outside. Perhaps the excitement itself served as her addiction or just the basic human desire to finish life in a different way than it had begun.

Her mistake the second time was to live as she had learned from Aces. He taught that men were out only to do women wrong. She found this to be true time after time. Soon time itself began to pass quickly between the men and also briefly with them as she searched for the right one.

In the French Quarter, her habit of promiscuity turned profitable easily. The career of prostitute started with Aces' training. When she worked at the Blue Peacock, she had sex with his friends for his pleasure. Then he forced her to, or he would beat her. Later she rationalized the money she got paid for the previous free use of herself.

Now she no longer sang.

If she was seventeen again, she still didn't know the best decision. The solitude of the swamp or the excitement of the city? The waste of her talent or the misuse of it?

And often she actually wished to see her daughter to tell her the pain of life and the need to escape from it. But what would Oceola recognize? The child would be completely changed. O.C. named her Blue, after the place where she worked and the color of sky that she first saw outside the swamp. If Oceola thought about it, she could almost picture Blue's face, floating like a song travels, becoming a ghostly presence over the grey hanging moss. Except for the tinge, Oceola's image was very close to her child's real appearance.

The doctor pushed the black-painted glass door to the Blue Peacock Room and saw that the sign did not lie. The club, transformed from an old liquor store by distorted drawings of blue cocktail glasses and pink elephants, was one cubical. Its proportions of length and width were equally small. The ceiling was not very high.

The room was dark, not unusual. But it smelled slightly fresher than other barrooms.

"Well, business," the bartender said absently out of surprise when the doctor entered. The bartender did not expect company lately, he said. As he explained to the doctor, the clientele now came mostly on Thursday and Friday. Most of them would finish their paycheck in that one night, or the majority of it. So he had few customers at other times.

The doctor had not yet sat. He strolled the room slowly, close to the walls. There hung photos of entertainers in the Blue Peacock's better days, the bartender said. He pointed out names, "Johnny Taylor, Ernie K-Do, Lee 'Ya-Ya' Dorsey." It was an opportunity for the doctor to ask, "You ever heard of O.C. and Aces?"

"You mean Aces and O.C.," the bartender corrected. "They had a day or two. Look over there."

As the doctor walked to the corner and leaned over one of the four or five blue formica-topped tables in the room, the bartender continued, "Everyone know he done her bad. I was here then. Long time ago. Don't seem like it 'cause I was here then. But I was just a child." The bartender laughed in a husky voice that brought phlegm to his throat that he spit in a coffee can. "I was here to see Miss O.C. herself. She was so beautiful and so sweet. And not much more than my age." The bartender threw his index finger harder in the doctor's direction, "See them, there?"

"No. I can't tell," said the doctor.

The bartender came out from behind the bar. He limped on the left. "From the war," he explained. He and the doctor exchanged cordial and tight-lipped smiles and dropped their eyes. "There she is. Look," the bartender was the first to recover. "She wouldn't have nothing to do with me. When I begged her. Before my stuff happened." The doctor and bartender glanced at the floor together. "When I was young and pretty myself, that Aces had her locked up. And when I come back," the bartender pulled the tail of a soiled white rag out of his waistband and dusted the black drugstore frame of the photo, "I was scared to even wish it. Like I was." He mumbled the last sentence. Then he grew loud, "That Aces, man. I hate him. I swear I hate him. I'm glad he's dead and I know what that means. But it wasn't my wish that killed him. I guess I don't wish it on nobody anyway. Was the horse took him out. You know, heroin."

The last part, that there would be no Aces to talk to, the doctor heard. Most of the rest, he half listened to. He stared intently at the small photo of a thin, slick-haired man and a young girl on his lap wearing a dress with a slit on the side opened up further to show the photographer most of her left leg.

Except for her hair bob and lips opened in a provocative smile, the face of O.C. was the same as of the girl, Joan, who now waited in the room in the French Quarter for word of whether her mother would provide a home.

The other resemblance the doctor hadn't expected. Joan's eyes that curved into almonds, even the slight bags below them, belonged to the man. Aces looked to be very much Joan's father, although that place on her birth certificate was blank.

"Dead, huh? His people around here bury him? Who?" the doctor asked.

"The city, far as I know, and ain't nobody to care." The bartender moved back behind the counter.

The doctor bought him a beer. "You know where Oceola is now? She's not dead, is she?"

"You know her? Is she all right?" the bartender responded. Realizing that he too was searching—asking a question while not realizing the question was directed at him, the bartender said, "Not since that last night, twelve, fifteen years ago? I couldn't look at her after that." The bartender leaned down and closer, "See I always wanted her. And, man, I needed it bad when I come back from the war, some love and affection. And me and O.C., we were—before I went, anyway—like joking friends. And I come back like I am and she say she don't mind. And we do it, and I think, 'God, let me marry her.' But you know what she say when I'm leaving up out the door, even saying 'Baby, thank you.' She say, 'Fifteen dollars.' I ask, 'What?' She say, 'Fifteen dollars for that. I give you a good deal.'"

The bartender drank out of his beer, put his hand up to his face, and balanced his elbow on the arm across his chest. He stood slack, all of him leaning now to the right. "I just couldn't keep up with her after that. I changed and she changed. Maybe they ain't no real difference because we both poor off. But there is. I feel there is."

The men were both silent for a long time. Both sipped beer and looked at anything in the room but the faces of each other. Neither wanted to turn the corner on sadness. That would be like staring at the attachment of skin chewed by the shells.

The doctor spoke first, "You think I could have that picture?" He pointed to O.C. and Aces against the wall. "Her daughter is looking for her. . . ."

The bartender cut in excitedly, "She had a child?"

"Here, give her this." The bartender reached to his back pocket and took out a very old wallet. Out of a broken and yellowed plastic sleeve, he took a photo of Oceola. She was young with a clear face and a smile that showed no lipstick and much more sincerity. On the back was written in a shaky hand with fountain pen, "To George. From O.C." The bartender said, "Oh. I wrote that in the war."

The doctor looked at the picture in his palm. She was almost a different person than the one on Aces' lap.

"Give her this picture, not the other one. Tell her you found it or something. Don't tell her about Aces. That was a bad time," the bartender said.

"I don't know." The doctor started to hand the photo back.

"Keep it, please."

The doctor agreed slowly to that.

"Maybe, in a few years," the bartender stammered, "if you don't find her mother, you could tell the child—what's her name? . . ."

"Joan," the doctor said.

"Maybe in the future, you could tell her to look up George, if she need to. Not now. Now you speak for me."

The doctor nodded yes and went to the door after placing the photo in his own wallet. He thanked the bartender.

"If you see O.C., tell her George say, 'How you doing?'" the bartender asked.

"You know, that could have been my baby," he said as the doctor pulled open the door. They both nodded agreement and looked in their different directions.

The photo in the doctor's pocket had life of its own. Energy radiated from it, making him feel touched and tense. All the way back to the French Quarter apartment, the doctor tried to decide whether to show the picture to Joan now or to wait until they found her mother.

He did not want to get the girl's hopes too high. But the photo felt as if it wanted to be seen. The doctor was compelled to pull it out of his pocket again during the cab ride. The driver asked if the doctor came from out of town and whether he wanted a "date." The driver's talk was distracting. Finally, the doctor asked, "Please be quiet."

"You some kind of priest?" the cabdriver said. The doctor ignored him. Oceola's face showed so much hope. She could have picked any man before Joan was born. Perhaps she remained in New Orleans to find someone again. And not having found anyone, she stayed away. Or maybe she did find a man and she lived with him now, and with the children they made.

From the photo, he could see Oceola was once as childlike as Joan.

It must have been very hard for them both not to grow up around others. In his childhood home were so many brothers and sisters that worldly wisdom increased to the youngest, as it was passed down. But Joan was barely socialized. When they went to a restaurant in New Orleans, Joan picked up the meat with her fingers and broke it with her teeth. She chewed roughly, the way the doctor imagined Eskimos ate blubber. But even they, far in the North, had community in these manners.

Joan's mother was probably equally out of place when she arrived in New Orleans. The doctor saw from her picture, she vainly tried to be a sophisticate. She wore a small sequined hat like a soup bowl placed askew on her head. Net gushed out from the top like a fountain, the veil going up hopefully but then cascading.

Joan got the photo from the doctor as soon as he walked in the door. She guessed he had found something. Then she ran into her room to examine the picture alone. Joan did not turn on the light to the bedroom. She could see clearly enough because in the swamp she relied most times on lamps. Plus, she felt more comfortable without the buzzing and spitting of manmade illumination. Instead, Joan went to the window and pulled the long drapes aside so she could see by the moon.

But the streetlights overcame the cosmos. The moon was apparent but not usable. So Joan pretended the conditions were natural under which she first saw her mother.

The face was like Joan's in the oval shape of the bones and innocence of the smooth skin. But the eyes were almost tearful in their pretended joy. The mouth smiled. But there was tension across the top of the parted lips. Joan could see that her mother tried to please and was fearful of not succeeding.

Joan wept when she saw it. This is the way she imagined her mother. Joan thought her mother was weak. Her death, as she was in Joan's mind for many years, was proof of Joan's mother's inability to survive. And if her mother was alive, Joan imagined protection was still needed. Joan would say, "Mother, come home to the swamp where it is more peaceful."

"Mother, come home," she whispered now to the picture. She held the photo close to her face and stared at it until she could imagine the mouth spoke. "I miss you, Joan," the picture said. "I would do anything to be with you."

Joan folded her arms so that the picture lay close to her heart. Then she fell asleep. The doctor came into the room later and saw the girl on the floor next to the window, leaned against the wall. But he did not want to startle her. She had already had one shock. Plus, he did not want to spoil the movement in her dreams.

In them, Joan spoke with Oceola on the porch of the house in the swamp. The mother said, "Joan, I did not intend to leave you. I just got lost on the way home. I want you again."

"It's OK, Mother," Joan replied. "I knew you hadn't deserted me. It was grandfather's fault."

Joan began to feel very angry in her dream. She looked for her grandfather all through the house. But he would not come to her call and she heard a splash in the water off the side porch. She got there too late, only to see her grandfather's heels and then toes slipping into the swamp, as if in a dive. That made Joan madder. And she began to hear herself cry loudly, "I want ma mére. Where is she?" But instead of her mother the schoolteacher appeared. "In New Orleans," she said. Joan heard her, although she did not listen. Instead, she wept.

Joan awoke feeling bad. The room was very dark. She remembered the apartment in the French Quarter. She thought, how would the Bible advise her in this situation? "Seek to find," immediately came to Joan.

Joan stepped to the balcony and found the drainpipe nearby. She slipped down to the sidewalk. And when the doctor knocked on the door the next time, Joan did not answer.

There were no girls Joan's age walking through the French Quarter streets in the dark. There were men and women holding onto each other in most obvious ways. Many of them seemed mismatched, Joan could tell by their fashions. She noticed that one of the couple wore very bright clothes while the other had on dark colors. Pushed up against each other in doorways or heaped together in cars, they first appeared to Joan like sparrows nesting with bluejays.

Then Joan understood that their activities were just as private. Shocked, she rushed in the direction of noise. On Bourbon Street, the doorways blasted more sound than Joan's ears could stand. The reverberations of trumpets, drums, and loud off-key singers slipped right through her ears into her brain. She left that street where men called to her often and when she turned around to answer them, made what appeared to be mean signals with their mouths and their hands. Joan hurried on, getting farther to the back of Esplanade and near the French Quarter, feeling sadder and nearer somehow to her mother.

Actually, Oceola was near the vegetable carts in a doorway waiting for someone to respond. Her presence was felt by Joan as a feeling of overwhelming sorrow and melancholy. When Joan walked past the group of men lingering and making their minds up not far from her mother, she did not stop as they asked for her and then threatened. But she rushed away in tears and confusion.

She had walked in a circle. She discovered nothing she

wanted. Joan rang the bell of the apartment building to be let in. The doctor answered, "You can't do this running away no more."

They went upstairs to talk. "I'm shamed how you acting," the doctor said to her. "You got to think and act like an adult now. If you didn't find your mother, what, huh?"

"That's not possible," Joan's pride now lied to cover the realization she made on the streets. New Orleans was big and loud and hard. She might not find her mother among all these people. She tried hard to picture herself and her mother happy in New Orleans. But instead, she saw the day she sat on the porch feeling bad because her grandfather had said Joan had no mother alive. It was the day he and the schoolteacher argued. When her grandfather took her home, he came out to the front porch to comfort Joan.

She remembered pushing him. "I want ma mére," she said.

"What about me?" Joan remembered he looked hurt.

"You are a man," she said.

Then he put an old rag over his head and tied a knot under the chin. He began talking to Joan in a squeaking high voice. She could not help but begin laughing.

Her grandfather then made her happy just as the doctor was trying to now. They wanted to give of themselves to satisfy her emptiness. But they could not fill it. Her mother was special, Joan knew, although they had never met. Just that she bore Joan showed a connection the men would never understand.

Her mother gave life to Joan for a good reason, she felt. Why else would a woman have a child? Joan remembered once when her grandfather left the supply store first, the lady behind the counter offered a package of roots. "Make tea out of these if you ever need them. Then you won't have a baby," she said.

Why would a woman not want a baby, Joan wondered. And that time she said, "The babies are nice. They small and they soft. But me, I can't have one no way."

"The babies is trouble. You never heard of getting in trouble? Child, you too innocent." The store woman pushed the package of roots into Joan's hand, "for when you will need them."

Joan kept the roots for a very long time. She put them near her bed under the Bible in case they were bad magic and she needed protection from hell. Then one time, a boy at the school pushed Joan into the closet and kissed her. She was upset and knew then she would get pregnant. She thought about telling her grandfather, and how if she told him about the boy, he would take her away from school. Joan liked school. She wanted to go there as long as possible to read and then maybe to study with the nuns, as her teacher once suggested to her. The kiss would prevent her unless she did something about it. Joan decided to take the roots. If the kiss got her pregnant, that would rid it, make it go backwards, away. She prayed that the kiss would return out of her. It did, like vomit.

Joan was so sick her stomach ached for days. But she did not tell her grandfather or the doctor when he came what had happened.

But while she was ill and laying in some delusions, she forgot who she was. She dreamed that she was her mother, advising her grandfather, "Don't tell Joan who I am. Don't tell her they kissed me until I died." Joan did not tell her grandfather about this dream. And she came to understand the need for having a secret. Her mother had one too. Joan wasn't sure what the secret was. But it had to do with kissing, and babies and dying. And men could not feel about it the same way as women.

Joan rose at about six the next morning in the French Quarter apartment. The doctor had talked to her the previous night about not running away anymore, growing up and starting a new life. Joan understood that he did not want her to return alone to the swamp. He wanted her to live with him or go work for the nuns. He said they could still try to find her mother.

Joan stood on the balcony looking at New Orleans beginning to rise. The sun was not visible as she looked toward the river. But she already felt the morning heat. Below Joan on the balcony, a group of women walked and talked loudly. Their laughs sounded false, coming out of fatigue and despondency. One of them was a redhead. Joan immediately felt the same excitement as when she received the photo. She felt her mother among them.

Joan raced out of her bedroom, through the living room where Claudia and the doctor sat. She ran down the steps of the building and into the street. The first call she could think of was a mockingbird whistle, a high screeching imitation of cats.

Oceola heard the sound behind her. It was familiar. But she couldn't place it.

The doctor ran right after Joan into the streets. He yelled, "Stop."

Oceola Leontine, having lived the last eighteen years with an immediate response to that word from a man, began running. But before she ran she noticed the girl coming after her. Oceola thought, "What a shame, a kid that young in the trade." She was just about that age and probably not as pretty when she began, Oceola considered. She was running, but slower than the other women. Her night had been uneventful, unprofitable, and discouraging. Oceola wished she was as young as that girl running away from the man. She was not. Too many years had passed. She was old and broke down, and who knew how she would become?

The girl was beginning to gain on Oceola. She was crying, whistling loud like mockingbirds. She must be crazy, Oceola thought. That man might be trying to put her away. But the sounds were so familiar to Oceola they made her feel crazy and confused too.

"Hurry up. Get out of here, fool." The women ahead of Oceola told her to catch up. Instead, she stopped and leaned into her boot. She pulled out her long blade knife. She would give it to the child. If the girl was crazy, she could destroy the man. No big loss. If she needed only to get away from him, the knife was her diversion.

Oceola left the blade on the ground where it glimmered a streak of light back to the sun. Oceola ran, then stood on the corner to watch. The girl ran by the blade. But the man picked it up.

After looking at the blade in his hands, and hesitating, the man finally brought his arm back and threw it. He was a poor aim. But it still landed near O.C. He had tried to get her.

At the same time, the girl arrived. "You my mother?"

"God." Oceola took Joan's hand. They ran down the street out of the French Quarter and into the safety of her apartment.

The doctor stood in the sunlit street, now angered and upset by his decision. He had tried all along to save this girl's life, to do right by her and all of her kind. Hadn't he always ministered to those who had nothing and sympathized with their hopeless situations? But Joan deserted him just as he tried to help. That was her choice, he conceded. But the means he had chosen, that's what upset him. He was not a man to believe in the sword. Yet such was his decision if that innocent girl ran straight into the arms of harm. He would hurt whomever stood in his way to protect her. Maybe a good man did have to use violence for a better outcome. Or maybe each person had a violence in them that arose when faced with a situation they could not control. He had succumbed to his baser emotion.

Joan and Oceola Leontine, out of breath, rested in her living room on the old brocade couch. The daughter leaned back and looked around the room. Damask and aged curtains and furniture displayed an affinity for darkness in this first part of the house that did not fit with the outside Oceola.

Oceola's red hair, heavy makeup, and bright orange dress were colored so obviously to be out of place here where her walls, floors, and even decorations were in shades of deep blue, green, and grey. Additionally, an aquarium gave the room an odd light. The fish moved in front of the fluorescence like three-dimensional shadows.

Oceola rose and opened the curtains so that the room changed and so did she in it. The straight rays of sunlight coming in the length of the window seemed to throw into the house a cast of brightness almost artificial in its intensity. And only the fronts of the furniture and even Oceola herself were lit. The backs remained in shadow as if everything had a covered and undiscoverable side. The light on her mother, Joan thought, made a mask of her face—painted bright in the front and smiling with tension—over the true depth of her thoughts.

Joan wordlessly watched her mother, now energetically moving around the room. She appeared to be nervous with Joan staring.

"I knew I would find you. Granddaddy's dead," Joan said.

"Oh. I expected that happen some time," Oceola replied.

"Did you miss me?" Joan asked.

"As much as I knew of you I missed." Oceola did not look into Joan's eyes.

"I didn't know that you were around. So I guess I didn't miss you much either," Joan reflected her mother's statement. For Joan the words were said in truth.

Oceola, however, had lied. She knew her daughter existed and she could have visited Joan with her grandfather. Because of that Oceola did miss Joan and the opportunity of having a child. She knew that and she felt guilty. But she could not say it now, just as in the past she could do nothing about her own loneliness that kept her away from the people she loved.

As Joan continued to stare, Oceola moved to the record player. "This your first time to New Orleans?" Oceola fell back on her repertoire of meaningless statements, with which she was more confident and familiar.

"Yes. Didn't you want a daughter?" Joan continued with questions.

"I wanted you to be better than me."

"The fruit drops not far from the tree." Joan remembered her Bible, which had explained her mother's behavior while Joan was young and wondering.

"Oh. You don't know." Oceola began to speak of a life her daughter never discovered in her religious reading. Oceola spoke frankly, sparing no details about the life of a prostitute: Johns, living outside of the law, deaths, drugs, alcoholism in women. She told her daughter about selling the body and how the product cheapens with age. Oceola offered her life with candor as she had learned to speak to the women and men of the street. But this time, she told her story with sadness, since she finally had someone to hear her problems. In fact, Oceola was so overwhelmed by her own continuing trouble that she did not notice the face of her daughter.

The stories were wasted on Joan, who could not appreciate her mother's cleverness and skill as Oceola described her talent for staying alive. Her mother's behavior went strictly against the codes Joan learned from the Bible. Joan tried to understand and reminded herself that this was her mother. She should listen as the Lord would to sinners.

For her part, Oceola assumed her daughter already had similar experiences because of the man chasing Joan. Oceola had been out in the street so long she could not imagine the mentality of a virgin.

So Oceola just unburdened herself. She made herself a drink as she talked. The art of listening, so practiced by women in Oceola's profession, was also the job of listening. So on her own time and finally with someone to care, Oceola paid no attention to her audience.

When Oceola so easily said she had expected hell for considering the abortion and was happy to see her daughter alive, Joan fell sad, finally understanding her mother in a way her grandfather could never have explained.

Oceola had said, "See, I ran out of that place so fast. Shoot. I was a sight then. I didn't know nothing. But I knew enough that that old lady could have killed me with what she was planning. And Aces knew too. And you think he would have cared. Who? Honey, that man was shit. It's good he's dead and you never met him. Well, I got out all right. And when the baby was born, I said, I can't take care of that thing here in New Orleans."

Oceola had slipped. She had told the story so often. She had not made the connection between the "thing" and her daughter sitting in front of her. But Joan had. And then she decided that she was better off without a mother than with one like this.

As Oceola talked rapidly, still moving often from chair to record player to liquor cabinet, Joan rose slowly and deliberately.

"Could I have your address, so I can write you?"

"Where you going? We just getting to know each other. Baby, don't go back to no bad man. They not worth anything," Oceola said.

"Mama, Oceola. I'm just doing the best for myself." Joan walked toward the door, ready to memorize the numbers in case she ever wanted to return. But right then, she had to leave. She was not a thing. She was Joan. She was not city clever. But she was wise and alive. She did not feel she should have been thrown out because she disturbed Oceola's life either before she was born or after. Oceola had still not realized that.

"How could you kill me before I was born?" Joan asked.

"Baby, sit down. But I didn't. And I didn't know it was you

to come out. You were nothing to me then. I did not even see you."

"And you haven't seen me since." Joan opened the door for herself.

"Child, don't go now. I need to have you around now that I know you're alive."

"I can leave, Oceola, now that I know you."

Joan stepped out the front door of the apartment in the Marigny into the sunlight. Her mother stood in the frame. She was slightly drunk from drinking and talking so fast. Joan looked around and waved from the sidewalk. But Oceola was distracted by something in her living room and did not see Joan turn back before walking away.

Joan felt older and grown. No matter what the doctor said, she was going to live again in the swamp. Joan was ready to take care of herself. She did not need her childish imagination anymore. She had seen the reality of her mother and could give her up.

Her mother had given Joan to her grandfather because for Oceola that was the best choice, Joan considered. Now she was better alone. Becoming a woman meant saving oneself, Joan suddenly realized, and maybe, if possible, another person.

Before she left, Joan had told Oceola, "If you get tired of money and men using you like you say, you could do different."

When Joan found her way back to the French Quarter apartment, the doctor and Claudia were waiting. Hearing her story, they decided to return to the country. The doctor agreed to let Joan go back to the swamp after he made some arrangements for her to be looked after and work for the supply store woman. Joan spent a few weeks in the doctor's house getting prepared to go home.

When Joan got in her pirogue, she didn't want anyone but the dog to return with her to the house. She paddled through the swamp, now smelling its decay compared to the open air outside. But she felt comfortable. The swamp showed little passage of time and none but the most dramatic of changes. But she was accustomed to it and she had more peace here than any place else.

Joan greeted in tears the house where her grandfather died. She tied her boat up to the side of the porch and climbed the stairs. She went to the screen to undo the zipper of bent nails. But it was already open. The dog ran in ahead. Joan came in more slowly, wondering what she would find after so many weeks. Was her grandfather back alive?

Oceola Leontine stood waiting for her daughter. "I will try," she said. "This is better for both of us." Oceola opened her arms and Joan fell into them like a child and also finally a woman comforted.

Fatima Shaik with the Mayor of New Orleans, Sidney Barthelemy

Fatima Shaik studied at Xavier University of Louisiana before graduating from Boston University in 1974. She received her masters degree from New York University in 1978. She also attended Ottawa University and the University of Chicago. In 1981, she received a fellowship from the National Endowment of the Arts. Fatima Shaik was a reporter for the *Miami News, New Orleans Times-Picayune* and a correspondent for *McGraw-Hill World News*. She is married to the painter James Little and lives in New York City. THE MAYOR OF NEW ORLEANS is her first book.

PRAISE FOR
THE LIFE-GIVING CHURCH

A gold mine of successful ideas born out of practical experience!
The Life-Giving Church is must reading for anyone who
wants to be part of a thriving, growing church.

DR. DON ARGUE

President, Northwest College
Seattle, Washington

Ted Haggard is one of the most "life-giving" guys I have ever met!
His teachings and insights have been a great inspiration and
help to our leadership team. *The Life-Giving Church*
is a must read for growing churches, their laypeople
and their pastors.

JOHN ARNOTT

Senior Pastor, Toronto Airport Christian Fellowship
Toronto, Ontario, Canada

Ted Haggard writes from a depth of practical experience.
His fresh, compelling style causes challenging truths to be
renewed with grace. A man of prayer and a true pastor with
a shepherd's heart, Ted has learned how to combine the
spiritual and the practical in his life and ministry. I recommend
Ted's book with enthusiasm to anyone seeking to learn more
about Christ-centered ministry that releases the
vibrant life of the Holy Spirit.

MIKE BICKLE

Pastor, Metro Christian Fellowship
Kansas City, Missouri

THE
LIFE-GIVING
CHURCH

———

THE
LIFE-GIVING
CHURCH

—

TED HAGGARD

Regal

A Division of Gospel Light
Ventura, California, U.S.A.

Published by Regal Books
A Division of Gospel Light
Ventura, California, U.S.A.
Printed in U.S.A.

Regal Books is a ministry of Gospel Light, an evangelical Christian publisher dedicated to serving the local church. We believe God's vision for Gospel Light is to provide church leaders with biblical, user-friendly materials that will help them evangelize, disciple and minister to children, youth and families.

It is our prayer that this Regal book will help you discover biblical truth for your own life and help you meet the needs of others. May God richly bless you.

For a free catalog of resources from Regal Books and Gospel Light please call your Christian supplier, or contact us at 1-800-4-GOSPEL or at www.gospellight.com.

Cover Design by Kevin Keller
Interior Design by Britt Rocchio
Edited by Karen Kaufman

Library of Congress Cataloging-in-Publication Data
Haggard, Ted.
    The life-giving church / Ted Haggard.
      p. cm.
    ISBN 0-8307-2135-5 (Trade paperback).
    1. Church management. I. Title.
    BV652.H26 1998   98-27599
    253—dc21   CIP

1 2 3 4 5 6 7 8 9 10 11 12 13 14 15 / 04 03 02 01 00 99 98

Rights for publishing this book in other languages are contracted by Gospel Literature International (GLINT). GLINT also provides technical help for the adaptation, translation and publishing of Bible study resources and books in scores of languages worldwide. For further information, contact GLINT, P.O. Box 4060, Ontario, CA 91761-1003, U.S.A., or the publisher. You may also send e-mail to Glintint@aol.com, or visit their web site at www.glint.org.

DEDICATION

In 1971 Pastor Jon Gilbert was sent by the Home Mission Board of the Southern Baptist Convention to Yorktown, Indiana, to plant a church. While the church was temporarily meeting in the American Legion hall, some of my high school buddies invited me to visit. That visit resulted in a group of us driving with Pastor Jon to Explo '72 in Dallas, Texas, where I accepted Christ as my Savior.

As I continued in high school, my Christian life was shallow and lacked commitment. Then just after I graduated from high school, I was enjoying an exciting weekend night with my friends when my life was suddenly changed.

It was the summer of 1974, and by this time, Jeff Floyd had come to pastor Yorktown Baptist Church. The church had recently built a new building and Pastor Jeff was temporarily living in a trailer nearby until a parsonage was prepared. My buddies and I knew that he was alone in the trailer, so late one night we drove our cars in circles around his trailer until we saw a light come on. Then we drove off only to return in another hour when we were sure the pastor had gone back to bed. After three or four episodes of this mischievous behavior, we unexpectedly saw Pastor Jeff standing in the glow of our headlights. Our cars screeched to a stop. Much to our chagrin, Jeff invited us in. With a gentle spirit and a well-worn Bible, he brought us to our knees on his living room floor. God touched us that night and our lives were forever changed.

Jon Gilbert and Jeff Floyd will probably never be on the cover of *Charisma*, *Christianity Today* or *Ministries Today* magazines—although I think it would be great if they were. And I doubt that either of them will aspire to writing a book that hundreds of thousands will read—although I think we would all benefit if they did. Nor will either of them pastor a megachurch and enjoy its attending benefits. But they and thousands of pastors like them will pray for us, silently sit with us while we cry, perform our weddings and funerals, answer the phone when we call and faithfully care for our families as well as their own. They will drive vans loaded with our kids to Christian events and bless us in countless other ways.

I think these pastors are heroes. It is because of them that more Americans attend church services every Sunday than attend all of our major sporting events for an entire year combined. As time passes, these pastors accumulate thousands of believers in myriad churches who are living healthy lives because of their godly example: teaching and loving us. Often we don't even acknowledge them with a warm thank-you.

It is to these pastors that we dedicate this book. Jon and Jeff are symbols of the thousands of faithful pastors who come when they are called, sacrifice all for the cause of Christ and unyieldingly service His kingdom.

Thank you, Jon Gilbert. Thank you, Jeff Floyd. We all thank you very much.

TABLE OF CONTENTS

SECTION I

FOUNDATIONS FOR
LIFE-GIVING MINISTRY

SECTION II

PHILOSOPHY FOR
LIFE-GIVING MINISTRY

SECTION IV
BUSINESS THAT STRENGTHENS
THE LIFE-GIVING CHURCH

FOREWORD

Back in 1985, a young pastor serving on the staff of Bethany World Prayer Center of Baker, Louisiana, which now numbers upwards of 8,000, sensed a clear call from the Lord to launch out and plant a new church in Colorado Springs. With the agreement, the support and the covering of his senior pastor, Larry Stockstill, Ted Haggard moved his family to Colorado Springs and began New Life Church. Colorado Springs was not then the center of evangelical Christianity that it is today, but 1985 is widely regarded as the year that things in the city began to change for the good. One indication of the influence that New Life Church now has in Colorado Springs is the fact that some 6,000 believers show up for worship every Sunday.

When Ted Haggard first arrived in Colorado Springs, then a New Age center that was economically and socially depressed, he had no district superintendent or home mission board to direct his activities and to give him a tried-and-true strategy for planting a new church. Rather than serving under a traditional denomination, Ted Haggard represented a new form of carrying out the life and ministry of the Church, which I have been calling the New Apostolic Reformation.

WHAT IS THE NEW APOSTOLIC REFORMATION?

The New Apostolic Reformation is an extraordinary work of God at the close of the twentieth century, which is, to a significant extent, changing the shape of Protestant Christianity around the world. For almost 500 years, Christian churches have largely functioned within traditional denominational structures of one kind or another. Particularly in the 1990s, but with roots going back for almost a century, new forms and operational procedures are now emerging in areas such as local church government, interchurch relationships, financing, evangelism, missions, prayer, leadership selection and training, the role of supernatural power, worship and other important aspects of church life. Some of these changes are being seen within denominations themselves, but for the most part, they are taking the form of loosely structured apostolic networks. In virtually every region of the world, these new apostolic churches constitute the fastest growing segment of Christianity.

Church planting is built right into the very fabric of new apostolic leaders. Nothing could be more predictable than a staff member of a new apostolic church in our nation and in scores of other nations around the world. But more often than not, the pioneer church planters are largely left on their own to figure out how to get the job done. A strong aversion to bureaucracy, control and standardization of polity have kept most new apostolic leaders from drawing up established principles and procedures for planting new churches and for managing the churches once they are planted.

Ted Haggard has now provided something that every new apostolic church leader has deeply desired—a practical operator's manual, so to speak, for starting and running a church. Many pastors and other church leaders within denominations have also wanted an answer to their question, How are these new fast-growing churches doing it? They will find their answer in *The Life-Giving Church.*

This book provides many practical lessons that are not usually taught in seminary, such as a chapter on etiquette: How do you restore the fallen? How do you take care of guest speakers? How do you hire and fire? Why are good manners so important?

I hope you don't miss the last chapter on Bylaws. I know that very few will read it from beginning to end, but keep in mind that these are new apostolic Bylaws, and therefore quite different from *traditional* church Bylaws. In new apostolic churches, however, it is assumed that the pastor is the *leader of* the church. There is a huge difference between the two mind-sets, and this is one of the first presentations of a model for new apostolic Bylaws provided for church leaders in the form of a book.

I can personally affirm that the advice in *The Life-Giving Church* is good advice. This is not just because I have read and evaluated the book with professional church-growth eyes. Even more, it is because my wife, Doris, and I joined New Life Church when we moved from California to Colorado Springs. Ted Haggard is our pastor. I thought that our wonderful church in California would be hard to replace. But New Life Church has done it!

I have found an incredible presence of the Holy Spirit throughout the life of the church. I have found a passion for the nations of the world that could hardly be surpassed. I have found an incredible love for the community and its people. I have found a spiritual freedom emerging from Pastor Ted's insistence that we live day by day under the tree of life as opposed to the tree of the knowledge of good and evil.

As you read this book, you will see what I mean. If you say, "I want my church to be like that!" you will have made a good decision.

C. Peter Wagner
Fuller Theological Seminary

Acknowledgments

This book reflects a lifetime of exposure to the church world and 13 years of personal experience as a senior pastor. During these years, my staff and I have accumulated ideas and materials from many sources. Our problem has been, though, that the vast majority of ideas within the church world sound good. But only by testing them in the Scriptures and through both personal and observed experiences can we determine which ones actually help.

So we're constantly observing great successes and unfortunately, devastating failures, because of contrasting ministry ideas. That's why I am grateful to the people listed below. They help me think and, as a result, have protected us from many hard lessons. I hope this book will do the same for you.

As you read *The Life-Giving Church*, our prayer is that it will help you avoid painful lessons and ease you into greater effectiveness in His kingdom. And, of course, I trust that it will inoculate you against bad ideas that would inadvertently limit the effectiveness of your ministry.

I believe in learning from others. It's less painful, and I like that. So the following are a few of the organizations and people who have contributed to the strengthening of the local church and have helped form some of the principles presented here:

ACKnOWLEDGMEnTS

- My wife, Gayle and our five children, Christy, Marcus, Jonathan, Alex and Elliott. (If these ideas aren't perfected at home, then they don't work at church either.)
- New Life Church staff members: Ross Parsley, Lance Coles and Russ Walker.
- Pastors Roy and Larry Stockstill of Bethany World Prayer Center, Baker, Louisiana.
- Dr. C. Peter and Doris Wagner, Global Harvest Ministries and The World Prayer Center, Colorado Springs, Colorado.
- Tim and Monica Amstutz, Living Word Christian Center, Brooklyn Park, Minnesota.
- Bob Sorge, Sally Morgenthaler and Kent Henry, all great worshipers.
- Martin Nussbaum, New Life Church legal counsel for policies and practices.
- The National Association of Evangelicals, Wheaton, Illinois.

SECTION I

FOUNDATIONS FOR LIFE-GIVING MINISTRY

1. My Foundation
2. Change the Church? Why?
3. Our Choice: Life or Death?
4. Our Mark: Innocence or Victimization?
5. Our Power: Spirit or Flesh?

This section explains both my personal and the biblical foundation for life-giving ministry. Even though all Christian churches assume that they offer life-giving ministry, the overview provided in this section ensures that we do, indeed, offer life.

1

My Foundation

So it is written: "The first man Adam
became a living being"; the last Adam,
a life-giving spirit.

[*1 Corinthians 15:45*]

FiRST iMPRESSiONS

Delphi United Presbyterian Church is where Mom and Dad took me and my three older brothers to church while growing up on a farm in Indiana. My dad was the town veterinarian and owned several businesses and farms. At church, he was a presbyter and enjoyed teaching the high school Sunday School class. Mom did a remarkable job, working at home. She had her home economics degree from Kansas State University in Manhattan, Kansas, the heartland of great food and strong families, and was a professional at making our home and family a work of art. So whether hosting the women's missionary circle, or preparing one of her great meals for our family, Mom was the best. And it was she and Dad who decided the farm and the church were to be the center of our lives.

A few pictures of those years are indelibly imprinted on my mind, and those pictures form the values that shape my view of the local church. I can still see myself sobbing while sitting on the cold tile floor under the table in the basement Sunday School room with the teacher sympathetically pleading with me to come out. I can also see the four of us—Teddy, that's me, the youngest; Timmy, the strongest; Danny, the smartest; and Johnny, the oldest—sitting up straight in our pews with our starched white shirts, dark jackets and clip-on ties.

With our hair perfectly in place, fingernails trimmed and teeth freshly brushed, we stood tall while singing with hymnals in hand. The church seemed huge to me as a little boy, and I was proud of its giant stones, stained-glass windows and towering ceilings. I was awed by the majesty of the pipe organ accompanying the beautifully robed choir, which communicated worship and tidy, Midwestern order.

We each knew that if we poked, punched, whispered, laughed or did anything to draw attention to ourselves, Mom would gently glance at us, which was the first warning. Failure to adhere to the unspoken family rules would lead to the second warning, a gentle touch or soft pinch. But after that, if we solicited even a giggle from another brother that distracted surrounding worshipers from the service, there had better be a loving God in heaven who would help us, because we were going to receive some wholesome encouragement as soon as we got home.

So we didn't. Instead, we always looked forward to the big family meals after church. Sometimes we would go to a little one-room restaurant on the highway that could seat a dozen or so people at a time. Babe, the owner and chef, could make the best fried chicken, mashed potatoes and gravy, corn on the cob and green beans in the world. But most Sundays we would go home to an even better meal prepared by Mom. Sunday meals were always fun and loud, because we all wanted to eat and talk at the same time. I can still see Mom and Dad laughing hard with us during our Sunday dinners.

That's why Delphi Presbyterian Church was such a cornerstone for our family. It was the only time we were consistently formally dressed, starting with Saturday-night baths. And Mom and Dad always made the routine of Sunday worship special. Mom called it the best day of the week. Throughout the week she would count the days until Sunday, which caused all of us to look forward to church.

One time when I was six, everyone was so excited to get home for Sunday dinner that they left me at church. It's a childhood picture I hope I'll never forget. Little Teddy Haggard standing on the church lawn crying with family friends volunteering to drive me all the way to the Haggard farm. Then, when Daddy's Oldsmobile sped around the corner, I could see a look of relief on Mom and Dad's faces. But as the car approached, I could also see my three brothers laughing and pointing at me from the backseat. I was so embarrassed and angry that I jumped into the backseat with my brothers and tried to teach them a lesson by pounding on them.

They just held me and kept laughing at me as I struggled—just what good, big, mean brothers are supposed to do.

These were my first impressions of what a church should be. Our family never considered not going to church. I don't remember that the church service itself was ever anything spectacular and, as I think about it, I don't know that we went because of the services. Instead, we went because we were Christians. Certainly, we never thought of the church as a place for entertainment, or required the church to keep us happy. Rather, it was a major focus of our lives because of the decisions Mom and Dad made about the kind of people they wanted us to associate with and the kind of people they wanted us to become.

Years later when the Lord gave me the opportunity to pastor New Life, I was not particularly interested in building the church on events, entertainment or the most popular movement within the Body at the time. I enjoy those things very much, but I have built New Life on the Word and worship, full of life and power; and I've intentionally structured it to be a great place for parents to raise their children and to graciously mature together as a family. That idea probably came from Mom and Dad's unwavering consistency at Delphi United Presbyterian Church.

Another group of believers in Delphi that significantly impacted my impression of church, and thus the values of New Life Church, were the Dunkers. They were actually Old German Baptist Brethren, but most called them Amish. Like the Amish, they lived simple, rural lifestyles without electricity in their homes and used horses and buggies for transportation.

I was vividly aware of the Dunkers because they traveled to and from town on the road in front of our house. The largest Dunker family, the Royers, would stop from time to time to visit with Mom and Dad. Daddy was their veterinarian and felt very protective of their community because they were completely nonviolent. I remember hearing Dad on the phone telling people that it was our responsibility to protect them so they would have a safe place to farm and raise their families. We were probably as close to the Royers as any non-Dunker family could be. Living near them and knowing them gave me an opportunity to see their humility and sincere faith.

One night a group of drunken high school boys went out to the Royer farm after a football game and began breaking watermelons—the produce that provided the majority of their annual

---

[THE DUNKERS] WOULD NEVER ARGUE OVER MATERIAL POSSESSIONS, NEVER JUDGE ANOTHER OR EVER KNOWINGLY CAUSE ANOTHER TO SIN....THEIR HOMES WERE SIMPLE, THEIR CLOTHING PLAIN AND THEIR SPEECH SOFT AND KIND.

---

income. While the boys were yelling and cussing in the field, the light of a glowing lantern began flickering in an upstairs bedroom of the farmhouse. From the field the boys could see the light being carried down the stairs and then out onto the front porch. Then, as the light approached them through the darkness, the boys were ready for a fight. Instead, Mr. Royer told the boys they could have all the melons they desired, but that the melons they were breaking were not his best. He offered to lead them to the best field and give them as many as they wanted.

The boys were embarrassed and respectfully apologized before leaving. Mr. Royer invited them in for a glass of lemonade—he said they needed it. But the boys declined, trying to soak in their vivid lesson on Christian character. The Royers influenced many people. Instead of preaching with words, they communicated by living well. They would never argue over material possessions, never judge another or ever knowingly cause another to sin. That's why their homes were simple, their clothing plain and their speech soft and kind.

The Dunkers loved the Bible, and actually practiced the Scriptures. They would never dream of resisting an evil man, rebelling against authority or flaunting anything that might stir

———

BEING A CHRISTIAN MEANS...WE STOP
STRUGGLING AGAINST ONE ANOTHER IN
ORDER TO GAIN THE WISDOM TO WORK
TOGETHER IN HARMONY AND TRUST.

———

envy in another's heart. They believed that heaven was their home. Alcoholism, sexually transmitted diseases, divorce, violence and betrayal were unheard of in their community. The Dunkers were models of godly character and conviction for me.

So when I think of a Christian community, I think of the honesty, the generosity and the adherence to Scripture of the Royer family. I would never think of causing others to have to lock their cars, homes or businesses because of my presence. Being a Christian means that the reality of heaven affects every area of our lives, and that we stop struggling against one another in order to gain the wisdom to work together in harmony and trust. These are values I believe all Christians can embrace. Rural cultures don't produce these values, holy hearts do. And Jesus' holiness is available to all of us, no matter where we live—that's what should be evident in our churches.

In Delphi, I remember the back doors of businesses being left unlocked because someone might need something. Daddy used to go into businesses after hours to pick up an item and leave the money and a note on the cash register so the owner would know exactly what he had purchased. Stealing was never a thought. To take something you hadn't earned was shameful. The fabric of our community was woven with trust, honesty and a meaningful handshake. Caring for each other's children and humbly sacrificing for another person's good was the norm, not the exception.

As I write these first impressions of church and Christian people, I realize things couldn't have been as ideal as I remember them. I'm 41 now and know better. However, I do think it's great that these were the memories from the eyes of little Teddy Haggard. I want my kids to have memories just as wholesome. It makes adult life easier. That's why we need good churches.

TRUTH VERSUS RELIGIOUS INSTITUTIONS

Then, when I was in the seventh grade, our world began to change. Daddy's back started to bother him, making it impossible for him to work. Even though his friends tried to help, Dad's pain was so intense that he had to lie on a hard wooden surface without moving, thus we began selling farms and businesses. As the laughter in our home transitioned into caution, Dad saw Billy Graham on television and, for the first time in his life, heard about being born again.

After praying with Billy Graham, Dad went to talk with our pastor who told him that the term "born again" was irrelevant to our modern culture and didn't have any contemporary application. Our pastor warned Dad not to expose our family or his Sunday School class to anyone who believed in being born again.

Even though various people within the community offered to help our family, our financial condition worsened. Dad couldn't stand the thought of borrowing from people in our community, so in the dichotomy of his spiritual renewal and horrible back pain, he and Mom decided to move us to a larger community where they could build a small animal practice that would be easier on Dad's back.

When we moved, Dad found a Presbyterian church that was evangelical, where the pastor understood being born again. But because of his previous experience, Dad was compelled to read and trust his own Bible. While we were settling into our new church home, Dad read about being filled with the Holy Spirit. He asked our new pastor about it and was told not to pursue this experience because it might lead him into fanaticism.

Then, while praying about some of the Scriptures, Dad had a powerful encounter with the Holy Spirit. But because our new pastor had discouraged his seeking this wonderful experience, Dad began to doubt the spiritual integrity of our new church as well...so, we moved on.

Eventually Dad started associating with a group of believers who emphasized the gifts and the power of God's Holy Spirit, a major cultural move for our family. But while worshiping with this group, Dad discovered the Scriptures about deliverance. Because of some old negative patterns that had been deeply rooted in the Haggard family, Dad was very interested in personal deliverance. When he asked his new friends about it, they said Christians never need deliverance, only sanctification. They discouraged him from associating with anyone who believed that Christians could be candidates for deliverance. But Dad and I and some other family members did receive our much-needed deliverance from generations of bondage. Unfortunately, once again, people connected with institutional religion had attempted to thwart our family's growth in the Scriptures and in the power of God.

MY PASTORAL CALL

Therefore, when God called me into pastoral ministry, I was concerned about how Dad would respond. I was home from college after my freshman year as a telecommunications major with a minor in journalism. It was late, and I was by myself in the kitchen, pouring a bowl of cereal when God spoke into my spirit and called me. I was totally surprised.

I paused, smiled and told the Lord I wanted to serve Him. But before I mentioned this to anyone, especially my parents, I asked the Lord to assure me by using others to confirm His calling on my life. I felt as though He consented, so I went into the living room to watch TV and eat Cheerios.

The next morning I received a letter from Curry Juneau, my Sunday School teacher at the church I attended while away at college. Curry wrote that he had been asked by another church to become its senior pastor, and that he would accept the position if I would agree to join him as the youth pastor. I grinned as I read the letter. *Confirmation number one.*

Later that same day Pastor Jeff Floyd, one of the pastors eulogized in the acknowledgments of this book, dropped by the house. He had come to ask if I planned to be in church on Sunday. When I said yes, Jeff was pleased because he said the deacons had voted to license me into the ministry so I could officially begin preparations to be a pastor. They had never spoken to me about this, nor had I hinted at any interest. But Jeff smiled broadly as he told me what they had already decided to do. *Confirmation number two.*

Then that evening, Owen Crankshaw, one of my buddies from high school, came by to pick me up to go out for some fun. As we drove, Owen asked me why I was a telecommunications major when I was going to be a pastor. *Confirmation number three.*

That did it! Pastoral work had never been a subject with my friends before. And yet, after one quick encounter with the Holy Spirit in the kitchen over a bowl of cereal, it seemed everyone knew more than I did about my calling.

But I was cautious about telling Dad that God had spoken to me about becoming a pastor because three respected pastors had given him advice that was contrary to Scripture. Even though I had received three supernatural confirmations, I knew I would not violate my dad's counsel. In my mind I kept hearing him say, *Most traditional churches are worldly institutions that appease God's people and keep them from knowing the Scriptures or the power of God.* Dad no longer trusted pastors to be godly men of integrity, and now I wanted to be one.

The next day I was working in Dad's office and decided to tell him what had happened to me. When I told him, he dropped his head to think, looked up at me, and said he believed God had indeed called me. Then he cautioned: "If worldly church systems or politics ever begin to drain God's life out of you, you must get out quickly. Don't let others kill it." I gave him my word and he gave me his blessing. *Confirmation number four.*

The next Sunday I was licensed at Yorktown Baptist Church and returned to school as a sophomore. Upon my return I switched my major to Biblical Literature with a Christian Education minor, and began working with Curry Juneau at Phoenix Avenue Baptist Church. As I was finishing my bachelor's degree, Phoenix Avenue ordained me and hired me to be an interim pastor for a short time before graduation.

LOCAL CHURCHES WITH A GLOBAL VISION

As graduation approached, I was hired by World Missions for Jesus, a West German missions organization, to become their American representative. World Missions worked exclusively to assist the believers behind the Iron Curtain and in Third World socialistic countries. The risks believers were taking to assist other believers suffering under Communist dictatorships gave me personal insight into the universal Body of Christ, the importance of Christians working in harmony together, and the tragic results that are inevitable whenever Christians separate themselves from one another.

After one and a half years with World Missions, I became the American vice president, which was more administration than I liked. So I resigned from World Missions and joined the ministry team at Bethany Baptist Church, which is now Bethany World Prayer Center in Baker, Louisiana. During the five years at Bethany, my wife, Gayle, and I learned many of the principles for a life-giving church that are in this book:

- Rest.
- Keep your word.
- Don't think more highly of yourself than you ought.
- Churches are to care for others.
- Strong leadership combined with consistency, humility and honesty builds healthy churches.
- Churches are best when not swayed by Christian movements.
- No secrets.

COLORADO SPRINGS

After working with Bethany for five years, Gayle and I thought we would serve there all of our lives. But while on vacation in Colorado Springs visiting Gayle's family, I took a pup tent, a gallon of water, Scripture cassettes and my Bible to the back of Pikes Peak to pray and fast for three days. On that trip, God spoke to me about Colorado Springs and called me to pastor there.

Not long after my arrival in Colorado Springs, during times of praying and fasting, I saw four things:

1. A stadium full of men worshiping God (There were no children or women, but huge numbers of men worshiping God.);
2. A place where people could pray and fast without any distractions;

3. People coming from all over the world to pray for the lost in a world prayer center containing a huge globe;
4. A church where people could freely worship God and study the Scriptures with no strings attached. A hassle-free life-giving church.

After I saw these things in my heart, I believed that God let me see them for intercessory prayer, so I began asking God to bring them to pass. I did not dream that the Lord would actually use me to bring these visions to pass. In the case of the men in stadiums, I haven't had any direct involvement. In the other three, I have had direct involvement:

- The first vision was fulfilled when Coach Bill McCartney received the same idea about 10 years later as he was driving near Colorado Springs. That ministry is Promise Keepers.
- The second vision is Praise Mountain, a prayer and fasting center in Florissant, Colorado that started in 1987.
- The third vision is The World Prayer Center in Colorado Springs.
- The fourth vision is New Life Church.

When Gayle and I came to Colorado Springs in August of 1984, we had been blessed with positive church experiences. Neither of us had ever been involved with a church split, a mishandled moral failure, broken or wounded spirits because of betrayal or deception, or any other common abuses. Because of our history, we knew God had given us great models for ministry. We also knew that if we could just pastor the way we had seen others pastor, we could successfully serve people for many years.

On the first Sunday in January of 1985, New Life Church was birthed with a handful of people in the basement of our recently purchased home. Five months later we moved into our first public space—a little auditorium that sat 200 people with a small room for a nursery and children's ministry.

In May of 1986 we moved down the street to another office building. We reconstructed the inside of the building into a 650-seat auditorium with room for a few classrooms and offices. In 1987, Paul and Geri Fix from Florissant, Colorado gave the church a 70-acre field as a seed toward Praise Mountain, a prayer and fasting center. The church bought two adjacent pieces of property, which resulted in a beautiful 110-acre facility where people pray and fast to this day.

Again in May of 1988, the congregation moved into a larger storefront that was constructed into a 1,500-seat auditorium with a small youth chapel, 12 classrooms and a small office space. That space, like the others before, was quickly filled to capacity, but we couldn't find a space in the city large enough to hold the expanding congregation. It was time to buy land and build.

But because of our strong missions philosophy and our determination not to be wasteful or ostentatious, the church bought land in the county that had to be annexed into the city before construction could proceed. In 1991, New Life Church purchased 35 rural acres on Highway 83 and constructed a simple concrete structure. Our new building had an auditorium that would seat as many as 4,000 with limited classroom and office space. The first service was held Christmas night, December 25, 1991, and since that time, attendance has steadily grown.

Recently we added some additional classroom space to help serve the more than 6,000 members that regularly attend. And, because of our emphasis on missions, the church gave more than $1,000,000 to missions last year (1997). We pray that this kind of giving will continue to increase.

Every church has its own personality and culture. And that personality and culture is composed of the gifts, calling, experiences and personalities of its leadership team and congregation. That's why the value of life-giving churches starts for me in

Delphi, Indiana, with the Presbyterians and the Dunkers. The values learned there, my dad's warning to avoid religious structures and to trust the Scriptures, and Bethany World Prayer Center's emphasis on integrity were fundamental to my personal development, and thus, the foundations of a life-giving church. These elements convinced me that church could and should be simple and effective.

I used to think we were somewhat unique; then I learned that life-giving churches all around the world have discovered how to practice freedom, trust, spiritual sensitivity and honesty in a simple format. In fact, innovative life-giving churches are the fastest growing churches in the world. The negative realities of the "god business" causes me to cling to the simplicity of the life-giving church. Certainly, not all life-giving churches are the same as New Life, many are more established and are of various sizes, but all of them emphasize the power of God, the integrity of the Scriptures and the life available in Christ.

2

CHANGE THE CHURCH? WHY?

EACH ONE SHOULD USE WHATEVER GIFT
HE HAS RECEIVED TO SERVE OTHERS,
FAITHFULLY ADMINISTERING GOD'S
GRACE IN ITS VARIOUS FORMS.

[*1 Peter 4:10*]

SOMETHING IS WRONG

New Life Church attracts people who love God but don't necessarily like the church world very much. I can relate. Sometimes I'm like that. I love the Bible, seek the manifestations of the Holy Spirit, enjoy the diversity of the Body and look forward to His Second Coming. Believers make me smile. Prayer is a delight, spiritual warfare is exhilarating and serving others is deeply satisfying. I am thrilled when I think of a good cell group. I like studying the Bible, going on Christian retreats and participating in powerful worship services. They are fun to me because they give me life.

But when most people think of church, they don't think of the life-giving experience that comes from knowing Christ;

TOO OFTEN CHURCHES MAKE NICE PEOPLE
MEAN, HAPPY PEOPLE SAD AND INNOVATIVE
PEOPLE WANT TO PULL THEIR HAIR OUT.

instead they often think of excessive introspection, irrelevant sermons and offerings. Baptisms, weddings and funerals are the only purpose of church for many. And most people draw security from knowing Grandma goes to church. But when thinking of church, few people smile. No one ever says, "I want to have a great party at my house this Friday, so I'm going to invite a group of pastors and church elders." Nope. Doesn't happen. Why? Because too often churches make nice people mean,

CHANGE THE CHURCH? WHY?

happy people sad and innovative people want to pull their hair out. Something is wrong on the main street of traditional church structures.

Transitioning Church Structures to Mobilize Ministry

The November 1996 issue of *Christianity Today* profiled 50 people, age 40 or younger, who have demonstrated leadership potential for the next generation of evangelicalism. I am one of those 50. I found it interesting that only 9 of us minister primarily through local church structures. Some of the reasons are obvious: one is a congressman and others are journalists, musicians, educators and professional athletes. But based on the discussions we had when we met at the 1997 National Association of Evangelicals convention, the rest discovered that even though they love their local churches and feel a part of the local Body, they cannot adequately minister through the local church structure. And they are right.

However, the Lord seems to be transitioning the structures He is using to mobilize Christian ministry. Many of us closely associated with local churches are rapidly embracing changes driven by the emerging megachurches and servant ministries. One indicator of this change is that seminaries, our traditional training system for Christian leaders, are not training the leaders of many of our most successful churches or successful servant ministries. Focus on the Family was founded and is prospering under the leadership of Dr. James Dobson, a child psychologist; Promise Keepers was founded and is being directed by Bill McCartney, a football coach.

I don't intend to comment here on the benefits or consequences of the evolving sources of our Christian leadership. But it is so notable that new technical terms are being developed to describe the emerging systems. Renowned missiologist, Dr. C. Peter Wagner, the Conservative Congregationalist from Fuller

[41]

Seminary, is regularly writing and speaking about the "new apostolic reformation." Dr. Wagner has accurately recognized the changes as so dramatic that they are creating an actual reformation within the Body of Christ. Without question, we are improving the way we administrate churches and improving the way churches relate to one another.

Dr. Wagner's new book *The New Apostolic Churches* is the most recent publication describing churches that have a powerful ministry of spiritual life and the ministry relationships that emerge around them. This book documents the transformation that is occurring in the way the church administrates ministry.

As I have already mentioned, these transitions are affecting the way churches relate to one another. Several years ago I wrote *Primary Purpose* about the new ways coalitions of churches are working together to promote more aggressive conversion growth in their cities. As a follow-up book, Jack Hayford and I coauthored *Loving Your City into the Kingdom* with Bill Bright, Ed Silvoso, George Otis, Jr. and others to explain how churches can work together to affect their entire city.

Obviously, the Holy Spirit is birthing this dramatic change. The public is seeking out churches that minister life and servant ministries that strategically advance Christ's kingdom. Thus, rapid changes are taking place in existing organizations that desire to grow, and new organizations are birthing from innovation and creativity.

We seldom look to traditional church hierarchies to teach us how to do church anymore. Instead, we look to those on the cutting edge, the thoughtful innovators who are creative and spiritually daring with proven successes. Rick Warren teaches us how to integrate people into our churches, Tommy Barnett teaches us how to illustrate sermons, and Bill Hybels teaches us to consider the seeker's point of view. We don't look to these people for our theological underpinnings, but we are experimenting with ways to communicate a proven gospel message within a rapidly changing culture. So Pentecostals freely receive from Southern Baptist Warren, Baptists unhesitatingly learn from Assembly of God Barnett, and charismatics drink fresh water from evangelical Hybels.

PRESERVING OUR DAVIDS AND INFANT KINGS

Because of improved communication within the Body of Christ, we can find those who know how to most effectively minister life and learn from them. Our entrepreneurs and innovators are rising to the surface, and when they do, we hear about them. That's why I was so fascinated with the 50 people *Christianity Today* chose. They are certainly a promising group, and no one knows which of these will actually make a positive contribution to the growth of evangelicalism.

But, as *Christianity Today* implied, many were not on the list because they are currently unnoticed shepherds. Many of these Davids are in local churches trying to find the mystery of true ministry while serving as youth pastors, music ministers, assistant pastors, cell leaders or volunteers. They love the purpose of the church, but my concern is that when the church bogs down in gossip and inefficiency, they will go where the water flows more freely—outside the local church.

Young Davids want structures that facilitate relationships which are conduits for His living water...the bread of life...the tree of life—that's what future leaders are looking for. But if true life is secondary to a well-intentioned but top-heavy bureaucratic structure that appears political, corrupt or hurts people, then our Davids will graciously excuse themselves. Even the world seems to have caught on to the need to disencumber from the oppressive weight of bureaucracy. The May 14, 1998 headline for *USA Today* reads, "Start-up Davids Don't Fear Goliaths" and the subtitle reads, "Big Can Mean Clumsy, Bureaucratic."

Stimulating greater opportunity within our local churches for our Davids of every age is the reason this book was written. Our future will be brighter when our Davids have a positive experience within their local church structures rather than, like so many other infant kings, being poisoned before they ever approach notable service.

Considering the young Davids, I can't help but think of Bill Gates's book *The Road Ahead*, which emphasizes the necessity of building a corporate atmosphere that attracts and retains the brightest and the best of the business—the entrepreneur. In his book, Gates says that the greatest threat to Microsoft is not NCR, Hewlett Packard, Ford Electronics or IBM, but some college student in a dormitory somewhere playing on his laptop computer, a David. Gates maintains that these Davids are learning what the major corporations already know, but are developing better ideas than paid researchers and developers usually generate.

His concern is that these innovators will get out of school, go to work for Microsoft for a few years until they branch off and start a competing organization that is highly focused in a particular field. That new organization, driven with the creative innocence of the young David, will probably provide a better product at a better price than Microsoft, the large established corporation.

So Gates is taking strong action now. Microsoft's foresight requires it to provide a healthy corporate structure that is not threatened by or passively hostile toward the entrepreneurs, but rather embraces its Davids, causing the entrepreneurs to want to stay within Microsoft. Then, Microsoft will become stronger because of a corporate environment that values the changes birthed by creative innovators. Bill Gates wants the Davids of the microelectronics business to stay, just as we want the Davids of the Body of Christ to be productive within our local churches, not driven from them.

Most young Davids within the Christian world start with an innocent heart before God and a trusting attitude toward churches. They love His life and are innocent before Him. But when they discover cumbersome systems and unnecessary processes that don't contribute to effective ministry, these disillusioned Davids quickly decide they can do more elsewhere. Therefore, our local churches may unnecessarily be losing some of our brightest and best future leaders.

It's no wonder that while we have more money, buildings, books, seminars, seminaries and support groups than ever, 80 percent of our North American churches have either plateaued or are declining. While the Body of Christ is growing three times faster than the population growth rate globally, why hasn't the North American church experienced any net growth in more than 20 years? I think one reason has something to do with how our Davids are being treated within our local church structures. Fortunately, we are changing.

This book offers four sections of information about the life-giving church:

- First is the foundation of life-giving ministry in contrast to ministry that appears godly but doesn't offer life.
- The second is the philosophy, which is vitally important to transitioning from a corporate, highly structured mentality into a dynamic, relational mentality that creates healthy ministry.
- The third discusses some of the ministries of the life-giving church. These are neither simple programs nor departments, but rather tracks that allow apostles, prophets, evangelists, pastors and teachers to enable people within the local church in their ministries.
- Then the fourth section discusses the business structures of the life-giving church, emphasizing how the corporate can serve the spiritual functions of the Body.

Too often church structures restrain godliness and inadvertently provide a voice for ungodliness. We've all grimaced when our structures have unnecessarily given platform to the whiners, manipulators and controllers within the Body, while our strongest innovators gently begin moving toward the door because they don't need to tolerate unnecessary and unproductive systems.

———

LOCAL CHURCH STRUCTURES TOO OFTEN
STEAL OUR INNOCENCE AND PRODUCE
BONDAGE, SLOWLY DRAINING US OF THE
VERY SPIRITUAL LIFE AND JOY WE ARE
SUPPOSED TO MINISTER TO OTHERS.

———

We have a paradox. The message of the gospel provides spiritual freedom, but our local church structures too often steal our innocence and produce bondage, slowly draining us of the very spiritual life and joy we are supposed to minister to others. Eventually we become like our predecessors: whitewashed tombs looking good on the outside but powerless and maybe even deadly on the inside.

There is no reason to allow these repressive, encumbering systems to continue to drive the church. What are we protecting? Small bastions of a culture that were squeezed out of mainstream society years ago? Our local churches can be spiritual power-houses of effective ministry *to people*. They should be stable, but not so stable that they are dead. Therefore, our churches must provide simple structures that are tracks for effective ministry rather than restrictive barriers. In the midst of America's spiral away from its Judeo-Christian foundation, God is preparing strong leaders with creative dreams and aspirations for the next generation of local churches to reverse this negative trend.

Attracting and retaining our future leaders within existing local church structures will require some risks as we rearrange the ways we minister with and to the congregation. Certainly, we need the necessary checks and balances to prevent abuse. But we must also recognize that those with the greatest potential require the freedom to test their own wings in order to either fly or fall. If we protect them too much from falling, that same overprotection may keep them from flying. Then we're stuck with more status quo and no net growth in plateaued local churches. We can't afford this any longer. Thus, the transition to *The Life-Giving Church.*

3

Our Choice:
Life or Death?

And the Lord God made all kinds of trees
grow out of the ground—trees that were
pleasing to the eye and good for food. In
the middle of the garden were the tree of
life and the tree of the knowledge of good
and evil....And the Lord God commanded the
man, "You are free to eat from any tree in
the garden; but you must not eat from the
tree of the knowledge of good and evil, for
when you eat of it you will surely die."

[*Genesis 2:9,16,17*]

Many Faiths,
One Life-Giving Spirit

Mrs. Morgan has been enjoying the Body of Christ from the same pew of St. Peters practically every Sunday for more than 30 years. The slope in the wood grain eternally marks the exact location from which this faithful church secretary observes weddings, funerals, baptisms and boys fidgeting in their seats. For years she has been watching people come and go, children grow up and marry, and their parents age. From her pew she watches widows grieve the departure of their spouses and children's choirs sing special Christmas songs. Mrs. Morgan faithfully teaches her Sunday School class from the quarterly. At times the church has been healthy and growing with the strength of young men and an atmosphere created by bustling young families. Other times the church has felt tired and solemn, but Mrs. Morgan has never wavered. She loves her church.

Just a few minutes drive from St. Peters is another church of the same denomination. Even though the theology is the same and the people are from the same neighborhood, some even from the same families, the church feels different—its atmosphere is the opposite. For some mysterious reason, people fight easily in that church. They are contentious, defensive and often demanding. Mrs. Morgan has never mentioned anything negative regarding this "sister" church, but when asked, with great sensitivity she graciously changes the subject.

The contrasts between the two churches are evident, despite the fact that the signs in front of their buildings and their listings in the yellow pages indicate that they are of the same faith. But they aren't. The spiritual climate is too different, even though they believe the same creed and read from the same Bible. It is that difference that people notice but can't identify.

This subtle contrast in spirit must be understood in order to build a life-giving church.

When we talk about a life-giving church, we all understand that the life of God is available through faith in the Lord Jesus Christ. By His sacrifice, we have access to the Father, and it is the empowering Holy Spirit who indwells all believers as a deposit

———

IN THIS WORLD OF BLINDED EYES, DULL EARS AND HARDENED HEARTS, THE LIFE OF GOD ISN'T IMPARTED ACCORDING TO FORMULAS...BUT RATHER BY DYNAMIC RELATIONSHIPS.

———

guaranteeing our inheritance in Him. So all churches that believe Jesus is the only solution to our sin problem and that the Bible breathes His revelation into our hearts and minds should be life-giving. Theoretically, all of them are life-giving.

But in this world of blinded eyes, dull ears and hardened hearts, the life of God isn't imparted according to formulas, biblical or not, but rather by dynamic relationships. Most churches that believe the fundamentals of the faith are truly life-giving, but unfortunately, others believe the same things and are deadly. Why?

CREATION AND EDEN

The first two stories in the Bible give us the foundation for our relationship with God and the basis upon which we interpret the balance of Scripture. The Creation account teaches us, among many other things, that God *is*, He is big, and He created everything. No way to avoid it, He's in charge. The account of Adam and Eve in the Garden of Eden gives us insight into the major choice Adam and Eve had to make. They could have obeyed God and continued to enjoy the benefits symbolized by the tree of life, or disobeyed God and died because of the consequences of partaking of the tree of the knowledge of good and evil. This account, for the purpose of our study, provides us with a metaphor that is a picture which helps us see the choice we have to make between those same two trees. And, as in the case of Adam and Eve, one tree gives us life while the other oozes death.

Even though I believe the Eden account is literal, it also provides a figurative lesson for us. As we all know, the Old Testament is full of types and shadows that can be used to strengthen our Christian lives. When we choose the tree of life, we are choosing the life that God offers all of us through Jesus, His Son. The tree of life is a picture of walking and talking with God, living in His provision, protection, fellowship, friendship and lordship. It's a picture of living life full of His Spirit, and having a clean conscience—innocence. But innocence is quickly destroyed when we choose the forbidden, the tree of the knowledge of good and evil. When we choose the tree of the knowledge of good and evil, it brings death.

George Washington Carver, one of our greatest American heroes, exemplified living in the tree of life. Because he was the son of slave parents and raised in abject poverty, he could have been bitter and angry. But he chose not to let the knowledge of good and evil infect his spirit and poison his heart and life. As a result, he said, "I will never let another man ruin my life by making me hate him." Consequently, his brilliant mind was not limited by a bitter spirit, which released him to become one of the greatest inventors in American history.

By choosing the tree of life, George Washington Carver was able to maintain the vitality of the Holy Spirit in his heart and freely minister life to others. If he would have misunderstood and chosen to live according to the knowledge of good and evil, he and those within his influence would have been poisoned by the injustices of his day and would have died spiritually. This is the difference between living according to the tree of life (see Gen. 3:22) and responding according to the tree of the knowledge of good and evil (see Gen. 2:17).

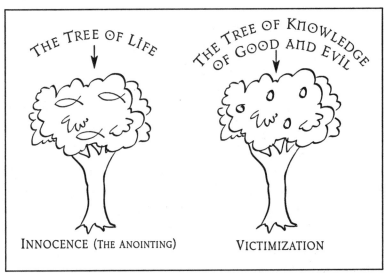

THE TREE OF LIFE

THE TREE OF KNOWLEDGE OF GOOD AND EVIL

INNOCENCE (THE ANOINTING)   VICTIMIZATION

In this chapter I am going to compare the tree of life to the tree of the knowledge of good and evil. Chapter 4 will focus on the attitudes that emanate from these two trees—innocence from one and victimization from the other. Then, chapter 5 will show how these attitudes result in the fruits and gifts of the Spirit or in demonic opportunity, both at individual and church levels.

> Now the serpent was more crafty than any of the wild animals the Lord God had made. He said to the woman, "Did God really say, 'You must not eat from any tree in the garden'?"
> The woman said to the serpent, "We may eat fruit from the trees in the garden, but God did say, 'You must not eat fruit from the tree that is in the middle of the garden, and you must not touch it, or you will die.'"

"You will not surely die," the serpent said to the woman.
"For God knows that when you eat of it your eyes will be
opened, and you will be like God, knowing good and evil"
(Gen. 3:1-5).

In the opening verses of Genesis 3, we hear the serpent's
cunning when he asks, "Did God really say?" This same question, is still the question the serpent asks us today to steal
God's plan.

And, like too many of our discussions with the serpent, Eve's
dialogue quickly digressed from a simple question about the
content of God's Word to a direct contradiction of His Word.
When the serpent said, "You will not surely die," he was no
longer simply questioning the Word of God, but saying that it
was wrong, and offering bait that appealed, oddly enough, to
Eve's love for God.

Notice that when the serpent was appealing to Eve to participate in the knowledge of good and evil, he did not directly
encourage her to rebel, become her own person, find herself, do
her own thing or go her own direction. Instead, he offered her
the knowledge of good and evil that would "open her eyes" and
make her more "like God." Satan appealed to Eve's love for God
and her desire to be like Him. The serpent appealed to her godliness to cause her to abandon the life God had given her and
enter into the knowledge of good and evil that had an appearance of godliness but in reality was void of His life.

When the woman saw that the fruit of the tree was good
for food and pleasing to the eye, and also desirable for
gaining wisdom, she took some and ate it. She also gave
some to her husband, who was with her, and he ate it.
Then the eyes of both of them were opened, and they realized they were naked; so they sewed fig leaves together
and made coverings for themselves (Gen. 3:6,7).

When I was a little boy my mother would sit me on her lap and read Bible storybooks to me that included the story of Adam and Eve. Throughout the years the pictures in these storybooks have been similar, and I think they have influenced the way we read the actual biblical account.

I vividly remember the picture of Adam standing behind a bush and Eve with long hair eating an apple. Because of that picture, every time I read Genesis 3, without thinking I would read "tree of knowledge of good and evil" as "apple tree." Whether this was a literal tree or not, no one knows. I still tend toward a literal interpretation. However, we must not neglect that the point here is consuming "knowledge of good and evil," not a piece of fruit.

I can understand why artists draw apple trees to portray this scene. The woman saw that the fruit of the tree was good for food and pleasing to the eye. With that sentence alone, it could have been an apple, orange, pear or peach tree. But when the Bible says that the tree of knowledge of good and evil had fruit that was desirable for gaining wisdom, it is obviously talking about more than fruit. The fruit that Eve partook could have actually been knowledge. Thus, for our purposes in contrasting the two trees, the tree of the knowledge of good and evil is a worldview, a system of thought, a set of ideas or values that we wrongly think will "open our eyes" and make us "more like God."

Without a doubt, different knowledge produces different outcomes. As medical students study, their eyes are opened to medical realities and, as a result, they are able to assist us with our physical bodies. Trained car mechanics have their eyes opened to the principles that make a car function properly, and the effect is that they know more about cars and trucks than the average person. Some brilliant minds understand the theories associated with Communism, and when they come into power a very different economic and social outcome surfaces than when others with brilliant minds who respect individuals and believe in free markets come into political power.

Knowledge always produces fruit of some kind. The fruit from the tree of the knowledge of good and evil was pleasant to consume and looked fine, and truly was desirable because it appeared to be "wisdom," but consuming this wisdom wasn't as positive as Eve believed it would be. She thought it would open her eyes and make her more like God. She trusted her own misguided judgment instead of trusting God's Word. As a result, she shared the knowledge of good and evil with her husband and their eyes were opened, and both of them were poisoned and began to die.

But the Bible says that they ate the fruit, and the pictures in Mom's storybook showed them eating apples. To eat something means to consume it, ingest it or devour it. Eating means that we take something that is outside ourselves and absorb it into our bodies or lives, to utilize it or take it for our own use. When we read our Bibles, we sometimes refer to it as "eating the Word." When we watch a video, read a book, listen to a teacher or engage in a lively discussion, we are eating knowledge, and that knowledge changes the way we see our world.

Just as the serpent promised, when Adam and Eve ate the knowledge of good and evil, their eyes were indeed opened and they realized they were naked. No doubt about it, they were indeed naked, and always had been. It was never an issue before, but now, with the knowledge of good and evil in their lives, it became a point of shame, and the Lord knew it would affect them that way; that's why he didn't want them to know it.

In Genesis 2:25 the Bible says that "The man and his wife were both naked, and they felt no shame." But in Genesis 3:7, after their eyes were opened because they consumed the knowledge of good and evil, the Bible says "they realized they were naked, so they sewed fig leaves together," in an inept attempt to cover themselves. In other words, they were ashamed of themselves and wanted to cover up. Their innocence was gone. Death had subtly entered through an errant attempt to "be more like God."

Then the man and his wife heard the sound of the Lord God as he was walking in the garden in the cool of the day, and they hid from the Lord God among the trees of the garden. But the Lord God called to the man, "Where are you?"

He answered, "I heard you in the garden, and I was afraid because I was naked; so I hid."

And he said, "Who told you that you were naked? Have you eaten from the tree that I commanded you not to eat from?" (Gen. 3:8-11).

HEAVEN'S SEARCH AND RESCUE TEAM: THE FATHER, SON AND HOLY SPIRIT

God in His sovereignty had to have known that neither Adam nor Eve had the capacity for an open, transparent, childlike relationship with Him any longer. They chose to reject His instructions, but He still came to find them. Here we have the beginning of God's search for disobedient, high-minded, self-reliant humankind. God did not shield Himself or isolate Himself from them. His holiness did not reject them, but rather His heart seemed to long for them. That's why He came looking for them, just as He does today.

God searching for wayward humanity in the garden is the reason most life-giving churches are missions-oriented, outreach-focused churches. God intentionally came to find Adam and Eve even though they sinned. When Jesus confirmed in John 15:16, "You did not choose me, but I chose you and appointed you to go and bear fruit—fruit that will last," He was confirming one more time that He searches for lost humanity.

God's attitude toward fallen humanity is clearly displayed in Philippians 2 where Paul describes Jesus coming as a servant to rescue humankind. Jesus says it Himself in Matthew 20:28 when He turned traditional authority structures upside down by saying, "Just as the Son of Man did not come to be served, but to serve, and to give his life as a ransom for many." Timothy repeats His heart again in 1 Timothy 2:3,4 where he writes, "This is good, and pleases God our Savior, who wants all men to be saved and to come to a knowledge of the truth."

As is our condition today, it was humankind that was hiding from God. Adam says that he was hiding because he was naked, and God doesn't dispute that fact. But there is a tone of hurt in God's voice, I think, when He says, "Who told you that you were naked?" And then the logical conclusion, "Have you eaten from the tree that I commanded you not to eat from?"

[WHEN] MY CHILDREN SHIELD THEIR
HEARTS FROM ME...I SEEK THEM OUT
AND TRY TO GET THEM TO TALK TO ME...
SO SHAME NEVER BOXES THEM INTO
ISOLATION FROM OTHERS.

Gayle and I have five perfect children, as you might imagine—four of whom are boys. On more than one occasion Gayle and I have been sitting in our living room with friends while our three youngest boys were supposed to be taking baths, only to have them come running down the stairs completely naked. Everyone always laughs as these little men dash through the house with their uncovered little bodies being hotly pursued by their embarrassed mother. It's all right because it's innocent. They're children.

On the other hand, sometimes I notice that my children shield their hearts from me. They hide. When that happens, I seek them out and try to get them to talk to me. Usually, something has happened that has placed a barrier between us, or maybe between them and everyone else. It's my responsibility as their father to coach them in living an honorable life so shame never boxes them into isolation from others.

I believe that's why God came looking for Adam and Eve. He knew they had filled themselves with knowledge of good and evil in their attempt to be more like Him. They had allowed the first ungodly stronghold in the human race to enter their lives in their ignoble pursuit of God. But they pursued Him according to what appeared to be "good" and "pleasing" and "desirable." Their pursuit didn't appear to be bad, painful or repulsive, but it was. It was a way of thinking that led to a set of poisonous conclusions.

Throughout the Old and New Testaments, the Holy Spirit clearly requires godly people to change their ways of thinking. The knowledge of good and evil is so deceptive and subtle, if we don't guard His life in our hearts by obeying His Word, we can become quickly deceived and find ourselves separated from life, which always has the same result: victimization. We either blame ourselves for everything going wrong, or we blame another. In Adam's case, he blamed Eve.

> The man said, "The woman you put here with me—she gave me some fruit from the tree, and I ate it."
>
> Then the Lord God said to the woman, "What is this you have done?"
>
> The woman said, "The serpent deceived me, and I ate" (Gen. 3:12,13).

THE KNOWLEDGE OF GOOD AND EVIL: THE TREE THAT CREATES SPIRITUAL ORPHANS

Here we see the second evidence that death was entering their hearts: They were blaming each other because they were not content with simple obedience and the life it afforded them. In

Paul's first letter to the church in Corinth, he discusses the war of ideas that must be fought. It's a battle of values, thoughts, principles and systems that either clears the way to find His life, or subtly begins to enslave us with a deceptive knowledge of good and evil that produces death in our spirits.

These systems of ideas are so strong and controlling that Paul calls them strongholds that must be demolished. But once we understand that life does not come from expertise in good and evil, but rather in revelation of life and death, then the mystery of genuine life is within our grasp and we may find the kingdom of God. Unless we understand the flow of life in contrast to the mechanics of death, we have little hope of ever leading a life-giving church.

> For though we live in the world, we do not wage war as the world does. The weapons we fight with are not the weapons of the world. On the contrary, they have divine power to demolish strongholds. We demolish arguments and every pretension that sets itself up against the knowledge of God, and we take captive every thought to make it obedient to Christ (2 Cor. 10:3-5).

It's the knowledge of good and evil that gives us a value system which tells us that we are naked and should hide from God. It's also the knowledge of good and evil that gives us the parameters with which to judge another so we can say "Eve did it," and "The snake did it." Disobedience gave Adam and Eve the ability to know, blame and judge, which led to God having to clearly articulate the consequences of their search for godliness in disobedience. The serpent was cursed (see Gen. 3:14,15), and both the man and the woman had the consequences of their disobedience listed for them by God (see vv. 16-19).

Then God displays, in type, that their own garments won't cover their sin because no blood was involved. So as another act of mercy, He covers them with garments of skin to remind us all that it is only through the blood of another that our shame can be covered. Then, at the end of the chapter, God limits humankind's access to the tree of life, so they won't live forever on their own without finding life in Christ Himself. Humankind no longer has access to life on their own, but now by knowing life Himself, Jesus, we can find eternal life.

> And the Lord God said, "The man has now become like one of us, knowing good and evil. He must not be allowed to reach out his hand and take also from the tree of life and eat, and live forever." So the Lord God banished him from the Garden of Eden to work the ground from which he had been taken. After he drove the man out, he placed on the east side of the Garden of Eden cherubim and a flaming sword flashing back and forth to guard the way to the tree of life (Gen. 3:22-24).

I love to travel all around the world, taking teams of intercessors to spiritually strategic sites to pray for the outpouring of the Holy Spirit. On those journeys, we've visited the places of worship of every major religion. In these sites, I find sincere people searching for God. Mosques, temples, churches and religious sites are used by millions of people daily, touching the spiritual world. Most of these worshipers pray, read holy books, burn candles, rub beads, give offerings, dip in rivers and pour water over statues in their deep pursuit of a relationship with the Almighty God. Few actually find Him, but they don't realize it because they experience a sense of spiritual fulfillment through the soulish satisfaction that comes from the tree of the knowledge of good and evil.
Most religious people know they have had a spiritual experience because it has enlightened them; it has opened their eyes and they know good and evil. They also know that their spiritual journey has given them satisfaction; it's been "good for food."

And, as with Eve, their spiritual devotion produces a positive change in their lives; it's "pleasing to the eye."

Unfortunately, these characteristics are universal in all religions, including Christianity. Many "Christians," Jewish believers, Islamic worshipers, adherents to Hinduism and Buddhism all enjoy the benefits and the consequences of the tree of the knowledge of good and evil. Only those who have pressed beyond religious practice and have come to know Him, the God of Abraham, Isaac and Israel, through His Son, Jesus, can know God. For it's in knowing Him that the mystery of genuine godliness starts to unfold. And it is, indeed, a relationship that is a narrow path—a path that can only be navigated according to the Scriptures by the Holy Spirit. It's easy, but it requires understanding relationships, not just creeds. That's why, after Genesis 3, the Bible begins telling the stories of God's encounters with people to teach us about Him. He's a person, we're people, and to have His life we must learn to know Him.

4

Our Mark: Innocence or Victimization?

And he [Jesus] said, "I tell you the truth, unless you change and become like little children, you will never enter the kingdom of heaven. Therefore, whoever humbles himself like this child is the greatest in the kingdom of heaven."

[*Matthew 18:3,4*]

It's a Heart Attitude

We all love to hear the children sing at Christmas time. I used to wonder why because they usually can't sing very well. They fidget, can't remember the words and are often so enamored with the crowd that they are usually distracted. But those things don't matter. They are cute, innocent, little children and we all love innocence.

In Matthew 19:14 Jesus said, "Let the little children come to me, and do not hinder them, for the kingdom of heaven belongs to such as these." Even David in Psalm 103 advances this idea when he writes, "Praise the Lord, O my soul...who satisfies your desires with good things so that your youth is renewed like the eagle's."

Many times when I see people come to Christ, they have a sinless look on their faces that communicates childlike innocence. They always look clean. Through the years I've noticed that believers who understand living in the tree of life have this same childlike purity about them. I'm convinced that innocence is the by-product of knowing Jesus, and the conduit for His anointing.

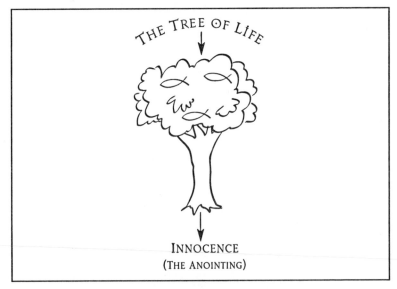

THE TREE OF LIFE

INNOCENCE
(THE ANOINTING)

From the lips of children and infants you have ordained praise (Matt. 21:16).

Men such as Billy Graham, T. L. Osborn and John Arnott from Toronto are great examples of the strength of innocence. They have remained untainted throughout years of ministry, which actually disturbs their critics. They respond to criticism with simple honesty, preventing it from hardening their hearts and ruining the anointing.

ONE OF THE GREATEST MARKS OF OUR
CHARACTER IS OUR RESPONSE TO
SOMEONE ELSE'S SIN.

Women such as Katherine Kuhlman, Ruth Graham and Freda Lindsey are the same way. Even though they are aware of their shortcomings, they have stayed above the seductions of the knowledge of good and evil and have remained free to minister His freedom. Throughout the years, all of these have maintained a simple childlikeness that allows the Holy Spirit to freely flow through them, and God likes that. Like children, they have more fun than most, and that's refreshing.

Two women can be standing outside an abortion clinic holding signs saying "Stop Abortion Now." Even though they are similarly dressed and are protesting the same problem, one may be in the tree of life and the other in the knowledge of good and evil. The difference is the motivation of their hearts.

The tree of life protester is there because of love and compassion for the mother, unborn child and even the father. She wants to try to help those struggling with their pregnancies. In contrast, the tree of knowledge of good and evil protester is there because abortion is evil, those who participate in it are evil, and they must be stopped. The tree of life protester will enjoy a sense of innocence and peace of heart, and the Lord will use her in a special way. She reflects Him. The other protester has fallen into the tree of the knowledge of good and evil and has squarely placed blame. She has identified the victim of her wrath and, in her self-righteousness, has inadvertently fallen into sin. This subtle difference of the heart is one of the most important biblical messages.

One way we can tell if we are enjoying the tree of life or suffering under the consequences of the knowledge of good and evil is our response to sin. Our response to our own sin can only adequately be settled in the life of Christ, but one of the greatest marks of our character is our response to someone else's sin. If we respond to our own sinfulness and to others' sin with life, then we can enjoy great power and freedom. If, however, our sin or someone else's sin traps us with a negative response, then we've eaten the wrong tree and have begun to die.

God warned Adam that eating from the tree of the knowledge of good and evil would kill him, and in Genesis 3 and 4 we see shame in Adam and Eve as they hide from God. Later, we see Cain killing Abel. Their eyes were opened, but they didn't become like God. Instead, they became like the one they chose to obey: The serpent. The accuser.

The serpent has not stopped. He still asks, "Did God really say?" and continues to offer anything that will draw people away from the life Christ offers. For some it's a good, religious life. For others it's good works in the secular world. For others, it's blatant evil. The serpent doesn't care as long as people don't find Christ's empowering life. Then he has accomplished his task of keeping people in darkness so they will spend eternity in hell. Jesus, however, wants people to come to Him and to receive life, knowing that His life is the only way we can live forever.

INNOCENCE

Staying innocent does not mean that we ignore or reject ideals of good and evil. In Genesis 4, God speaks clearly to Cain and explains that if he will do the right thing, then he will be accepted. God is not saying that doing the right thing is the life of God, but He is saying that there is a path to life. He continues in the same paragraph by explaining that sin is crouching at the door of our hearts and that we need to resist sin in order to pursue the will and plan of God.

Some people grow in their understanding of right and wrong from the tree of life and find great insight, wisdom, victory and joy in the stream of Jesus' righteousness. These people have a high view of right and wrong and use it to direct themselves and others toward life. Others, though, base their understanding of right and wrong in the wrong tree. This results in frustration, judgmental attitudes and ultimately death.

Both good and bad people are dead without life. Life comes from Christ alone, and His fruit is righteousness. His righteousness is the only place where we can find absolute right, which is our plumb line for right and wrong. If we don't understand His righteousness, as revealed both in the Scriptures and in our hearts through His Spirit, then any standard of right and wrong is merely subjective to our culture or our personal preferences. If we do, though, use a religious standard for right and wrong outside of Christ's life, we have found the knowledge of good and evil and will unknowingly begin going down the path that leads to death.

This process explains why some good people get so mean being good. We've all heard jokes about church secretaries, deacons' meetings and leaders who "love God" but can't constrain anger, bitterness or other areas of their sinful nature. All of these people have a form of godliness, but many times their attempt to be godly produces such anger and frustration that their actions deny the very power of God they had hoped to represent.

For as the Father has life in himself, so he has granted the Son to have life in himself (John 5:26).

In Galatians 5, the apostle Paul lists for us the acts of the sinful nature (see Gal. 5:19-21) and the fruit of the Spirit (see vv. 22-26). Most who study these two lists think of them as a list of evil things to avoid and a list of good things to do. Not so. Each list is a mirror that helps us see if we are living a spirit-filled life or not. Should our lives fall short, the message of the book of Galatians is to discover the truth of the gospel and be increasingly filled with the Holy Spirit so genuine freedom in Christ can be found (see v. 1).

That's why neither the Old Testament nor the New could simply give us a creed by which to live. It's more personal than that. The Scribes and the Pharisees, the Bible scholars of Jesus' day, didn't come close to understanding. So Jesus told them in John 5:39, "You diligently study the Scriptures because you think that by them you possess eternal life. These are the Scriptures that testify about me, yet you refuse to come to me to have life" (italics added).

It seems as though these good people studied the Scriptures diligently and missed the point completely, just as we so often do. They were neither studying the Scriptures nor living their lives in the tree of life, but were studying and living according to the tree of the knowledge of good and evil. That's why Jesus called them whitewashed tombs and vipers (see Matt. 23:27,33). Jesus rebuked the Bible scholars of His day for missing the primary messages of the Scriptures, but He loved the humble worshipers who had childlike hearts.

"I praise you, Father, Lord of heaven and earth, because you have hidden these things from the wise and learned, and revealed them to little children. Yes, Father, for this was your good pleasure" (Matt. 11:25,26).

It's important to understand that Jesus was not speaking against thoughtful examination of the Scriptures. Nor should we construe that God's warning about the knowledge of good and evil could be an exhortation to keep us from studying and gaining knowledge. He was simply emphasizing the necessity of a heart submitted and open to Him. That's why Jesus Himself had to display for us that the Word must be written in our hearts so believers actually become living epistles. We don't just read the Word and believe it, we become it through knowing Him. We're resurrected in His life.

To clarify this, Jesus emphasizes:

- "I am the *bread of life*" (John 6:35,48, italics added).
- "I am the *living bread* that came down from heaven. If anyone eats of this bread, he will live forever. This bread is my flesh, which I will give for the life of the world" (John 6:51, italics added).
- "I tell you the truth, unless you eat the flesh of the Son of Man and drink his blood, you have no life in you. Whoever eats my flesh and drinks my blood has *eternal life*, and I will raise him up at the last day. For my flesh is real food and my blood is real drink. Whoever eats my flesh and drinks my blood remains in me, and I in him. Just as the living Father sent me and I live because of the Father, so the one who feeds on me will live because of me. This is the bread that came down from heaven. Your forefathers ate manna and died, but he who feeds on this bread will live forever" (John 6:53-58, italics added).
- "I am the resurrection and the *life*. He who believes in me will live, even though he dies; and whoever lives and believes in me will never die. Do you believe this?" (John 11:25,26, italics added).
- "I am the way and the truth and the *life*. No one comes to the Father except through me" (John 14:6, italics added).

Jesus' teaching had to transition those who wanted a relationship with God from the tree of the knowledge of good and evil to the tree of life. Because much of Judaism had become a religion of "godly" action instead of a relationship with God, Jesus had to challenge the fundamental way the Scriptures were being applied. So He emphasized that without a relationship with Him, a relationship with the Father was impossible. That's why He said we had to eat His body and drink His blood. Christianity is more than an intellectual assent to the principles of the Bible; it requires actually consuming Him so His life dominates our lives. To gain life takes believing and more, it requires dying and becoming again, in Him. That's why He said He is:

- The Messiah (see John 4:26);
- The Light (see John 9:5);
- The Gate (see John 10:7);
- The Son of God (see John 10:36);
- The Lord (see John 13:13);
- The Way, the Truth, the Life (see John 14:6);
- The Vine (see John 15:1);
- The Alpha and the Omega (see Rev. 1:8,17).

Jesus gives us these metaphors to help us understand that only by knowing Him can we know His life. He is the source of living water (see John 4:10), which gives life (see Ezek. 47; Rev. 2 and 21). Paul communicates the necessity of knowing Him for the Jewish culture by contrasting attempts to be saved through obedience to the law and the assurance of salvation promised through the grace made available by the Cross. Genesis introduces the same principle with our choice between the tree of life, Jesus, and the tree of the knowledge of good and evil.

JOY VERSUS JUDGMENT

On occasion I have appeared to be like a monkey jumping between these two trees. I've been in the tree of life with the joy, innocence and anointing, only to have someone come up and say something critical to me. Immediately, I jumped out of the tree of life into the tree of the knowledge of good and evil and became sinfully defensive. I could feel a cloud of death starting to grow in my heart, and part of me liked the fight. But I was using the knowledge of good and evil to demonstrate how I was right and they were wrong. But in fact, I was right and wrong at the same time. At best, empty victory. I technically won, but I didn't. I started to die. I was right, *dead* right!

Now I've learned, though, when I'm criticized, to remain in the tree of life while responding. The innocence of that response leaves my heart clean and gives my critic a greater opportunity to find the tree of life as well. What a relief! With the tree of life I am still able to respond and explain, but everyone stays clean. That's genuine victory.

When we go to church in the tree of life, we are grateful for the congregation, grateful for the staff, grateful for the leadership, and want to make ourselves available to serve. It's a joy to give, a delight to worship, and easy to pray and fellowship with those around us. But attending church in "the tree of knowledge of good and evil" attitude is quite different: We go because of duty or obligation, not because we draw life from church. When we get there, we attend with a critical eye. So if the pastor, the volume or the temperature isn't correct, a sour spirit starts developing in our hearts. And, if a need surfaces somewhere in the church, rather than helping we criticize.

Bible reading can have the same dynamic. When I read the Bible from the tree of life perspective, joy is always evident. Like a child I submit to the Scriptures and let them speak deeply into my heart. I can always tell when I'm in the tree of life because I want to mark lots of the verses and make prolific notes. But I've had other times when I've read my Bible from the knowledge of good and evil point of view where I read it out of a duty or a goal or an obligation. The struggle of trying to get through a certain number of chapters or trying to read for a certain time period every day can be a source of death.

When I was in high school, I read a chapter from the Bible every night before I went to sleep, no matter where I had been, how late it was, or how tired I was. That was a blessing to me. Since then I have set goals that didn't add fresh life to my spirit but instead became a religious duty and obligation which actually darkened my spirit. If I were trying to read a certain number of chapters, I would find myself resenting long chapters rather than learning from them. Or, if I were trying to read my Bible for a certain time period, I noticed that time seemed to stop. It was hard work. But if I would stay in the tree of life, I found that I read more of the Bible for longer periods of time, using chapter goals or time goals simply as guidelines but never as the end in themselves. If the goal is anything other than Him, it quickly degenerates into religious legalism, which causes us to judge.

Prayer is the same way. "Tree of life" praying is when worship, intimacy, communion with the Father and an easy connection with the Spirit is natural. It's getting into your prayer closet and worshiping and praying until you are done. Tree of knowledge of good and evil praying is different. When you are driven to do it because you ought to do it, it becomes a miserable trap. You get into your prayer closet knowing that you have to pray for a certain period of time or get a certain list covered. It's dry, rote and lacks connection. It's satisfying to a degree, because it makes us feel as though we have done something good. This, however, is not nearly as satisfying as knowing His life.

- The purpose of serving is to reflect the life of God.
- The purpose of Bible reading is to learn the personality of God so His life can freely flow through us.
- The purpose of prayer is fellowship, friendship and communion. In prayer we confront demonic schemes

and commune with God. We engage darkness and grow in the Holy Spirit to become more effective vessels of His life.

However, in the tree of knowledge of good and evil, we mistakenly believe that doing good is an end in itself. It's good to go to church, protest abortion, pray and read our Bibles. It's good to be good. It's satisfying to be good. It looks good, tastes good and feels better than being evil. But goodness is not life unless it is a result of His life.

Living in the tree of life includes constructive discipline that makes us better people. When I pray, I ask God to convict me strongly so I can live in the refreshing of His Spirit and walk in His life. That conviction keeps me clean, and His discipline motivates me toward life.

Childlike innocence has an optimistic view of the future and learns the lessons from the past but doesn't let the failures or negativity of the past dictate our futures. It focuses on learning, growing and developing for a stronger future. It highlights sanctification as a positive process that protects our lives and ministries, and seems to always embrace light. Confession, healthy relationships and willingness to accept responsibility in order to correct a difficulty is inherent in tree of life living. Forgiveness, gratefulness, appreciation with its attending joy and peace allow innocence to reign as we live in the tree of life.

VICTIMIZATION

But the dangerous sword of victimization is birthed when we live according to the knowledge of good and evil. Sometimes victimization convinces us that we can't obey God because of someone else's actions or our personal weaknesses. Adam blamed Eve, Eve blamed the snake and Cain blamed Abel. Displacing responsibility never helps. As soon as we place blame, we are saying that

Jesus is not actually our Lord, but whoever or whatever it is that we are blaming really is.

Adam admitted that Eve was his lord instead of God. He obeyed her voice, not God's. Eve admitted that she allowed the serpent to be her lord instead of God. By Cain killing Abel, Cain let Abel

---

THE TREE OF KNOWLEDGE ALWAYS

MAKES US POINT AT SOMEBODY AND SAY,

"I CAN'T, BECAUSE THEY DIDN'T."

BUT THE TREE OF LIFE SAYS,

"I CAN, NO MATTER WHAT THEY DO."

---

become the lord of his attitudes and actions rather than God. We do the same thing when we blame the economy, deacons, the devil, witchcraft, negative social trends, our parents or our spouses. Whatever or whomever we blame, we place in lordship over us.

We are often more victimized by our own hearts than by what has happened to us.

The tree of knowledge always makes us point at somebody and say, "I can't, because they didn't." But the tree of life says, "I can, no matter what they do." That keeps them from being your lord, consuming your thoughts and controlling your life. The tree of life says, "If someone slaps you on one cheek, turn the other cheek, walk a mile with them, give them your cloak, and kiss them as you invite them to church." That drives demons crazy.

As a matter of fact, it drives people crazy who want to manipulate you into hating them. Some people will actually try to do something bad enough to you to gain control in your life. They will say bad things about you, knowing you will hear about it. If you respond according to the tree of the knowledge of good and evil and are hurt by them, they have, in effect, taken control of you. But if you stay in the innocence of the tree of life, they are frustrated because they can't get into you because you forgive and maintain your freedom.

That same deceptive sword of victimization can cut the other way as well. When it's not cutting against us, dethroning Christ in our hearts, it's causing us to use seemingly good things to cut against others around us. We become convinced that we have achieved some position in God that others haven't achieved; or that we are more obedient, disciplined or blessed. That superior tone will always backfire. Proverbs 16:18 says, "Pride goes before destruction, a haughty spirit before a fall."

For example, if I believe it is godly to read five chapters of the Bible a day, and I successfully read five chapters every day, I'll establish this as the standard for godliness. My knowledge of good and evil tells me that when I read my five chapters a day, God likes me and that I am walking secure in Him. When I meet other people, if they are reading their five chapters a day, then they meet the godly standard. But when I meet people who say they are Christians but are not reading five chapters a day, I somehow make sure they know that they should be reading five chapters a day in order to be a successful Christian. And, until they do that, they will not be as successful as I am. Even though that sounds good, it's deadly.

Victimization produces guilt and insists upon punishment. It provides fertile soil for the serpent to accuse and condemn. It always uses fear and causes people to focus on the past and dread the future. It finds fault, places blame and demands retribution whenever possible. Victimization loves the darkness so it entices us to hide portions of our lives, cover for failure and avoid personal responsibility.

Because victimization uses guilt, it prompts us to make promises that can't be kept, vows that will soon be broken and powerless ideals that cannot be fulfilled. Once broken, failure begins to define our view of ourselves and our relationship with God and others, causing us to lose the joy and peace that Christ intends through His sacrifice.

CHOOSE LIFE

When we choose life, we receive refreshing innocence that is a conduit for His anointing, which manifests by producing the fruit of the Spirit and His gifts. The mark on our lives is either innocence or victimization, and each receives strength from either the Holy Spirit or the darkness of our sinful natures. Life-giving churches freely operating in the gifts and displaying the fruit of the Spirit are what we all desire. The next chapter explains how we can grow in this dimension of His life.

5

Our Power: Spirit or Flesh?

He has made us competent as ministers
of a new covenant—not of the letter
but of the Spirit; for the letter kills,
but the Spirit gives life.

[*2 Corinthians 3:6*]

BE ON THE ALERT

A young graduate from seminary feels called by God to plant a church. He pursues this call with all his heart, knocking on doors, inviting people and meeting in a school cafeteria. The Lord blesses, and the little fellowship grows. People are saved, baptized, healed, delivered and the fruit and gifts of the Spirit flow beautifully.

Finally, several hundred people are attending regularly, and a permanent meeting place is clearly needed. The first building committee is formed. The members of the committee search for sites prayerfully, but a major split soon develops. Some want to build in the prospering suburbs, where most parishioners live, while others want to establish a place downtown to reach out to a needy community.

People take the debate very personally. One side argues, "We are going to lose people if they have to drive 45 minutes to get to church."

The other side responds, "God calls us to minister to those in need. A church in their neighborhood is the best way to do that."

The young pastor is in the middle, trying not to offend either side. Meanwhile, he finds his prayer life suffering. His chief concern is the next business meeting. He finds himself looking hard at the amount in the offering and wondering how to increase it.

Many churches and pastors start out in innocence with the Spirit of God moving there, but then an issue arises where people start judging and taking sides, and sinful bickering in God's name soon develops. At this point, demons have an opportunity to wreak havoc. On the other hand, this challenge provides an opportunity for a demonstration of the fruit and gifts of the Spirit. The power to choose lies with the pastor and the people.

This chapter will tell how the fruit and gifts of the Spirit increase when believers stay in the tree of life. It will also help you spot the warning signs that demonic opportunity has been allowed. Finally, I will briefly overview some specific issues that can either bring life or death to a church body as a whole.

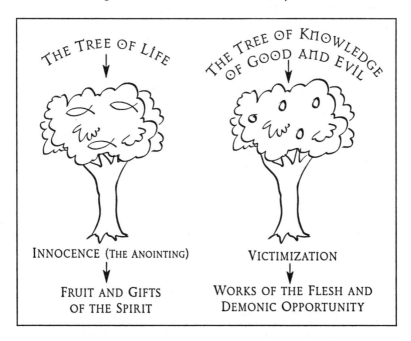

THE TREE OF LIFE

THE TREE OF KNOWLEDGE OF GOOD AND EVIL

INNOCENCE (THE ANOINTING)

VICTIMIZATION

FRUIT AND GIFTS
OF THE SPIRIT

WORKS OF THE FLESH AND
DEMONIC OPPORTUNITY

Then the angel showed me the river of the water of life, as clear as crystal, flowing from the throne of God and of the Lamb down the middle of the great street of the city. On each side of the river stood *the tree of life*, bearing *twelve crops of fruit*, yielding its fruit every month. And the leaves of the tree are for the healing of the nations (Rev. 22:1,2, italics added).

Bad decisions, regardless of the motivation, produce unintended consequences. If you don't make an effort otherwise, offenses will grow, become cancerous, destroy relationships and infect other people, and potentially the entire church. The Scripture warns about the root of bitterness that pollutes many (see Heb. 12:15).

When we make a decision to stay in the tree of life, any situation can refine our character and make us stronger people of God. Problems won't grasp us and control us and determine our futures. Instead we stay innocent so we can fulfill God's plan. When we stay innocent, the anointing of the Holy Spirit is free to flow.

The first step is to be filled with the Holy Spirit.
When I repented and asked Jesus to come into my heart, the Holy Spirit came into me and made me a new creation (2 Cor. 5:17; Rom. 8:16). The first people to experience this new birth, as we understand it as members of the New Testament Church, were the disciples. In John 20:22, Jesus breathed on them and said, "Receive the Holy Spirit." In that instant the disciples were just like we are as born again believers:

1. They had received the Holy Spirit (see John 20:22).
2. Their names had been written in heaven in the Lamb's Book of Life (see Luke 10:20).
3. They had already established a personal relationship with Jesus because He was with them physically (see Matt., Mark, Luke and John).

But Jesus commanded them to have an additional encounter with the Holy Spirit: "Do not leave Jerusalem, but wait for the gift my Father promised, which you have heard me speak about. For John baptized with water, but in a few days you will be baptized with the Holy Spirit" (Acts 1:4,5). Because they didn't understand the significance of what Jesus was asking them to do, the disciples began talking about Jesus' political takeover of Israel.

So Jesus redirected their attention by saying their role did not necessitate knowing the times and the dates, instead He pointed out that this baptism in the Holy Spirit was of supreme significance. In Acts 1:8, He returns to the subject and describes what will happen to them when they are baptized in the Holy Spirit:

"But you will receive power when the Holy Spirit comes on you; and you will be my witnesses in Jerusalem, and in all Judea and Samaria, and to the ends of the earth."

Because Jesus had already breathed on them and commanded them to receive the Holy Spirit in John 20:22, they already had the Holy Spirit. But Jesus wanted them to wait in Jerusalem for the gift the Father had promised. What gift was He talking about? The disciples already knew Jesus, so we know His relationship with them wasn't the gift. And they already had their names written in the Book of Life, so we know that eternal life wasn't the gift referred to here. In addition, they already had the Holy Spirit working in their lives, so that wasn't the gift of which Jesus was speaking. The only thing they hadn't received was this baptism in the Holy Spirit, which Jesus was comparing to John's baptism in water.

To ensure clarity, Jesus emphasized that the gift the Father had promised could be compared to the water baptism of John. Jesus said, "John baptized with water, but in a few days you will be baptized with the Holy Spirit" (Acts 1:5). The word baptism means to dip, immerse, sprinkle, submerge or dunk. In some cases it means to anoint. So Jesus' meaning was clear. Just as John the Baptist had been dipping, immersing, sprinkling, submerging and dunking people in water, in a few days the disciples were going to be dipped, immersed, sprinkled, submerged and dunked in the Holy Spirit. Just as the baptism of John had an anointing about it that prepared people for the coming of Christ, so the baptism in the Holy Spirit would carry its own anointing of fire.

Acts 2 tells the story that established the Church, as we know it today:

Suddenly a sound like the blowing of a violent wind came from heaven and filled the whole house where they were sitting. They saw what seemed to be tongues of fire that separated and came to rest on each of them. All of them were filled with the Holy Spirit and began to speak in

other tongues as the Spirit enabled them...."We (Jews who
spoke various languages) hear them declaring the wonders
of God in our own tongues!" Amazed and perplexed, they
asked one another, "What does this mean?" Some, however, made fun of them and said, "They have had too much
wine" (Acts 2:2-4,11-13).

Immediately Peter stood up and began preaching to the crowd
and explained, "These men are not drunk, as you suppose" (v. 15).
Then he began quoting from Joel 2:28-32 and explained that they
had been filled with the Holy Spirit, which was a fulfillment of
Jesus' instruction.

"In the last days, God says, I will pour out my Spirit on all
people. Your sons and daughters will prophesy, your young
men will see visions, your old men will dream dreams. Even
on my servants, both men and women, I will pour out my
Spirit in those days, and they will prophesy" (Acts 2:17,18).

It had happened. Humankind, fallen from the innocence of
the Garden of Eden, had now rediscovered the full measure of
life flowing from their hearts toward God. Jesus prophesied it in
John 7:38 and 39 when He said, "'Whoever believes in me, as the
Scripture has said, streams of living water will flow from within
him.' By this he meant the Spirit, whom those who believed in
him were later to receive. Up to that time the Spirit had not been
given, since Jesus had not yet been glorified."
But now Jesus has been glorified and we have the privilege of
being filled with the Holy Spirit. So to have life-giving churches,
we must have Spirit-filled people.
In order to maintain a Spirit-led attitude in my own life and
church, I pace myself with great care by scheduling my time according to priorities. I have a Bible and prayer plan that is life-giving and
refreshing. I enjoy praying and fasting, both alone and from time to

Encouraging Scriptures
About the Holy Spirit

I baptize you with water for repentance. But after me will come one who is more powerful than I, whose sandals I am not fit to carry. He will baptize you with the Holy Spirit and with fire (John the Baptist speaking, Matt. 3:11).

If you then, though you are evil, know how to give good gifts to your children, how much more will your Father in heaven give the Holy Spirit to those who ask him! (Jesus speaking, Luke 11:13).

I am going to send you what my Father has promised; but stay in the city until you have been clothed with power from on high (Jesus speaking, Luke 24:49).

And I will ask the Father, and he will give you another Counselor to be with you forever—the Spirit of truth. The world cannot accept him, because it neither sees him nor knows him. But you know him, for he lives with you and will be in you. I will not leave you as orphans; I will come to you (Jesus speaking, John 14:16-18).

But I tell you the truth: It is for your good that I am going away. Unless I go away, the Counselor will not come to you; but if I go, I will send him to you (Jesus speaking, John 16:7).

time with friends. I love praying with people in our church to assist them in being born again, filled with the Holy Spirit, and victorious over the sinful nature and demonic resistance. We are the Church, the only ones who can help others find liberty. And to fulfill our call, we must be filled with the Holy Spirit.

Unfortunately, this experience has been debated so much in the tree of the knowledge of good and evil that most believers think they are filled with the Holy Spirit if they simply believe what they view as the "correct interpretation" about this subject. But the Bible says we will know if we've been filled with the Holy Spirit by our fruit (see Matt. 7:16; John 15:2). The evidence doesn't lie (see Luke 6:43-45). So, if we don't have the fruit, we aren't filled. We will exhibit whatever is in our hearts. So if we are full of the Holy Spirit, we will demonstrate His life like rivers of living water.

The super-megachurches in Asia, Central and South America, and Africa that are experiencing exponential growth all encourage their people in lifestyles that cooperate with the power of the Holy Spirit. None of them are afraid of the person of the Holy Spirit or His manifestations. They understand that the gifts and fruit of the Spirit are vital necessities for the powerful life that Christians require.

Follow the way of love and eagerly desire spiritual gifts, especially the gift of prophecy (1 Cor. 14:1).

The Bible has several lists of the gifts or manifestations of the Holy Spirit's presence in our lives. The following are two of the passages with their references:

Now to each one the manifestation of the Spirit is given for the common good. To one there is given through the Spirit

- the message of wisdom, to another
- the message of knowledge by means of the same Spirit, to another

- faith by the same Spirit, to another
- gifts of healing by that one Spirit, to another
- miraculous powers, to another
- prophecy, to another
- distinguishing between spirits, to another
- speaking in different kinds of tongues, and to still another
- the interpretation of tongues.

All these are the work of one and the same Spirit, and he gives them to each one, just as he determines (1 Cor. 12:7-11).

We have different gifts, according to the grace given us. If a man's gift is...

- prophesying let him use it in proportion to his faith. If it is...
- serving, let him serve; if it is
- teaching, let him teach; if it is
- encouraging, let him encourage; if it is
- contributing to the needs of others, let him give generously; if it is
- leadership, let him govern diligently; if it is
- showing mercy, let him do it cheerfully (Rom. 12:6-8).

Once we are filled with the Holy Spirit and are operating in His gifts, the streams of living water flow naturally. We're to choose the tree of life, live in childlike innocence and seek the gifts of the Holy Spirit. As we enjoy the attending benefits, one of the greatest joys we can experience is the natural outcome of His power in us.

But the fruit of the Spirit is love, joy, peace, patience, kindness, goodness, faithfulness, gentleness and self-control. Against such things there is no law (Gal. 5:22).

The wonderful truth about the fruit of the Spirit is that it is just that, fruit. We can't ask for it, receive it through divine impartation, learn it or create it. It is the result, the effect, the product of His power working through us in normal life situations. And it is always tested.

- Love is tested by our desire to take care of ourselves or those near to us in preference to those who are outside of our own circle of friends.
- Joy is tested when everything goes wrong.
- Peace is tested when we have too much to do.
- Patience is tested when we're in a hurry.
- Kindness is tested when someone needs a firm hand.
- Goodness is tested when we want attention ourselves.
- Faithfulness is tested when loyalty has run out.
- Gentleness is tested when we're feeling harried.
- Self-control is tested when no one is watching.

Unfortunately, some have read lists like this from the tree of the knowledge of good and evil and have attempted to attain these virtues through their own strength, only to fail. Rather than enjoying life and easily producing fruit, they are actually living in death while trying to produce godly fruit—and it doesn't work. The resulting frustration opens the door to the acts of the sinful nature and demonic opportunity, which is the final consequence of choosing the wrong tree.

Throughout the Bible we see supposedly godly people dominated by their old sin natures oftentimes becoming influenced by demonic activity. Even our current generation has been embarrassed by Christian leaders whose personal lives revealed that they didn't know the power of God in a life-giving way and were trapped in ungodliness.

Not only individuals but entire churches and movements can also fall into this rigid, religious trap. Remember the story of

Mrs. Morgan, the church secretary at St. Peter's church, who was faithfully serving in a life-giving church. St. Peter's had a sister church that believed the same creed but didn't enjoy the anointing of the Holy Spirit and thus, had lost its innocence, and neither the fruit nor the gifts were evident within that Body.

ONCE WE FALL INTO VICTIMIZATION...IT'S ONLY A MATTER OF TIME BEFORE THE SINFUL NATURE AND THE EVIDENCES OF DEMONIC INVASION BEGIN TO MANIFEST.

Once we fall into victimization and lose the childlike freedom that Jesus provides, it's only a matter of time before the sinful nature and the evidences of demonic invasion begin to manifest. Many times we'll try to maintain a clean exterior appearance but in our hearts greed and self-indulgence slowly take root. As time progresses in the knowledge of good and evil, hypocrisy, public positioning, secrecy and at times seeds of blatant wickedness begin to grow. The Bible says in Galatians 5:19-21: "The acts of the sinful nature are obvious: sexual immorality, impurity and debauchery; idolatry and witchcraft; hatred, discord, jealousy, fits of rage, selfish ambition, dissensions, factions and envy; drunkenness, orgies, and the like."

Lists such as this that warn us are common in the Scriptures. Revelation 21:8 says, "But the cowardly, the unbelieving, the vile, the murderers, the sexually immoral, those who practice magic arts, the idolaters and all liars—their place will be in the fiery lake of burning sulfur. This is the second death."

Jesus emphasized the importance of clean living when He said,

"If your hand causes you to sin, cut it off. It is better for you to enter life maimed than with two hands to go into hell, where the fire never goes out...And if your foot causes you to sin, cut it off. It is better for you to enter life crippled than to have two feet and be thrown into hell...And if your eye causes you to sin, pluck it out. It is better for you to enter the kingdom of God with one eye than to have two eyes and be thrown into hell, where 'their worm does not die, and the fire is not quenched'" (Mark 9:43,45,47,48).

How then can we be saved? Only by consuming Jesus as He is found in the Scriptures and being empowered by His Spirit, the Holy Spirit. Every other attempt leads to failure.

GOD'S POWER VERSUS HUMAN GOODNESS

Islam has a well-meaning but harsh religious code that attempts to keep people holy. Because of their attempt to please God, they pray five times a day, wrap their women in black robes and limit exposure to every potential vice. They block the sale of alcohol and pornography. They teach and try to practice many notable disciplines, but haven't found life. Many are angry, bitter religious zealots; others go through the motions but in actuality have given up. They can't do it.

Every other religion is the same. From the Hindu and Buddhist temples to the Jewish synagogues to many Christian churches, we find people learning to live better lives, but finding at best a "knowledge of good and evil" which satisfies to a degree but does not offer the liberating life that transforms hearts.

Last October while in Nepal we observed the sacrifice of chickens and goats to idols. No life. No healing. No power. The worshipers even admitted to us that their gods never answer prayer and the blood of the goats doesn't help them. But they still do it because the knowledge of good and evil satisfies their soulish desire to seek God.

In the same way some Christians recite words, rub beads, pray to statues and give, hoping that God will respond to them. Their religious rituals offer no more life than those of an Islamic, Buddhist or Hindu worshiper. All are worshiping out of the tree of the knowledge of good and evil unless they go beyond the routine and find life Himself, Jesus. To know Him and the power of His resurrection requires openness to His Spirit and a freedom in His life, so His gifts and fruit can freely develop. Then and only then is God's life adequately infused into the worshiper and displayed in genuine ministry.

The apostle Paul said it clearly when he wrote in Romans 8:1-8,12-17, "Therefore, there is now no condemnation for those who are in Christ Jesus, because through Christ Jesus the law of the Spirit of life set me free from the law of sin and death. For what the law was powerless to do in that it was weakened by the sinful nature, God did by sending his own Son in the likeness of sinful man to be a sin offering. And so he condemned sin in sinful man, in order that the righteous requirements of the law might be fully met in us, who do not live according to the sinful nature but according to the Spirit.

"Those who live according to the sinful nature have their minds set on what that nature desires; but those who live in accordance with the Spirit have their minds set on what the Spirit desires. The mind of sinful man is death, but the mind controlled by the Spirit is life and peace; the sinful mind is hostile to God. It does not submit to God's law, nor can it do so. Those controlled by the sinful nature cannot please God.

"Therefore, brothers, we have an obligation—but it is not to the sinful nature, to live according to it. For if you live according to the sinful nature, you will die; but if by the Spirit you put to death the misdeeds of the body, you will live, because those who are led by the Spirit of God are sons of God. For you did not receive a spirit that makes you a slave again to fear, but you received the Spirit of sonship. And by him we cry, 'Abba, Father.'

The Spirit himself testifies with our spirit that we are God's children. Now if we are children, then we are heirs—heirs of God and co-heirs with Christ, if indeed we share in his sufferings in order that we may also share in his glory."

This passage explains why life-giving churches must be saturated in the Word of God and filled with the Spirit. If not, the sinful nature takes over and demonic activity becomes evident. The apostle Paul warned the church at Ephesus not to give the devil a foothold (see Eph. 4:27) before he emphasized to them that their struggle was not with one another but against spiritual forces looking for an opportunity to weaken, and if possible destroy, the church (see Eph. 6:10-18). James repeats this warning when he writes "Submit yourselves, then, to God. Resist the devil, and he will flee from you" (Jas. 4:7).

How do we know when the enemy has been given a place in our lives and our churches? When we see people becoming critical, unsatisfied, beginning to be hypersensitive and harsh in their defense of what they believe is "godly." When I pray for the believers who worship at New Life, I ask God to protect them and keep them in life-giving relationship with Him and with their brothers and sisters in Him. I also pray the Word will stay alive in them and that all demonic forces will be thwarted in their schemes to paralyze Christians.

The enemy is aggressive and powerful, ready to capitalize on every area of weakness. So if we allow religious footholds to begin in our hearts and consequently in our churches, it's only a matter of time before our church will no longer be life-giving but rather dead, regardless of our creed. Therefore, we must be diligent to pursue His life, His innocence, His anointing, His gifts and allow the fruit of His Spirit to freely flow so the kingdom of God is manifested in people's hearts with the accompanying evidence of good works birthed by His Spirit.

SECTION II

PHILOSOPHY FOR
LIFE-GIVING MINISTRY

6. Relationships That Empower

7. Characteristics That Protect

8. Etiquette That Sustains

This section provides practical examples of life-giving ministry that apply to every area of life. With relationships, characteristics and etiquette well understood, nothing can prevent us from continuing to grow and minister in His life.

6

———

RELATIONSHIPS
THAT EMPOWER

TWO ARE BETTER THAN ONE, BECAUSE THEY HAVE
A GOOD RETURN FOR THEIR WORK: IF ONE FALLS
DOWN, HIS FRIEND CAN HELP HIM UP. BUT PITY
THE MAN WHO FALLS AND HAS NO ONE TO HELP
HIM UP! ALSO, IF TWO LIE DOWN TOGETHER, THEY
WILL KEEP WARM. BUT HOW CAN ONE KEEP WARM
ALONE? THOUGH ONE MAY BE OVERPOWERED, TWO
CAN DEFEND THEMSELVES. A CORD OF THREE
STRANDS IS NOT QUICKLY BROKEN.

[*Ecclesiastes 4:9-12*]

THE DIVINE FLOW OF RELATIONSHIPS

Moses knew he couldn't do it alone. He didn't speak well; he knew Pharaoh was the most powerful man in the world; he also knew that Egypt would not release the children of Israel. God strengthened Moses by adding Aaron to Moses' calling. Aaron strengthened Moses, and together, they liberated Israel.

"Relationships are the only thing we take to heaven with us," an old Baptist preacher once said. I've heard businesspeople say that everything they know is subordinated to their people skills. If they can't relate well with people, their ability to provide goods and services to others is greatly hampered. A board member of one of the world's largest corporations told me that people who understand relationships are the ones who enjoy true success.

Some grumble that success is too often based on "who" we know rather than "what" we know. I think it's a fact. Even our eternal destinies are determined by our personal relationships with Christ. If we know Him, we go to heaven. If we don't, we don't.

Several years ago I read a little booklet by John Osteen, a pastor in Houston, Texas, entitled *The Divine Flow*. This booklet explains how the Holy Spirit creates a divine flow between people's hearts that, if responded to properly, can supernaturally build relationships. He explains that we can often determine God's perfect plan in building purposeful relationships for His kingdom by learning to respond to the divine flow in our hearts.

Pastor Osteen develops the idea further by applying it to our relationships within the Church. He says we should learn to sense God's divine flow toward other people because it may mean we are supposed to work together in a meaningful way in His kingdom. Sometimes this divine flow feels like a welling up of love, or a desire to devote special attention toward a particular person. Other times the divine flow causes us to have an unusual interest in another person.

Several years ago I was asked to speak for the Godly Men's Conference at Oral Roberts University. During the meeting I noticed a divine flow in my heart toward the worship leader, Ross Parsley, who is now a trusted friend and the worship pastor here at New Life. In that same series of meetings, a student working outside the chapel, Russ Walker, caught my attention. He is now my associate who oversees our small group ministry.

The flow can happen both ways. Another student who attended the conference, John Bolin, had a miracle happen in his heart that touched his spirit. He felt a sense of being connected with me, even though we hadn't met. Now, years later, he and his wife, Sarah, have moved to Colorado Springs and serve as our youth pastors. Joseph Thompson, another associate pastor, read my book *Primary Purpose,* and experienced a powerful sense of connectedness with me. As a result, he and his family are now here powerfully serving in God's work.

Life-giving ministry flows through godly relationships, not corporate structures. Corporate structures give us order and define our roles, but relationships empower us. It's the relationships with family members, elders, staff members, community leaders, the press and volunteers that are the core of life-giving ministries. When God creates supernatural relationships to make us more effective—if they are honorably maintained—they can empower and enable us to fulfill God's calling.

The following are seven sets of relationships that empower successful life-giving ministry. All of these relationships funnel people toward eternal life through Christ, and the more levels we understand, the more effective our ministries. As you read the list, notice that each additional level of relationships has increased breadth of impact, and each level requires its own revelation. These relationships are the way God strengthens us to fulfill His calling. He wants us to understand and flow in relationships that empower us to do what He wants done.

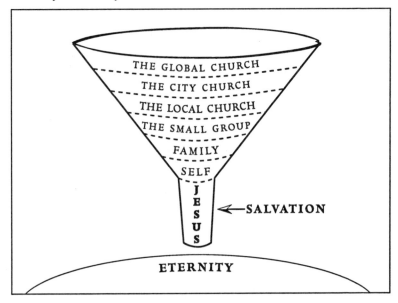

Relationship #1: Jesus
Result: Salvation

> "I am the good shepherd; I know my sheep and my sheep know me—just as the Father knows me and I know the Father—and I lay down my life for the sheep" (John 10:14,15).

In order to have a life-giving ministry, we must be confident that we have been born again into a vital relationship with Christ. In this generation of "easy-believism," many people think they have been born again, when in fact, they have not. Jesus said in Matthew 7:21-23, "Not everyone who says to me, 'Lord, Lord,' will enter the kingdom of heaven, but only he who does the will of my Father who is in heaven. Many will say to me on that day, 'Lord, Lord, did we not prophesy in your name, and in your name drive out demons and perform many miracles?' Then I will tell them plainly, 'I never knew you. Away from me, you evildoers!'"

When Jesus gave us the Great Commission to reach the world, He said, "Go and make *disciples* of all nations, *baptizing them* in the name of the Father and of the Son and of the Holy Spirit, and *teaching them* to obey everything I have commanded you" (Matt. 28:19,20, italics added). Note that He did not say, "Go into all the world and have people repeat a salvation prayer."

Because many misread the Great Commission, millions of people believe they are born again, but they neither know Him nor live lives that have been transformed by the power of the Holy Spirit (see 2 Cor. 5:17). Philippians 2:12 says, "Therefore, my dear friends, as you have always obeyed—not only in my presence, but now much more in my absence—continue to work out your salvation with fear and trembling, for it is God who works in you to will and to act according to his good purpose."

Prayer, expressing our heart's repentance, is without a doubt the way we are all born again. But being born again is only the doorway to the ultimate purpose of knowing Him. If we guarantee people that they have begun a relationship with Christ and have received eternal life just because they repeated a prayer, we might be assuming too much. There is no way for any of us to know the condition of another person's heart. So when repeating or reading a prayer, some do begin their relationship with Christ, but others don't. The horrific reality might be that if they were just repeating words and we tell them they are now guaranteed eternal life, we might be giving them false assurance that could contribute to their going to hell. We as life givers point the way and direct people to Christ, but each individual must faithfully pursue his or her own relationship with Christ and work out his or her own salvation with fear and trembling.

In 1972 I prayed to receive Christ along with thousands of other high school students at Explo '72 in Dallas, Texas. In that prayer, I expressed my love for Christ and my desire to have Him live in me. Upon returning home, I started going to church and reading my Bible, but my internal life did not change. I didn't stop any of my normal non-Christian high school student activities. I was fully liv-ing in the world but involved in the Bible and church. Then, after my senior year of high school, my pastor led me in a prayer to "sell out," to commit my entire life to Christ. After that prayer, my life dramatically changed—evidence of becoming a new creation.

So, when did I become a Christian? I tell people I got saved at Explo '72, but something makes me wonder if Explo '72 didn't begin a process that led to a genuine conversion experience two years later. I don't know with assurance, and I don't want to endlessly discuss the salvation process here. But I do want to emphasize that in order to have life-giving churches, we need to know, with absolute assurance and evidence in our hearts and lifestyles, that we are securely and verifiably in a dynamic relationship with Christ.

Jesus is the cornerstone of the Church. Our relationship with Him is foundational to every other relationship we have; it empowers us to assist others. Once our relationship with Him is secure and growing, then He is able to create and maintain all of our other relationships, which will create healthy ministry. He is the life giver for all life-giving relationships. He is the foundation of every life-giving church.

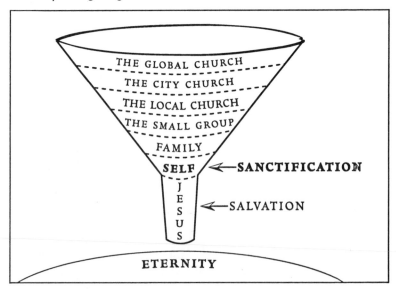

Relationship #2: Self
Result: Sanctification

> May God himself, the God of peace, sanctify you through and through. May your whole spirit, soul and body be kept blameless at the coming of our Lord Jesus Christ (1 Thess. 5:23).

Every growing Christian knows the war that can sometimes develop between our spirits, our souls (sometimes defined as our minds, wills and emotions) and our bodies. When we come to Christ, our spirit becomes a new creation, but the soulish portions of our lives and bodies are still just as they were before conversion. That is why Christian growth over time is required to settle internal conflicts so we can safely minister to others. The reason the Bible lists qualifications for eldership and standards for Christian leaders is not because of God's struggle in dealing with sinful humanity, but because certain lifestyles give us credibility in the hearts of other people. Personal sanctification validates His message through us. Therefore, if we attempt to minister without internalizing His life to some degree of comfort, we can horribly embarrass the Body of Christ.

First Thessalonians directly addresses this issue by saying, "It is God's will that you should be sanctified: that you should avoid sexual immorality; that each of you should learn to control his own body in a way that is holy and honorable, not in passionate lust like the heathen, who do not know God; and that in this matter no one should wrong his brother or take advantage of him. The Lord will punish men for all such sins, as we have already told you and warned you. For God did not call us to be impure, but to live a holy life" (4:3-7).

Only time, trial and error, failing and trying again, thinking, praying, talking and sharing with others in the Body can work sanctification into our lives.

Jesus emphasized the role of the Word in the process of sanctification in His John 17:17 prayer, "Sanctify them by the truth; your word is truth."

Peter emphasized the role of the Spirit when he said that we have been chosen "according to the foreknowledge of God the Father, through the sanctifying work of the Spirit, for obedience to Jesus Christ and sprinkling by his blood: Grace and peace be yours in abundance" (1 Pet. 1:2).

The book of Hebrews emphasizes the role of the relationships within the Body of Christ (see 10:19-39) by explaining how God's righteousness is integrated into every area of our lives. Within the heart of this discussion, Hebrews 10:25 says, "Let us not give up meeting together, as some are in the habit of doing, but let us encourage one another—and all the more as you see the Day approaching."

As we grow in Christ, He establishes His lordship over our bodies, minds, wills and emotions, so our lives become increasingly productive. If these internal conflicts are not settled, we may become spiritual time bombs, potentially destructive to His kingdom. Thus, in order to build a life-giving church, we must consistently allow the Word, the Spirit and healthy relationships within the church to keep our lives in harmony so His life-giving Spirit can flow unhindered through us.

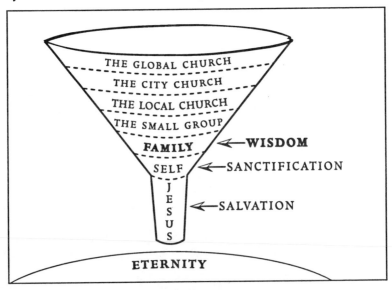

Relationship #3: Your Family
Result: Wisdom

> He [an overseer] must manage his own family well and see
> that his children obey him with proper respect. (If anyone
> does not know how to manage his own family, how can
> he take care of God's church?) (1 Tim. 3:4,5).

Even though the traditional family is under siege by western culture, the relational dynamics of a traditional family are invaluable
and must be preserved within our Christian community. A husband and a wife in relationship with their children have a greater
potential for success because the home is the primary place God
designed to train all of us in positive, healthy relationships.

Every relational dynamic we need can be developed within the
school of the home. For example, Paul says in Ephesians 5:22-33
that the relationship between the husband and the wife is to
model the relationship that exists between Christ and the Church.
This dynamic provides the insights into God's love for His people,
servant-style leadership, our love for one another, compassion,
caring, intimacy, respect and giving. Biblical references to intimacy, acceptance, boundaries, affection and rejection, and other significant emotions and attitudes reflect God's love for His people
and His desire for intimacy with them. These characteristics are
most powerfully integrated into our lives through our marriages.

Gayle and I have five children. Before our children came along
I thought the role of parents was to help their children grow up. I
have discovered that this is only partially true. I now know that the
role of children is to force their parents to grow up. You can't be
selfish and successfully raise children.

Children teach us how to live for others and how to relate to
various ages. Babies don't care about income, titles or influence.
They demand our attention and respect. If we withhold it, they'll
punish us. And these lessons apply to every child in relationships
with siblings as well.

In our home, Christy is 16, Marcus is 15, Jonathan is 10, Alex is 7 and Elliott is 5. When any of them fight, they must settle their differences without leaving. Divorces are not allowed. No one can leave home while fighting. Everyone must realize that in order to play happily, we all have to adjust to and understand one another. And we have to know who is in charge. If any of us becomes selfish, the home becomes unhappy for everyone. If a job needs to be done, it is accomplished with greatest ease when we all work together.

Family dynamics provide the wisdom for successfully leading a healthy church. The home should spawn rules of decency, kindness, respect, honor and contentment—all necessary for a life-giving church. The balance of law and grace, autocratic rule and group dynamics, giving justice and the positive role of discipline are principles we all must learn in order to have a healthy home and church.

If the discriminating insights required to maintain long-term relationships are not learned at home, divorce or hurt will follow. The same holds true for the church, and the potential for separation, broken relationships and wounded hearts increases. I am not saying that our families must be perfect to function normally in a life-giving church. I am saying, though, that the wisdom learned

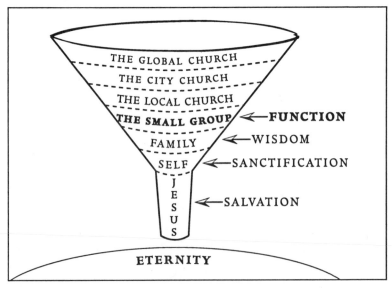

through the family dynamic is invaluable to understanding how to build and maintain the relationships required to have a long-term, life-giving church.

Relationship #4: The Small Group
Result: Function

> As iron sharpens iron, so one man sharpens another (Prov. 27:17).

Every successful church has some method for helping people to meet and form dynamic friendships within the Body. Some

———

ANY DEMON, NO MATTER HOW WEAK,

CAN PENETRATE A CORPORATE STRUCTURE.

BUT NO DEMON, NO MATTER HOW STRONG,

CAN PENETRATE A GENUINE FRIENDSHIP.

———

churches use cells or other small groups to accomplish this goal, while others use Sunday School classes. But every successful pastor knows that friendships within the Body are what hold the church together and cause it to function.

To emphasize my strong belief in friendships, I often say, "Any demon, no matter how weak, can penetrate a corporate structure. But no demon, no matter how strong, can penetrate a genuine friendship." At New Life, 392 small groups meet every week. Because of those groups, new friendships are constantly forming, helping our church family to stay strong and healthy.

Many of the great Bible heroes understood genuine friendships. Ruth 1:16 says, "Don't urge me to leave you or to turn back from you. Where you go I will go, and where you stay I will stay. Your people will be my people and your God my God." First Samuel 20:17 is one of many verses that talk about the way David and Jonathan strengthened one another. Here the Bible says, "Jonathan had David reaffirm his oath out of love for him, because he loved him as he loved himself."

The Gospels make note of several of the friendships Jesus maintained. Some just wanted to serve the Lord, while others were His disciples. Matthew 27:55 says, "Many women were there, watching from a distance. They had followed Jesus from Galilee to care for his needs." In the Garden of Gethsemane, Jesus wanted His closest friends, Peter, James and John, with Him. He drew strength from His friends, just as we do (see Matt. 26:36-46).

Strong healthy friendships make all of us more secure, positive, productive and effective than we could ever be alone. They produce an upward synergy that activates strength. Paul was very frank about his relationships with the church at Philippi when he wrote in Philippians 1, "I thank my God every time I remember you. In all my prayers for all of you, I always pray with joy because of your partnership in the gospel from the first day until now,...It is right for me to feel this way about all of you, since I have you in my heart;...God can testify how I long for all of you with the affection of Christ Jesus. And this is my prayer: that your love may abound more and more in knowledge and depth of insight" (vv. 3-5,7-9). Paul understood the importance of the divine flow and genuine friendships.

These friendships teach us how to function in the calling God has given us. In small groups we refine the righteousness God is working into our lives in a practical way. In small groups we learn how to apply the lessons we have learned in our walk with Christ to our family relationships. In small groups we incorporate life lessons into our public lives. Honest friendships keep us from being deceived or diluted into hypocrisy. My friends sharpen me and help me see the blind spots, making me a more capable person. Small groups are the strength of the local church. They keep it from evolving into a simple religious organization, and keep it functioning as a life-giving Body linked together with positive relationships.

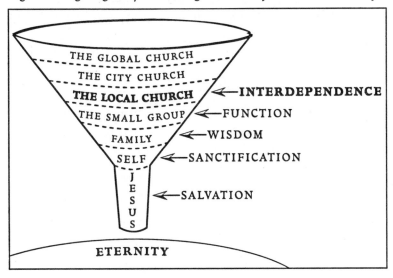

Relationship #5: The Local Church
Result: Interdependence

> It was he who gave some to be apostles, some to be prophets, some to be evangelists, and some to be pastors and teachers, to prepare God's people for works of service, so that the body of Christ may be built up until we all reach unity in the faith and in the knowledge of the Son of God and become mature, attaining to the whole measure of the fullness of Christ....From him the whole body, joined and held together by every supporting ligament, grows and builds itself up in love, as each part does its work (Eph. 4:11-13,16).

Our local churches are God's storehouses of dynamic power for learning to function in the strength of interdependence. In 1 Corinthians 12, the Bible reminds us that we are a Body with many members, which only functions when working together. By worshiping, giving, learning and growing together as a local church, our cumulative impact dramatically increases. In local churches, our unified prayer, financial strength and mutual encouragement causes us to form a Body of Christians capable of accomplishing tasks that would be impossible in small groups.

Ephesians 4:16 emphasizes the role of interdependent relationships within the local church when it talks about the Body being "joined and held together by every supporting ligament." Those supporting ligaments are the healthy relationships within the Body that cause it to grow, build itself up and work. God's plan for His people cannot be fulfilled unless we gather as a local church so the apostles, prophets, evangelists, pastors and teachers can equip us to effectively work in His kingdom.

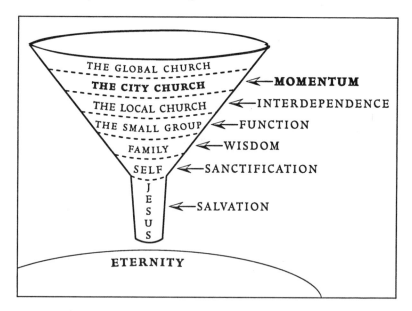

Relationship #6: The City Church
Result: Momentum

To the angel of the church in Ephesus, Smyrna, Pergamum, Thyatira, Sardis, Philadelphia and Laodicea write (see Rev. 2:1,8,12,18; 3:1,7,14).

All around the world the Holy Spirit is speaking to the Body about forming citywide coalitions of local churches to promote evangelism. These coalitions are groups of churches that strengthen one another by forming strategic alliances. The coalition of churches in Colorado Springs has three goals:

1. We pray for every person in our city by name at least once a year;
2. We communicate the gospel, in an understandable way, to every person in our city at least once a year; and
3. We want an additional 1 percent of our city's population attending church on an average weekend by the end of each year. For our city, that means an additional 3,500 people saved and discipled in our churches citywide every year.

To achieve these goals, we have several networks of churches that coordinate our citywide efforts. Individually, our churches could not have accomplished these goals; but as a group of churches, we can achieve them with relative ease. This network of relationships makes all of our jobs simpler, and causes our churches to grow through conversion growth rather than competing for transfer growth.

Just as individual Christians need to connect with others in a healthy local church in order to grow strong, so local churches can connect with other local churches to become increasingly effective. My book *Primary Purpose* (Creation House) discusses "how to make it hard to go to hell from your city." Jack Hayford and I coauthored a book on city strategies entitled, *Loving Your City into the Kingdom* (Regal Books), an excellent resource for all Christians. Bill Bright, Peter Wagner, Ed Silvoso, George Otis, Jr., George Barna and others contributed to this book. Another recommended resource for city strategies is Ed Silvoso's book *That None Should Perish* (Regal Books).

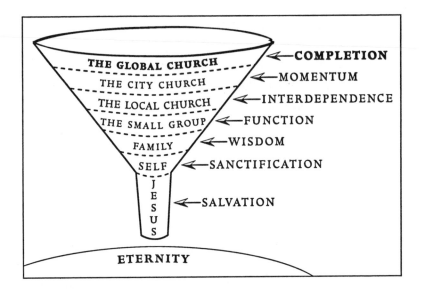

Relationship #7: The Global Church
Result: Completion

> After this I looked and there before me was a great multi-
> tude that no one could count, from every nation, tribe,
> people and language, standing before the throne and in
> front of the Lamb. They were wearing white robes and
> were holding palm branches in their hands (Rev. 7:9).

The final set of relationships needed to empower us for effective
ministry is the network of relationships we as local churches
form to enable missionary activities. These efforts require local
churches to take a portion of their tithes and strategically use the
money to ensure that every person living in our generation has
an opportunity to hear the gospel. This level of relationships fur-
thers our efforts to fulfill the Great Commission: "Go and make
disciples of all nations, baptizing them in the name of the Father
and of the Son and of the Holy Spirit, and teaching them to obey
everything I have commanded you" (Matt. 28:19,20). To fulfill this
task, we must work in harmony with the other members of the

Body of Christ in increasingly broader relationships. By working as members of the global church, the city church, the local church, the small group and the family, we can see Jesus' calling on our lives fulfilled.

Some will argue against various levels of these increasingly empowering relationships. However, I believe as we receive the revelation from His Spirit and the Scriptures about our purpose in His kingdom, it becomes evident that each of these sets of relationships are vital to His purpose and are dependent upon one another. Relationships are not optional for any of us as Christians. Productive, empowering relationships make ministry easy, delightful and efficient with maximum breadth of impact— they are foundational to building a life-giving church.

7

CHARACTERISTICS
THAT PROTECT

YOU [CHRIST] ARE THE MOST EXCELLENT OF MEN
AND YOUR LIPS HAVE BEEN ANOINTED WITH GRACE,
SINCE GOD HAS BLESSED YOU FOREVER. GIRD YOUR
SWORD UPON YOUR SIDE, O MIGHTY ONE; CLOTHE
YOURSELF WITH SPLENDOR AND MAJESTY. IN YOUR
MAJESTY RIDE FORTH VICTORIOUSLY IN BEHALF OF
TRUTH, HUMILITY AND RIGHTEOUSNESS; LET YOUR
RIGHT HAND DISPLAY AWESOME DEEDS.

[*Psalm 45:2-4*]

Systems That Wound

Pastor Bowen watched from an upstairs window as one of the volunteers from the nursery got into her car with her three children. With snow blowing all around her, the mother carefully buckled each child safely into their old, rusted family vehicle with balding tires. After the car had a chance to warm up, it slowly crept out of the church parking lot headed for home.

Because this mom had been faithfully serving in the nursery, and obviously needed better transportation, the pastor wanted to buy the family a new set of tires, or maybe even replace their car with a newer model. Then the process started....Board members wondered if they were setting a precedent that would result in trouble with other moms in the church. Others wondered if helping this family was the wisest expenditure of church finances. Some even questioned the true faithfulness of the mother!

Pastor Bowen understood the reasoning for systems that would not allow him to randomly spend money for parishioners, but today it didn't make sense. He just wanted to help quickly and quietly, and yet now that the issue had become a major discussion, he feared the family would hear about it and be embarrassed. The board denied the money. The mom did hear about it and was embarrassed and, a few months later, quietly left the church.

This incident illustrates the need for certain characteristics within our local churches that will protect our ability to minister life. Psalm 45 prophesies about the coming Christ, and explains how Christ in His majesty will ride forth victoriously in behalf of truth, humility and righteousness, displaying awesome deeds by His right hand.

Our churches are His right hand, which is to display awesome deeds—that is why we need to be undergirded with *truth, humility* and *righteousness*. In this chapter I will discuss these three qualities which reflect the characteristics of our life-giving churches, and, in a sense, provide protective armor for them. But before we review these characteristics, it's important that we contrast and clarify the roles of the spiritual Body and the corporate structure.

SPIRITUAL MINISTRY SERVED BY CORPORATE STRUCTURE

All modern churches have two structures within them. One is the spiritual Body; the other is the corporation. Jesus Christ is the head of the spiritual Body with pastors who teach, elders who support, deacons who serve, apostles who lead, evangelists who win the lost, and overseers and bishops who bless and protect. The Bible is their guide and the Holy Spirit provides the life for this living organism, the true Church.

Membership within this spiritual Body is based on being born again. Heaven, not this world, is the home of the Church. Believers, therefore, do not have the same values as nonbelievers.

It doesn't take any money to perform the functions of the spiritual Body. Spiritual Bodies study the Scriptures and minister to others in the power of Jesus' name by the anointing of the Holy Spirit. We lead people to Christ, pray and worship—all paid for by Christ on the cross.

But if the believers who make up the spiritual Body want to use their tithes to finance missions, own a building or hire people to coordinate meetings, then the spiritual Body must form a corporation to perform these functions.

Corporations perform practical functions that do cost money. They have officers, boards and members that govern them. Corporations own assets, incur liabilities, employ personnel and set budgets. Even though the corporate side of a church is important, the corporation is the servant of the spiritual Body.

Many churches effectively use their corporations to further the ministry of the church. Too often, however, as years pass, the corporation slowly starts dominating the spiritual Body. Once this happens, the spiritual Body becomes the servant of the corporation and the purpose of believers' meetings becomes the receiving of offerings, the selling of religious products and increasing assets.

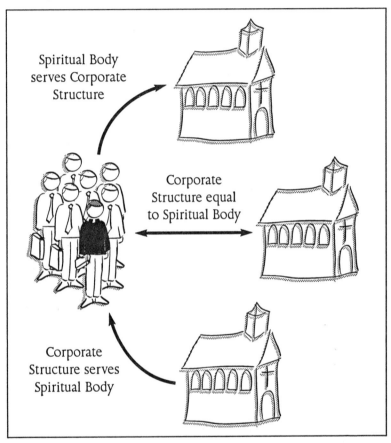

Spiritual Body serves Corporate Structure

Corporate Structure equal to Spiritual Body

Corporate Structure serves Spiritual Body

The values of most churches are usually revealed by the objectives of their leaders. If leaders focus on people coming to Christ and the stirring of faith and freedom for the Holy Spirit to minister, then the corporation is only a tool of the church. If, however, emphasis transfers to church attendance, the offering, gaining new members and/or trying to avoid offending anyone, then the church becomes no more than a resource of the corporation. Understandably, the Holy Spirit is grieved when this reversal occurs.

Recently I had lunch with a man who had just been hired by a large mainstream church as its director of evangelism. He said his primary responsibility was to bring people to membership. Because I knew that agnostics, humanists and Universalists held membership there, I realized that this church was no longer a spiritual Christian Body at all. Instead, it had become a group of members working for the corporation—to expand assets and influence by enlarging the membership.

In an attempt to prevent this process, some churches place their spiritual leaders in corporate positions, hoping to ensure that the corporation always serves the spiritual needs of the congregation. As a result, churches are sometimes poorly managed. Certainly, many spiritual leaders are competent corporate executives, but others are not. Because a person is honest, dependable and qualified as a spiritual leader, we should not assume that the person is fully equipped to buy and sell real estate, sign leases or borrow money. Many are not.

Therefore, various attempts have been made to develop systems that protect the spiritual Body while utilizing the strength of the corporation. Thus, we now have a combination of four major church governance systems: (1) strong pastoral leadership, (2) board, eldership or presbyter authority, (3) congregational control or (4) outside denominational oversight. Every church is governed by one or some combination of these systems.

Much of the confusion within the church is caused by tension over money, struggles over the control of assets and influence over others. Therefore, life-giving churches must wisely distinguish between the legal corporation and the spiritual Body. By clearly defining these roles, the resulting order and peace will allow members to stay in the tree of life and perform the ministries of the spiritual Body. This distinction is clearly articulated in chapter 14, "Bylaws."

The following characteristics are necessary for both the corporate structure and the spiritual Body of the church. When truth, humility and righteousness are in operation, the freedom and innocence of the church are protected. With the discussions of each characteristic, I have given tips for implementing these characteristics into the lives of the leadership and the church.

Truth

When Jesus spoke again to the people, he said, "I am the light of the world. Whoever follows me will never walk in darkness, but will have the light of life" (John 8:12).

1. Be honorable and honest.
Paul says in Ephesians 4:1 and 2, "I urge you to live a life worthy of the calling you have received. Be completely humble and gentle; be patient, bearing with one another in love." Living a life worthy of the calling includes obeying the commandments: Don't lie and steal. Don't be deceitful. Demonstrate integrity through actions rather than honorable words.

As leaders, we communicate commitment to the church and community when we *buy* a home rather than *rent*. This says we're here to stay; we're not just passing through. We are wise to drive a moderately priced car rather than one that communicates extravagance or unnecessary spending. And we demonstrate prudence when we refuse to dress like a television personality, especially since we aren't one. Even when we do appear on television, it's best to dress reasonably. And as for the flattering words that may come our way, we must not believe them—they're exaggerations. Scripture warns us against thinking more highly of ourselves than we ought (see Rom. 12:3). We are to humbly serve the Body by actually being who God wants us to be, and doing what He wants us to do. We are to reflect Him, not the world.

2. Fast and pray.
Regularly scheduled times of constructive, proactive, private prayer and fasting are a powerful way to rest, recharge your spir-

it and clarify God's plan and power in your heart. While praying and fasting, don't get introspective and depressed, instead let the truth of the Word and the power of His blood cleanse you so you can effectively serve in His kingdom for many years.

The strength of prayer and fasting combined with regular Bible reading and prayer will help establish priorities. As a result, you'll get more done. A godly pace established by accurate priorities keeps us from ever having to be deceitful or fake, and it protects us against burnout.

3. No secrets.

I believe *there is no such thing as a secret*, which helps me stay clean. When opportunities are presented that require secrecy, I don't do them. That's the way we keep our consciences clean and, as a result, the light of truth is our friend, not our enemy.

4. Be purpose driven.

Successful leaders know why they do what they do. The apostle Paul maintained his ministry purposes in the midst of complex church situations. Paul was motivated by the love of Christ and the terror of hell, and that revelation propelled his ministry (see 2 Cor. 5:11,14).

Keeping a clear perspective about why we're doing what we're doing is vital. Many people who truly love God have become disillusioned with church because we often fail to articulate why we meet together. Understanding and pursuing clear-cut objectives without unnecessary clutter has great public appeal.

5. Financial integrity is a close friend.

Many people love giving to God but resent the schemes some churches use to raise money. When believers see honesty, integrity and genuine spiritual values reflected in the business of the church and the lifestyles of their church leaders, they are much more willing to give generously. Every year we publish our cash-flow statement and send it to all contributors with their contribution statements. Why not?! We have nothing to hide.

6. Honor the tithe and don't get greedy.

Jesus said, "Come to me, all you who are weary and burdened, and I will give you *rest.* Take my yoke upon you and learn from me, for I am gentle and humble in heart, and you will find rest for your souls. For my yoke is *easy* and my burden is *light*" (Matt. 11:28-30, italics added). Did He say easy and light?

IT'S OUR RESPONSIBILITY TO MANAGE THE

DISTRIBUTION OF THE TITHE IN A GODLY WAY.

IT'S NOT OUR RESPONSIBILITY TO GET

PEOPLE TO GIVE MORE.

In 2 Corinthians 11:9, the apostle Paul reveals that he refused payment for ministry because he didn't want ministry expenses to be a burden for believers. Did he say he didn't want ministry to be a burden?

Obviously the Bible teaches powerful principles about sowing and reaping, and every Christian must participate in sowing seed into God's storehouse in order to receive the full blessings God wants to give.

The giving of tithes and offerings is worship to God. If any one of us ever tampers with or defiles worship, God will respond. For that reason, I am very cautious. In order to avoid the pressure to become manipulative with offerings, we set our budgets based on past history rather than upward projections. And as a result, even though we have grown more than 10 percent every year for 13 consecutive years, the financial support of the church has never been a burden to the believers.

It's our responsibility to manage the distribution of the tithe in a godly way. It's not our responsibility to get people to give more.

7. Don't drain baby churches dry.
Some church plants unnecessarily struggle because all of the financial resources are absorbed with the pastoral salary and/or a building. I recommend using a percentage system in the beginning. We used a scale such as the following:

35%	Pastor and/or staff
10%	Missions
10%	Youth
10%	Outreach (to promote the gospel in our city)
35%	Facilities (building, utilities, etc.)

This scale was excellent in the early stages to infuse life into our birthing baby church.

8. Whatever you build it on, you'll have to maintain it on.
If you build the church on Sunday School, you will have to maintain it with Sunday School. If you build the church with great guest speakers, you will have to maintain it with great guest speakers. If it's powerful preaching, you'll have to maintain it on that. If you build on prophecy, you're in trouble if the Holy Spirit doesn't want to give a prophecy. Let all these ministries be tools, but build the church on worship and the Word of God so you can maintain steady growth. Remember, "flesh gives birth to flesh, but the Spirit gives birth to spirit" (John 3:6).

Humility

Humility and the fear of the Lord bring wealth and honor and life (Prov. 22:4).

The one characteristic God positively responds to from Genesis through Revelation is humility. Humility does not mean weakness or powerlessness, but instead indicates clear understanding of authority, spiritual power and holiness. Thus, the humble are meek, modest and submissive.

These attitudes always activate supernatural favor. Thus, the Bible promises that as we understand how to relate to others with humility rather than arrogance, it opens the door for our ministries to enjoy wealth, honor and life (Prov. 22:4).

The following are seven practices that require humility and provide protection for our churches:

1. Foster freedom with simple structures.

We must set people free, both spiritually and within the structure of the church. To offer freedom in Christ and, at the same time, force people to navigate through complex ministry structures is counterproductive. They won't do it.

The gospel message is simple enough to be grasped by all, and we certainly should not cloud participation in the church with structures that are excessively bureaucratic.

2. Promote membership in Christ's Body.

Jesus is the Head of the Church, and people are ultimately responsible to Him. Life-giving churches emphasize the goodness of knowing Him, not necessarily the church. Because of this fact, we at New Life emphasize membership in the Body of Christ and a commitment to Him above membership in our specific church and commitment to us. We are at best the instrument God will use to save, heal or restore people, but God actually does the work.

3. Give others the freedom to choose.

Because the Lord gives people the freedom to make decisions and then receive the benefits or the consequences, we stay in the tree of life with greater ease when we respect their decisions.

The primary responsibility of the pastor and other staff leaders is to equip believers for ministry, to encourage good choices through Bible teaching and counsel, to pray, and to lovingly correct and administer the day-to-day affairs of the church. These roles do not include personal control or manipulation of people's lives. This freedom allows people to feel respected, responsible and accepted.

Everyone needs a pastor, Pastor! Every pastor should have another pastor that he or she looks to for wisdom, counsel and spiritual covering. My pastors are Roy and Larry Stockstill of Bethany World Prayer Center in Baker, Louisiana. Every year one of them visits New Life and is introduced as my pastor. Their covering provides stability, consistency and security for both the congregation and me.

4. Develop and maintain the heart of a servant.

Make sure a servant's attitude saturates the entire church Body. People don't owe the leadership anything. On the contrary, leaders owe service to everyone the Lord sends across their path. Treat all people as though they were gifts from God. Serve people in such a way that God can trust you; then He will add more to you.

The balance to this is the reality that sometimes people will take advantage of you, drain your energy and steal your time. Even these people can be dealt with from a servant's attitude, but this doesn't mean you're always soft and fluffy. To serve people, it is often necessary to be firm and direct, in love.

5. Promote Jesus, not the church.

Churches often waste huge amounts of money advertising themselves. I know it's hard to believe, but people don't care as much about you or your church as you think; they do care about God. So by promoting what He does, the Holy Spirit may choose to promote you. And when He does, it will be because you are His representative, not your own.

6. Laugh more and enjoy people.

Laughing at things that, if taken seriously, could become major issues, makes ministry much more fun. Just laugh and go on. When God is in control, circumstances can't move out of His hand and become crises. Trust God. Enjoy the variety of people. Never put them down or become critical. Avoid classifying groups of people. Remember that they are individuals, not groups. Every person is the way he or she is for a reason. Should you be tempted to err in relationships, always err on the side of grace.

7. Learn.

In order to be increasingly effective for many years, we have to be humble enough to identify those who know certain areas of ministry better than we do and learn from them. Read their books, attend their conferences and study their churches. My practice is to learn from others and wait six months to see what ideas still impact me—then apply them. The fresh input keeps us growing, while the six-month waiting period prevents us from swinging from trend to trend too quickly. We don't want to be movement-oriented churches; we want to be steady, increasingly effective churches.

Another set of teachers that helps us improve our influence on others is our critics. In our office, we refer to our critics as our Tuesday mail: We upset them on Sunday, they write on Monday, and we read on Tuesday. These people give us helpful information if we'll look past their anger and determine whether or not they have a point. I think Tuesday mail can sometimes be our best friend. My practice is to read all mail that is signed. If it is anonymous, I don't read it. For me to hear them, they must believe it enough to identify themselves.

Righteousness

> "For I tell you that unless your righteousness surpasses that of the Pharisees and the teachers of the law, you will certainly not enter the kingdom of heaven" (Matt. 5:20).

Every believer enjoys the way the Word of God and the Holy Spirit breathe Jesus' righteousness into our lives. That righteousness, which is freely given to us by God, is not only reflected in our personal lifestyles but also in the ministries we are able to influence. Life-giving churches have additional strength because of the righteousness reflected in their foundational philosophies. The following are six of those ideas:

1. Establish efficient church governments.

As I mentioned previously, godly people often become disillusioned with the carnality of church politics and business meetings. Therefore, we encourage:

- Strong pastoral leadership in the day-to-day operations of the church;
- Board-of-trustee control in major financial decisions;
- Full congregational rule in the selection of a new senior pastor; and
- Outside eldership (overseers) jurisdiction when disciplining the senior pastor.

This system clearly separates the various roles within the Body, and allows us to benefit from the most positive elements of the four primary types of church government. With the peace this balance brings, believers are free to grow without the burden of an excessive church government. The church was designed to be a place of liberty, healthy growth and development, not a burden. Relax and keep it simple.

2. Structure and plan for the church to last longer than you do.

Remember, we are working in God's kingdom, not our own. If Jesus doesn't return soon, others will inherit the churches we serve. To ensure that our work will continue long after we die or retire, we must structure our churches so others can minister through them for generations to come.

Because the church belongs to Jesus and not to a pastor or a particular group of people, it should be structured to provide ministry through a variety of people. The Bylaws explained in chapter 14 were written with that thinking in mind.

3. Conservatively address the senior pastor's salary.

It seems as though we have two streams of thought. One group underpays pastors, and their families suffer as a result. The other group pays the senior pastor so well that his lifestyle seems contradictory to the mission of the church.

To balance those extremes, I recommend that pastors have the ability to set their own salaries with certain provisions and restrictions. That way the pastor is rewarded for successfully serving a church, and his other associates are adequately paid as well. Chapter 14 explains the details of this approach.

4. Focus on the gospel.

Extremely positive, healing messages should be taught in conjunction with regular personal power ministry. Teach life, not law. Display greater wisdom than Adam and Eve. Reject the temptation to feed your followers from the tree of knowledge of good and evil, but instead let them grow from the tree of life. Stick with living water, the bread of life and His fruit in their lives.

If you start teaching the knowledge of good and evil, your people will be poisoned and die. If you teach life, they will live and prosper and grow. Remember as you teach that the issues are life and death, not good and evil. No matter what your subject is, always edify.

5. Fight the devil; serve people.

Don't fight with city hall, the neighbors, other Christian groups or the atheists. Serve them. Obey the law. Fight only the devil and serve people. "For our struggle is not against flesh and blood, but against the rulers, against the authorities, against the powers of this dark world and against the spiritual forces of evil in the heavenly realms" (Eph. 6:12). Do battle in your prayer closet and serve in public.

6. Encourage free-market ministry.

Free-market ministries always produce creative and innovative ministry methods. Anywhere in the world where the government allows a free-market economy, people produce goods and services that make prosperity possible. In contrast, where central-command economies are dictated from a central office, the result is always poor quality, poor service and outdated products—unhappy people.

Our local churches have some of the same characteristics. When we allow the Holy Spirit to work within people to create effective ministries, we have an abundant supply. If, on the other hand, we want to monitor every ministry from our central office, then the ministries of the church will eventually lack creativity and fail to adequately meet the needs of the congregation.

So life-giving churches should give people systems to use for their ministries. Our responsibility is to enable people to birth ministry; it is not our responsibility to make their ministries work. If they do work, praise God.

This free-market ministry style is used to one degree or another through every super-megachurch in the world. Cell systems allow people to creatively minister to others without having to initiate a program within the church. Rather than having the church leadership team create a ministry and enlist people to participate in it, cell churches allow the needs of people to create the ministries.

As we teach people to spot needs and fill them as servants, effective ministries are constantly birthing within our churches. Make sure all ministry programs center on taking care of people, not people taking care of the programs.

Together these three characteristics, truth, humility and righteousness, shield the flow of life within a church. And each of these characteristics contributes to longevity in ministry. But before we close this section on the philosophies of life-giving churches, we need to address the sensitive subject of etiquette.

What do we do when people want to leave our churches? What should we do when we want to leave? How should we treat an associate who wants to quit? All of these questions and more need to be answered if our hearts are to stay clean throughout years of ministry.

Offensive behavior among coworkers in the Body often disappoints people and hardens their hearts, causing them to make horrible mistakes. With common courtesy, though, mistakes can be avoided so, in the midst of difficult decisions, an atmosphere of harmony and life can prevail.

8

ETIQUETTE THAT SUSTAINS

DO NOTHING OUT OF SELFISH AMBITION OR VAIN
CONCEIT, BUT IN HUMILITY CONSIDER OTHERS
BETTER THAN YOURSELVES. EACH OF YOU SHOULD
LOOK NOT ONLY TO YOUR OWN INTERESTS,
BUT ALSO TO THE INTERESTS OF OTHERS.

[*Philippians 2:3,4*]

BAD MANNERS MOCK OUR
MINISTRIES AND MARK OUR FUTURE

Several years ago, Bruce Jefferson, the youth pastor at Mountain View Assembly, received what he believed to be a call from the Lord to serve as a senior pastor. He began discussing his plans with several church members who offered support, and before long, Bruce was assured that the time had come for him to plant a church. He hadn't spoken to his senior pastor about the matter until the day he met in the pastor's study to announce his departure. The senior pastor was surprised but accepted the decision.

Bruce started a new church with his supporters from Mountain View. Now, years later, Bruce has moved to a different town to serve in another church, and the small church he birthed struggles to survive. Mountain View has never regained the momentum it lost from the departure of Bruce and his followers. Bruce's lack of understanding about etiquette resulted in an improper response to God's call upon his life and diminished his reputation. Security in ministry is no longer an option for Bruce because he didn't practice a code of behavior that enables healthy long-term relationships.

My major fear in writing this chapter on etiquette is that I don't want to sound like the Miss Manners of the church world. God help me! But at the same time, we've all seen people who have effectively ministered the life of God to others and yet were unable to sustain their ministries because they didn't understand the social graces of the church world. The kingdom of God suffers when a believer violates decorum within the Body.

Long-term relationships cannot survive without manners. Families that enjoy harmony do so because of a code of behavior in the home. Public gatherings cannot be successful unless people have courtesy toward one another. Respecting others and knowing how to make people feel comfortable is what causes society to work smoothly. That is why we in the church world need a protocol as much as any other group.

This chapter will briefly review two sets of etiquette for Christian leaders. The first set is for the senior pastor, the second for associates. As with any other relationship, both parties must use wisdom and take responsibility for their own attitudes and actions.

PROTOCOL FOR THE SENIOR PASTOR

Inter-Pastoral Friendships

When arriving in a new city, I recommend locating the ministers' gatherings and attending them regularly for at least the first year you are in town. If the pastors of the large churches attend those meetings, make a point to meet them. If they don't, call and make an appointment to meet personally with them. These pastors are the gatekeepers of the city, and their views will help you quickly orient to the community. Your presence at the meetings will help to establish a solid set of friendships that will strengthen your entire tenure in the city. After one year, go to the pastors' meetings only when you want to.

After your first year in town, you are in a position to welcome new pastors into your city. I try to get the phone numbers of pastors who will be moving to Colorado Springs so I can call to welcome them before they arrive. I offer to answer any questions they might have and assure them that they will enjoy the spiritual climate and pastoral relationships within our city. These phone calls dispel a great deal of fear and apprehension between the pastors and their new assignments, and give them a friendly point of reference once they get here.

Another courtesy that promotes inter-pastoral friendships is offering financial assistance to expanding churches. New Life doesn't generally send financial assistance to struggling church-es, simply because it's important that free-market dynamics determine whether or not churches survive. But if a pastor's family is suffering because of a downward spiral in the church, we will sometimes send money to the pastor so his family can experience some relief.

If a neighboring church is doing any kind of construction to upgrade its facilities, we send some money to help. Or, if a church is celebrating an anniversary or a grand opening, we always send flowers and a card. Once a few churches start displaying this kind of support for one another, it becomes the culture of your city, which facilitates longevity in pastoral positions and the life of God flowing through churches...because of good manners.

Resigning

I believe senior pastors need to find their life call and stay in the same church and community as long as possible. I also believe it takes four years to meet someone, which means it also takes four years to meet a church and, in fact, it takes four years to begin substantive ministry within a church.

The standard I use to determine longevity in a church is whether or not it is growing. After the first four years of orientation, the church should begin growing steadily by at least 10 percent a year. If it does, stay. If it doesn't, try to correct the problem within the next year. If the church still won't grow, move on. Don't blame anyone or anything, just humble yourself and learn from the experience, then try again in another city.

The exceptions to this four-year standard are obvious: a declining population in the region, a limited population base or some other influence totally outside of your control. But in most situations, this standard works.

That being said, I understand that situations do arise when it is the genuine leading of God and/or a practical necessity to resign from a church. In those instances, always talk with the church leadership first, announce your departure to the congregation, and leave fully supporting the church. Nothing negative, critical, judgmental or offensive should be said in this process. And if negative attitudes have taken root in your heart, don't leave because of them. Hurt or bitterness will prevent you from growing in Christlikeness and can be the springboard for a long season of barrenness. Senior pastors should only leave when their hearts are clean.

STRUCTURES DON'T RESTORE
PEOPLE TO GODLY LEADERSHIP,
FRIENDS DO.

If you are moving because of the weather, don't tell the congregation that God is calling you somewhere else; tell them you're moving because of the weather. If you were fired, don't say you received a better opportunity; tell people the church leadership felt the position was not suited for you, and that you agree. If you are tired, just say it.

Graciously, wisely, and with discretion tell the truth. Don't cloak your departure in religious deception. And, don't be unkind. Instead, be gracious and truthful so every possible positive relationship can be sustained.

Hiring and Firing Staff Members

I believe senior pastors should work for the church, and staff members should work for the senior pastor. To have an effective team, senior pastors must be able to build and trim their own staff. I hire people who have both skill and personality. I enjoy ministering with people I like, therefore, I hire my friends. I hire people toward whom I have a divine flow.

Ten people at New Life report directly to me, and they are a delight for me to work with. I encourage each of them to hire people they enjoy, so the atmosphere in the office is pleasant, and we can work hard together. The friendships make the work relationships fun.

My responsibility to my friends is to assist them in fulfilling God's best plan for their lives. When their positions do not appear to be suitable, I wait six months to make sure that my assessment is correct. If it is, I talk and work with them to help find the best possible alternative. In some instances we try a different position within the church; in other cases, that is not possible.

I attempt to be flexible in this process so, together, we can find the role for that person which will be most productive for God's kingdom. Sometimes while we're searching, people continue in their positions at the church; other times, we let them go so they will have more time to locate a new position. Either way I maintain close communication and finance them beyond reason to assist in their transition.

Oh, one last note: no resignations or dismissals on Mondays.

Restoration of the Fallen

Structures don't restore people to godly leadership, friends do. I've never known of anyone who has fallen into sin and been successfully restored by the formal church structure. Nor have I ever seen a formal church structure wisely deal with sin, enabling ministry to continue without interruption. I do, however, know of many instances where a leader has fallen and that leader's friends have helped to heal and restore the person, while the church itself didn't skip a beat.

The greatest test of character is our response to someone else's sin. If our responses are from the tree of the knowledge of good and evil, which emphasizes punishment instead of restoration, judgment instead of redemption or justice instead of mercy, then our responses might sow seeds that will ultimately destroy our own lives. But if our responses are out of the tree of life, we will not only protect our own hearts from subtle deception, but will give the one who is in trouble maximum opportunity to find liberating life.

DON'T PUNISH PEOPLE WHO REPENT; HEAL THEM.

In my view, healthy relationships best contain the temptation to unknowingly develop sinful attitudes while dealing with someone else's sin. But simple corporate roles seldom withstand the pressure and collapse into arrogance or religious high-mindedness. Friends cry with friends over failure and get people healed; supervisors without strong relationships seldom do.

So how do we restore the fallen? First, sin only needs to be repented of as far as it has actually gone. Forgiveness doesn't have to be asked for from people who don't know that the sin ever occurred. So if a brother or sister falls, get him or her with trusted friends and have the person repent to everyone who has been violated. If the person repents, establish a simple but purposeful restoration plan and have friends assist and monitor the recovery.

Don't punish people who repent; heal them. I don't believe private sin requires public rebuke or removal from office if repentance is taking place. However, when no evidence of true repentance exists, then discipline is in order.

In every step of restoration, be sure to ask: *What do we hope to accomplish from the action we are considering?* And, *Will this produce positive results for the kingdom of God?* When repentance is present, there is a time when love should cover sin.

In these situations, mercy prevails over justice (see Jas. 2:13). But if repentance is not evident, then and only then should justice and judgment prevail.

Visiting Speakers

Before inviting guest speakers to our church, we make sure the following five questions have been answered:

1. *Can we pay them well?* When speakers accept our invitation, leaving their normal routines, families and all other duties to be with us, we recognize that the opportunity costs began when they started packing for the trip and those costs won't end until they are settled back into their routines at home. So we cover all of their expenses, except phone calls and personal purchases, and reward their families for their time away from home. When we invite pastors to speak in one of our Sunday services, we understand that they must be away from their church on Sunday—a major opportunity cost that deserves to be rewarded.

2. *Can we host them well?* Different people like to be hosted differently. I like to be picked up at the airport and driven to my hotel room. Or, if I must travel a long distance from the airport, I prefer to rent a car with a good map. But I don't like staying in people's homes unless absolutely necessary. Why? Because they want to host me when I need to rest or work. I don't mind, though, meeting with as many people as possible who are associated with the reason for my visit.

3. *Can we communicate with them well?* When I travel, I want to know why I'm there, how many people I'm going to be speaking to, the appropriate dress for the event and any protocol issues that might be relevant. If communication is not clear, then I'll choose the topic I

teach on, which might not fulfill my host's expectations. Therefore, clear written communication in advance is very important.

4. *Can we introduce them well?* The purpose of an introduction is to prevent speakers from having to spend the first 15 minutes of their talk connecting with the crowd. If the introduction is warm and includes meaningful information, it will communicate the speaker's right to be heard. Reading from a biography is acceptable, but reading it for the first time in front of the crowd is not.

5. *Will inviting this speaker hurt any of the nearby churches that have previously hosted this person?* Sometimes we would like to have a certain speaker but, because that person has often been with another local church, we might appear to be doing something unethical if we were to ask that person to speak at our church.

Responding to Those Who Are Leaving

One of the most difficult situations a senior pastor ever faces is the departure of a valued staff member or family from the church. I believe in dialoguing with people when they are considering a major transition. With some, the discussions should occur as friends. With others, it should occur as a pastor talking with an associate or parishioner. Unfortunately, with some staff members, the dialogue is purely a discussion between an employer and an employee. Each of these roles has its own standards of etiquette and rules of conduct.

Most tension, however, develops when the culture of the church does not allow easy entrance and comfortable exit. My experience has been that if people have the freedom to go in good graces, they will sense a greater freedom to choose to stay. I encourage full discussion when thoughts of leaving first develop, unless of course the departing staff member or parishioner chooses not to communicate and has already made a decision to go. In those instances, the pastor should not dialogue extensively with the person, but cordially accept the decision. Don't be cold, just graciously accept it.

The only exception to this standard is when, for valid reasons, you know the decision is wrong. Then, you can protest, but not as a pastor or as an employer, only as a friend. Friends can passionately discuss delicate issues such as this; however, it violates every sense of dignity, courtesy and good taste to have a pastor or employer resist the departure of a staff member or parishioner.

So how do we treat those who have gone? With decorum: kind words, gracious conversation and cordiality. Never should the senior pastor become harsh, judgmental or condemning. Instead the senior pastor should treat those who have gone with respect and affection.

But what about rejection? I feel rejected when people just disappear or announce their decision to depart. I do, however, understand that those things will happen for good reasons, and I respect that. But it is easier if I, or someone else on the staff, is part of the process and was a part of the conclusion. Then, no matter how we feel about the decision, at least we can understand it.

PROTOCOL FOR ASSOCIATE PASTORS

Your First Day on the Job

Every church has a secret code of conduct that everyone on staff knows about, except you, the new associate.

I'll never forget my first day of work at Bethany World Prayer Center, the megachurch of Baton Rouge, Louisiana. I arrived early as the new associate pastor: clean shoes, crisp shirt and sharp suit. I was ready to minister. But it didn't happen. Instead, Brother Roy, the senior pastor, began educating me in the culture of Bethany by gently saying with a grin, "Brother Ted, go home and get some work clothes on; we'll be picking up sticks today." I understood perfectly. I was in for a series of lessons about social graces that were going to have to be caught through observation, not taught with words. It took two years.

The first day for every associate pastor lasts about two years. During this time, three relationships have to be developed. The first is your relationship with the senior pastor. Learn his personality, his moods, his likes and dislikes. Don't judge him, just serve him. Make him glad you are there.

The second significant relationship to cultivate is with other associates. They know all of the unspoken rules, so watch them closely. They understand how and when to dress; when to be visible and when to disappear; and how to get the job done. But they won't know what to think of you until you've been there a while, so stay steady. Have a servant's heart, and yet serve with confidence. Don't be arrogant, but don't be a puppy. Just stay humble.

As these first two relationships are developing, the door will open for a significant relationship with the congregation itself. As the pastor gets to know you and the other associates begin to respect you, you will enter into effective ministry within the congregation. It will feel great, but remember the process takes about two years.

These first two years will include lessons on personality styles, power, wisdom and patience. Building for a successful future is tied closely with your ability to patiently stay innocent as you learn. If you give the impression that you are impatient, disloyal, high-minded or just waiting for a better offer, people will only superficially connect with you. Conversely, if you make a decision to relate with people as if you're going to stay for the rest of your life, you might actually receive that option.

As you work through your first two years, develop a healthy pattern of praying and fasting, daily Bible reading, and serving with confidence and humility. Don't brag or even talk much about your spiritual discipline, just do it. Make the senior pastor's job easier, and understand that both you and the senior pastor will have different expectations as time passes. Don't let your original expectations limit you, instead stay flexible so your strengths can find your most productive role within the church.

Multiple Roles in Relationships

If your goal is to develop a positive and healthy relationship with the pastor, you must understand the multiple roles he will have in your life: associate in ministry, friend, intercessor, defender, confidant, employer, traveling companion and basketball buddy—all at the same time. These different roles can become very confusing.

To successfully serve as an associate pastor, you will have to learn these various roles. Early in the day, the senior pastor may be your friend. When he calls you that evening, he is your boss. The next morning when you see him in church, he's your spiritual leader. But on Monday when you play basketball with him, he's an old man with a bad back.

Occasionally when meeting with my staff, decorum requires that I distinguish our roles. I'll openly say that this conversation is friend to friend, or church business, or whatever. Clarifying the roles can help, but most associates usually know which role I'm in at the time.

But I Have a Call on My Life Too!

For churches to grow, many more people must be called to be associates than senior pastors. New Life Church has many pastors, but only one senior pastor. Because of my style, we function as a team; however, the buck stops with me.

Every pastor on our staff has a strong sense of purpose, and I pray that their purpose will be fulfilled at New Life. Out of love and respect for them, I do everything I can to see that their dreams are fulfilled and that the desires within their hearts are satisfied. Therefore, the vast majority of our pastors have served in various roles within our church. Communication and flexibility allow the transitions to protect everyone's dignity as the years pass and as our ministries grow.

I deeply love and appreciate every day of working with the pastoral team God has placed at New Life. Yet I understand that as they go through the various stages of life, their hearts can become restless and at times they sense the call of God to go pastor a church themselves. Even though I hate it, my responsibility as their friend and pastor is to assist them in doing what's right for themselves and the kingdom of God.

Can I Work at Another Church in Town?

Yes, but certain rules apply. For example, it is improper for any leader to take a position in another church within the same city unless the senior pastor has made the arrangements to do so. When the associate has independently arranged the move to a nearby church, a major violation of protocol and a betrayal of the Kingdom occurs. It feels too much like a divorce. It betrays a sacred trust.

The sacred trust is also violated when an associate takes a senior pastor's position in a nearby church without the senior pastor's initiative. A pastor moving to a neighboring church should never confuse relationships established in another local church. Subjecting believers to awkward situations such as these is unwise and unproductive. It's poor judgment, and causes believers to feel like children whose parents are divorcing. Don't do it.

I Think God Is Calling Me to Plant a Church

A worse violation of common courtesy occurs when an associate leaves to plant a church nearby. This is the ultimate violation of any sense of social grace and is an offense to God.

Associates who resign or are dismissed should not serve in a church or plant a church within a one-hour drive of their previous church. *The Haggard one-hour rule.*

But what if the senior pastor is wrong? Gene Edward's book

The Tale of Three Kings, beautifully addresses this situation. I suggest reading it if you have a moral dilemma regarding the senior pastor.

How do I quit so I can move on? If you want to consider becoming a senior pastor or taking another position outside of the church which would require a resignation, talk with your pastor about it. If open communication is established with the pastor, and the change is the right thing to do, resigning should not be uncomfortable. It is important to leave the church in good standing. The pastor can tell you if the timing is good, or if he would rather you stay for an additional few months. A request to stay more than a year would be excessive, however, I have found that when I have asked an associate to stay a few months to help the church through a particular season, the delay has generally benefited both of us.

Longevity in Ministry

Later in this book we discuss pay schedules and structures that encourage longevity in ministry. Staying in one location for an extended period of time is not only personally beneficial to growing our ministries, but is also beneficial for the kingdom of God.

Unless you know, without any doubt, that you are supposed to serve as a senior pastor, ask God to place you in a church with a strong calling, and faithfully serve there. As the years pass, the church will develop and strengthen, and you'll find that staying with the same people year after year in a growing church is deeply satisfying.

No matter where you serve, you will be successful if you remain in the tree of life, flowing in innocence and the anointing. You will then be able to maintain an environment where the gifts and fruit of the Holy Spirit provide life-giving nourishment for others and a reputation that reflects Kingdom values and Kingdom etiquette.

Section III

Ministries of a Life-Giving Church

Even though life-giving churches have a variety of ministries, I have selected four from New Life Church that reflect the philosophy of life-giving ministry. These four—Missions, Worship, Free Market Cells and Elders—are just examples of light, innocent, life-giving ideals to study and apply.

As you read this section, pay close attention to not only the practices described but also the philosophy behind them. Then apply that philosophy to any ministry to make it increasingly life-giving.

9

—

MULTIPLICATION OF LIFE: MISSIONS

ASK THE LORD OF THE HARVEST,
THEREFORE, TO SEND OUT WORKERS
INTO HIS HARVEST FIELD.

[*Matthew 9:38*]

ONE LIFE TO GIVE

The soldiers forced the family to stand on the beach for more than an hour without telling them why they were there or what they were going to do. The family members only knew that Mom had been summoned to school earlier that day for questioning about her faith. She had been accused of telling her children about God—accusations that were true. A month earlier during their evening meal the mother of these seven children had told them about the Savior and His great love for them.

Everyone in the family knew the school had heard about their discussion from one of the youngest children, but no one dared say anything about it. As they stood on the beach glancing nervously at one another and, at times, looking away in anguish, fear began to mount.

The silence was suddenly interrupted by the rumble of converging military trucks. After coming to a dusty halt on the beach, the officers sternly exited their vehicles and approached the family, visually inspecting each family member, especially the parents. A group of young soldiers began to unload a barrel from the back of a truck and rolled it toward the water. The barrel was open on one end.

For no apparent reason, the guards lifted their rifles toward the family, forcing them to stand in a row. Then the dreaded command came, ordering the mother to step forward. She handed the youngest, who had been tightly clinging to her, to her husband. Her body quaked with fear as she began slowly walking toward the guards. Father watched in terror. And the youngest, knowing that everything was very wrong, started to cry. With several rifles pointed in her direction, the officers ordered this godly woman into the barrel where her frail body was forced into a fetal position.

Mother was affectionately studying her family when her head disappeared into the barrel. The children screamed. Daddy shouted something, but one of the guards threatened him, and he stopped. Then a guard approached the oldest boy, 17-year-old Palucha, pointing a pistol at his head and ordering him to step forward. Palucha reluctantly obeyed. The guard handed Palucha the lid to the barrel with a hammer and nails, and commanded him to seal his own mother in the barrel.

Palucha refused at first, but caught his mother's eyes and listened as she softly beckoned him to obey the soldiers. She said she understood and wanted him to obey, explaining that they would see each other in another world. Palucha heaved in sorrow as he placed the lid on the barrel and nailed it shut.

The soldiers forced the family to watch as they rolled the barrel into the sea. Older family members held the littlest ones in their arms to keep them from running after their mother. Then, with the sudden crack of rifle shots, the guards started shooting at the barrel.

This family has never known whether their mother died from gunshot wounds or drowning. There were never any sounds from the sinking barrel. They only knew that the same fate awaited anyone in their communist state who expressed a belief in the living God.

Afterward, the guards turned to the family and said, "There is no God. He didn't help her, and He won't help you." The trucks drove off, leaving the grieving family standing alone on the beach while their dead mother sank to the bottom of the sea in her coffin, a crude barrel. They were alone; their mother was a martyr.

FULFILLING THE PRAYERS OF THE MARTYRS

Since the fall of Communism in Europe, no one has been able to confirm this story, but when I heard it and others like it in college, my worldview changed dramatically. As a 20-year-old college student, I would walk around the campus in the evenings, asking God to use me to serve the suffering Church. I knew the martyrs had asked God to protect their families and save their countries. As I considered their bravery and sacrifice, I realized there could be no greater honor in this life than to be used by God to answer some of the prayers that were prayed in those barrels.

Just before graduation from college, I received a phone call from World Missions for Jesus, a West German missions organization, saying that they were looking for someone to help establish a stronger North American office. When I heard that World Missions served the suffering Church in atheistic countries, I agreed to meet with them.

I accepted the position with World Missions for Jesus, and the perspective I learned there and in my subsequent position at Bethany World Prayer Center convinced me that every church should take advantage of every opportunity to impact the world for Christ. Life-giving churches don't exist for themselves, but for those who don't know life Himself, Christ. God has spoken that same message to lots of people. That's why many life-giving churches are missions churches.

Others, the Focus of the Church

The Bible teaches that all believers should tithe to the storehouse, which I believe is the local church. I also believe local churches should tithe to missions. At New Life, we budget at least 10 percent for missions. But because of the way God always blesses our church, we usually find ourselves giving more than 20 percent of our total income to missions. Our church gave more than $1 million to missions last year to help answer some prayers that were prayed in the barrels.

When Jesus was exhorting His disciples just before His ascension, He said, "But you will receive power when the Holy Spirit comes on you; and you will be my witnesses in Jerusalem, and in all Judea and Samaria, and to the ends of the earth" (Acts 1:8). His exhortation applies to every one of us.

In chapter 5 we discussed how this verse prepared the disciples to receive the power of the Holy Spirit. But the power of the Holy Spirit was not given to enable the Early Church to have better church services; it was given to provide the Church with the power to reach unbelievers. Outreach starts in our "Jerusalems," our hometowns, then our "Judeas," the state or nation surrounding our hometowns. "Samaria" is a neighboring state, in this case a despised state to the north of Judea. And "to the ends of the earth" exhorts us to ensure that every people group is reached!

———

THE REASON GOD GIVES US HIS LIFE
IS TO IMPACT OUR WORLD.

———

The reason God gives us His life is to impact our world.

New Life has a very specific strategy for staying outreach oriented. We have flags hanging in the living room, our main auditorium, from every nation on earth. We also fly the flags of Native American nations, the United Nations, the Presidential Seal, Palestine and all 50 states. Our church is charismatic, and because charismatics look at the ceiling of their auditoriums more than anywhere else, we hung the flags from the ceiling as a constant reminder to the congregation of the reason we do what we do in our living room: others, not ourselves.

In addition, we are currently building The World Prayer Center directly in front of our building. This center will gather information on Church growth from all around the world and feed that information to intercessors. The purpose is to keep the intercessors of the world praying for the lost, and to provide them with feedback information so they know that their prayers are being answered. Because the kind of praying that emanates from there is for the expansion of God's kingdom, and for the continued outpouring of the Holy Spirit worldwide, the World Prayer Center is a symbol of evangelistic prayer. We want everyone who drives into our church parking lot to be reminded to pray for the lost and to focus their attention on others rather than themselves.

OUR ĴERUSALEΠ

The first step in helping our congregation to become aware of outreach is to lead people in praying for their "Jerusalem," Colorado Springs. We often distribute a copy of the obituaries to each member of the New Life staff on a paper that says, "Today some people from Colorado Springs will be going to Heaven and some will be going to Hell. Our work today will affect the percentage going to Heaven or Hell tomorrow."

We pray through the phone book, over maps and for other churches. We pray for government leaders, schools and neighborhoods. And, probably the most effective way we help our congregation touch the lost of our city is by having them prayerwalk our city.

We coordinate our prayerwalking efforts with scores of other local churches to ensure that every street in the entire city is prayerwalked at least once a year.

One night my friend and I were prayerwalking through downtown Colorado Springs at about 1:30 in the morning. We were walking on a bridge high over some railroad tracks when we heard a noise on the tracks below. We leaned over the edge and saw a group of skateboarders playing on the concrete beneath the bridge. I yelled in the gruffest voice I could muster, "Hey you boys! What are you doing down there?"

The students looked up and, after a pause, one of them sheepishly questioned, "Pastor Ted, is that you?"

I was shocked! After composing myself and feeling a little embarrassed, I acknowledged to this young man, playing with his buddies in the middle of the night, that his senior pastor from the church in the suburbs was downtown playing too. My friend and I walked down to the railroad tracks to speak with them. It turned out that the boy from our church had slipped out of his bedroom window without his parents' knowledge so he could meet his buddies. And wouldn't you know it, his senior pastor showed up! How do you explain that to Mom at breakfast?

PRAYERWALKING CAUSES THE PEOPLE OF OUR CHURCH TO TOUCH, SEE, SMELL AND FEEL OUR COMMUNITY AT LARGE; IT MAKES US WANT TO SERVE OTHERS, NOT JUST OUR OWN LITTLE WORLD.

As it turned out, the boy told his parents, and his mom and dad were very grateful. Sadly, several months later his mom died and I was asked to participate in the funeral. Because of our meeting under the bridge, this young man and I were unusually connected, which made the struggle of burying his mother much easier for both of us. We weren't strangers, nor were we limited to our church roles, because of prayerwalking. Prayerwalking got me into his world so I became human, and I hope, a friend.

Similar stories are often told around our church. We have prayerwalking teams that target schools, certain businesses, teenage hangouts, government buildings, high places, power points and occult sites. Sometimes we prayerwalk a geographical area, and other times we strategically target a site or series of sites. Either way, prayerwalking causes the people of our church to touch, see, smell and feel our community at large; it makes us want to serve others, not just our own little world.

Therefore, some of our missions money goes to our Jerusalem. We give to various community organizations that serve our community in Jesus' name. We don't have to create any organizations ourselves, instead we partner with those that already exist but need financial assistance. Incidentally, I make a point of financing neighboring organizations with no strings attached. I don't want to serve on their boards or organize their ministries, I just want our church to help them fulfill their calling, thus our Jerusalem is moving a little more in the right direction.

OUR JUDEA

The second charge of the Great Commission is our Judea, which is to us our state, or our nation. Several years ago the Lord spoke to me and told me to send prayer teams to every county seat in the state of Colorado. As a result of that effort, our church has enjoyed expanded relationships with churches throughout our state. Not only have many of our counties improved spiritually, but members of our congregation have connected with counties outside their normal sphere of influence and, in many cases, developed a heartfelt concern for others.

OUR SAMARIA

The next groups are outside our region: "Samaria, and to the ends of the earth." In Jesus' day, Samaria was a despised group of people from the north of Judea. When Jesus said that the power of the Holy Spirit would give His disciples power to be witnesses in Samaria, He was sending them with the gospel to people of a different culture. To do this, we send people in our congregation on prayer journeys and in a few cases, to be missionaries in the traditional sense.

In my experience, prayer journeys are the most effective way to expose the people within our congregations to the mission field. Training is unnecessary in cross-cultural communications, witnessing, conducting services or any of the other issues that would otherwise cause people to be hesitant to go. Instead, prayer journeys enhance their prayer lives. People begin praying together with others from their home church; they practice by participating in prayerwalking in their own community; then they travel and pray for those living in a dark region of the world.

I enjoy prayer journeys not only because they always open the door for powerful spiritual advances, but also because they are fun. They have been packed with adventure and are too numerous to recount in detail within the pages of this short chapter. We have prayed through caves lined with bloody altars that have been used to sacrifice animals for more than 1,500 years; prayed through secret underground prisons once used by the communists; and stood on the dome of Islamic Mosques with both arms raised, claiming the building and the Islamic worshipers for Christ.

Perhaps I should take the time to tell about slipping through the dark streets in the capitals of closed Islamic nations to meet secretly with members of the underground church in order to train them in warfare prayer. There was also the time God supernaturally opened the clouds so our helicopter could seemingly appear out of nowhere to pluck our prayer team off the top of a mountain just in time.

Maybe it would be more interesting if I wrote about the prayer journeyer who was supernaturally protected from being hit by a bus that might have killed her without divine intervention, or the team members who were praying in tongues in an Islamic hospital only to discover that the patients understood them and started speaking back to them in their own language, just as in the book of Acts. The supernatural physical miracles that took place among the patients in that hospital didn't just lead to the healing of the patients, but also to the conversion of many doctors and nurses who were treating them. These high-adventure experiences are some of the reasons why prayer journeys are motivating for the people of our churches.

Prayer journeys are the penetration of God's commando forces—that's you and me, and the people of our churches—into enemy territory. I've led teams to the heart of Islam, Buddhism, Hinduism and other non-Christian religions. Why? Because I don't want even one more barrel cast into the sea.

We have watched too many people bow to Mecca, burn incense, dip in rivers, slaughter animals and construct idols only to have them become worse off after their futile attempts to find God. To cancel the effects of demonic opposition and open the windows of heaven, prayer must be the number one charge. Prayer is the way to produce a global impact.

Then we follow with strategic evangelism. In one of the nations we targeted with prayer, the Body of Christ grew 600 percent during the 12 months that followed; the growth rate the next year was 300 percent. In another nation we targeted for prayer, the underground church was soon networked, mobilized and trained to pray through the homes, recreation sites and worship sites of its Islamic masters. We are trusting God for revival there. In our most recent "target" nation, the Body of Christ is doubling every year! Prayer journeys combined with strategic partnerships for evangelism produce tangible results, every time.

The mission statement of our outreach office "is to spiritually and financially support, equip and empower missionaries and national workers who serve primarily in the 10/40 Window and among the least evangelized people groups."

To do this, we begin with a strategy. We want to touch those areas of the world that have the greatest need and, at the same time, have fertile spiritual soil. If they are hard, we send prayer teams. If they are prepared for evangelism, we send prayer teams and develop alliances with organizations or churches that already have some work in the region we can support.

"10/40 WINDOW"

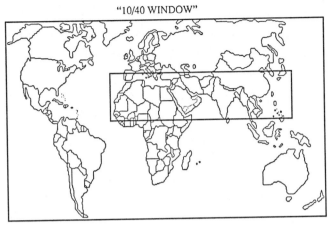

For example, in 1993 Albania was a predominantly Islamic nation ripe for the gospel. New Life Church sent our prayer team there, along with many other teams from other organizations, and enjoyed great encouragement from the Lord about the prospects for the Church among the Albanian people. Thus, upon our return home, we partnered with Every Home for Christ and the Gideons. We didn't have much financial strength at the time, so we made arrangements with both of these organizations to work through them in Albania. As a result, the kingdom of God received much greater strength through partnering than we could have ever have achieved working independently.

Currently, I believe Nepal is ready for revival. So, New Life Church is working in Nepal through five organizations that were already making headway there. We haven't had to train missionaries, buy land, build anything, hire anyone or fly anyone over there. Instead, we are working through organizations we know and trust that already have an infrastructure in place. As a result, we are seeing great results from our investment for the kingdom of God.

Strategy and partnership are the two strongest ideas behind our missions philosophy. In order to be strategic, we focus our efforts on the least evangelized people in the world. And to maximize effectiveness, we never launch into projects alone. New Life Church always partners with other ministries, such as Youth

With A Mission, Every Home for Christ, International Bible Society and others, or trustworthy national brethren. With the combination of being strategic and multiplying our efforts through partnerships, we have been able to maximize our impact among some of the most difficult to reach areas of the world.

I am writing this chapter today in Denver, Colorado, where I just finished a meeting with Eric Watt, missions strategist for the Christian Broadcasting Network; Charles Blair from Calvary Temple in Denver; Howard Foltz from AIMS; and about a half dozen leaders of networks of churches. We were developing strategy that would incorporate literature distribution, church planting and media efforts among unreached people groups. Together, we are all more effective than we ever could be alone.

When we consider training or sponsoring missionaries, we want to know:

1. Are they strategic in their thinking and planning? We recognize that every place has need, but is their destination a location of particular darkness, and are they the best resource we can send to penetrate that darkness?
2. Are they interested in training and enabling national workers to reach their own people? There is some value in direct cross-cultural ministry, but any value that is there impacts the culture most and continues multiplying for years if it includes training and empowering nationals to work within their own culture.

Once we have decided to support a missionary, we have certain guidelines that keep the relationship healthy. They are as follows:

• We don't support more than 35 percent of any missionary's total income. The only exception is if the missionary comes from our church. Then, we will support that person 100 percent for the first two years to give them time to build a support base. After two years, we limit our giving to 35 percent.

- We send all missions support on a monthly basis whether the money is sent to a missionary or to an organization that we are partnering with on a specific target.
- Occasional one-time gifts toward specific efforts and projects are given.
- Our missions-support structure is simple. At the end of every year, we review the amounts and the ministries of everyone receiving missions support. We decide to either increase, decrease or eliminate their support at the end of each year.
- Then we have a balance of how much more we want to commit to missions for the next year. At that time, we review all the applications and opportunities we have received from the previous year and decide which new projects or people we will agree to help for the following calendar year.
- Some of the selection criteria we use include:
    a. Personal integrity of character;
    b. Established work;
    c. Good stewardship of gifts and funds;
    d. Personal relationship with the senior pastor or missions director.

Once a missionary or project is on the support list, we maintain simple but informative communication with them so those on the field can spend their time doing mission work and we at home can spend our time strengthening the Church here.

INVESTING FOR FUTURE IMPACT

I believe one of the reasons families enjoy raising their children at New Life is because of our missions emphasis. Our church has a very distinct missions philosophy that purposefully directs the young people of our church.

Our newborn through fifth-grade children's cells emphasize primary Bible education, which consists of basic Bible stories. We tell the stories of the Bible again and again, in every possible way. Many of our children's cells are held in bright rooms with puppets, actors and sometimes popcorn. We provide maps, globes, missionaries and every possible tool to communicate the gospel message. We tell Bible stories, act them out, draw them and sing them. We use every method we can think of to tell Bible stories to this age group.

Sixth through eighth-grade cells emphasize secondary application. We teach how the Bible applies to the lives of young people in this age group. In other words, we explain that because Abraham did this, we need to do it, too. Or because Paul said this, so must we. Our goal is that the Bible becomes personal and powerful in the daily lives of our youth. The middle-school meetings and cells all focus on learning and applying the Scriptures.

Ninth through twelfth grades teach personal purpose and local church participation with a global perspective. This group emphasizes the compelling call and purpose from God for every student's life.

In these cells, the emphasis is our personal role in the global church. We try to take at least 100 of these high school students overseas every year. To stimulate a global conscience, they carry passports to their meetings and receive encouragement to discuss the condition of the Church in various parts of the world. They understand that God has called them to global evangelization. We teach them strategy, city-reaching techniques, intercessory prayer, warfare prayer, networking, evangelism, and prayer and fasting.

This group is the fertile soil into which we plant seeds of loving leadership to produce a crop of Christian leaders who will love the local church and understand its role in the global church. These students learn holiness, calling, purpose, dying and anointing. Most churches retain about 30 percent of their high school graduates for the kingdom of God by the time they graduate from college; New Life retains more than 95 percent because of its global emphasis.

Our college meetings and cells deal with strongholds. This group tackles the major economic, theological and philosophical issues of our day and learns the Christian worldview in response. They are learning to pull down strongholds in people's minds. They are preparing to enter into adult life and either become missionaries or support missions for the rest of their lives because, after all, they are from a life-giving church, which means they are called to have a global impact.

Life-giving churches make it hard for God's children of every age to forget the bravery and sacrifice of those who have given all to lead a lost and dying world back to the giver of all life, Jesus Christ. They make it hard to forget that God gives us His life so we can be His life givers "in Jerusalem, and in all Judea and Samaria, and to the ends of the earth."

10

İmpartation of Life: Worship

By Ross Parsley, Worship Pastor

Let the word of Christ dwell in you richly as you teach and admonish one another with all wisdom, and as you sing psalms, hymns and spiritual songs with gratitude in your hearts to God. And whatever you do, whether in word or deed, do it all in the name of the Lord Jesus, giving thanks to God the Father through him.

[Colossians 3:16,17]

THE WORSHIP LIFE

Life-giving worship is not just singing, nor is it a three-song warm-up for the sermon. Life-giving worship doesn't only happen when we gather for Sunday services, nor is it an event; it's our lifestyle.

When we define worship as devoting our time, attention and affection to Him, every area of our lives is involved. Playing with our kids, encouraging friends, working conscientiously, and gathering together with other believers to sing, read the Word and express our love for God and one another are all forms of worship.

Jesus said the Father is seeking those who will worship in Spirit and truth. We worship in Spirit through our communication and relationship with Him. And we worship in truth as we authentically reflect who He is in us to others. Our goal then is to have a constant demonstration of His presence in our lives so others can join with us. This is the foundation upon which life-giving praise and worship is built.

THE WORSHIP LEADER

Worship is a high and holy calling. Every believer is called to be a worshiper. But when called to lead others into worship, we have an added responsibility. We must evaluate whether our hearts are pure, wholly submitted to Him and focused on glorifying Him.

Our motives and intentions need to be scrutinized as we consider what an honor and privilege it is to administrate the worship of others' hearts toward God. As we embrace this calling, it quickly becomes evident that if we ever treat worship as a hobby or something routine, God will replace us.

He is life, and worship to Him brings life. In order to keep worship from being polluted, God must graciously mold His worship leaders into holy vessels. He wants worshipers to receive His life as they worship Him, life Himself.

Our first responsibility as life-giving worship leaders is to minister to the Lord. Jesus is the center of attention at all life-giving services. There is no other good reason for us to gather than to meet with Him and study His Word. Without the Lord as our primary focus, we become ritualistic and social, but with Him at the center of attention, we are able to minister life to those around us.

Worship is not a monologue, it is a dialogue. It's not telling God what we think of Him, or giving Him a laundry list of what we want from Him. Praise and worship begins a spiritual dialogue through which He breathes His life into our hearts and minds, which conforms us into His image. As we engage in this wonderful conversation, the Lord imparts His heart, which leads to conviction, revelation and intercession. God's heart is fixed on rescuing the lost, and when we worship Him, our focus shifts from ourselves to others; consequently, we are led to intercede and work to reach others.

Jesus said, "the Son of Man did not come to be served, but to serve, and to give his life as a ransom for many" (Matt. 20:28; Mark 10:45). Musicians find it easy to get sidetracked and concentrate on performance, talent or personal recognition. However, our attitudes need to be the same as that of Christ Jesus who laid down His rights, His reputation and His preferences in order to take on the nature of a servant to all humankind.

As musical servants to the Body of believers, we must give up our rights, our agendas and our preferences so we can concentrate on the Lord's purposes. We don't sing and play our instruments to be served and seen, but to serve and give our lives for others.

That's why we worship, not just in our hearts but with our lives as well. Worship is a physical demonstration of the spiritual realities in our hearts. Just as communion reminds us of Christ's body and blood, and water baptism is where we identify with Christ's death, burial and resurrection, so our physical actions in praise and worship reflect the surrendering of our hearts to God.

When we praise the Lord with clapping, singing, shouting, dancing, lifting our hands, kneeling, bowing or standing, we are demonstrating with our bodies what our spirits already know: God is absolutely worthy of our praise. We demonstrate through our bodies His truth in our hearts. These physical manifestations of praise are the gateway for releasing our spirits to worship God. When we make our bodies serve our hearts, we fulfill the command to love God with all our hearts, minds, souls and strength.

Just as we use our bodies to demonstrate worship, we can also use our emotions for worship. God is emotional. If you doubt it, just read the Old Testament. He created us in His image and wants us to interact with Him in an emotional way.

Many people think that emotionalism is defined as showing a lot of emotion. But, the true definition of emotionalism is allowing our emotions to dictate our actions. We don't do that. Instead, we allow the realities of eternal life to dictate our worship. We worship, no matter what our emotions are. Often deciding to worship first results in becoming joyous or contemplative, but we worship.

One of the best examples of a passionate worshiper is King David, writer of the Psalms. Many times David used his emotions as the impetus for worshiping God. No matter what frame of mind he was in, David did not allow his emotions to determine his response to God. Instead, he used his emotions to press in to meeting with God. When David was sad, he found hope in God. When he was afraid, he ran to God for refuge. When he was grateful, he declared the greatness of God. Regardless of circumstances, David found the place of worship each time. He knew how to encourage himself in the Lord, because no matter how he felt, David understood the truth of God's worthiness and His faithfulness to him (see Ps. 42).

David not only modeled for us the way to worship in the midst of various emotions, he also modeled humility in worship. Throughout the Bible we see God resisting the proud and giving grace to the humble. Have you ever wanted to do something in praise and worship but didn't because you were embarrassed? Have you ever heard others talk about the depth of their personal worship experience or the freedom for worship in their local church with just a subtle hint of arrogance?

Our focus in worship should never be ourselves, and yet too many times in our own minds we become the central issue during worship. Whether it's feeling unworthy or just unruly, in order to worship, we must take our eyes off of ourselves or what others may think, and fix them upon the true subject of our worship, Jesus.

The more I realize that worship is a gift God grants me by His grace, the more that realization makes me want to capitalize on every opportunity to worship Him. Romans 11:36 says, "For him and through him and to him are all things." This is central to understanding our position in worship. The desire is *for Him*; the ability and gifting come *through Him*; and our purpose is to bring all the glory back *to Him*.

THE WORSHIP TEAM

Leading worship requires both heart and skill. Clean hearts are essential to successfully leading others to the life of God. Worship is a heart connection with God that relies upon the transparency and vulnerability of our hearts when we come to Him. This is important for leaders to understand, because our primary responsibility is to model openness of heart as we stand before the Body of believers.

Skill, on the other hand, has to do with our God-given abilities to accomplish what He has called us to do through music.

Music, just like preaching or plumbing, has an element of skill-fulness that either increases or decreases our effectiveness with others. The parable of the talents illustrates for us that we are stewards responsible to cultivate the gifts or talents we have received. When we don't, we are called lazy and wicked servants. Yikes!

With the privilege of leading worship comes the responsibility to develop our craft; however, we must keep the motivation pure. Excellent music on its own will not do anything eternal for our souls, but meeting with Jesus changes us every time. Therefore, excellence is only useful in our music for one reason: to provide an atmosphere for people to enter into God's presence, free from distractions. Great music under the inspiration of the Holy Spirit is an unparalleled combination to lead people into His presence.

Every one of us influences those around us. We are all leaders. The choir is not the background for the leader. The band does not just accompany the person in front. We don't have backup singers; we are all worship leaders. As worship leaders, we live worship, always. We sing with a purpose because we have a responsibility as leaders to be prepared, both musically and spiritually. When we stand before the congregation, we are the instruments of the Holy Spirit to inspire, motivate and encourage hearts to enter into worship. Each of us must embrace the idea that we are accountable to the Lord for this ministry, which causes us to be leaders who are motivated, instead of just participants depending on someone else.

Auditions

So why can't just anyone be on the platform? Are auditions OK?

Yes, auditions are OK, really! Heart attitude and various ability levels are the reason we need an audition process for the music ministry. Everyone cringes at the thought of auditions, but we don't intimidate people, we help them to discern where God wants to use them in their gifts. If leading others in praise and worship is a high and holy calling, then there should be some prayerful consideration given as to who should be involved.

Psalm 66:1 says, "Make a joyful noise unto God" (Ps. 66:1, *KJV*), and this exhortation is completely appropriate for every believer. But when we aspire to stand before the Body and inspire worship in others, we have to balance the desire of our hearts with our talents for specific roles within the Body. Luke 12:48 says, "From everyone who has been given much, much will be

---

IN THE PROCESS OF FINDING OUR ROLES
WITHIN THE BODY, WE MUST NEVER CONFUSE
WHAT WE DO WITH WHO WE ARE.

---

demanded; and from the one who has been entrusted with much, much more will be asked." Every one of us has been given much, and God expects us to work within the Body to find the area where we can best serve. For those who have musical skills that are recognized by others, the Bible says, "Sing to him a new song; play skillfully, and shout for joy" (Ps. 33:3).

As the music pastor, the Lord has given me the responsibility and spiritual authority to assist Him in inviting people to join the worship ministry in our local church. With this understanding, I ask each person to trust God and to trust me in helping to find his or her best place of ministry in the church. Therefore, when I don't invite people to be part of the worship leadership team, I believe I am encouraging them to discover the place where their giftedness will better serve the Body in order to release the fullness of God's call in their lives.

In the process of finding our roles within the Body, we must never confuse what we do with who we are. Musicians are a strange breed. I know because I am one. We are very creative, sensitive and emotional people, who at times wear our feelings on our sleeves. We often confuse who we are with what we do because our music is such a deep expression of our lives. But if we never learn to separate the two, we set ourselves up for heartbreak.

The truth is that we are all children of God created in His image. We are all the righteousness of God in Christ, and we are all citizens of heaven. This is who we are.

The gifts God has given us are His. They are simply what we do in the Body, not who we are to Him. We don't rely on our roles to give us worth or to make us feel as though we have significance. We don't use our gifts for the prestige or the applause of people. When we separate what we do from who we are, then we can allow others to speak into our lives, to give us direction, to properly place us according to our talents and the needs within our churches, and to instruct us and make us better at what we do.

If we do not separate these issues in our lives, then we become resistant, controlling, obstinate and proud, or we move in the other direction and become too timid or threatened to try. Yes, it is possible for us to both submit our gifts and talents to the Lord, and to allow others to input into our lives to make us more effective in the kingdom of God. When we do this, we stay humble, openhanded and can be a blessing to everyone.

The basis for the team relationship as well as the audition process is Ephesians 4:15 where Paul tells us to speak the truth in love so we can all grow in Christ. Mature relationships require the truth, but not the truth without love.

Usually we either get the ooey-gooey love with no truth, or the brutal truth without love. You may have heard the saying

People don't care how much you know, until they know how much you care. Consider that quote when interacting with musicians. They will respond positively, even to difficult news, if they know that you care about them, if they know you have the courage to shoot straight with them, and if they see your willingness to take the time to invest in them. It's hard work, but well worth the investment.

Rehearsals

Music is the tool to help people worship Him. If the music is not well done, it becomes distracting. If it is well done, people don't notice either those of us who are leading or the music; they notice Him instead, and that is our goal.

Oh, I know it's easy to get bogged down in all the work of rehearsals and preparation and planning, but we do it for a higher purpose. The rehearsals are important because the better we are rehearsed, the easier it is to use the tool of music to encourage worship in others. The sharper the ax, the faster the tree falls, but remember...the music rehearsal is only the tool being sharpened for the greater assignment. The reason for learning music and working hard is so we can internalize the message and be free to embrace the bigger picture of what we do.

Our purpose is bigger than Sunday morning. The reason for having a choir is not the choir. The reason for our church is not the church itself. The reason we're here is that vast numbers of lost people within our city need the power and presence of God in their lives. The ministry exists so they will meet Him.

Once the worship team, choir or orchestra is formed, that group must mold into a family of worshipers. The praise and worship ministry is both outward and inward in its focus and function. Our primary responsibility is to lead the congregation into His presence. At the same time, we must invest in one another and develop relationally so we can become a healthy, vibrant Body of believers.

Cells

To strengthen the interpersonal connections within the worship team, New Life's praise and worship ministries function as a section within the cell system. We have cells entitled Basic Music Stuff, Children's Choir, Youth Choir, Choir, three Exploring Worship cells, a Learning to Sing cell, a Prayer Team for Worship Ministries cell, etc. Through these cells we develop the relationships that keep people connected as a body, as a family of worshipers.

Each cell is a family within a family, and we treat each other as such. Singing with a bunch of people you don't know is neither powerful nor dynamic. But when you've developed a bond of relationships and experiences, worship comes alive.

Our effectiveness in leading worship is genuinely increased when surrounded by people we know, love and trust. When we're connected to each other, we play better, we sing better and we minister with more confidence and authority. After all, relationships are what we're all about, loving God and loving people.

Because of this structure and philosophy, it's easy to embrace the team mentality. As the music pastor, I am the section leader over all the worship cells and the cell leader over the choir. Because I have the heart of a pastor, I love doing what I do with the team. I wouldn't want to do it by myself. An understanding of team dynamics is essential to effective music ministry, and a requirement for receiving God's blessing.

Psalm 133:1,3 says, "How good and pleasant it is when brothers live together in unity!...For there the Lord bestows his blessing, even life forevermore." These verses highlight the pleasure the Lord receives when we live and work together for a common purpose. The team mentality requires everyone to give up their rights as individuals for the good of the whole. We surrender ourselves to bigger goals and objectives, and because we are teammates, we each fulfill our different roles, allowing God to use us as one.

Our numbers provide strength, both physical and spiritual. Of course, this means that we have no tolerance for hot shots or prima donnas. But when we serve each other in humility, then together we accomplish more than we ever could on our own. When we flow together in unity, we get stronger anointing, greater power and most importantly, God's blessing.

THE WORSHIP SERVICE

Two major ingredients for a life-giving church service are corporate worship and the public reading of Scripture.

We come together to give our hearts to the Lord, to minister to one another and to share the Word, all in the context of worship. We attend God. We celebrate His attributes. We worship His majesty, and our hearts are changed in His presence. This is who we are and what we do as believers.

When the life of God is flowing, there should be lots of smiling and laughing. People should be relaxed and feel at home. I'm convinced many people have difficulty enjoying church, simply because they take themselves too seriously. The reason we go to church is to enjoy being with God and with other believers as we function as his Body. There is great delight in that.

A life-giving worship service should feel like a gathering of friends. You know, like when the family is having dinner together and there's a roar of conversation and laughter. People who always approach God with a wrinkled forehead and tight hair miss out on the joy and pleasure of being with the family of believers in worship. Take a drink of living water. Enter into His rest and enjoy Him. And whatever you do, don't become so serious that you lose sight of why you're there.

I was in a church not long ago where the senior pastor was not even in the auditorium during the praise and worship. Then, toward the end of the worship time, he was ushered into the room. While the worship was finishing, he was reading his Bible and seemed to be waiting for worship to finish.

I'm confident that this brother loves to worship the Lord. But his actions came across to me a little self-absorbed and rude to the worship leader. He was reading while others were worshiping, communicating that the worship was to prepare the crowd for the main event, his sermon. It made me appreciate the norm in most life-giving churches, where the senior pastor understands his role in loving the worship leader and helping him lead the congregation in worship.

———

NOT ONLY DO PEOPLE LOOK *TO* THEIR SENIOR PASTOR FOR THE VISION OF THE CHURCH, BUT THEY LOOK *AT* HIM DURING SERVICES TO SEE HIS VISION FOR WORSHIP.

———

It is wonderful when the senior pastor has the heart and passion for leading the church by example in worship. As the one who has been given the spiritual authority to lead the local church, the senior pastor communicates the vision and direction for everything from style to our theology of worship. Not only do people look *to* their senior pastor for the vision of the church, but they look *at* him during services to see his vision for worship.

The worship leader might be trying to lift the people to a higher place in worship, but they won't go unless the senior pastor models worship in his lifestyle. When people see their senior pastor abandoning himself in freedom to praise God wildly, and to worship God in humility, they follow him.

As the spiritual leader, the senior pastor profoundly affects the focus and participation of everyone in attendance. So, senior pastors, lead on! It will be a great blessing to your church and especially to your worship leader.

Worship is making a heart connection. Preaching is not just for transferring information; it is connecting people's lives with the Word of God. The offering is not just a collection, but an act of worship. The singing of songs and our expressions of praise have one ultimate purpose: to open our hearts to the Holy Spirit's ministry and dialogue with us. This affects the kind of songs we choose, as well as the style and format we use to communicate them. Some people ask me, "Why do we have to sing these songs so many times through?"

My response is simple: Most of the time we don't grasp the concept or meaning of the songs until we've sung them a couple of times through, then we want to internalize them and use them to express our hearts to the Lord. Remember, the songs are not worship, but making a heart connection is!

What God thinks is most important. In the final analysis, what we think about our services is not the issue. When we step off the platform on Sundays, our observations of how people responded or what the tone of the meeting was or even how we *felt* about our "performance" are irrelevant. When all is said and done, it's what God thinks that counts.

No matter what happens musically or emotionally during a service, I have learned through experience that God gets the glory anyway. Again and again, I've finished a service that I thought was...let's say less than anointed, but when people approached me afterwards they have said, "That was the most anointed service I've ever been in. God met me and ministered to me in such a powerful way."

Then I think to myself, *Were you in the same service I was in?*

The point is this: Does God get the glory from our services, or do we shortchange Him by thinking it all depends on us? The answer is obvious. God's opinion is the final authority. We want Him to not only be pleased with us, but to receive glory from everything we do.

11

Integration of Life: Free Market Cells

With Russ Walker, Pastor of Small Group Ministries

Get rid of all bitterness, rage and anger, brawling and slander, along with every form of malice. Be kind and compassionate to one another, forgiving each other, just as in Christ God forgave you.

[*Ephesians 4:31,32*]

Disciples, not Spectators

Life-giving bodies of believers can thrive within any structure. They are found in networks of house churches as well as facility-based churches. Some are in denominations; others are independent. In North America, most churches are program based; internationally, most churches are cell based. Having a life-giving church is not contingent upon any particular structure or affiliation. The life of the church is based, instead, upon the spirit that operates within the group itself.

New Life Church represents an unusual combination of structures. I am a Southern Baptist pastor serving in an independent charismatic church. We as a church, though, are highly networked with other churches, locally, nationally and internationally. Our growth throughout the years, however, has dramatically changed the way we do church. We started as a home church, grew through a series of storefronts and became a facility-based program church. Now, as we've continued to grow, the church has become a facility-based cell church. In other words, we have great Sunday services that we all enjoy very much, but the majority of the pastoral care and discipleship occurs in the cells that are led by the ministers of our church, the laypeople.

When New Life was a program-based church, we had a series of departments that coordinated events. We, the paid pastoral team, taught, spoke and built the congregation. The church was relatively large, but we were impersonal in our structures. As we grew, we noticed that our systems were serving lots of people, but we were also beginning to hurt people by not genuinely connecting with them or aiding them in their development in ministry. This resulted in uncomfortably high flow-through. We realized that even though we appeared healthy, our programs produced too many spectators and not enough disciples.

Then it dawned on us: The largest churches in the world are cell churches. Asia, Africa and South America had the largest numbers of people in their churches, and they were empowering them to minister in small group ministries while we in North America were struggling to find a cell-church model that worked for us.

At New Life, we failed twice at adopting cell ministries into the life of our church. I had given up on cells when Larry Stockstill, the Pastor of Bethany World Prayer Center in Baker,

———

EVERYTHING GOD HAS DONE IN OUR LIVES IS UNPROVEN UNTIL IT IS REFINED AND DEMON- STRATED IN THE MIDST OF RELATIONSHIPS.

———

Louisiana, developed an extensive cell system that, though constantly evolving, was working. We sent our staff and key leaders to Bethany to learn. We liked what we saw. After working with the Bethany model for two years, we had 80 successful cells and were seeing positive results.

Larry Stockstill's book *The Cell Church* (Regal) explains the transition from a program-based church to a cell-based church better than any book I've seen. In the book, Brother Larry tells the story of how Bethany World Prayer Center transitioned to a cell church by observing the super megachurches of the world, and how each one ministered to its people and evangelized its community through cell groups.

I knew we had to restructure the way we grouped people so they could minister more effectively to each other. Obviously, being in a small group is the primary way we exemplify godliness.

Everything God has done in our lives is unproven until it is refined and demonstrated in the midst of relationships. There is no way to verify the work of His grace in us if we are independent of others; nor is there any way to demonstrate godliness to any other than God except through interaction with others.

PRESERVING THE LOCAL CHURCH

My difficulty was dealing with those who emphasize the role of small groups for enabling ministry without an adequate understanding of the vital role of the local church. I am an advocate of the local church. I believe in both the institution and its function. I never did, nor do I now, believe that the need for small groups should diminish or threaten the vital and irreplaceable role of strong, healthy local churches. Other groups, though, that emphasize the importance of weekend, facility-based, clergy-led worship services without productively linking believers together are just as problematic.

In the Early Church, even the participants of home meetings went to synagogue on a weekly basis, and still remained networked together through the council at Jerusalem. It seems that when alienation occurs at any level, the effectiveness of both the individual and the Body of Christ as a whole is limited.

I have become convinced that God is preparing to send revival. Therefore, we at New Life want the flexibility that cells provide so we can respond quickly to a rapid influx of new believers. We want to be structured to effectively train those who come to Christ. In our view, the best models for successfully discipling significant numbers of new believers are cell churches. We have noted, however, that even the most successful cell churches throughout the world have powerful weekend believers' meetings. The only exceptions are for obvious reasons in communist or Islamic countries. But in the rest of the world, strong facility-based ministries on weekends led by those who function in the ministry offices listed in Ephesians 4:11 are essential to the effective work of the church. The purpose, however, as I said earlier, is for the weekend meetings to equip all Christian people in their ministries so they can then minister in their homes and workplaces throughout the week (see Eph. 4:12,13).

A NEW REVELATION

Then, I began to experience a revelation in my spirit. Larry Stockstill's message about the necessity for cell churches in North America inspired me to strengthen the role of the believers who had spent years developing personal relationships and godly character in our congregation. I realized that the wisdom of age and the strength of personal example were not being adequately utilized, and too many church attendees were unnecessarily failing in their families and other areas of their lives. I had to do more. We had a successful church by most standards, but I knew we could do so much more if our Body could only connect. With our combined experience and insight, there was no reason for anyone in our Body to fail in any area of their lives.

Then a supernatural series of events started to occur. Almost every morning for a period of several weeks I woke up with a fresh thought about how cells could work in Colorado Springs, or new ideas would come to me during my prayer times. I formed special dream teams to help me think through the impact of the new simple system we were ready to launch. Every day we would meet to refine the ideas.

Rather than eliminating any of our existing programs, we decided to transition them into a new structure that would allow unlimited creativity and innovation. Thus we were able to unleash our Davids (see chapter 2) without threatening anyone. We didn't impose the transition to cells on the church; we offered it. Our cells were so appealing that the church naturally transitioned, and we didn't lose anyone from the church or from any of our old programs because we didn't eliminate anything. We simply gave our old programs opportunity to evolve, and people liked the improvements.

One Sunday morning before the early service, I was standing in my office worshiping when, in a split second, the Holy Spirit came upon me and changed me. I was the senior pastor of thousands of people, and God suddenly changed the purpose of the Sunday services. Rather than going to the service to teach First Peter, I was now going to the service to teach all of those attending to teach First Peter. I understood. Rather than teaching the life of Christ, I was to use the Sunday services to equip the congregation to teach the life of Christ. Sunday services had become in my heart the training, equipping and preparation meetings for empowering those people God had sent to New Life to multiply. Sunday services themselves became the training time for ministers.

Now Ephesians 4:11-16 made sense. Paul wrote:

It was he who gave some to be apostles, some to be prophets, some to be evangelists, and some to be pastors and teachers, to prepare God's people for works of service, so that the body of Christ may be built up until we all reach unity in the faith and in the knowledge of the Son of God and become mature, attaining to the whole measure of the fullness of Christ.

Then we will no longer be infants, tossed back and forth by the waves, and blown here and there by every wind of teaching and by the cunning and craftiness of men in their deceitful scheming. Instead, speaking the truth in love, we will in all things grow up into him who is the Head, that is, Christ. From him the whole body, joined and held together by every supporting ligament, grows and builds itself up in love, as each part does its work.

My understanding of my role was instantly transformed, and so were the roles of those who attended New Life Church. I was to be added to their ministries, they didn't have to be added to mine. They were the purpose; I was to train them. It was my job to build them up and equip them to do what God called them to do. I was their coach, their preparer, their enabler. I was to teach them to minister. I was to teach them First Peter so they could teach First Peter. I understood multiplication. I got it!

A NEW BEGINNING: FREE MARKET CELLS

Free Market Cells were born. Within two months the number of cells increased from 80 to 345. Three months later, that number grew to 392 cells—and it was easy. We didn't have to sell, negotiate with or pressure people. Instead, people joyfully participated because they knew that cells only lasted a semester, which gave them freedom to change groups as their interests or lives changed, and since they were grouped according to interest, stage of life or task, people could easily involve their friends.

Within weeks we offered cells based on books of the Bible, marriage, missions, parenting and prayer. Cells that study the previous week's sermon, emphasize the family, train men and network singles all formed naturally. Suddenly we had cells for children, homeschoolers, young people and women. Praise and Worship cells began training budding worshipers; outreach cells began creatively serving the lost; and recreational cells began connecting people from various backgrounds. Oral Roberts University now offers correspondence classes for credit toward a bachelor's degree through our cells!

Our menu of cells covers practically every interest, subject, profession and stage of life, and they flow naturally out of the congregation. That is what makes them easy. We don't have to think of topics and recruit people, the free market within the church does all of that work, which makes it fun and effective to train many more people in godliness than we ever projected.

THE FREE MARKET PARADIGM

How do we do it? Free markets allow people to be innovative and creative, like they were created to be. Countries that have free market economies allow their citizens the freedom to produce goods and services, and find the marketplaces full of products and their citizens well fed—Free Market Cells do the same thing. They allow people to be innovative and creative with ministry ideas, which keeps people spiritually well fed and growing because of the endless number of ministry opportunities.

All of our churches already have the internal resources to provide great ministries and receive the resulting benefits, and Free Market Cells provide simple tracks that enable people to minister the wisdom God has already built into their lives.

We've found that Free Market Cells work in every area of the church except the nurseries. No longer do cells need to be confined to home-fellowship meetings. With Free Market Cells, the cells are the church rather than being a church with cells. For example, no longer does our children's ministry function as a program of the church with its own recruitment and leadership development. Now each class is a children's cell, with the leadership receiving training through the cell ministry training that goes on for all the other cell leaders. We have now converted every area of New Life Church, from the choir to the youth ministries, to cells, restructuring the programs into small-group philosophy.

Last year New Life grew 24 percent. Our back door, the number of people who left the church, was only 7/10 of 1 percent. The low numbers leaving are attributed to Free Market Cells. They work so well that our new mission is to "promote healthy relationships through small groups, which empower people for ministry." Since we transitioned our children's ministry from Sunday School to children's cells, we not only have children's cells that meet in classrooms during regularly scheduled service times, but we also have children's cells meeting in apartment complexes, parks, daycare centers and homes. It's wonderful!

In the Free Market Cell model, the number of people in each group is not limited, but left to the ability of the leader and the interest of the people. Emphasis is given to attracting people to the cell through their felt needs, so a multitude of topics are available in the groups. People choose the kind of group they want to go to based on relationships or an interest or a need they might have. And, because Free Market Cells provide easy entrance and easy exit, people join cells without hesitation, knowing that every cell has a predetermined transition date, when either the cell ends and members of that cell find a new cell or decide to continue on the next semester with that same cell.

Because these groups are free market, the best groups are the ones that survive and multiply, creating other similar groups, while the weaker groups must improve to survive or dissolve.

Advantages to Free Market Cells

- All participants know in advance the length of time the group will meet so they can comfortably attend, knowing they can cycle out without rejecting anyone or having to quit.
- All groups attract participants through people they already know who have a common interest, or new people who are attracted because of the subject.
- Free Market Cells allow people with various gifts, talents, experiences and personality types to lead. This increases the leadership pool and causes diversity in styles of groups.
- Leaders can teach or lead the group in whatever topic they are most interested in at the time, causing leaders to stay for longer periods because they can switch subjects and styles of groups from semester to semester.

- Because the cells have a time line, some groups stay together and switch subjects each semester, while others continue with the same study. This gives the participants the freedom to transfer to other groups, and keeps the groups vital and constantly expanding.
- Interpersonal relationships remain as the groups evolve and multiply because the participants initially meet around a common interest.
- Groups multiply naturally without effort. Free Market Cells reward success by creating more cells like the successful ones.

The Threefold Purpose of Free Market Cells

1. *To build long-term healthy relationships between people.* The cell meeting is the launching pad people use to develop relationships. In the cell, members meet one another and have an opportunity to dialogue regularly. Because people join a cell based on a common felt need or interest, relationships are built naturally and quickly. Once this foundation is laid, the relationships begin to diversify outside of the scheduled cell meetings. Outside the cell, situations occur that, when properly coached, lead to genuine discipleship and spiritual growth throughout the cell. A sense of genuine community begins to be established and, as a result, the entire cell begins ministering to itself in a healthy way. This is when believers learn *to live* a righteous life, rather than just learning *about living* a righteous life. Cells cultivate a lifestyle of integrity rather than people who just believe they should have a lifestyle of integrity. Major difference.
2. *To disciple people until they become disciplers* (see Heb. 5:11—6:3). We call our cell leaders "life coaches" because they have a great opportunity to coach the people in their

cells in every area of life and to pull them up into ministry. Regardless of their cell subject, we train all of our life coaches how to role model, mentor, motivate and multiply themselves in every cell member. As a result, we have hundreds of people each week strengthening others. This system allows us to reach thousands on the weekends, and thousands more thoughout the week who do not come to our church but are positively impacted by those who do attend. Everyone is to disciple other people until they become disciplers. Multiplication. Major improvement, and much easier than our old system.

3. *To provide the unchurched a safe way to become associated with Christians.* We believe God has a calling on every person, whether they know it or not. Christian people know more about their callings than non-Christians do, so to help people find God's plan for their lives, we invite nonbelievers to our groups and, along with everyone else, they grow in the revelation of why God created us. We encourage every group member to invite an unchurched friend or relative to the group. And because of the structure of the group—common interests, clear purpose and limited duration—those who don't know Christ are very comfortable in these cells.

STRUCTURING THE CELL MINISTRY

The levels of leadership are: cell leader, Section leader, Zone leader and District leader. Each of these leaders is responsible for being life coaches to the people they serve:

- At least two people and one coach form a cell;
- Five to 12 cells form a Section;
- Five to 12 sections form a Zone; and
- Five to 12 zones form a District.

This is not a corporate organizational chart; it is a diagram of relationships that enable people in ministry. Therefore, staff members may be cell leaders, Section leaders, Zone leaders or District leaders. For example, I am a cell leader. I have a cell for ministry leaders that meets at 10:00 A.M. on Wednesday mornings. Pastors from other churches and leaders from servant ministries (parachurch ministries) attend. So the senior pastor is also a cell leader. I love it!

TYPES OF CELL GROUPS

Every ministry of the church, with the exception of the nursery, is a cell ministry. From our children's ministry to our senior's ministry, these cells serve our church and our city. They provide a place for anyone to be equipped to do works of ministry. As I mentioned earlier, not only are cells discussing my Sunday sermons—we call them sermon cells—but they also cover topics such as books of the Bible, various Christian books, marriage enrichment, biblical enrichment, biblical foundations and parenting.

We also have cells for specific groups of people: men, women, singles, seniors, handicapped and youth. In addition we have cell groups that accomplish a certain purpose: ushers, door greeters, musicians and children's workers. Furthermore, we have cell groups that get together for the purpose of doing a specific activity. For example, we have cooking, biking, quilting, various sports and a number of other activity cell groups. All of our cell groups have a purpose!—to help people grow in godliness around their interests.

Characteristics of a Free Market Cell
The following characteristics are the consistent elements included in all cell groups:

1. All cells must engage in one or more of the following:
   - Prayer
   - Worship

- Bible study
- Testimonies

2. All cells must welcome new people unless otherwise designated. For example, some of the marriage cells cannot be joined after they have begun.

3. All cells must have life coaches and assistant life coaches committed to providing pastoral-type support, equipping the cell members in spiritual growth, and intentionally empowering the people in their groups to be more successful in every area of their lives.

4. All cells are to develop members into future leaders.

5. All cell members are encouraged to bring unchurched people who have the same interest as the group within the first month of each new semester. The only exceptions are those groups that close to newcomers after the first week because of the nature of the cell.

6. All cells must have completed their study and be ready to either change subjects or receive additional people by the beginning of the next semester.

7. All cell leaders must communicate with their Section leaders weekly so the Section leaders can coach them for increasing effectiveness.

8. All cells must honorably reflect the ministry, spirit and theological position of New Life Church.

CELL-MINISTRY TRAINING

Three times a year we distribute sign-up cards throughout the congregation to encourage people to become cell leaders. These cards say that, to be a cell leader, a person must commit to:

1. Serve people;
2. Meet weekly with friends;

3. Receive initial training;
4. Get leadership coaching with the senior pastor;
5. Tithe.

If they are willing to do those five things, their next step is to attend an initial training class on a Sunday afternoon.

Training

1. Initial Training Class

The purpose of this class is to provide the future cell leader with the vision, purpose and structure of the cell ministry. Additional training is provided regarding small-group dynamics as well as training for each leader's specialized interests within the cell ministry (i.e., children's, music, Bible, sermons, etc.). These training classes are offered three times a year, approximately one month before the next semester begins on Sunday afternoons.

At the end of this class, applicants complete a form, indicating what topics they want to teach or facilitate. They are then interviewed by a Section leader and/or meet with a Zone leader or District pastor for approval. Once the topic or type of group has been approved, and the application has been approved, the person becomes a cell leader and his/her group will be listed on the menu for the next semester along with the appropriate information to advertise the group.

2. Weekly Leadership Training Class

Training takes place every Sunday night at 5:00 P.M., and every leader (cell leader, Section leader, Zone leader and District pastor) must attend this class. The purpose of this meeting is to provide ongoing leadership training for every leader in the church with the goal of improving their ministries to others. The senior pastor is primarily responsible for this training class; however, he may have a designated representative lead from time to time. The leadership training class format is as follows:

5:00 to 5:30 P.M.: Senior pastor or his representative will speak.

5:30 to 6:00 P.M.: Section leaders meet with their cell leaders (huddles).

5:30 to 6:00 P.M.: District leaders meet with their Zone leaders (huddles).

6:00 to 6:30 P.M.: Zone leaders meet with their Section leaders (huddles).

In addition, all leaders are to call their coaches once a week to give a report about their meeting(s). Thus, each person is in contact with the coach at least twice a week.

The Vital Link: Rally Week

To maintain continuity throughout the year, we use two Rally Weeks—one in January and the other in August—to launch the next semester's cells. Rally Week provides the focus, transition and entry points into cell groups. The Sundays prior to and following Rally Week are used to introduce the upcoming cell groups to the church. A menu with a list of all the cells is distributed in all services for an entire week. The menu includes the topic of each cell group, a brief description of the cell, a short profile about the person leading the group, and the day, time and location of the meeting. Unique characteristics are also listed such as possible costs involved (i.e., purchase of books or other materials), and whether childcare is provided or if a children's cell will coincide with the adult cell meeting. Rally Week consists of the following schedule:

Sunday A.M.: Explain the interrelationships among services, cells and our homes.

Sunday P.M.: Children's Rally Night

Monday: Men's Rally Night

Tuesday: Prayer and Outreach Night

Wednesday: Ladies' Rally Night
Thursday: Music/Praise and Worship
Friday: Singles' Rally Night
Saturday Afternoon: 55 and Wiser Rally
Saturday Night: Youth Rally Night
Sunday A.M.: Commissioning Sunday
Sunday P.M.: Celebration!

At each of these rally-night meetings, we highlight various cells so people can learn more about what is available in their areas of interest. We advertise these rally-night meetings in the community. This system is exactly like the free market in that it looks like chaos, but under closer scrutiny, is systematically discipling believers who are connected with others. Mission accomplished.

12

DEMONSTRATION OF LIFE: ELDERS

WITH LANCE COLES, PASTOR OF CHURCH ADMINISTRATION

THEREFORE I URGE YOU TO IMITATE ME.

[*1 Corinthians 4:16*]

DEFINING THE ROLE OF THE ELDER

Several years ago I was at a pastors' retreat when the subject of church elders came up. Initial responses to the topic ranged from groans to stories of reckless disasters. It was interesting to me, though, that as pastors told stories about elders within their churches who had actually created problems rather than solved problems, each of them was quick to defend the biblical role of elders.

Because these pastors were from various styles of churches, their elders served in a variety of functions. The worst stories came from churches where elders managed rather than served the church, or where they tried to help in delicate situations in which they could not possibly understand the relational subtleties of their decisions, thus creating havoc.

Some would offer a defense of the faithful elders who serve in churches all around the world. The consensus was that most elders were fine people wanting to serve the Body, but that they were poorly placed in structures that put them in situations unsuitable for their experience.

As part of this discussion, I presented the difference between the corporate and the spiritual functions of our churches, and asked whether their elders served spiritual roles, corporate roles, or both. Every one of them said both. I asked if they thought that was the problem. They thought it was. I asked for any suggestions, they had none.

But I did!

This chapter on the role of elders is just that—a suggestion. It's the way we structure the elders ministry at New Life and in our sister churches; it works well. I know that life-giving churches throughout the world structure the function of elders differently, and I'm not suggesting this is the way life-giving churches should operate. As a matter of fact, I'm convinced there is no "absolutely correct" way. But I do believe some structures are more helpful to effective ministry than others.

Our elders don't have any corporate power. On the chart of the corporate and the spiritual, our elders serve the spiritual Body of believers. Their role is to help the senior pastor and his staff keep the church spiritually healthy. They have well-defined functions they perform to keep our Body stable and consistent.

As all Christian leaders know, seemingly endless discussion continues about the title and role of elders. Therefore, the title has evolved to identify various offices and functions within the church, depending on the church's interpretation of Scripture and history. Despite these variations, though, individuals who either perform the function or are placed in the office of elder should always meet the biblical requirements for eldership:

> An elder must be blameless, the husband of but one wife, a man whose children believe and are not open to the charge of being wild and disobedient. Since an overseer is entrusted with God's work, he must be blameless—not overbearing, not quick-tempered, not given to drunkenness, not violent, not pursuing dishonest gain. Rather he must be hospitable, one who loves what is good, who is self-controlled, upright, holy and disciplined. He must hold firmly to the trustworthy message as it has been taught, so that he can encourage others by sound doctrine and refute those who oppose it (Titus 1:6-9).

Now, with 2,000 years of development since these Scriptures were written, elders fill three dominant roles for various groups.

Overseers
The first group oversees churches from outside the local Body. Some would call this group elders, others call them apostles, pres-

byters, bishops or denominational overseers. I call the outside group of elders who oversee churches overseers. Their purpose and authority are described in Article Eight of our Bylaws.

Pastors

The second group of elders is comprised of the pastoral team in a local church. Because of the nature of their roles, we believe the pastoral team should serve and be recognized as the elders who manage the day-to-day operation of the local church. To avoid confusion with the third group of elders, we refer to them as pastors, but often emphasize their ability and responsibility to also serve as elders.

Elders

The third group is the subject of this chapter. They consist of men and women within our local churches who meet the qualifications for an elder and are recognized by the congregation as functioning in that capacity, but they earn their living in the community, not from the tithes of the church members. In our church, they are able to function as elders once elected by the church Body.

In our church government, even though overseers, pastors and elders all meet the biblical qualifications for elders, we have distinguished these three roles with distinct functions. As I've already mentioned, the function of the overseers is described in Article 8 of our Bylaws and the functions of the pastors are discussed in various chapters of this book. Now let's discuss the functions of the elders.

Ten Unique Roles of the Elders

Those we call elders have 10 unique roles they fulfill within our church policy, as outlined in Article Nine of our Bylaws. Even though these elders must perform many more functions within the Body to serve it effectively, the following are identified as the 10 essential to the effective flow of ministry to the church.

I. Teach by Living a Godly, Christian Lifestyle

Elders should reflect a Christlike lifestyle that maintains the respect and confidence of the people whom they serve. We ask our elders to:

- Be responsible financially by living within their means. This idea includes prompt payment of all financial obligations, support of the church and faithfully caring for their families so they can model wise financial planning.
- Avoid the appearance of evil in every area of their lives, which means elders must be careful of what they watch, what they drink, their speech, how they dress, and every other attitude and action. This, too, is a stabilizing force within the church Body as the elders model mature Christian living.
- Demonstrate personal discipline. Personal habits, proper hygiene, appropriate dress and control of eating and exercise all model healthy Christian living for others.
- Show wisdom in their ability to bring others to maturity by successfully participating in the small-group ministries of the church.

We don't want to list every detail of what a godly Christian lifestyle is, and we certainly don't want to fall into the trap of policing others, but this list gives the elders an idea of what kinds of things are important in modeling godliness.

II. Provide a Prayer Shield for the Pastoral Team and the Local Church

Every Christian needs a prayer shield, but because pastors and other Christian leaders are at the spiritual hub of the church, they need even more spiritual protection than other members of the Body. The following reasons indicate why this may be so:

A. Pastors have more responsibility and accountability. James 3:1 says, "Not many of you should presume to be teachers, my brothers, because you know that we who teach will be judged more strictly."

B. Pastors are subjected to more temptation. Because a pastor's role requires that he be transparent and connect with people's hearts, he is subject to greater temptation than most.

C. Pastors are strategic targets for spiritual warfare. Servants of darkness single out pastors for their greatest onslaught of spiritual attack because they know that they can weaken thousands of Christians by getting just one leader to fall.

D. Pastors have more visibility. Because pastors are continually in the public eye, they remain under constant scrutiny and are too often the subject of gossip and criticism, which places an immense burden on them and their families.

Because of the responsibility to provide a prayer shield for the pastoral team and the church, we ask all of our pastors and elders to read and apply the principles in *Prayer Shield* (Regal) by Dr. C. Peter Wagner. This book is an excellent explanation of how to build protective prayer shields.

III. Defend, Protect and Support the Integrity of the Pastoral Team and the Local Church

Not only is the call to defend, protect and support the church and its leadership consistent with Titus 1:6-9, but this teaching is also consistent with James 3:5,6:

Likewise the tongue is a small part of the body, but it makes great boasts. Consider what a great forest is set on fire by a small spark. The tongue also is a fire, a world of evil among the parts of the body. It corrupts the whole person, sets the whole course of his life on fire, and is itself set on fire by hell.

Elders must always be conscious of their speech and not be silent in the face of verbal attacks against the pastoral staff or the local church. This means that elders are expected to speak proactively about the pastoral staff as well as the local assembly. Negative speech is like a cancer and once it spreads, it causes strife and a spiritually unhealthy Body.

I am not suggesting that any elder deny the reality of sin or abuse and ignore it. If for some unfortunate reason a just cause surfaces for criticism about the pastor, it should first be a matter of private prayer. If, after prayer, an elder discerns that pastoral discipline is necessary, then, the procedure is clearly outlined to confront the pastor under number IX of this chapter. But random discussions are not the way to correct problems, so the elders are to put out fires that might be in the congregation or community, and model wisdom in their speech.

IV. Pray for the Sick

The Bible is very specific about the role of prayer in the lives of the elders. James 5:14-16 says, "Is any one of you sick? He should call the elders of the church to pray over him and anoint him with oil in the name of the Lord. And the prayer offered in faith will make the sick person well; the Lord will raise him up. If he has sinned, he will be forgiven. Therefore confess your sins to each other and pray for each other so that you may be healed. The prayer of a righteous man is powerful and effective."

Elders are also included in the commission of the Lord Jesus when He commands all believers in Mark 16:18 to "place their hands on sick people, and they will get well." Clearly, Christ is the healer. Thus, the one who is laying hands on the sick person is an instrument through whom God's healing power can flow.

———

THE OUTCOME OF PRAYER IS NOT DETERMINED BY A SPECIFIC FORMULA OR APPLICATION, BUT BY GOD. THUS, THERE IS NO PRESSURE ON THE ONE PRAYING TO PERFORM A MIRACLE.

———

The outcome of prayer is not determined by a specific formula or application, but by God. Thus, there is no pressure on the one praying to perform a miracle.

Hospital Visitation Protocol

- Make sure the person in the hospital has requested or approves of receiving a visit.
- If someone else has requested a visit on behalf of the sick person, have the requesting party obtain permission from the patient or a family member (if the patient is not able) before the visit. This prevents the patient from being placed in the awkward situation of either having to tell you the visit is unwelcome, or being surprised when you drop in.
- If the patient does accept a visit that has been requested on his or her behalf, try to have the requesting party join you for the visit.

- Do not visit a young person or someone of the opposite sex alone. The exception might be an elderly person or a person with a terminal illness who has requested a private, personal meeting for spiritual reasons.
- Be patient and polite, not loud and self-righteous.
- Listen.
- Be encouraging and sensitive.
- Pray for and with the person, encouraging his or her personal relationship with the Lord.
- Do not attempt to give easy answers.

Procedures for Visitation

1. Before entering the room, ask God to anoint you with the power, wisdom and compassion of the Holy Spirit.
2. Ask the Lord for the gifts of healing and encouragement.
3. If the person doesn't know you, tell him/her who you are and that you are from the church.
4. Bring a gift, e.g., some candy, a Big Mac (if you know his or her diet allows it), a flower, or maybe a toy, a book or a knickknack to cheer up the room.
5. If other family members, friends or medical personnel are in the room, give them priority.
6. At the close of the visit, ask if you can help either the patient or that person's family in any way and follow through on your offer.
7. Convey your commitment to pray for the person and continue to offer support throughout their recovery.
8. Provide lots of opportunity for the patient to be exposed to the healing power of God's Word. The following are some verses you may want to share:

Exodus 15:26: "He said, 'If you listen carefully to the voice of the Lord your God and do what is right in his eyes, if you pay attention to his commands and keep all his decrees, I will not bring on you any of the diseases I brought on the Egyptians, for I am the Lord, who heals you.'"

Psalm 103:3: "Who forgives all your sins and heals all your diseases."

Isaiah 53:4,5: "Surely he took up our infirmities and carried our sorrows, yet we considered him stricken by God, smitten by him, and afflicted. But he was pierced for our transgressions, he was crushed for our iniquities; the punishment that brought us peace was upon him, and by his wounds we are healed."

Matthew 4:23: "Jesus went throughout Galilee, teaching in their synagogues, preaching the good news of the kingdom, and healing every disease and sickness among the people."

Matthew 8:16,17: "When evening came, many who were demon-possessed were brought to him, and he drove out the spirits with a word and healed all the sick. This was to fulfill what was spoken through the prophet Isaiah: 'He took up our infirmities and carried our diseases.'"

Acts 5:15,16: "As a result, people brought the sick into the streets and laid them on beds and mats so that at least Peter's shadow might fall on some of them as he passed by. Crowds gathered also from the towns around Jerusalem, bringing their sick and those tormented by evil spirits, and all of them were healed."

Acts 10:38: "How God anointed Jesus of Nazareth with the Holy Spirit and power, and how he went around doing good and healing all who were under the power of the devil, because God was with him."

1 Peter 2:24: "He himself bore our sins in his body on the tree, so that we might die to sins and live for righteousness; by his wounds you have been healed."

Another way to expose people to the Word of God is by giving them a book. I suggest *Healing the Sick* by T. L. Osborn, *Christ the Healer* by F. F. Bosworth, or a little booklet we have available entitled *Healing Scriptures*, which is an excerpt from the *Full-Life Study Bible*. The booklet is replete with Scriptures regarding healing.

For those who either don't want to read or cannot read because of their illness, you might want to provide a cassette tape player and cassette tape of healing Scriptures being read. Another helpful tool to provide is a set of Scripture posters the person can read while recovering. The posters need to be large enough to be read from across the room, and made with brightly colored pieces of paper and then laminated. Hang them on the walls of the hospital room in view of the patient to build faith.

V. Organize, Implement and Execute Licensing and Ordination Requirements and Procedures

Because ours is an independent church, our elders oversee the licensing and ordination of ministry candidates. Materials explaining licensing and ordination are available from the church office.

VI. Mediating Disputes Among the Brethren

Mediating disputes is one of the greatest provisions we have in our church administration. This provision leaves the pastors in a position to minister to the people involved in a dispute without becoming embroiled in it. And, it protects individual elders.

We use this system not only within our church, but also when believers from our church have major disputes with believers from other churches. In those instances, the case is heard by elders who are selected by our church and the other church. The senior pastors select elders who are not known to the people involved in the dispute so neither party is quite sure which elders are from their respective churches.

According to the Scriptures, believers in Christ are to settle disputes with other believers outside of secular courts of law. The following passages give us clear instructions about how we are to respond to those who disagree with us:

> Therefore, if you are offering your gift at the altar and there remember that your brother has something against you, leave your gift there in front of the altar. First go and be reconciled to your brother; then come and offer your gift.
>
> Settle matters quickly with your adversary who is taking you to court. Do it while you are still with him on the way, or he may hand you over to the judge, and the judge may hand you over to the officer, and you may be thrown into prison. I tell you the truth, you will not get out until you have paid the last penny (Matt. 5:23-26).

> You have heard that it was said, "Eye for eye, and tooth for tooth." But I tell you, Do not resist an evil person. If someone strikes you on the right cheek, turn to him the other also. And if someone wants to sue you and take your tunic, let him have your cloak as well. If someone forces you to go one mile, go with him two miles. Give to the one who asks you, and do not turn away from the one who wants to borrow from you (Matt. 5:38-42).

> If your brother sins against you, go and show him his fault, just between the two of you. If he listens to you, you have

won your brother over. But if he will not listen, take one or two others along, so that every matter may be established by the testimony of two or three witnesses. If he refuses to listen to them, tell it to the church; and if he refuses to listen even to the church, treat him as you would a pagan or a tax collector (Matt. 18:15-17).

If any of you has a dispute with another, dare he take it before the ungodly for judgment instead of before the saints? Do you not know that the saints will judge the world? And if you are to judge the world, are you not competent to judge trivial cases? Do you not know that we will judge angels? How much more the things of this life! Therefore, if you have disputes about such matters, appoint as judges even men of little account in the church! I say this to shame you. Is it possible that there is nobody among you wise enough to judge a dispute between believers? But instead, one brother goes to law against another—and this in front of unbelievers! The very fact that you have lawsuits among you means you have been completely defeated already. Why not rather be wronged? Why not rather be cheated? Instead, you yourselves cheat and do wrong, and you do this to your brothers (1 Cor. 6:1-8).

Prior to the mediation, all parties involved must be willing to voluntarily accept the decision of the elders as binding. The elders may invite the participation of other church members who are experts in the area of disagreement. And, when a dispute is being heard by the elders, those having the dispute must agree to allow the elders to confidentially speak with members of the pastoral staff who may have some insight.

If a dispute involves money, the number of elders required will be based on the following criteria:

Amount of Dispute

- $1 to $10,000: Three elders are to hear and decide this dispute or any disputes that don't involve monetary damages. Each party will select one elder, and the coordinating elder will select one elder. Two of the three elders must agree for a settlement.
- $10,001 to $100,000: Five elders are to hear and decide disputes of this size. Each party may select one elder and the coordinating elder is to select three. Three of the five elders must agree for a settlement.
- $100,001 or more: Seven elders are to hear a dispute of this size. Each party may select two elders and the coordinating elder will select three. Disputes of this magnitude require five of the seven to settle.

The individuals experiencing the dispute may ask people to send letters relating any pertinent information to the elders who are hearing the case. No limit is imposed on the number of letters that may be solicited or reviewed by the elders.

Each person involved in the dispute may bring two people to testify and answer questions during the mediation. One of the elders should open the meeting with prayer. Each side may take no more than one hour to present their case. Then the elders may question those present for as long as they feel is appropriate or necessary.

When the elders are satisfied with the information they have received, the elders should go to a private place to make a decision. Then they are to collectively communicate their decision to the parties involved at the same time in the same room. The opinions of individual elders are NOT to be expressed. Instead, all elders are only to express the final decision of the board.

After the decision has been communicated, the meeting should be closed in prayer, and the elders should remain for ministry if necessary.

VII. Counsel

Elders are to make themselves available as often as is reasonable to assist people within the church with biblical counsel or wisdom from their own experiences.

VIII. Confirm or Reject Pastoral Appointments to the Board of Trustees and the Board of Overseers

To maintain the highest level of accountability, we must have procedures that force us to check and balance one another. One of the ways we do this is by having our elders confirm or reject the people whom the senior pastor appoints as new members of both the board of trustees and the board of overseers.

The decision to either confirm or reject an appointment to these boards is done in accordance with Article Six, Section 4, Paragraph 1 and Article Eight, Paragraph 3 of our church Bylaws.

IX. Contact the Board of Overseers to Initiate Investigation and Potential Discipline of the Senior Pastor

Once again, accountability should always be a top priority, especially in the lives of those who are in positions of great responsibility and leadership. There should never be so much oversight that creativity and ability to lead with efficiency are hindered, but also, never so little that a leader is made unnecessarily vulnerable to the snares of the enemy.

In our system, the senior pastor may only be disciplined or removed for one of the following offenses:

1. Teaching that violates the creed of the church;
2. Misappropriation of funds;
3. Sexual misconduct.

If an elder is alerted to allegations against the senior pastor regarding any of these three offenses, the elder should meet with the pastor according to Matthew 18. If that meeting does not satisfy the elder, the elder and senior pastor may contact any member of the board of overseers to express their concerns. The overseers may then investigate the situation in compliance with Article Eight, Paragraph 3 of the church Bylaws.

X. Represent the Church to Other Churches

Most churches need representation from time to time at special events and with sister churches. In these situations, an elder may be the appropriate representative.

Section IV

Business That Strengthens the Life-Giving Church

Proper planting and organizing are vitally important to the protection of a life-giving church. Regardless of the role you have in ministry, understanding the subtitles of the next two chapters will assist your healthy participation in ministry for the rest of your life.

13

CHURCH PLANTING:
FIRST THINGS FIRST

WITH JOSEPH THOMPSON, ASSOCIATE PASTOR

IT [THE KINGDOM OF GOD] IS LIKE A MUSTARD
SEED, WHICH IS THE SMALLEST SEED YOU PLANT IN
THE GROUND. YET WHEN PLANTED, IT GROWS AND
BECOMES THE LARGEST OF ALL GARDEN PLANTS,
WITH SUCH BIG BRANCHES THAT THE BIRDS OF
THE AIR CAN PERCH IN ITS SHADE.

[*Mark 4:31,32*]

A Biblical Pattern

Just as children always reflect some of the attributes of their parents, so churches usually reflect the strengths and weaknesses of their founding. Here in Colorado Springs, we've seen many churches grow into powerful places of worship, while others have failed miserably. The reasons for the successes and failures are numerous, but the Bible does give us some hints to guide us in the planting of a healthy church. Exodus provides an amazingly helpful series of events that directly parallels the process necessary for planting a strong local church.

I. Recognize an Area of Need: Exodus 1

Exodus 1 portrays God's chosen people as needy and horribly oppressed. When planting a new church, we too must locate people with unusual needs. Chapter one of Exodus gives us an example for the placement of a church plant: a place where people are being harshly enslaved by darkness. Verse 11 says that Pharaoh "put slave masters over them to oppress them with forced labor." The Bible continues by reporting that the slave masters "made their lives bitter with hard labor in brick and mortar and with all kinds of work in the fields; in all their hard labor the Egyptians used them ruthlessly" (v. 14). This tyranny evolved into mass murder with Pharaoh ordering the slaughter of male babies born to Jewish mothers (see v. 22).

These verses canvass the ruthlessness of the powers of darkness enslaving people. Pharaoh, a type of Satan with his demonic influences, restrains God's people and, when necessary, murders any who might become a threat to his rule.

This scene, which demands God's liberating power, paints the backdrop for modern-day church plants; they should be strategically placed in oppressive, dark areas where the voice of God is only a whisper. The greater the darkness, the greater the need for light. For example, because of the darkness that oppresses people with such ruthlessness in so many cities, it might not be sound spiritual judgment to plant a church where an abundance of churches are already doing an effective work. Certainly, a need probably still exists in those areas, but the degree of need does not compare to those cities where there is less Christian influence.

This kind of thinking is standard in the world of missions. Currently, Dr. C. Peter Wagner of Fuller Seminary is coordinating prayer efforts specifically targeted at the world's darkest areas. Millions of intercessors from more than 120 countries are networking to focus their prayers toward the darkest areas of the earth.

At the same time, many outreach-evangelism groups are working on the heels of the prayer effort to follow up with tract and Bible distribution designed to promote church planting. Many believe that this generation can be the first to have the gospel available to every person on earth in his or her own language and culture. Because of the possibility, missiologists such as Dr. Wagner and others have wisely called all local churches to strategically focus their outreach efforts where they are most needed. As of this writing, 1,739 of the least evangelized people groups are being targeted with prayer and evangelism to bring at least a flicker of light to the darkest regions of the world.

Those efforts do not negate the fact that people in so-called reached areas have needs too. They do. All are needy. Some, however, are more needy than others. And God is calling us as believers to penetrate the darkness of the world with His light.

Sometimes, though, light tends to enjoy other light. It's more comfortable being one more light in a room with some light than going into a dark room to create only enough light to cast a shadow. We are called to be salt and light. Salt is better on food than in the shaker, and light shines brightest in darkness. Thus, when the spark that we carry is ignited by the wind of God's Spirit, we are neither burned out nor overcome by the foul breath of

———

WE ARE CALLED TO BE SALT AND LIGHT.
SALT IS BETTER ON FOOD THAN IN
THE SHAKER, AND LIGHT SHINES
BRIGHTEST IN DARKNESS.

———

demonic forces. Instead, we are fanned into life-giving flames that set the darkness ablaze.

So step number one should be to locate people who are in great need.

II. Appropriate Spiritual Authority: Exodus 2

Exodus 2 gives the account of when Moses "saw an Egyptian beating a Hebrew, one of his own people" (v. 11). In haste Moses killed the Egyptian, which embittered the Jewish people as well as the Egyptians against him. Because he was premature in his actions, Moses failed in providing any relief to his people. He didn't have the spiritual strength to confront Pharaoh, nor the spiritual authority to lead the Jewish people.

Moses was a good man, and he had been well trained. If being a man of God with fine training and good intentions had been the necessary combination for success, Moses would have achieved victory at this point. But Moses failed because he greatly lacked the spiritual authority needed to liberate others.

Being a well-trained, well-meaning Christian trying to do a church plant is not enough. We must be assured that God has appointed the timing, anointed the man and allocated a divine sense of spiritual strength for the task. When people show up and get excited about a new church plant, we can easily mistake their enthusiasm as a false signal for God's timing. And false starts do generate a degree of gratification, but they do not bring lasting results: Moses did kill the evil Egyptian, but that did not give him victory over Egypt, nor did it give him the right to lead the Jewish people to liberty. He won a little battle that, in fact, hurt rather than helped.

Many church plants start the same way, and usually lead to hurt feelings and discouraged leaders. "Unless the Lord builds the house [church plant or ministry], its builders labor in vain" (Ps. 127:1). Moses took the only sensible course of action available— he aborted the plan, got alone with God and allowed God to raise him up. If Moses had stayed, he would have been destroyed and God would have had to call another.

III. Receive a Divine Charge: Exodus 3

In Exodus 3 Moses encounters God through a burning bush. It is here that Moses receives a mandate and a blueprint from God for delivering the people of Israel out of their suffering. This is an essential step in successfully fulfilling God's call to plant churches. Only God's mandate can provide the spiritual strength and authority needed to win the war for the souls of men.

When God says, "Take off your sandals, for the place where you are standing is holy ground" (v. 5), He is demonstrating our need to have a divine, holy experience with Him. Part of that holy experience is God sharing His burdens with us. God explains in verses 7 and 8, "I have indeed seen the misery of my people in Egypt. I have heard them crying out because of their slave drivers, and I am concerned about their suffering. So I have come down to rescue them from the hand of the Egyptians" (emphasis added).

God is speaking to Moses about His concern for His people. He wants to partner with Moses in fulfilling His plan for Israel. But because Moses has learned the lesson so well from his hasty first mistake, he responds, "Who am I, that I should go to Pharaoh and bring the Israelites out of Egypt?" (v. 11). God likes that response. Moses' impulsive flesh and self-generated strength has now surrendered to the Master so God's plan can unfold. He starts giving Moses supernatural insight and strategy—fresh ideas.

I will never forget praying and fasting in a pup tent on the back of Pikes Peak. During those three days, God spoke deeply into my heart some things that burn in me to this day, 12 years later. He spoke to me about Praise Mountain, a prayer and fasting center that now exists in Florissant, Colorado. He spoke to me about New Life Church, which now exists in Colorado Springs. And He spoke to me about the World Prayer Center, which is currently under construction.

That was my burning bush experience, and because of it, the city looks different to me than it does to many. God spoke into my spirit what He thought of Colorado Springs and what He wanted the city to look like. He shared His plans. As the bush burns, it is never consumed. It just keeps speaking...forever.

To do a church plant without a divine charge creates a soulish church that lacks spiritual strength. But when the bush burns, it produces a humility that combines with boldness to create a foundation for action that is difficult to crack.

IV. Make Practical Preparations: Exodus 4

Even though God had spoken to Moses about His desire to liberate the Jewish people through his leadership, other practical issues still had to be settled. As those issues surface in Exodus 4, notice how they parallel those of the modern-day church plant. Moses needed:

A tangible sign from God (vv. 2-7). Moses' staff became a snake and then a staff again. God caused his hand to become leprous and restored it to normal. This same kind of supernatural confirmation is fundamental to pioneering a church plant. I don't believe the confirmation must always be as dramatic as that of Moses, but it must be enough to convince the church planter that there is enough empirical evidence to prove God has indeed spoken to him.

A friend (vv. 14-16). Note here that Moses does not need a board, a committee, government or structure to confront Pharaoh; he needs a friend. Moses feels inadequate, and his feelings frustrate and anger God. Nonetheless, God allows Moses' brother and friend, Aaron, to stand beside him to give strength and confidence. We learn later that Aaron alone is not strong, and we see here that Moses alone is not strong, but *together*, they can fulfill God's calling. In the same way, the success of a life-giving church plant will require the strength of loyal, sacrificial friendship. Genuine friendships empower people.

Submission to God's delegated authorities (v. 18). Even after this dramatic experience with God, Moses asked Jethro, his father-in-law for whom he was working, to give him permission to return to Egypt. God commands us to pray for all who are in authority over us so "we may live peaceful and quiet lives in all godliness and holiness" (1 Tim. 2:2). If we fail to pray for those in authority over us and fail to receive their blessing, the result can be unnecessary vulnerability. But Moses asked permission from his authority to do what God had commanded him to do, and God granted Moses' request through Jethro. This was, in effect, additional confirmation.

After my burning bush experience on the back side of Pikes Peak, I went to Roy Stockstill, my senior pastor for whom I was working at the time, and asked permission to move to Colorado Springs so I could fulfill my calling. He then flew from Baton Rouge, Louisiana, to Colorado Springs to meet with pastors and observe the city. When he returned, he told me that he could indeed see why God was calling me and he released me to go.

Obedience (vv. 24-26). Moses' wife, Zipporah, rescued Moses from the consequences of disobedience to God. When God called me to Colorado Springs, I was watching a baseball game as the Lord unexpectedly spoke into my spirit: *If you'll obey me, your effectiveness in Colorado Springs will be like this.* Immediately, the team I was watching started doing everything perfectly. It looked as though a professional team were playing against elementary school students. Then God said, *If you disobey me, you'll still be somewhat effective because of my grace, but your life will be like this.* Remarkably, the same team lost all ability. They couldn't hit, throw, catch or even communicate clearly. The game became a miserable, horrible experience for them. I got the picture. Obedience is a must.

Initial positive reception by the core of friends who shared his vision (vv. 29-31). Moses and Aaron met with the elders of Israel to share the vision, and God confirmed His plan to use Moses by performing the signs before them. The elders, therefore, believed that Moses was sent to them in answer to their prayers and worshiped God for his provision. Unity was established. We see here that, in order to do a church plant, a sense of unity, focus and purpose must be established among those who help to plant the church.

As soon as the practical preparation was complete, Moses, with Aaron at his side, was ready to confront Pharaoh.

V. Boldly Confront Demonic Strongholds: Exodus 5—11

Moses leads through influence, not corporate power. He gains his strength directly from the Lord and his relationships with his friends, not a formal committee. Notice, however, that when Moses is confronting the false gods of Egypt and demanding that they release the Jewish people in chapters 5 through 11, he does not call for a board meeting or a consultation to determine *what*

FRIENDSHIPS ARE AN IMPENETRABLE FORCE

BECAUSE OF THE FLEXIBILITY AND POWER

OF AN UNSPOKEN COVENANT.

God may be saying. Instead, Moses forcefully confronts the demonic strongholds that are empowering the Egyptians. That demonic hold on Israel is ultimately broken and then, with the Passover, comes the type of liberation through Christ.

These chapters on confrontation provide types of engaging prayer for us. Prayer is both communion and confrontation. Chapters 5-11 show the strength appropriated through Moses' communion with God for *confrontation* with darkness.

The confrontation begins when God instructs Moses to have Aaron throw down his staff before Pharaoh. The fact that Aaron is to throw down the staff, not Moses, is a testimony to the necessity for friends in the midst of battles.

When we were beginning New Life Church, a core of us worked together as friends. The relationships that formed because of our common purpose were much more important than any corporate positions, job descriptions or salaries. The innocence of the early days is very important as everyone works together, eats together, prays together and ministers together. No one worries about who should do what because of the friendships.

Without this understanding about relational ties, the spiritual battle required for the birthing of a local church in a needy area may be substituted with a corporate structure. When that happens, the forces of darkness easily infiltrate that birthing church and either kill it or at least control it, rendering it powerless.

Friendships are an impenetrable force because of the flexibility and power of an unspoken covenant. We see this type of empowering friendship with Moses and Aaron; David and Jonathan; Jesus and John; and Paul with his friends in Philippi. The list could go on and on, but the vital power of friendships must not be underestimated if we are to win the spiritual battles that will confront us as we begin a church plant.

The most important friendship of all, of course, is our relationship with Jesus Christ. He is the friend "who sticks closer than a brother" (Prov. 18:24), and it is the strength and connectedness we have with Him through a healthy, ongoing prayer life that will ultimately conquer our enemies.

Systematically, the Lord sent 10 different plagues to demonstrate that the God of Israel is more powerful than any of the gods of Egypt. In Colorado Springs a religious god of control had enslaved many churches. We had to confront it. We have also had to deal with other gods (evil spirits) in our area. Every community has demonic strategies that will attempt to enslave people. If that were not so, there would be no need for church plants.

These Egyptian gods were dealt with one at a time through the plagues that God sent. Sometimes demonic forces would respond to God's plagues by demonstrating their powers. Other times the demonic forces chose to hide or leave. That same pattern is consistent in any strong church plant. Threatened demonic powers may resist, not exist or simply surrender.

When the Nile turned to blood, the impotence of the water deity Iris was exposed. God sent a multitude of frogs and then killed them to demonstrate victory over Ptha and Heka, the Egyptian gods that glorified the supremacy of human life. Leb, the earth god, was embarrassed when God sent lice (gnats). The plague of flies was a blow against Khepara, the beetle god, god of the insects. The next plague was a plague of *murrain* (a general term implying a plague upon domestic animals) and was aimed at Apis (or Seraphis), the sacred cattle god at Memphis.

The plague of boils kept people from worshiping Neit, the Egyptian goddess, queen of heaven. Iris, the water god, and Osiris, the fire god, were proven inept when God sent the hail. And the locusts proved God's superiority over Shu, the god of the air. The final blow came when God demonstrated His sovereignty over Ra (or Atun Re), the sun god, the supreme god of Egypt, represented by Pharaoh himself. God sent darkness to the earth and brought death upon the firstborn of all Egyptians, including the son of Pharaoh.

Only after this awesome display of spiritual might did Pharaoh surrender and let God's people go. Similarly, the true effectiveness of church planting (delivering people from bondage to sin and death) is only realized after major confrontations with the forces of darkness have resulted in a supernatural display of God's might.

VI. Publicly Emphasize Jesus' Victory—Celebrate!
Exodus 12—17

Confrontation with the demonic will always yield good fruit, tangible evidence. The first Passover demonstrates for us the ministry of Christ's sacrifice, which opens the door for the liberation of the people from Satan's grasp. Moses leads the people out of Egypt and when they reach the Red Sea, the Lord causes it to supernaturally part, allowing the Israelites to cross over to the other side. This crossing through the Red Sea symbolizes a rebirth of the people of Israel—a metaphor for conversion growth in the New Testament Church.

In chapter 15 we see demonstrative praise and celebration—happy people. Victory and deliverance from oppression are celebrated as bitter water turns sweet, healing is promised and received, and springs and palm trees appear—all pictures of the celebration and the innocence that should engulf people in every church as they rejoice over their newfound freedom in Christ.

Chapters 16 and 17 give us a type of the New Testament Church complete with signs and wonders. God miraculously provides food in the form of manna from heaven and water from the rock to satisfy thirst. Both the manna and the rock point to Christ, and the water refers to the Holy Spirit.

Spiritual growth within the Body of Christ is where the strength of established friendships becomes even more apparent. We see Moses observing the Israelites in battle with the Amalekites from his vantage point on top of a hill. As long as his arms are raised to the heavens, Israel is victorious. As soon as Moses begins to tire and his arms start to drop, Amalek begins to win. Enter Aaron and Hur. They place a large rock under Moses so he is able to sit down. Then they hold up his arms, one on either side, to provide strength. Israel is victorious.

Joshua is fighting on the battlefield for Moses. Aaron and Hur hold Moses' hands up when he grows weary. Friendship increases the strength and integrity of the early victories in any church plant. Once the early battles have been won, the resulting growth is so overwhelming that soon a fully functioning church government needs to be in place. Thus, Moses is overwhelmed by his ministry load and Jethro recommends the establishment of a formal government.

VII. Now, Establish a Functional Church Government: Exodus 18

Now that the church has begun to experience numerical and spiritual growth, a system of governance should be put in place to serve the needs of the larger Body. Exodus 18 paints a clear picture of this process.

Moses is spending all of his time adjudicating disputes among the people when his father-in-law suggests that there is a better way to minister to their needs:

> Listen now to me and I will give you some advice, and may God be with you. You must be the people's representative before God and bring their disputes to him. Teach them the decrees and laws, and show them the way to live and the duties they are to perform. But select capable men from all the people—men who fear God, trustworthy men who hate dishonest gain—and appoint them as officials over thousands, hundreds, fifties and tens. Have them serve as judges for the people at all times, but have them bring every difficult case to you; the simple cases they can decide themselves. That will make your load lighter, *because they will share it with you*. If you do this and God so commands, you will be able to stand the strain, and all these people will go home satisfied (vv. 19-23, italics added).

This is a perfect illustration of some of the attendant problems with numerical growth. There comes a time when the weight of ministry needs to be shared simply because it is too overwhelming for one person. Under these circumstances the formation of a church government or corporation becomes essential for effective ministry to the Body.

The problem is further reiterated by Jethro's statement in verses 17 and 18:

What you are doing is not good. You and these people
who come to you will only wear yourselves out. The work
is too heavy for you; you cannot handle it alone.

When we started New Life Church, we had a basic church-
government system for processing funds and purchasing a few
small items, but the church didn't really function through the
church-government system in those early stages. Instead, the
governing process was similar to what Moses went through.

God called me for a specific task and my friends helped to
empower me to take risks. I was not rebellious. I was submissive
just as Moses was, but I was also decisive and directional. It was
not the time yet for boards and committees because I knew that,
even though others were called to join with me, they had not
heard what I had heard, nor seen what I had seen, nor were they
responsible for what God had told me to do. We did pray together, and many times in the midst of engaging prayer, we would
talk about what the Lord was doing. What little government we
had at that stage was not to make decisions, but to enable vision.
We only had enough government to serve, not to lead.

As in the case of Moses, in every successful church plant there
eventually comes a time to delegate areas of responsibility to
people who have proven themselves to be mature and faithful. At
that stage a defined corporate and spiritual structure must be set
in place to serve the Body.

Furthermore, after working through the steps of church planting right up to establishing a church government, a need arises to
provide a written law or statutes for the people. This process of
"receiving" the law is outlined in Exodus 19 and 20.

Moses meets with God on Mount Sinai and is given the Ten
Commandments as a guide for the people. The "Sinai experience"
only becomes relevant at the time a corporate structure is being
instituted. This enables the house vision to be clearly articulated
with defined roles and parameters established for every individual.

Exodus describes the step-by-step procedures we must go through to plant a church. If we can keep from bogging down in unnecessary complexity and unproductive structures, the life-giving flow that birthed the church will continue on into its maturity. Don't organize the corporate structure too soon. Instead, let life attract so many people that organization demands formation because of the volume of ministry required.

14

BYLAWS:
JETHRO'S REQUEST

THERE IS A TIME FOR EVERYTHING, AND A SEASON
FOR EVERY ACTIVITY UNDER HEAVEN.

[*Ecclesiastes 3:1*]

PEACE, PEACE, WONDERFUL PEACE

This final chapter is where the rubber meets the road. As I said earlier, staying in the tree of life is possible within any church structure, but some structures make ministry easy, while others unnecessarily complicate it.

This chapter is a set of recommended Bylaws with footnotes that explain the reasoning for the Bylaws. Some of these ideas you will like; others you will not. That's fine. Mark the ones you like and, if you decide to adopt them, consult an attorney to adapt the correct wording for the laws within your state. Take what you like and leave the rest. I would suggest, though, that spiritual freedom could be short-lived without structural freedom. These simple Bylaws give people the freedom to minister without providing a license to sin. Good combination.

Bylaws are the rules that govern an organization. I've seen some organizations that overemphasize their Bylaws and strangle the life out of everyone, and others that don't have any Bylaws; therefore, they find themselves in trouble when the unexpected happens. The Bylaws that follow are simple but thorough. I think you'll actually enjoy them. I know they can save you great heartache and provide the protection needed for effective ministry. So get a cup of coffee, a pen in hand to make some notes and sit back to enjoy them. Smile.

ARTICLE ONE

Offices

The principal office of [church name], hereinafter referred to as the Corporation, shall be located at the address set forth in the Articles of Incorporation. The Corporation may have such other offices, either within or without the State of Incorporation, as the board of trustees may determine.[1]

1. If you are leasing, it is important that the principal office of the Corporation be an address that is consistent. Most states allow a residential address to be used if the meeting location is transitional. However, if you have a permanent church location, that is the address to use.

ARTICLE TWO

Membership

Members shall be all people who contribute financially to the Corporation (church). Membership is granted and recognized with voting powers when a person has attended the church long enough to receive an annual contributions statement. A contribution statement is the certificate of membership. Should one year pass without a record of contribution, membership is automatically terminated. Members' voting rights are described in Article Nine, Paragraph 5, relating to nominations for the board of elders and Article Five, relating to the selection of a new senior pastor. Members shall have no other voting rights.[2]

2. This bylaw is the balance between those who strongly emphasize church membership and those who have no formal membership at all.

   I believe people need to know what determines their membership in their local church, and I think the pastor needs to know who is a member and who is not. But membership should be structured so the leadership team is 100 percent consumed with drawing people into a relationship with the Lord, not the church. Once people establish a relationship with the Lord, their natural responses signal that they have become members of the Church.

I don't think it's wise to have too many hoops to jump through or barriers to hurdle to become a member. Actually, I've observed that when people start referring to the church in the first person, "my church" or "our church" it means that their hearts have been added to the church Body. Once again, strive for balance. People need to be strongly committed to the local church without a hyper sense of obligation. That is what this article allows.

ARTICLE THREE

Statement of Faith[3]

Holy Bible: The Holy Bible, and only the Bible, is the authoritative Word of God. It alone is the final authority for determining all doctrinal truths. In its original writing, the Bible is inspired, infallible and inerrant (see Prov. 30:5; Rom. 16:25,26; 2 Tim. 3:16; 2 Pet. 1:20,21).

Trinity: There is one God, eternally existent in three persons: Father, Son (Jesus) and Holy Spirit. These three are coequal and coeternal (see Gen. 1:26; Isa. 9:6; Matt. 3:16,17; 28:19; Luke 1:35; Heb. 3:7-11; 1 John 5:7).

Jesus Christ: Jesus Christ is God the Son, the second person of the Trinity. On earth, Jesus was 100 percent God and 100 percent man. He is the only man *ever* to have lived a sinless life. He was born of a virgin, lived a sinless life, performed miracles, died on the Cross for humankind and, thus, atoned for our sins through the shedding of His blood. He rose from the dead on the third day according to the Scriptures, ascended to the right hand of the Father, and will return again in power and glory (see Isa. 9:6; John 1:1,14; 20:28; Phil. 2:5,6; 1 Tim. 2:5; 3:16).

Virgin Birth: Jesus Christ was conceived by God the Father, through the Holy Spirit (the third person of the Trinity) in the virgin Mary's womb; therefore, He is the Son of God (see Isa. 7:14; Matt. 1:18,23-25; Luke 1:27-35).

Redemption: Humanity was created good and upright, but by voluntary transgression, it fell. Humanity's only hope for redemption is in Jesus Christ, the Son of God (see Gen. 1:26-31; 3:1-7; Rom. 5:12-21).

Regeneration: For anyone to know God, regeneration by the Holy Spirit is absolutely essential (see John 6:44,65).

Salvation: We are saved by grace through faith in Jesus Christ: His death, burial and resurrection. Salvation is a gift from God, not a result of our good works or of any human effort (see Rom. 10:9,10; Acts 16:31; Gal. 2:16; 3:8; Eph. 2:8,9; Titus 3:5; Heb. 9:22).

Repentance: Repentance is the commitment to turn away from sin in every area of our lives and to follow Christ, which allows us to receive His redemption and to be regenerated by the Holy Spirit. Thus, through repentance we receive forgiveness of sins and appropriate salvation (see Acts 2:21; 3:19; 1 John 1:9).

Sanctification: Sanctification is the ongoing process of yielding to God's Word and His Spirit in order to complete the development of Christ's character in us. It is through the present ministry of the Holy Spirit and the Word of God that the Christian is enabled to live a godly life (see Rom. 8:29; 12:1,2; 2 Cor. 3:18; 6:14-18; 1 Thess. 4:3; 5:23; 2 Thess. 2:1-3; Heb. 2:11).

Jesus' Blood: The blood Jesus Christ shed on the cross of Calvary was sinless and is 100 percent sufficient to cleanse humankind from all sin. Jesus allowed Himself to be punished for both our sinfulness and our sins, enabling all those who believe to be free from the penalty of sin, which is death (see John 1:29; Rom. 3:10-12,23; 5:9; Col. 1:20; 1 John 1:7; Rev. 1:5; 5:9).

Jesus Christ Indwells All Believers: Christians are people who have invited the Lord Jesus Christ to come and live inside them by His Holy Spirit. They relinquish the authority of their lives over to Him, thus making Jesus the Lord of their lives as well as Savior. They put their trust in what Jesus accomplished for them when He died, was buried and rose again from the dead (see John 1:12; 14:17,23; 15:4; Rom. 8:11; Rev. 3:20).

Baptism in the Holy Spirit: Given at Pentecost, the baptism in the Holy Spirit is the promise of the Father. It was sent by Jesus after His Ascension to empower the Church to preach the gospel throughout the whole earth (see Joel 2:28,29; Matt. 3:11; Mark 16:17; Acts 1:5; 2:1-4,17,38,39; 8:14-17; 10:38,44-47; 11:15-17; 19:1-6).

The Gifts of the Holy Spirit: The Holy Spirit is manifested through a variety of spiritual gifts to build and sanctify the Church, demonstrate the validity of the Resurrection and confirm the power of the gospel. The lists of these gifts in the Bible are not necessarily exhaustive, and the gifts may occur in various combinations. All believers are commanded to earnestly desire the manifestation of the gifts in their lives. These gifts always operate in harmony with the Scriptures and should never be used in violation of biblical parameters (see Rom. 1:11; 12:4-8; 1 Cor. 12:1-31; 14:1-40; Eph. 4:16; 1 Tim. 4:14; 2 Tim. 1:5-16; Heb. 2:4; 1 Pet. 4:10).

The Church: The Church is the Body of Christ, the habitation of God through the Spirit, with divine appointments for the fulfillment of Jesus' Great Commission. Every person born of the Spirit is an integral part of the Church as a member of the Body of believers. There is a spiritual unity of all believers in our Lord Jesus Christ (see John 17:11,20-23; Eph. 1:22; 2:19-22; Heb. 12:23).

Two Sacraments:

Water Baptism: Following faith in the Lord Jesus Christ, the new convert is commanded by the Word of God to be baptized in water in the name of the Father, and of the Son, and of the Holy Spirit (see Matt. 28:19; Acts 2:38).[4]

The Lord's Supper: A unique time of communion in the presence of God when the elements of bread and grape juice (the body and blood of the Lord Jesus Christ) are taken in remembrance of Jesus' sacrifice on the cross (see Matt. 26:26-29; Mark 16:16; Acts 8:12,36-38; 10:47,48; 1 Cor. 10:16; 11:23-26).

Healing of the Sick: Healing of the sick is illustrated in the life and ministry of Jesus, and included in Jesus' commission to His disciples. Healing of the sick is given as a sign that is to follow believers. It is also a part of Jesus' work on the cross and one of the gifts of the Spirit (see Ps. 103:2,3; Isa. 53:5; Matt. 8:16,17; Mark 16:17,18; Acts 8:6,7; Rom. 11:29; 1 Cor. 12:9,28; Jas. 5:14-16).

God's Will for Provision: The Father's will is that believers become whole, healthy and successful in all areas of life. But because of the Fall, many may not receive the full benefits of God's will while on earth. That fact, though, should never prevent all believers from seeking the full benefits of Christ's provision in order to serve others.

- Spiritual (see John 3:3-11; Rom. 10:9,10; 2 Cor. 5:17-21).
- Mental and emotional (see Isa. 26:3; Rom. 12:2; Phil. 4:7,8; 2 Tim. 1:7; 2:11).
- Physical (see Isa. 53:4,5; Matt. 8:17; 1 Pet. 2:24).
- Financial (see Deut. 28:1-14; Josh. 1:8; Ps. 34:10; 84:11; Mal. 3:10,11; Luke 6:38; 2 Cor. 9:6-10; Phil. 4:19).

Resurrection: Jesus Christ was physically resurrected from the dead in a glorified body three days after His death on the cross. As a result, both the saved and the lost will be resurrected—they that are saved to the resurrection of life, and they that are lost to the resurrection of eternal damnation (see Luke 24:16,36,39; John 2:19-21; 20:26-28; 21:4; Acts 24:15; 1 Cor. 15:42,44; Phil. 1:21-23; 3:21).

Heaven: Heaven is the eternal dwelling place for all believers in the gospel of Jesus Christ (see Matt. 5:3,12,20; 6:20; 19:21; 25:34; John 17:24; 2 Cor. 5:1; Heb. 11:16; 1 Pet. 1:4).

Hell: After living one life on earth, the unbelievers will be judged by God and sent to hell where they will be eternally tormented with the devil and the fallen angels (see Matt. 25:41; Mark 9:43-48; Heb. 9:27; Rev. 14:9-11; 20:12-15; 21:8).

Second Coming: Jesus Christ will physically and visibly return to earth for the second time to establish His kingdom. This will occur at a date undisclosed by the Scriptures (see Matt. 24:30; 26:63,64; Acts 1:9-11; 1 Thess. 4:15-17; 2 Thess. 1:7,8; Rev. 1:7).

3. The statement of faith should say exactly what you want the church to believe throughout the generations. Your statement of faith is the way to protect the church, because no senior pastor can ever serve the church who does not believe and teach the creed of the church. To violate the creed is reason for dismissal.

4. We have chosen not to fight over our baptism formula. Matthew 28:19 says, "Therefore go and make disciples of all nations, baptizing them in the name of the Father and of the Son and of the Holy Spirit." Acts 2:38 says, "Peter replied, 'Repent, and let every one of you be baptized in the name of Jesus Christ for the remission of sins; and you shall receive the gift of the Holy Spirit.'"

   So when we baptize in water, we say, "I baptize you in the name of the Father, and of the Son, and of the Holy Spirit, in the name of Jesus Christ." That way we cover all of the scriptural instructions regarding water baptism.

ARTICLE FOUR

Government

[Church name] is governed by the congregation, the trustees of the Corporation, the office of the senior pastor and the overseers. The congregation determines the spiritual tone, strength and direction of the church by wisely selecting the senior pastor. The trustees are to serve the church by setting policy in the management of the church Corporation and making the major financial decisions for the church. The senior pastor's office is responsible for overseeing the day-to-day ministry of the church, and the board of overseers is to protect the church through counsel, prayer and, if required, the discipline of the senior pastor.[5]

5. This article formally introduces the balanced combination of the four primary methods of church government. All churches use these basic systems to one degree or another, but we use each of these in their most positive function, resulting in an excellent separation of power and clearly defined roles.

ARTICLE FIVE

Congregation

Section 1. General Authority to Select a New Senior Pastor[6]
Should the church need a new senior pastor, two methods are provided for the congregational selection of a new senior pastor. One method involves the participation of the departing pastor; the other method does not. The founding pastor of the church need not be officially confirmed by the congregation; therefore, he is exempted from Article Five.

Section 2. Congregational Process with the Participation of the Departing Pastor[7]

(Paragraph 1) Departing Pastor Participates in Replacement
If the senior pastor is in good standing with the church and is removing himself because of retirement or relocation, the following is the selection process:

(Paragraph 2) Congregational Vote
The senior pastor may choose up to two candidates. The first candidate is to speak in three or more of the primary church services. Then the senior pastor is to formally recommend this candidate during a Monday night meeting of the membership. The meeting is to be announced in the primary services of the church and held eight days later on a Monday night. Any meeting of the membership for pastoral selection requires that members bring their contribution records from the previous year and display them at the door in order to verify membership. At that meeting, the departing senior pastor and the candidate must leave. Then the secretary/treasurer is to conduct a secret ballot vote and, with a minimum two-thirds (2/3) vote, the candidate shall be accepted. If that can-

didate fails, the second candidate chosen by the senior pastor is afforded the same opportunity as the first. If the second ballot fails, the process outlined in Section 3 shall be followed.

Section 3. Congregational Process Without Departing Pastor's Participation[8]

(**Paragraph 1**) Departing Pastor Unavailable
If the senior pastor is removed by the overseers, is deceased, or cannot or will not participate in the selection process of the new senior pastor for any reason, the following shall be the process for selecting a new senior pastor:

(**Paragraph 2**) Meeting of the Membership
The secretary/treasurer or another person appointed by the board of trustees is to immediately call a meeting of the membership by making an announcement during the primary service(s). The meeting is to be held in the church building on a Monday night, eight days later. At the meeting of the membership, a Pastoral Selection Committee of nine people will be elected by the membership—to include three men and three women from the general membership and the three most senior full-time pastoral staff members. If there are not three full-time pastoral staff members, the membership may elect people who are familiar with the day-to-day work of the church. The committee itself is to vote and select a chairperson and cochairperson.

(**Paragraph 3**) Formation of Pastoral Selection Committee
The duty of the Pastoral Selection Committee is to

provide an interim pastor or guest speakers to conduct church services. However, neither an interim pastor nor a replacement speaker shall have the corporate powers of the president.

(Paragraph 4) Congregational Vote
The committee is to recommend a new senior pastor as soon as an acceptable candidate is available. That person must be a licensed or ordained minister of the gospel. He must be approved by three of the five members on the board of overseers before being presented to the church. Once the committee recommends a senior pastoral candidate, that person may speak to the church in every service for three weeks or in at least three of the primary church services. Afterward, a meeting of the membership shall be publicly called on a Monday night, chaired by the secretary/treasurer or by a member of the board of trustees selected by that board. At that meeting church members shall vote by secret ballot to either accept or reject the pastoral candidate. Trustees and their spouses are to count the ballots. A minimum two-thirds (2/3) vote of those attending the meeting is required to elect the next senior pastor. When a two-thirds (2/3) majority in favor of the candidate does not occur, the Pastoral Selection Committee shall seek another candidate.

(Paragraph 5) Staff Administration During Transition
During the selection process, members of the church staff are to continue in their positions. Should staff or financial problems arise, the secretary/treasurer has authority to alter the roles of staff members, including dismissal if necessary in the judgment of

the secretary/treasurer. When the new senior pastor is in place, he has full authority to select his own staff, replacing existing staff members, if he should choose, according to the severance agreements (Article Seven, Section 2, Paragraph 5).[9]

6. This section allows congregational government in the selection of a new senior pastor. This process is vitally important in light of the great freedoms the senior pastor is given under these Bylaws. Those freedoms are necessary for effective and powerful leadership, which places a great deal of responsibility on the people who select him. Remember, once the senior pastor is selected, he will direct the spiritual countenance of the entire church for potentially many, many years.

   Don't rush the process. The easiest way to fire someone is to never hire him. And, with this form of government, the person cannot be fired unless a serious offense has been committed. And even then, the overseers are the only people who can dismiss him. So be wise.

   Because of its importance, this selection process has two parts explained in Sections 2 and 3.

7. This process is to be used if the current senior pastor is leaving in good standing. That means he is trusted and respected, and therefore should be fully involved in the appointment of the person who will succeed him.

8. This process is more cumbersome than the first because it provides for the situation where the most recent senior pastor is not present due to death, dismissal or a resignation when the pastor chooses not to participate. The goal is to select God's man as the senior pastor. Don't become sidetracked by the process. Always remember the goal.

9. It is proper and right for employees hired by the previous senior pastor to make themselves available for resignation anytime within a two-year window of the new senior pastor's placement. The new senior pastor should have the freedom to replace past employees at will during his first two years. This courtesy by the employees is a great contribution to the continued health of the church.

ARTICLE SIX

Trustees of the Corporation
Section 1. General Powers[10]

The major financial affairs of the Corporation shall be managed by

the board of trustees, hereinafter referred to as the trustees, whose members shall have a fiduciary obligation to the Corporation.
Section 2. Functions[11]

(Paragraph 1) Provide Facilities
The trustees vote in accordance with these Bylaws in order to conduct the major business decisions of the Corporation. The trustees oversee the provision of the physical facilities needed by the church Body. They also coordinate any construction projects that require a loan.

(Paragraph 2) Exclusive Authority
The trustees are the only body within the Corporation or church Body with the authority to (1) buy and sell real estate, (2) borrow money and/or (3) secure real estate leases.

(Paragraph 3) Counsel[12]
The trustees are to provide counsel to the senior pastor regarding the major financial affairs of the church.

(Paragraph 4) Staff Loans
Any employee of the church requesting financial assistance from the church in the form of a loan must first obtain permission from the senior pastor to apply for the loan. The trustees shall then review the application. All terms and conditions of the loan must be approved by a majority (four or more) of the trustees.

No loans shall be made to any officer or trustee of the Corporation.

Section 3. Financial Guidelines[13]

(**Paragraph 1**) Moneys Available to Trustees
In order to provide for the physical needs of the church, the trustees have available to them 100 percent of all unrestricted moneys accumulated in any type of savings account (including stocks, bonds, CDs, mutual funds, etc.) and all assets in land and property. In addition, the trustees may direct any expenditures up to 35 percent of the unrestricted income of the church from tithes, offerings, interest and investments. (Current undesignated income is 90 percent of the undesignated income of the previous year.) From the 35 percent of church income at the trustees' disposal, payment must be made on all debts and real estate leases of the Corporation.

(**Paragraph 2**) Debt Restrictions[14]
Before the trustees may authorize the church to borrow money or incur a lease obligation, the following conditions must be met:

1. <u>Minimum 25 percent down.</u> Should the trustees choose to borrow money to facilitate the growth and/or work of the church, they must first accumulate 25 percent of the total price for the project as a down payment. Two variables apply when determining whether sufficient funds have been accumulated. One, amounts previously expended on the project to be financed from the proceeds of such indebtedness will be deemed accumulated. And two, amounts previously expended as principle reduction payments above minimum required payments on preexisting loans during the 12 months prior to incurring addi-

tional debt will be deemed accumulated and credited toward the 25 percent.

2. <u>Maximum 35 percent payment ceiling</u>. The combined totals of all monthly debt service and lease payments, following the incurring of the indebtedness or lease obligation under consideration, will not exceed 35 percent of the average monthly undesignated income. The percentage shall be based on, but not be limited to, tithes, offerings, investment income and unrestricted gifts of the church.

3. <u>Lease to purchase allowance</u>. If indebtedness is being secured to build a structure that will relieve the church of its need for a leased facility to be vacated when the new building is completed, then the current lease commitment need not be calculated into the 35 percent expenditure limitation for 18 months. Thus, the church is allowed 18 months for both construction and lease payments that combined, exceed the 35 percent limit, but only if compelling assurance is evidenced that by the end of the 18-month period reasonable relief can be expected from the burden of the lease payment.

4. <u>Income projections</u>. The church may *not* set budgets, meet conditions for borrowing or make any financial commitments based on upward projections of income.

5. <u>Audit requirements.</u> If the church wishes to borrow more than $250,000, the trustees must base their financial limitations on information provided by an audit of the previous year.

6. Church plant exception. If the church has less than
12 months financial history and wishes to borrow less
than $250,000, that decision may be based on the
most current 3 months of financial history provided
by the church treasurer. Even in this situation, the 25
percent down and 35 percent debt service ceilings
must be met.

(Paragraph 3) Annual Audit
If the income of the church exceeds $250,000 per year,
the trustees shall obtain an annual audit performed by
an independent public accounting firm in accordance
with Generally Accepted Auditing Standards (GAAS),
with financial statements prepared in accordance with
Generally Accepted Accounting Principles (GAAP).

(Paragraph 4) Audit Review Committee
The trustees shall appoint the secretary/treasurer and
two other members of the trustee board to serve as
an audit review committee. After reviewing the
annual audit, committee members are to report their
findings at a trustee meeting.

(Paragraph 5) Conflict of Interest
In order to avoid a conflict of interest, all the following criteria must be met to complete any business
transaction between a trustee and the Corporation:

1. The trustee with whom the transaction is being
considered is excluded from any discussions for
approving the transaction.

2. The trustees consider competitive bids or comparable
valuations.

3. The trustees act upon and demonstrate that the transaction is in the best interest of the Corporation.

4. The transaction must be fully disclosed in the end-of-year audited financial statements of the Corporation.

Section 4. Appointment, Number, Term and Qualifications[15]

(Paragraph 1) Number and Selection
The trustees shall be composed of seven members, who are appointed by the senior pastor and approved by the board of elders. Trustees may not be employees of the Corporation or staff members of the church, nor can they be related or married to employees or staff members. Any trustee appointed after [insert appropriate date] shall be approved by the board of elders (see Article Nine). The term of office for each trustee shall continue until such trustee resigns from office or from membership in the church, dies or is removed. All trustees must be selected from the membership of the church.

(Paragraph 2) Removal
The pastor may dismiss trustees without cause, but at a rate that does not exceed one dismissal every six months. The elders are not required to approve pastoral dismissals of trustees. In the event that the office of pastor is vacant, the secretary/treasurer may appoint or dismiss trustees subject to the same limitations that apply to appointments and dismissals by the senior pastor in accordance with this paragraph and Article Six, Section 4, Paragraph 1.

(Paragraph 3) Exclusive Role

Because the trustees are responsible for the major financial decisions of the church, they must resign their positions on the board if they ever become staff members or take any other paid position within the church. Volunteer work within the church is encouraged, but paid positions may constitute a conflict of interest.

Section 5. Meetings[16]

(Paragraph 1) Frequency of Meetings

A meeting of the trustees shall be held at least twice a year. The senior pastor, or any trustee may call a meeting at any time, under the condition that a majority (four or more) of the trustees attend the meeting.

(Paragraph 2) Leadership of Meetings

If at all possible, the senior pastor is to attend and lead each trustee meeting. If not possible, the secretary/treasurer shall lead the meeting. If neither the pastor nor the secretary/treasurer is able to lead the meeting, the trustees must choose a leader for that meeting and proceed in order, with an appointed member keeping minutes for the record. Any motions passed and recorded in a meeting without the pastor or the secretary/treasurer may not take effect until the following meeting with either the pastor or the secretary/treasurer present when the minutes of the previous meeting are approved.

(Paragraph 3) Location of Meetings

Any meeting of the trustees may be held at such place or places as shall from time to time be determined by the trustees or fixed by the senior pastor and designated in the notice of the meeting.

(Paragraph 4) Written Notice of Meetings
Whenever a written notice is required to be given to any trustee, these three rules apply: (1) Such notice may be given in writing by fax or by mail at such fax number or address as appears on the books of the Corporation and such notice shall be deemed to be given at the time the notice is faxed or mailed. (2) The person entitled to such notice may waive the notice by signing a written waiver before, at or after the time of the meeting. (3) The appearance of such person or persons at the meeting shall be equivalent to signing a written waiver of notice.

(Paragraph 5) Regular Meetings
The trustees may establish regular meetings. No notice shall be required for any regular meeting.

(Paragraph 6) Trustee Action Without Meeting
Any action that could be taken at a meeting of the trustees may be taken without a notice if at least four of the trustees participate with either the pastor or secretary/treasurer present. Such action shall be effective as of the date of the meeting.

(Paragraphs 7) Teleconferencing
At any meeting of the trustees, any person may participate in the meeting by telephone provided all members of the trustees present at the meeting or by telephone can hear and speak to each other. Participation by telephone shall be equivalent to attending the meeting in person.

(Paragraph 8) Quorum

A majority (four or more) of the trustees shall constitute a quorum for the transaction of business at any
meeting. The act of a majority of the trustees shall be
the act of the board of trustees. In the absence of a
quorum at any meeting, a meeting of the trustees
present may adjourn the meeting without further
notice until a quorum shall be established.

Section 6. Compensation

Trustees, as such, shall not receive any salaries for their services.

10. This section clarifies that the board has the fiduciary responsibility for
    the Corporation.
11. This section explains roles that only the board of trustees can fulfill.
    Most churches could have avoided problems over the exercise of
    authority if this section had been in their Bylaws. This section firmly
    establishes the Corporate board as the servant of the spiritual Body of
    believers, and will only allow the board to take action once the spiri-
    tual Body has demonstrated financial strength. This section is a great
    protection for the senior pastor and the church Body at large.
12. Counsel for the senior pastor can be interpreted as pressure. Therefore,
    the trustees are responsible for discussing with the senior pastor items
    helpful to his decision-making processes. I talk regularly with board
    members in stand-up meetings before or after a church service, dis-
    cussing different issues. This does not require a board meeting format
    or setting. Because different members on the board have different areas
    of expertise, I casually talk with our trustees when I see them at the
    church to get input. This is always helpful.
13. This section provides the framework the trustees can use to serve the
    church. It is a provision to keep anyone from placing too much money
    in buildings and not enough in direct ministry toward people. All
    moneys saved, and up to 35 percent of the income of the church, can
    be used by the trustees, but the amount cannot exceed these limits.
    This limitation is a protection for the ministry aspects of the church.
    People love knowing that their tithes and offerings are going to min-
    istry, not just buildings, and that even in times of expansion, no more
    than 35 percent of their tithes and offerings to the church go toward
    construction and debt service. This provision is a great motivator for
    the people in their giving. And it does allow the pastor to choose to

save as much as he would like toward a project. The limitation is only on indebtedness, not savings.

14. This section including its six subparagraphs keeps the church from incurring too much debt. It requires past performance before borrowing. Really, it keeps the church from making a financial mistake based on a dream, speculation or what people perceive as God's direction. These requirements do not unduly restrict, but provide a realistic constraint from overly aggressive financial commitments. With the 25 percent minimum down, 35 percent limit on payments, the congregation is secure and the business people will perceive the church as wise and conservative. This plan works well for all.

15. Some complain that in a beginning church, it is impossible to have seven people who could fulfill the role of a trustee board. If that is the case, you might not be ready to have a church structure. (Some rural communities would be one exception.) Maybe a Bible study format would be adequate with a club account at the bank. Then, when your group has grown to the point that seven people could fill trustee positions, incorporate and begin the actual process of establishing a working church structure.

    Remember that this board is not an elder board or a deacon board, so these people do not have to meet the biblical requirements for spiritual leadership in the church. This is a business board. Choose people who have a steady, consistent walk with Christ, have long-lasting, positive relationships and are financially responsible. Select people who have proven themselves responsible in other, natural areas of life. If a person wants authority or says he/she would like to be a trustee, respectfully decline. Watch out for subtle forms of pseudo-submission to win your favor. Choose people who are genuine servants and love God. They will always be a blessing. Lastly, make sure they love you so they will utilize the Corporation to serve the Body of believers in a way that glorifies Christ.

    Balance is achieved through the pastor's responsibility to appoint trustees. Should a pastor, however, want to change the board too quickly, he is limited in that he can only appoint and dismiss one trustee every six months. This stipulation protects everyone, and leaves proper balance of power in case of a difficulty. Provision is also made here should the pastor no longer be with the church. In that case, the overseers can appoint or dismiss trustees, keeping the church functional for a long interval without a pastor.

16. Don't have unnecessary meetings. If the church is building or moving, meet once a month. We meet on the second Sunday afternoon of every month at 4:00 P.M. when there is business. If not, we meet at the beginning of the year to review audit reports and in the fall for an update.

That's all that needs to be done unless money is being borrowed, land purchased or buildings being built. Keep it simple.

ARTICLE SEVEN

Senior Pastor of the Church/
President of the Corporation
Section 1. The Office of the Senior Pastor[17]

(Paragraph 1) The Dual Role
Because [church name] has two complementary branches-the spiritual Body of believers and the legal Corporation-it is the senior pastor who administratively bridges the gap between the two branches. This dual role can sometimes be awkward: The senior pastor is primarily responsible for the spiritual life of the church, therefore, he must be in a position corporately to ensure that financial strength is directed toward the ministries of his choice.

(Paragraph 2) Responsibilities of the Senior Pastor
It is the senior pastor's responsibility to:

- Provide biblical vision and direction for the congregation;
- Define and communicate the church's purpose;
- Oversee and coordinate the day-to-day ministry of the congregation and administration of the church;
- Appoint a board of overseers pursuant to Article Eight;
- Recognize and enlist apostolic, prophetic, evangelistic, pastoral and teaching ministries, along with elders, deacons and additional staff members as he deems biblical and necessary for the healthy spiritual development of the Body of believers;

- Select trustees pursuant to Article Six who will help oversee the business of the Corporation;
- Staff the church as he deems necessary to help administrate the affairs of the Corporation;
- Veto any nominations to the board of elders pursuant to Article Nine.

(Paragraph 3) The Pastor's Spiritual Leadership
The senior pastor may work with overseers, elders, deacons or anyone serving in the functions or offices as outlined in Ephesians 4:11-13 in whatever way he determines is biblical to serve the spiritual needs of the congregation. Additionally, the senior pastor may budget moneys, hire staff, develop projects, create cell groups, programs or other ministries according to his convictions and biblical understanding. He shall have the authority to appoint and approve any assistants necessary to properly carry on the work of the church.

(Paragraph 4) The Pastor's Responsibility for Services
Times, order of services and the leadership of services are to be determined by the senior pastor or by the spiritual church structure he establishes. No person shall be invited to speak, teach or minister at a service held in church-owned facilities, or in the name of the church, without the approval of the pastor or the appropriate member of the established church ministry team.

Section 2. The Office of the President[18]

(Paragraph 1) The President
The Corporation finds its leadership under the Lord

Jesus Christ and in its president. The senior pastor shall serve as the president and chief executive officer of the Corporation. If possible, he shall preside at all meetings of the board of trustees and shall see that all orders and resolutions of the board are put into effect. He shall execute in the name of the Corporation all deeds, bonds, mortgages, contracts and other documents authorized by the board of trustees. He shall be an ex-officio member of all standing committees, and shall have the general powers and duties of supervision and management usually vested in the office of the president of a corporation.

(Paragraph 2) The President's Role with Trustees
The president is the nonvoting chairman of the board of trustees. He calls meetings and determines the agenda in consultation with the trustees. The president shall make selections to the board of trustees from the church membership at a rate not to exceed one new appointment every six months in accordance with Article Six. The president may also dismiss trustee members, but at a rate that does not exceed one dismissal every six months in accordance with Article Six, Section 4, Paragraph 2.

(Paragraph 3) The President's Administrative Role[19]
The president is the senior administrator of the church. He is ultimately responsible for all day-to-day administrative decisions of the church.

(Paragraph 4) The President's Role with Staff[20]
The president hires, directs and dismisses staff. As the senior pastor, his call is confirmed to the church

through the congregation, and those hired by him are to assist him in fulfilling this calling.

(Paragraph 5) The President's Role in Establishing Salaries

The president determines all salaries and writes pay scales for full-time salaried employees. Pay scales shall be explained to new full-time salaried employees. Changes in pay scales will be given in writing to the affected employees. If a severance-pay agreement is established, that too must be given to the employee in writing. In addition, all part-time salaries and hourly wages are variable and are to be determined between the president and the employee.

(Paragraph 6) The President's Salary Exceptions[21]

The salary of the president is to be on the same pay scale consistent with the pay scale established for the other members of the pastoral team with the following two exceptions:

1. Housing: The president (senior pastor) may live in a parsonage owned and maintained by the Corporation. The board of trustees shall choose the parsonage.

2. Transportation: The senior pastor shall be provided with two automobiles, which will be maintained by the Corporation. The trustees shall determine the cost of the automobiles. The Corporation shall then purchase or lease the vehicle of the pastor's choice within the budget allowed. Each automobile is to be kept for six years. During his first three years of service at the church, only one automobile shall be pro-

vided; then, at the beginning of the fourth year, the second shall be purchased or leased. Henceforth, a new vehicle is to be purchased or leased every three years. If the president chooses to replace a vehicle before six years expires, the value remaining in the previous vehicle is the maximum that may be spent unless the president contributes personal funds toward the purchase of the replacement vehicle. No additional funds may be added by the Corporation for the purchase of a vehicle out of sequence.

(Paragraph 7) Optional Benefits
After the senior pastor has served for a minimum of 10 consecutive years, the trustees may provide additional benefits unique to the senior pastoral position. They may, for example, choose to provide an additional retirement benefit to compensate for the senior pastor's inability to build equity in a home while living in a church-owned parsonage. The trustees may also choose to reduce the amount of time the senior pastor is required to keep a vehicle before replacing it. These benefits and others like them must be initiated by the trustees rather than the senior pastor because these benefits are optional and not required. They are purely an attempt to reward many years of faithful service.

(Paragraph 8) Budget[22]
After the church is one year old, an annual budget must be prepared. The budget is to be based on 90 percent of the previous year's undesignated income. The president is to write the budget for 65 percent of the 90 percent in order to finance the basic ministry needs of the church (salaries, taxes, bills, missions,

benevolence, department financial allocations, etc.). He is free to reflect his values and wisdom in his budget portion. Then, the president is to work with the trustees to add their 35 percent to the budget.

(Paragraph 9) Expenditures

Budgeted amounts are not to be considered actual moneys available. The president can only spend actual funds that are available, and those moneys are to be spent according to the budget. The president may not borrow money, sign leases, buy or sell real estate, or make any agreements that could force indebtedness upon the church. Should the church borrow, the trustees may give the president authority to spend those moneys on the project for which the funds were borrowed. All undesignated moneys available to the Corporation above budgeted amounts are deemed discretionary and are available to be spent by the president, but he may only obligate funds currently on hand.

17. This section emphasizes the senior pastor's role as the spiritual leader of the local church. It distinguishes the two branches that must work in harmony—the Corporation and the spiritual Body. Then it clarifies that (a) the Corporation exists to serve the spiritual Body, and (b) that the senior pastor is responsible for leading the spiritual Body and using his influence to cause the corporate structure to serve that Body. So Section 1 emphasizes the role of senior pastor, and Section 2 explains the senior pastor's role as president of the Corporation.

18. The distinct role as president in contrast to pastor is significant. Remember that churches worship God, communicate the Word, pray for people, minister the life of the Holy Spirit to others and foster additional ministry. Corporations, on the other hand, hire and fire people, pay taxes, process money, buy and sell buildings, accumulate assets, etc. These two roles are distinctly different, but they overlap in every ministry. These Bylaws distinguish the two roles. And, as you can see, the corporate roles, when implemented with simplicity, facilitate ministry.

The Corporation, though, is not the purpose of the organization—the spiritual Body is.

So this section explains the corporate role of the senior pastor. As we have already seen, the trustees make the major financial decisions for the church. But in Paragraph 2, we notice that the pastor nominates trustees, the elders approve the nominations, and, if necessary, the pastor removes trustees. But the pastor cannot dismiss trustees at a rate faster than one every six months. This provision is needed in case the pastor's heart becomes sinful and he wants to "stack the board." Also, if the pastor has a conflict with the trustees, he can't do too much too quickly, thus everyone is protected. Remember, we want churches that remain strong and healthy for years—generations. So, the senior pastor can change the board, but not too fast. With this time delay, it would take three and a half years to change the entire board—enough time for the condition of heart to become evident to all. At the same time, should a trustee's heart become sinful, the senior pastor has the authority to remove that person quickly.

19. This paragraph clarifies that the senior pastor is the senior administrator. When a church is small, the pastor himself will often have to do all of the administration. When a church becomes large enough to afford it, a full-time administrator should be hired to serve the day-to-day ministries of the church and report directly to the senior pastor.

20. Paragraphs 4 and 5 clarify that the senior pastor, unless he is the founding pastor, is selected by the congregation, but all other staff members are hired by the senior pastor to help him serve. Therefore, according to these Bylaws, the senior pastor is ultimately accountable to the board of overseers while the rest of the staff is ultimately accountable to the senior pastor.

"I work for the church, and the staff works for me." This causes the staff to work together in great harmony and prevents unnecessary problems with staff members who might become disgruntled and try to undermine the senior pastor.

The ability of the senior pastor to set salaries is vitally important. Many church systems allow the pastor to set salaries for everyone but himself, and allow a governing board to set the pastor's salary. Not good. This could imply that the senior pastor works for a church board. He does not. The trustees already determine the home and the value of the automobiles the church will provide for the senior pastor and his family. The same problem exists if the congregation sets pastoral salaries. The implication is too strong that the senior pastor is an employee who can be hired or fired by anyone other than the board of overseers.

Most churches have four primary classifications of workers: (1) pastoral staff; (2) salaried support staff; (3) hourly support staff and

(4) volunteers. The senior pastor must design a universal pay scale for the pastoral staff. This way he knows that his base pay, experience-credit ratio and dependent allowance will be the same as the other pastors. Therefore, if he wants to pay himself a certain amount, the other pastors will need to be paid on that same scale. (Two exceptions do exist, and we will discuss them in detail later.) This provision creates a beautiful balance, and greatly reduces any sense of unfairness in pay among the pastoral team.

Our universal pay scale has evolved throughout the years, and you may be able to develop a better one than ours. But currently, our pay scale for pastoral staff starts with a $2,000-per-month base. To that base we give credit for work experience at a ratio of three to one. For every three years of experience, we give a 10 percent compounded raise. This must be experience that has helped train for the current position and does not include years in school. Thus, if someone had 12 years of qualified experience, we would give that person 4 years credit. Compounded at 10 percent a year would equal an additional $928 per month. We also give a $65-per-month allowance for every dependent. So if the pastor is married with two children, another $195 per month would be added. In this example, the pastor's gross monthly salary would be $3,123. This figure includes the pastor's housing allowance, which is nontaxable. In addition to salaries, the pastors are provided family medical insurance, retirement benefits and paid vacation. Even though this isn't an official agreement, we give at least a 10 percent raise to everyone if the church has grown 10 percent or more, which means that every person who has ever worked at New Life has received at least a 10 percent raise every year for 13 years now.

If this pay package is not enough, it is increased for all the pastoral staff. If the senior pastor can't live on the allotted amount, then the youth pastor can't either. This system has remarkable secondary benefits to the entire staff and church. For those who use it, it works very well.

Everyone would agree that the senior pastor is worthy of his hire because of his calling. Why, then, would we think a youth pastor or an administrative pastor should be paid less? If these pastors are fulfilling their callings, and God has placed them in their positions, shouldn't they also be compensated appropriately? How many youth pastors have had to become senior pastors because as their families grew, they needed to increase the family income? What a crime. Who would dare say the senior pastor works harder or longer hours than the youth pastor? No one who has been one.

The primary differential for income among the pastors should be in regard to tenure. If a pastor serves in a church for a longer period of time, that pastor will know more people and have been proven worthy of influence in more people's lives. His pay, therefore, should be raised to reflect his extended time of service. Not everyone at New Life makes the same, but all pastors are paid from the same scale.

21. The following exceptions are the only differences between the associate pastoral staff and the senior pastor, with the reasoning that the senior pastor holds corporate and spiritual responsibilities. The associate pastors and the support staff work exclusively under the senior pastor. The values of these extra benefits, though, are solely at the discretion of the trustees and outside the direct control of the senior pastor.

The two exceptions to the pay-scale system are clearly stated in Paragraph 6. Note, though, the balance in selecting the house and the vehicle(s). The trustees select the house the church will provide, so regardless of church size, if the church hires a full-time pastor, it can determine the value of the housing for the pastor and his family. In addition, the trustees determine the value of the cars the pastor receives.

If a car is wrecked during the six years, the pastor may use the remaining value in the car to replace it from insurance. These two paragraphs are very sensitive and, of course, may be changed. Some pastors already have their own homes, others prefer driving their own cars. In those cases, adjustments need to be made in this provision. For example, the trustees may choose to allow the pastor to use the financial allowance to increase his retirement. Whatever the case, make sure the senior pastor is on the same pay scale as other pastors, and that these two exceptions are not stumbling blocks.

People on the support staff are also fulfilling God's call by serving throughout the church. Support-staff pay scales are set according to job classifications, experience, responsibility, performance, etc. All of our pay rates are usually fair and in compliance with good stewardship of the tithes and offerings entrusted to us.

The view we hold regarding wage is: It is impossible to place a value on a calling. We could never afford to pay people what they are worth. So, paychecks are given to our staff out of the tithes and offerings to enable their ministries. If the church did not pay the staff, these people would have to work elsewhere to earn a living. This would greatly affect the amount of time and energy they would have available to answer their calls to ministry. Therefore, our wages are a gift, not compensation for services rendered. Hopefully, all of our staff believes so much in their callings versus their jobs, that if it were impossible for the church to pay them, they would find a way to make a living and still dedicate themselves to fulfill their callings through the church.

That brings us to volunteers. Without volunteers we could not continue to minister as effectively as we do. The fact that volunteers don't get paid does not mean they are not called. On the contrary. Volunteers themselves have clearly settled in their hearts that what they are doing is not a job. There is no hireling mentality among volunteers.

Volunteers are as much a part of the team as any paid staff member and should be treated with respect. Volunteers must be as carefully screened as staff members. You don't want to discourage good people, but trouble can occur when the volunteer process is too loose. Whether paid or not, you want the people God has called and added to your ministry team.

22. This paragraph is packed full of philosophical positions we believe are vital to protect good Christian people from overzealous leadership. Note: Budgets are prepared based on 90 percent of the previous year's unrestricted income. Why? So believers won't be constantly pressured by the church leadership to come up with extra money to meet a budget.

Too many books, tapes and videos are available on how to extract money from Christians. We receive "Christian stewardship" magazines regularly that, in essence, are teaching Christian leaders how to get money from the Body of Christ. Currently, one of the most popular speakers to the Christian-leadership world operates a for-profit ministry and is known to be extremely effective at raising money.

What's wrong with this? Christian people should be able to work, raise their families, pay their tithes to their local churches and trust that the churches are run well enough and disciplined enough to operate within their budgets. Then, if additional money comes in, that money can be used above and beyond the budgeted amounts.

In this 90-percent budget plan, even if the church income is the same as the previous year, the pastor will have 10 percent discretionary spending. If the church grows at least 10 percent, the pastor will have 20 percent discretionary spending. In 1997, New Life grew 24 percent. Therefore, we had 34 percent more income than our monthly budget, which provided flexibility toward debt reduction, missions, savings, etc. This provides great freedom for all!

In the preparation of the budget, the senior pastor has available 65 percent of the 90 percent figure. He meets with the trustees to offer his suggestions for the remaining 35 percent. We suggest the senior pastor have a proposal prepared and then, with the wisdom of the trustees, set the budget for the upcoming year. Budgeting should be done annually.

We don't publish our budgets. They are in-house documents that give our Administration Department direction for allocations to all departments. We only publish our cash-flow statements at year-end and make our audit reports available to the public—although within the past 12 years, no one has ever requested our audit reports.

ARTICLE EIGHT

Overseers[23]

(Paragraph 1) [church name] Requirements for Overseers
The members of the board of overseers must be active senior pastors of respected congregations who know and love [church name] and the pastor. They must agree to make themselves available at their own expense to serve [church name] if requested by the elders (Article Thirteen, Section 2), and must be willing to provide spiritual protection to the church through prayer and by exemplifying honorable Christian lives.

(Paragraph 2) Biblical Qualifications for Overseers
"Now the overseer must be above reproach, the husband of but one wife, temperate, self-controlled, respectable, hospitable, able to teach, not given to drunkenness, not violent but gentle, not quarrelsome, not a lover of money. He must manage his own family well and see that his children obey him with proper respect. (If anyone does not know how to manage his own family, how can he take care of God's church?) He must not be a recent convert, or he may become conceited and fall under the same judgment as the devil. He must also have a good reputation with outsiders, so that he will not fall into disgrace and into the devil's trap" (1 Tim. 3:2-7).

(Paragraph 3) Selection and Function of Overseers
A board of overseers will be nominated by the pastor

and confirmed by the elders. The pastor will be accountable to the overseers in the event of alleged misconduct in compliance with Article Thirteen.

(Paragraph 4) Installing New Overseers
The senior pastor and the elders may replace overseers at the rate of one per year and enter that change into the minutes of a trustees meeting. If disciplinary action is being considered, changes in the board of overseers may not be made until its work is completed.

23. This provision is unique for independent churches. Here, an outside board is given authority to discipline the senior pastor. These Bylaws allow checks and balances to all leadership groups. Additional details are given in Article Nine.

    Members of the overseers must be pastors of local churches that know and love your local church and the pastor. They must be pastors who would make themselves available at their own expense to your church to help during difficult times. This provision is vitally important for the security of an independent church, resulting in its greater health and success. When believers in an independent church know that their pastor can be disciplined or fired, they are willing to place greater trust in him.

ARTICLE NINE

Elders[24]

(Paragraph 1) Spiritual Role
The elders are to serve the congregation and the senior pastor for the development of the spiritual life of the church. These people and their spouses are to help create a positive spiritual climate within the church Body. They are neither a governing or corporate board, but a spiritual body called to create and maintain stability in potentially negative situations.

(Paragraph 2) Definition

The elders are people who function within the local church but are <u>not members of the pastoral staff of</u> the church. They meet the biblical qualifications for eldership and function in that calling, but derive their income from sources other than the church. The number of elders shall be determined by the senior pastor but shall not be less than 12.

(Paragraph 3) Functions[25]

The functions of the elders are to:

1. Maintain and teach by living a godly, Christian lifestyle;
2. Provide a prayer shield for the pastoral team and the local church;
3. Defend, protect and support the integrity of the pastoral team and the local church;
4. Pray for the sick;
5. Organize, implement and execute licensing and ordination requirements and procedures;
6. Mediate disputes among the brethren;
7. Counsel;
8. Confirm or reject pastoral appointments to the board of trustees and the board of overseers;
9. Contact the board of overseers to initiate investigation and potential discipline of the senior pastor;
10. Represent the church to other local churches.

(Paragraph 4) Biblical Qualification for Eldership

"An elder must be blameless, the husband of but one wife, a man whose children believe and are not open to the charge of being wild and disobedient. Since an overseer is entrusted with God's work, he must be blameless—not overbearing, not quick-tempered, not given to drunkenness, not violent, not pursuing dishonest gain. Rather he must be hospitable; one who loves what is good, who is self-controlled, upright, holy and disciplined. He must hold firmly to the trustworthy message as it has been taught, so that he can encourage others by sound doctrine and refute those who oppose it" (Titus 1:6-9).

(Paragraph 5) Nomination and Appointment to the Board of Elders[26]

Selection of the elders will be preceded by the senior pastor's teaching on the biblical requirements for eldership at a Sunday service. Each adult present at the service will make one anonymous nomination for the position of elder in writing immediately after the sermon on eldership. The pastor and his associates will tally these nominations, and the elders will be selected from those with the largest number of nominations. The senior pastor can veto anyone's nomination. This nomination process should occur once every four years unless needed to add additional elders to complete a four-year cycle.

(Paragraph 6) Four-Year-Service Terms

Once selected to serve on the elder board, the elder and spouse are to serve for four years. After that time of service, the selection process is to be repeated and anyone renominated and appointed may serve as many times as the congregation and pastor choose. However, should the congregation fail to renominate any certain elder, the pastor may not select that person for service.

(Paragraph 7) Removal of an Elder

Should anyone in the congregation, including a staff member or another elder, bring accusation against an elder, charging that the person does not qualify for eldership, a seven-member group from the staff and the elder board may hear the accusations and any response from the accused elder. Three of the seven-member group are to be chosen by the accused elder, and four are to be chosen by the senior pastor. The senior pastor may not serve on the panel judging the elder, but may oversee the procedures if he chooses. Then, in an anonymous vote, if five or more agree that the elder does not meet the qualifications for eldership, that elder may no longer serve on the elder board.

(Paragraph 8) Replacement of Elders

During the four years of service, those elders who are no longer able to serve for any reason need not be replaced unless the total number of elders is decreased to less than twelve.

24. This is the only "board" that includes the spouses in its function. All elders meetings and functions should fully include the spouses because of the function they have within the Body. We see the elders as the rudder on the bottom of the boat—keeping it upright in the midst of a storm. We also see the elders as the primary prayer shield for the church.

25. The ten functions of the elders are listed in the Bylaws for a specific reason. The elders do not have the same responsibilities as the trustees—even though from time to time they may want to—nor do they have the same responsibilities as the overseers. They are, instead, colaborers with the senior pastor and his staff to fulfill the spiritual direction and calling of the church.

26. This paragraph explains the process for selecting elders. We think it's best not to announce when this service will take place so lobbying does not occur. You want an honest, impromptu response from the congregation.

    Here's how to do it: The senior pastor should preach about the qualifications for an elder. Then have the ushers hand out three-by-five cards and ask the congregation to clearly write the name of one person in the church who most fits the qualifications of an elder. Read the Bible text one more time while people are thinking and writing. Have the ushers pick up all the cards and give them to a member of the pastoral team.

At that point, no one knows if they were nominated or how many times. It's important that the senior pastor's office tally the nominations confidentially. During the sorting process, some people may need to be disqualified by the pastoral team. Because of the nature of their positions, they will know about some people in the congregation who will be nominated who, in fact, should not serve as elders for personal reasons. Those facts should not be made known to anyone.

Then you can create a list of potential elders. Send the select nominees letters explaining that they have been nominated as elders. Include the scriptural basis for eldership and delineate the 10 eldership responsibilities (like a job description). Ask the nominees to evaluate their own lives to see if they think they qualify to serve for a four-year term.

Should they need to decline, they do not have to give a reason. Should they accept, they should call the office and let you know. That group and their spouses may serve for four years. Schedule a time during a Sunday service to recognize and commission the new elders and their spouses. Explain briefly the responsibilities of elders and have the congregation pray over them.

We suggest that if an elder develops difficulties, that person not be removed from office too quickly. There may be exceptions, and thus the provision in Paragraph 7. When elders face difficulty in their families or personal lives, they will usually resign. However, if the board is large enough to absorb the temporary unavailability of an elder(s) working through personal conflict, the benefits gained will outweigh removing the person(s). It is best to stay in the tree of life in these groups as much as possible. Relax and be full of grace.

ARTICLE TEN

Officers
Section 1. Officers[27]
The officers of the Corporation shall be a president and a secretary/treasurer and any other officers that the trustees may authorize from time to time.
Section 2. Appointment, Election and Term of Office

(Paragraph 1) Appointment of the President
The appointment responsibilities of the president are listed in Articles Five and Seven.

(Paragraph 2) Appointment of Secretary/Treasurer
The secretary-treasurer is to be nominated by the president and approved by the trustees. The term of this office is indefinite. Should the trustees fail to approve of the nomination from the president, other nominations must be made until a candidate suitable to the trustees is nominated. The president may remove the secretary/treasurer.

(Paragraph 3) New Offices
New offices may be created and filled at any meeting of the board of trustees. Each officer shall hold office until his successor has been duly elected and qualified.

Section 3. Removal of Officers

(Paragraph 1) Overseers' Responsibility for the President
The overseers of the church may discipline or remove the president according to Article Thirteen.

(Paragraph 2) Trustees' Responsibility for All Other Officers
Any officer elected or appointed by the board of trustees may be removed by the board when the best interests of the Corporation would be served thereby, but such removal shall be without prejudice to the contract rights, if any, of the officer so removed.

Section 4. Powers of Officers

(Paragraph 1) The President
The powers of the president are listed in Article Seven.

(Paragraph 2) The Secretary/Treasurer
As secretary, the secretary/treasurer shall attend all sessions of the board of trustees, and shall act as clerk thereof to record (or have recorded) all votes and the minutes of all proceedings in a book to be kept for that purpose. This person shall oversee the keeping of the membership rolls of the Corporation, and in general perform the duties usually incident to the office of secretary, and such further duties as shall be prescribed from time to time by the board of trustees or by the president.

(Paragraph 3) The Secretary/Treasurer's Role over Accounting
As treasurer, the secretary/treasurer shall oversee the keeping of full and accurate accounts of the receipts and disbursements in books belonging to the Corporation. The secretary/treasurer shall also oversee the deposit of all moneys and other valuable effects in the name and to the credit of the Corporation in such banks and depositories as may be designated by the president. The secretary/treasurer does not determine expenditures, but does oversee the disbursement of the funds of the Corporation as may be ordered by the trustees or the president. This person shall perform the duties usually incident to the office of treasurer and such other duties as may be prescribed from time to time by the board of trustees or by the president.[28]

(Paragraph 4) Audited Financial Statements

The secretary/treasurer shall serve on the Audit Review Committee and report to the trustees after its review of the annual audit. If the church does not have an annual audit, the secretary/treasurer is to provide to the board a report on the previous year's income and disbursements.

(Paragraph 5) Cash Flow Statements

The secretary/treasurer is to work with the president to provide an annual cash flow statement that must accompany all giving receipts to members. That report is to include the specific amounts of cash remuneration received from the church to specific pastoral staff members. Benefits, support staff salaries and other items may be grouped together, but the cash portion of the pastoral pay packages must be itemized individually.[29]

(Paragraph 6) Public Availability of Annual Financial Statements

The secretary/treasurer shall insure that current audited financial statements are available to anyone upon written request, and that the previous year's cash flow statements are available to all contributors to the church.

Section 5. Trustees' Selection of Additional Officers[30]

In the absence of any officer of the Corporation, except the president, or for any other reason that may seem necessary to the board, the board of trustees, by a majority vote, may delegate the duties and powers of that officer for the time being to any other officer, or to any trustee.

27. In Colorado, the law requires only two officers. Check your own state law to see what is required. Avoid having vice presidents, because the

implication is that the vice president will become president should the president no longer be in the church. And this is not true. If three officers are required by your state, I suggest appointing a president/pastor, secretary and treasurer. However, if possible, combine the secretary/treasurer position.

The secretary/treasurer is appointed by the president and approved by the board of trustees. That appointment is permanent unless the person resigns or is removed by the president.

28. There is a subtle safety measure here that some don't catch. The secretary/treasurer is responsible to oversee the bookkeeping of the church. The secretary/treasurer is not responsible to determine expenditures, but is responsible to make sure accurate records are being kept and reported. The financial office does our bookkeeping. The financial office works under the senior pastor but is also accountable to the secretary/treasurer.

Why is that important? Because if the senior pastor became dishonest or began to do something unusual with finances, the accounting staff would be responsible to tell him without any fear of recourse. If he did not correct the situation, they would then bring it to the attention of the secretary/treasurer. A safety measure such as this protects the pastor from a greedy, deceptive heart, and protects the accounting staff in the midst of a potentially difficult situation. It is very important that someone not paid by the church oversees the financial records. This system works very well.

The provision's requirement that the secretary/treasurer attend all sessions of the board of trustees does not mean the board cannot meet and do business when the secretary/treasurer is absent. It means the secretary/treasurer's functions must be performed when the secretary/treasurer is absent, and that if the secretary/treasurer is in town, every effort must be made on this person's part to attend.

29. This paragraph is vitally important. We believe that everyone who gives to the church should be able to know exactly how much money the church received, how much was spent and for what (i.e., each pastoral staff member's salary on a line-item basis). Believing that the funds given to the church are people's worship to God and knowing that cash-flow statements must be mailed out at the end of every year makes those who spend the tithes and offerings much more thoughtful. They know that the missions support, internal payroll, benevolence gifts, operations expenses and other expenditures will be openly accounted for and not "hidden" in a pie chart or percentage graph.

30. Section Five allows for additional officers. I don't recommend this because I think every circumstance should be covered with the already

existing provisions. However, if something unforeseen develops, this provision does allow flexibility.

ARTICLE ELEVEN

Business Practices
Section 1. Fiscal Year
The fiscal year of the Corporation shall be the calendar year.
Section 2. Contracts
The board of trustees may authorize any officer or officers, agent or agents of the Corporation, in addition to the officers so authorized by these Bylaws, to enter into any contract or execute and deliver any instrument in the name of and on behalf of the Corporation. Such authority may be general or may be confined to specific instances.
Section 3. Checks, Drafts or Orders
All checks, drafts, orders for the payment of money, notes or other evidences of indebtedness issued in the name of the Corporation shall be signed by such officer or officers, agent or agents of the Corporation, and in such manner, as shall from time to time be determined by resolution of the board of trustees. In the absence of such determination by the board of trustees, such instruments may be signed by either the secretary/treasurer or the president of the Corporation in accordance with their duties outlined in these Bylaws.
Section 4. Deposits
All funds of the Corporation shall be deposited to the credit of the Corporation in such banks, trust companies or other depositories as the board of trustees may select in accordance with these Bylaws.
Section 5. Gifts
The president/pastor may accept on behalf of the Corporation any contribution, gift, bequest or device for any purpose of the Corporation.
Section 6. Books and Records
The Corporation shall keep correct and complete books and records of account. The Corporation shall also keep minutes of the

proceedings of its members, board of trustees, committees having and exercising any of the authority of the board of trustees and any other committees. It shall keep at the principal office a record giving the names and addresses of all board members entitled to vote.

ARTICLE TWELVE

Church Ministry
Section 1. Minister Ordination and Licensing

> **(Paragraph 1)** Role of the Board of Elders
> The elders may ordain and/or license a person as a minister of the gospel after first examining the applicant's background, moral and religious character, and previous Bible courses and/or independent studies completed. Final determination shall be within the absolute discretion of the board of elders.

> **(Paragraph 2)** Application Through the Board of Elders
> Application for ordination and/or licensing as a minister of the gospel shall be supplied on the form provided by the elders. An application shall be either approved or denied within 90 days of the completion of the investigation of the applicant by the board of elders. Those applicants who are approved shall receive a certificate evidencing the approval.

> **(Paragraph 3)** Ability to Limit Ministry Validation
> The spiritual leadership of the church may at its own discretion limit any licensee ordained to an area of special emphasis.

Section 2. Ministry Training
The senior pastor and his staff may establish a School of Ministry,

setting forth a prescribed curriculum and course of study leading to ordination and licensing of ministers. The School of Ministry shall prepare students in the knowledge of the Word of God and in ministering to people's needs through the gospel of Jesus Christ.

ARTICLE THIRTEEN

Church Discipline
Section 1. Disciplining Church Members[31]

Only members are subject to church discipline.

Section 2. Disciplining the Pastor[32]

(Paragraph 1) Criteria for Discipline
Should the senior pastor demonstrate immoral conduct, financial practices or theological views, which the majority of the elders believe may require either personal correction or termination of his position, the elders shall contact the senior pastor and then, if the problem remains, be the overseers for investigation and evaluation of any appropriate discipline. (See Article Nine, Paragraph 3.)

(Paragraph 2) Process for Investigation
Should the overseers be asked to investigate alleged pastoral misconduct, a consensus of three of the five overseers is required to take disciplinary action. With such a consensus, the overseers shall assume complete authority over the senior pastor. They may decide to remove him from his position or to discipline him in any way they deem necessary. The overseers have no authority in [church name] unless contacted by the elders, and then only insofar as permitted under these Bylaws.

[266]

(Paragraph 3) Motivation
It is the intention of the Corporation to protect the hearts of all involved in matters of pastoral discipline. Using the method outlined in these Bylaws, the "sheep" never have to pass judgment upon their "shepherd."

31. This section provides for those occasions when the spiritual leadership of the Body needs to discipline a member of the congregation. Because worship services are open to anyone, the opportunity for church discipline is limited to those who are members in accordance with Article Two. Thus, an immoral or dishonest member may be disciplined. There is a biblical requirement for this function, and it simply provides a legal limitation of who would be protected by practical church oversight.

32. The disciplinary procedures in this section can be applied in one of three situations:
    - *Questionable moral conduct* such as elicit sexual activities, etc.
    - *Questionable financial practices* such as stealing money, tax fraud or some type of intentional dishonest activity with church or personal funds, properties or assets, which also includes a flagrant lack of good judgment in personal business decisions and/or allowing business schemes to affect the church fund-raising, causing harm to the spiritual life of the church.
    - *Questionable theological views* the pastor believes and teaches that are contrary to the theological views outlined in Article Three. This is to protect the church from heresy.

        The senior pastor should never be disciplined for simple personal preferences. Decisions such as guest-speaker selection (unless the speaker is invited to teach a heresy with the support of the senior pastor), scheduling services, selection of carpet color or anything purely subjective are not the bases for pastoral discipline. Sound judgment is to be evaluated before he is given the position of senior pastor. Once in office, the senior pastor can only be questioned and disciplined for a major mistake as outlined in Article Nine. This guarantees him freedom to boldly lead the spiritual Body of believers.

        This section also provides a benefit that is usually found only in denominational churches. It prevents the congregation, board or church members from having to judge or even talk about the discipline of their own senior pastor. Your Bylaws or minutes of a board meeting should include a current list of five overseers who know the church and the senior pastor. All five overseers should currently be pastors of local churches, and should be respected by your church and your senior pastor. These overseers have full authority, once contacted by an elder. Contacting the overseers is the only way within the church to discipline a senior pastor.

ARTICLE FOURTEEN

Amendment of Bylaws[33]

These Bylaws may be altered, amended or repealed, and new Bylaws may be adopted, by a five-to-seven (5/7) vote of the board of trustees at any regular board meeting. At least five days advance written notice of said meeting shall be given to each member of the board. The written notice must explain proposed changes. These Bylaws may also be altered, amended or repealed, and new Bylaws may be adopted by consent in writing signed by all members of the board of trustees.

Bylaws were approved by the board of trustees of [church name] on [date].

[Attach names of officers and trustees.]

33. This provision is for the amendment of the Bylaws of the church, but only under extreme circumstances. Notice that written notice of such changes must be made five days in advance and that the majority (five to seven) of the trustees must agree. This is the only time a quorum does not have the authority to take official action.

The information in this chapter should give you a starting point. Remember, take what will prove useful to you and discard the rest. We think it works well as a package and has philosophical continuity. However, each church is unique and state laws do differ.

Now you have a strong philosophical basis for a life-giving church. In addition, you have a brief overview of some of the ministries and a foundation for the business of the church. The foundation is ready, now let's give life together.

BLESSED ARE THOSE WHO WASH THEIR ROBES, THAT
THEY MAY HAVE THE RIGHT TO THE TREE OF LIFE
AND MAY GO THROUGH THE GATES INTO THE CITY.

[*Revelation* 22:14]

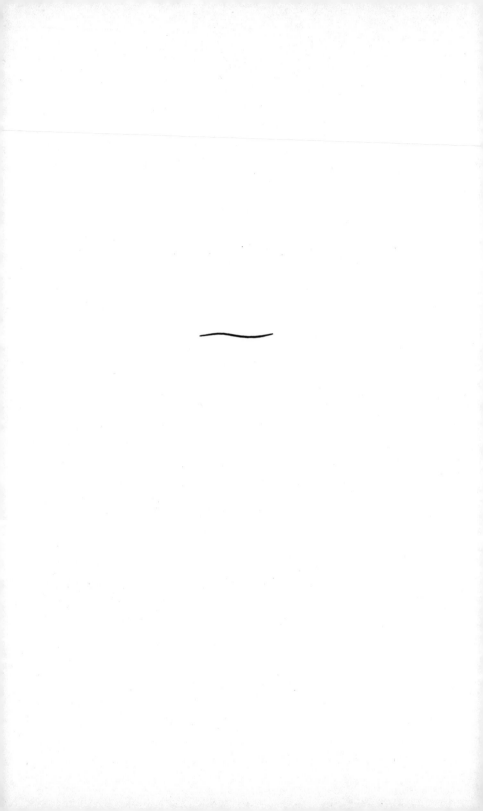

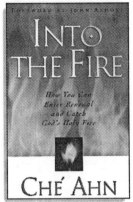
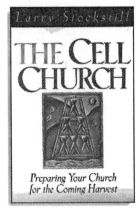
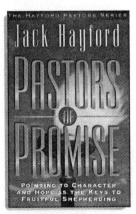
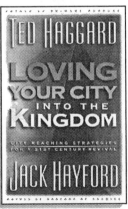
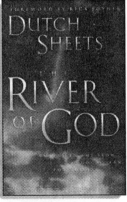

Great Ways to Keep Churches Growing

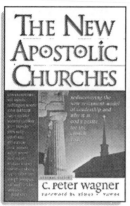

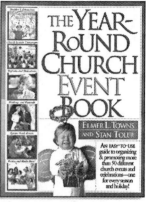
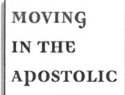

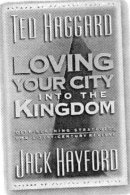